"Jam packed with action, suspense, kickass girls - brace yourself Cecy fans, *A Cursed Bloodline* will take you for an emotional roller-coaster ride. It left me not only without any sleep but stripped of every energy to function the day after reading this book. And with that said, *A Cursed Bloodline* is one of my Top Picks of the year."
 - *Under the Covers Book Blog*

"I can only advise you to start this series if it is not done already, it's one of my favorites. You will be completely blown away by the story, the characters and the pace without being able to stop reading it. And I can tell you now that I am again very excited to be able to read more!"
- *Between Dreams and Reality*

"The fourth book in The Weird Girls series is the best yet. Cecy has outdone herself. I have long loved the way that she writes, but this book was amazing. It was action packed and filled with all the drama that you know you love. For those of you who might not be into the supernatural, this series would be the perfect way to give it a try. *A Cursed Bloodline* grabs you, throws you to the wall, and then leaves you wanting more. Who else is ready for book five?" - *Art, Books, & Coffee*

"Once again I am blown away by Robson's ability to bring out both the best in me and the worst. She delivers in another spell binding addition to the Weird Girl series that had me constantly on the edge of my seat never knowing what to expect next...I think Robson may have ruined all other UF books for me."
- *My Guilty Obsession*

"Cecy Robson is one of my absolute favorite authors and each book that she writes becomes more gut-wrenching and brilliant than the last. *A Cursed Bloodline* is an amazing addition to the Weird Girls paranormal series and after finishing it, I'm dying to read the next installment."
 - *Books-n-Kisses*

"My legs are still shaking from this powerful, fast-paced, and violent tale. *A Cursed Bloodline* will make your heart race and you will shed friggin' tears."
-Caffeinated Book Reviewer

"Overall, *A Cursed Bloodline* is the proof that Cecy Robson and her Weird Girls series deserve its place on the prize list of the best paranormal romance series. I recommend this title to every Weird Girls series lover. Of course, to anyone out there who are looking for something new, hot, intriguing and refreshing to read, Cecy Robson will fulfill your desires!"
- Proserpine Craving Books

"*A Cursed Bloodline* is one of those books that is going to shock fans. I think you are going to love it! I am looking forward to the next book."
- Paranormal Cravings

"*A Cursed Bloodline* had me completely gripped from the very beginning, so much so that I stayed up all night reading and finished it just before 7am! The book brought out so many intense emotions in me, I was shocked, angry, horrified, angry, hurt, angry, devastated, angry and heart broken. "
- Feeling Fictional

"As always, Cecy's writing is top notch, she kept us engaged in this adventure with twists and turns that were completely unexpected, she brought us heartbreaks and joyous moments, and made her characters grow and evolve page after page."
- The Bookaholic Cat

"I absolutely LOVED Celia. She is brave and strong and loves those in her life so big. I so hated that not even her sisters could be with her to fight this battle. And an epic battle it turns out to be once a witch gets involved as well. I couldn't put it down until the very last page and I can't wait to read the rest of the books in the series."
- She Hearts Books

BY CECY ROBSON

The Weird Girls Series
Gone Hunting
A Curse Awakened: A Novella
The Weird Girls: A Novella
Sealed with a Curse
A Cursed Embrace
Of Flame and Promise
A Cursed Moon: A Novella
Cursed by Destiny
A Cursed Bloodline
A Curse Unbroken
Of Flame and Light
Of Flame and Fate
Of Flame and Fury (coming soon)

The Shattered Past Series
Once Perfect
Once Loved
Once Pure

The O'Brien Family Novels
Once Kissed
Let Me
Crave Me
Feel Me
Save Me

The Carolina Beach Novels
Inseverable
Eternal
Infinite

APPS

Find Cecy on *Hooked – Chat stories APP* writing as
Rosalina San Tiago

Coming soon:
Crazy Maple's Chapters: Interactive Stories APP:
The Shattered Past and Weird Girls Series

A Cursed Bloodline

A WEIRD GIRLS NOVEL

CECY ROBSON

Copyright © 2014 Cecy Robson
Cover design © Kristin Clifton, Sweet Bird Designs
Formatting by BippityBoppityBook.com

Excerpt from *Sealed with a Curse* by Cecy Robson, copyright © 2012 by Cecy Robson

This book contains an excerpt from *Sealed with a Curse* by Cecy Robson, the first full length novel in The Weird Girls Urban Fantasy Romance series by Cecy Robson.

eBook ISBN: 978-1-947330-23-8
Print ISBN: 978-1-947330-24-5

Acknowledgments

To my three children who occupy my mind, soul, and heart, and to the one I never had the chance to meet.

To my fans. This novel is my Magness opus, the first time I realized the depth and range of my writing. I never thought I'd write a better novel, until the next one came along. Thank you for standing by me and Celia, always.

To my gracious and wonderful editor, Sue Grimshaw, who gave me the opportunity to continue Celia's journey. Thank you, Sue, you'll never know the extent of my gratitude.

To my agent and dear friend, Nicole Resciniti, who fought to make my dream a reality. Nic, thank you. Just . . . thank you!

And finally, to my husband, Jamie, who believed in me from the very first words to the last. I thank God every day for you and our babies.

Dedication

To my husband, Jamie, who watched me create this story and hugged me when it was done.

Chapter One

I continued to stare at the tiny heartbeat on the screen. "How did this happen?" I asked stupidly. "Have you been sexually active, Celia?"

Dr. Belman's voice was soft and surprisingly patient. I thought about all the times Aric and I had been intimate in the last few weeks. "Um. Yes."

"Did you use birth control?"

"Yes." He raised his eyebrows. "It's true," I insisted.

I had started back on the Pill when Aric and I resumed our relationship. Dr. Belman pointed to the monitor. "Every time, Celia?"

"Well, no. But it was only one night." That was the truth—sort of. Granted that one night we'd made love four times, but that didn't matter, right? I looked back at the little beating heart. *I guess it does . . . matter.*

Tears streamed down my face. Although I completely freaked, I couldn't help smiling.

Aric and I are having a baby.

Dr. Belman removed the internal monitor, the same monitor I insisted he use to disprove the pregnancy test results. I thought he was just in obstetrician mode when I explained my symptoms and he had me give a urine sample. Extreme fatigue and nausea could have been related to anything I might have contracted on my recent international trips.

"Are you all right, Celia?"

I sat up and wiped my trickling tears. "Yes. No. I'm not sure, but I will be." "Do you feel the young man responsible will be supportive?"

Don't you mean the young werewolf? "In time. Aric is just going through a lot at the moment." *You see, Dr. Belman, he was severely burned and disfigured three days ago, in Chaitén, Chile, trying to save the world from a seven-headed fire-breathing demon.*

"Regardless of what challenges he's facing, if he's worth keeping, he'll make you and his child a priority." He sighed and placed his hand on my shoulder. "I apologize, Celia. I know it's not my place to speak to you like this, but you are a nice young lady and deserve a good man."

"I appreciate your concern, Dr. Belman, but Aric *is* a good man." *He's just hurting.*

Dr. Belman tapped my arm and regarded me thoughtfully. "If you say so, I believe you." He helped me off the exam table. "So, miss, the plan is you will stop taking birth control at once and you will see me in four weeks. Here is a prescription for some prenatal vitamins."

I pushed my long wavy hair from my face and stared at the script. Somehow the piece of paper officially announced I was becoming a mommy. Another tear escaped my eye. "Thank you, Dr. Belman."

On the way home, different scenarios of Aric's reaction played in my head, and I wondered how to tell him. He hadn't called, though he'd said he would. It was rare for him not to stay true to his word, and even more rare for him not to check on me.

My head spun with worry. The demon hadn't just marred Aric physically, he'd brutalized his self-esteem. I drummed my fingers against the steering wheel and entertained my options. I couldn't call his Warriors. If Aric's Pack Elders found out, his friends would surely be punished and so would Aric. I also couldn't involve my sisters. They would suspect something, and in this case, Aric should know my news first.

Will you be happy for us, Aric?

Four days ago, I wouldn't have asked myself that question. I would have known based on the depths of our feelings, and from the intimate moments in our past. I remembered one day in particular when we first began living together. We lay in bed facing each other. Aric traced my jawline with his finger as he spoke. It tickled and made me smile. "I wanted to talk to you about something."

"What is it, love?"

He'd returned my smile. It made him happy whenever I used that term of endearment. "I've noticed you haven't had your cycle. Do you think you could be pregnant?"

My fingertips playfully danced against his muscular chest while I tried in vain to suppress my blush. "My periods are irregular. They only come about every nine weeks. Don't worry, I should be getting another one soon."

"I wasn't worried," he'd replied. At the time, I could have sworn he seemed disappointed.

Another time I recalled, Aric and I had run into a family whose baby I'd delivered when I was still a nurse. We each took turns holding the baby and had exchanged heartfelt glances. Although neither of us had articulated our feelings, I knew we'd wondered about our own family one day.

Well, it looks like the day has come a little sooner than expected.

I was stopped at a light when my phone buzzed. My heart clenched when I read the incoming text.

I'm sorry. I need some time alone. Aric

The obnoxious car horn behind me snapped me from my stupor and made me drop the phone. It was just as well, I probably would have thrown it with how frustrated I felt. *Damnit, Aric. Don't do this . . . not today.*

I drove to my house in Dollar Point to gather some personal items following my doctor's appointment. I was about to take a walk along Lake Tahoe to clear my head, when someone knocked on my door. Anara waited on my doorstep, holding a charm similar to the one Genevieve had given me to pass through the wards. My hackles instinctively rose. "What are you doing here, Anara?"

A long, vicious growl rumbled through his chest. "I'm here to tell you that if you ever see Aric again I'll—"

"You'll what? Kill me?" I was livid. How dare he come to my home and threaten me!

Anara just laughed. "No, you stupid woman. *I'll kill him.*"

His response incensed me. I crouched and readied myself to attack. *"Not if you're already dead."*

Anara threw out his hand as if batting a fly, sending me slamming into the portrait-filled wall. Glass from the frames cut into my skin, stinging and piercing my flesh like the jagged teeth of a shark. Warm blood trickled down my back and soaked through my thick cotton sweater. He held me a few feet off the floor with just his will. I jerked my shoulders, trying to move, to kick—*anything* to break from his hold. My limbs failed me. I reached into my tigress for strength, but Anara's power caged her within me.

He walked inside, slamming the door behind him. Invisible fists struck my face with each step he took. He broke my nose and bloodied my face without ever lifting a finger. My ears rang from the jolts and from the eerie call of howling wolves.

"Do you think me merely a vampire or a Tribemaster you can so easily defeat?" he spat. "I am an *Elder*. I can summon the power of the Pack and use it to my liking. I can kill Aric and anyone I wish from miles away. No one can stop me—and no one can help you!"

He lifted his palm and squeezed his fingers, choking me slowly from where he stood. Spots speckled my vision. I thought he would kill me until he dropped his hand and released the pressure burning my throat. He paced in front of me, rubbing his jaw, seemingly pleased with the amount of magic at his fingertips. I spat out blood and tried to speak. "Why Aric?" I croaked.

His hot breath stirred against my face. "I will not allow you to taint his bloodline. He is a king among wolves and you are nothing but a whore. I'd rather see him dead than with an abomination like you!" His stare traveled the length of my body with the deepest of loathing. He lifted the edge of my sweater, before yanking it down with disgust. "I never understood what he saw in you," he scoffed. Anara's hold continued as he stalked away. "My followers are everywhere, Celia. I can manipulate them to do my will, just as I did Virginia. I will know if you see him, I will know if you speak to him."

The realization of his words struck me like a thunderbolt and washed my bleeding form with cold dread. *He* was the one who believed me the key to his destruction . . . and to all he led.

Anara stopped at the door, the muscles of his back tightening until they bulged against his red shirt. "If you *dare* tell anyone about this, your sisters will share Aric's fate."

As a testament of his power Anara didn't release me until about an hour after he left. I crashed to the floor, coughing and shaking. The only thought racing through my head was the need to protect Aric, my sisters, and the baby growing inside me.

Chapter Two

My legs trembled when I struggled to stand. Heavy footsteps pounded at the door. I thought Anara had returned to kill me and hurried to rise. I slipped on my blood and on the scattered pieces of broken wood and glass. My back slammed hard on the floor as the door swung open and a furious Liam charged in. He crouched next to me, poised to protect and growling ferociously.

Liam surveyed the damaged wall and the splintered glass and wood. I couldn't tell him what happened. Aric and my sisters would be hurt—or worse. But I couldn't lie to Liam. Like most preternaturals, he could smell a lie. So, I worked to calm my racing heart and tried to gather my words carefully.

He helped me to stand once he failed to sense any immediate danger. His eyes widened as he took in my state. "Good Lord, Celia. What happened?"

"I was attacked," I gasped, still unable to speak clearly.

Liam swept me into his arms, moving me away from the shards of glass. *"Tell me who did this to you!"*

"Our . . . enemy."

Liam sniffed the air. I panicked, thinking he'd detect Anara's scent. "Wolves. Wolves have been here," he said.

Wolves?

"I don't recognize their scent." Liam threw a blanket on the couch and gently laid me over it. "Hang on, Celia. I'll call Aric—"

"No! Liam, you can't call Aric."

"Celia, I have to, you're hurt."

My throat ached and it burned to talk. "I don't want him to see me like this. He's already dealing with a lot. Please, Liam, just get me to Misha's house. Emme can heal me there."

Liam's face split with guilt and uncertainty. As one of Aric's Warriors, he was blood- bound to protect me as Aric's mate, but he was also obliged to obey him. "Celia, I know he's in his own personal hell, but you're his priority. He'll want to be here."

"*Emme* is who I need right now. There's still blood running down my back."

In an instant, Liam was behind me, examining my wounds. I wasn't a *were*. I couldn't heal. "Oh, shit. I'll get you to Emme right away."

Liam lifted me and raced toward the door, kicking the empty boxes he'd dropped on the porch out of his way. He must have arrived to remove his belongings from the bedroom he and Emme had shared.

The bright sunlight burned my eyes. I shut them tight until we reached Liam's SUV. The moment he strapped me in, he stomped on the accelerator and roared out of our cul-de-sac. "What exactly happened, Celia? And why did I only smell your blood?"

"I was caught off guard."

Liam frowned. "What the hell? You're always on guard."

"I've been distracted because of . . . everything.

Look, I can't keep talking. It hurts too much." It was true, but mostly I was running out of ways to be creative with my answers.

"Sorry, Celia—I wasn't thinking. I'm just trying to figure things out. Don't worry. You'll be with Emme soon."

The relief I felt was short-lived. Almost immediately, he called the one person I dreaded most.

Aric's voice pulsed with strain from the moment he answered. "Liam, I told you now's not a good time—"

"Celia's hurt."

"*What?* Is she all right?"

"She's not dying." Liam gave me the once-over. "At least, I don't think she is. But she's pretty fucked up. Near as I can figure she was attacked by a bunch of Tribe wolves."

The Tribe were the evil band of bastards who had awoken the even more evil and bigger bastard demon. In stopping them, we'd decimated their numbers, but they were still out there— thankfully providing the perfect scapegoat.

Aric's breath came out fast. "When did this happen?"

Liam sniffed the air around me. "By the way the dry blood on her smells, about an hour ago."

Aric let out a string of swearwords. "By the way the *dry* blood smells on her!"

"Well, yeah, she's still bleeding."

"How bad is it?"

"Pretty bad, but I think she'll live." He shook his head when he took another look at me. "Damn, you should see her. She looks like hell."

I groaned. *Way to keep Aric calm, Liam.*

". . . her face is smashed in and her back is cut up like breakfast sausage…"

I glared at him. I couldn't believe he was being so

8

descriptive or how quickly Aric flipped out, smashing and destroying what sounded like heavy furniture.

". . . anyway, I'm taking her to Emme. She's at the master asshole's house."

"Let me talk to her."

I shook my head frantically and grabbed my throat when he tried to pass me the phone. Liam nodded his head in supposed understanding. "She can't talk right now, Aric. I think her larynx is partially crushed." My jaw dropped and I clutched my heart in shock. For once in his life, I wished Liam would shut his trap. Instead he smiled. "Aw, Celia, that's so sweet—I'll tell him. Aric, Celia sends her love."

If my head wasn't already pounding, I would have banged it against the window. "Tell her I love her, too. I'll meet you at the leech's house."

No!

Liam disconnected before I could protest. The rest of the way to Misha's my mind raced with what to say. Vampires were just as good at sniffing lies as wolves, but even if they weren't, Misha knew me well enough to tell the difference.

Liam turned onto the mile-long path that led to Misha's estate at warp speed, stopping only to slam on the brakes in front of the colossal wrought-iron gates. A vampire immediately abandoned his post and sneered at Liam through the window. "What do you want, mutt?"

"To smash your damn fangs in, asshole. Let me in. Celia's hurt and needs her sister."

The vamp did a double take when he saw me. "Oh, *shit*." He yelled to the group of vampires that had gathered behind the gate. "Let them through—it's Celia. Tell the master she's wounded!"

The gates had barely parted when several vampires disappeared toward the immense Mountain Craftsman mansion. Liam powered through the entrance and over the bridge. He swerved onto the circular stone driveway just as Misha sprinted down the stone steps, followed by Agnes, Maria, Liz, and Edith. The she-vamps wore their usual Catholic school uniforms. I always thought they looked creepy, but most males found it hot. Misha wore only black suit pants. I had probably arrived at a bad time.

My seat belt had just slid across my chest when Misha flung open the door and lifted me from the seat. Misha was about one hundred and forty years old. He normally didn't swear much, but, boy, he did then. His light Russian accent clipped every four-letter word.

Liam leapt out of the car and stormed toward us. "Keep your hands off her! She's only here for Emme."

"Shut up, hound. Emme is out, *I* will tend to her."

The schoolgirls blocked Liam when he charged, hissing through their elongating fangs. Daylight or dead of night, it didn't matter, the vamps were always ready to fight—especially *weres* who threatened their master.

"Don't hurt him," I croaked.

Misha responded in an ultra-deep, pissed-off voice. "No harm shall come to him so long as he knows his place." His eyes softened as they took me in. Without turning from my sight, he motioned to the crowd of vampires. "You three—locate Emme Wird and bring her back, *now*."

I placed my hand on his shoulder and squeaked out my words. "Misha, I don't want anything to happen to Liam."

Misha caressed my throat. "Rest your voice, my love. All will be well."

I glanced at Liam one last time before Misha rushed us inside. Liam hated vampires. As a member of the Alliance, he'd fought alongside them and the witch clans to help destroy the Tribe. They'd worked together because they had to—not because they enjoyed it.

We entered Misha's chambers faster than I could

take my next breath. Two sultry and very naked women lounged on his mammoth bed. "Leave us," he told them.

Misha shouted orders before his dinner and dessert could bolt. Edith removed my boots and socks while Misha carried me into the bathroom, her master's stress making her anxious. Maria filled the round tub and added salts that sizzled with hints of dry mint and thyme—the aroma of witch medicine.

Liz swept in, her arms packed with the first-aid supplies Misha had requested. As a former nurse, I thought Misha would allow me to dress my wounds. Sometimes I could kick my own ass for being so naïve. Misha tore off my clothes in one hard pull. As I stood there wearing only my tiny panties, I had the feeling he'd done this before.

I tried to cover my breasts with my arms and long hair. "Misha, what are you doing?" "Get on your knees."

"Excuse me?"

"Kitten, you must round your back. It's the only way to remove the glass embedded in your skin. Now do as I ask."

I sighed and looked to my closest Catholic schoolgirl. "Maria, may I have a towel, please."

She stopped in the middle of adding more salts and frowned. "For what?" she asked in her thick Brazilian accent.

"To cover myself."

My request seemed to confuse her. "Why? It's not like de master hasn't seen you naked before."

My face heated. "Just pass me a damn towel!"

Maria rolled her eyes and handed me a large cream bath towel to placate me. Had Misha not been present, she would have thrown it in my face. She might have dressed the part, but she was *not* a good Catholic.

I covered my chest and rounded my back, jumping when Misha removed the first large shard. Warm fluid spilled down my cold and sensitive skin. At once Misha's tongue ran over my open wound. He sealed it instantly, but wouldn't stop. Suddenly, I was no longer in pain—I was in trouble.

When vampires fed, both the 'sucker' and 'suckee' experienced emotional orgasms. As the 'suckee' who'd been body-slammed against a wall and pummeled into hamburger, I couldn't feel more than unease. Judging by Misha's deep intakes of breath as he continued to lick my skin, not only was he in the mood, he was full speed ahead.

"Misha, *don't*."

"I must," he groaned. "You are injured." Misha extracted another shard of glass near my right shoulder. His arms wrapped around my waist and his tongue moved in slow, seductive circles. My eyes widened, but it was a sound from his bedroom that had me bolting away.

Misha hissed. *"What is it, Edith Anne?"*

"Forgive me, Master. I was just trying to help." Edith fled the room as Marvin Gaye's "Let's Get It On" boomed over Misha's sound system. It appeared Edith's "help" consisted of "mood" music.

I stood at the opposite end of the bathroom when Misha turned back to me. The ravenous gleam etching its way across his handsome features made it clear I hadn't run far enough. I held out my hand when he took a step forward. "No more, Misha."

"My love—"

"Misha, I'm not your love. You know this."

I turned to wash my face in the sink, only to freeze at the sight of my reflection. My nose angled somewhere near my right cheek and the obscene amount of swelling distorted my features. Dry blood caked my face and long hair in thick streaks, and a cascade of bruises darkened my golden skin with ugly tinges of blue and purple. Anara had bashed my face in with the might of his hatred. I instinctively ran my hand over my belly, grateful my child had been spared his wrath.

The throbbing in my face and the relentless pounding in my head intensified as I relived the moment of the assault. The day had taken an array of unexpected turns, from the first moment I'd sat on the exam table until I'd opened the door to find Anara waiting for me. The disastrous outcome struck my battered body with a final blow, releasing my pain and terror in one mangled sob. I wasn't one for hysterics, nor did I want to be. I gritted my teeth so my tears ran silently and focused on that tiny heartbeat in order to calm.

Misha stepped next to me. Tension and fury darkened his beautifully masculine features. He turned on the water and soaked the washcloth gripped in his hand, then gently passed it over my face. "Whoever did this shall suffer," he promised.

A screeching of tires followed by the furious growls of my mate had me jerking away.

"Get out of my way before I kill you." Hisses and growls followed Aric's threat.

My sister Shayna's urgent voice surged over the chaos as she pleaded with her husband. "Koda, *don't*! This isn't helping Celia."

My other sister, Taran, also made her presence known. "I will jolt the shit out of anyone who starts a fight. Tim, where the hell is Celia?" she demanded of Misha's bodyguard.

"She's in the bedroom with the master," Edith taunted. "They're *busy*."

Of course, since the universe hated me, Marvin Gaye now sang "Sexual Healing." Tim, although not my biggest fan, took charge. "Let Celia's sisters through, but no one else shall pass."

Aric's growls cracked through the air like static. *"Celia is my mate. You will* not *keep me from her!"*

"She's my master's bride—"

A loud sizzle followed pained grunting.

13

Shit. Taran had just fired her lightning at Aric. Under other circumstances I would have ripped into her.

Anger riled Gemini's inner wolf and deepened his typically calm tone with an edge of anger. "Taran, I won't allow you to release your frustrations on Aric." Koda and Liam growled, furious Taran had attacked their Leader. "*Nor* will I allow threats upon my mate," Gemini snarled at them.

Taran ignored all of them. "Perhaps you didn't hear me the first time, Aric. I said I will jolt the shit out of *anyone* who starts a fight!"

"Damnit, Taran—"

"Aric, this bullshit with you and the vamps isn't helping Celia—stay here. Shayna and I will check on her."

"That's right. Stay, boy—" Liz didn't finish her insult. She was too busy screaming from whatever Taran zapped her with before she and Shayna barreled into the house.

I turned to Misha. "I don't want to see Aric. Please ask him to leave—*nicely*."

Misha angled his head, surprised by my request. Given that he hated Aric, I didn't need to ask twice. My sisters stumbled into the bathroom, where he had directed them on his way out. They screamed when they saw me.

Aric's growls returned full force. *"What's happening?"*

Shayna veered back toward the stairs. "You *have* to find Emme. Celia's in really bad shape!"

Taran approached me slowly, like she'd never seen me before. "Son of a bitch, Celia. What did this to you?" She reached to touch my face, only to yank it back as if it stung.

Tears streamed down Shayna's cheeks. I didn't want to lie to them, but I had to keep them safe. "I swung by the house to get some things. A pack of wolves broke in and attacked me."

Taran clasped her hand over her jaw. "Shit. Did you kill them?"

I lowered my head. "No. I was no match for them."

Taran took in the mangled mess of my face. "How the hell did you get away?" I was a horrible liar. "I didn't, they left me there when they were done."

Shayna's slender frame hunched and her long, silky black ponytail seemed to droop. She wiped her blue eyes on the sleeve of her white tunic. "Why would they just leave you like that?"

"You mean instead of just killing me?" I hated scaring them, but I wanted them to stop talking. I shrugged. "I don't know, I guess because they could."

Sleet splattered against the window and skylights, but it did little to muffle Misha and Aric. Damn, they were both furious. And Misha carrying the scent of his arousal from his snack time with me only made matters worse.

"What did you do to her?" Aric demanded.

I could almost picture Misha's wicked smile. "Tending to her wounds required me to taste her, and so I did."

There was some scuffling and growling. The wolves were struggling to hold back Aric. "Aric, listen to me," Liam grunted. "Celia was still bleeding when we arrived."

"I'm not leaving until I see her." Aric's deep timbre rang with anger, but Liam's words appeared to have stopped him from killing Misha. I was surprised Misha didn't rub his feasting more in Aric's face. Maybe he didn't want to upset me . . . or maybe he preferred that Aric jump to his own conclusions.

"Celia does not desire your presence, canine. Can you fault her? How many times have you reduced her to tears?"

A stillness grew over the worsening weather. "Those times are behind us," Aric growled. "Whether you like it or not, my future lies with her."

Aric wasn't leaving. I had to make him go before Misha did. The wolves were deadly, but so were the vampires. And Misha's house was full of vamps ready to kill anything that threatened their master. I clutched the towel against my chest, shaking from knowing what I had to do. I moved away from my sisters, who carefully worked to dig the shards of glass from my back. I barely felt the tugs and pulls. Fear and regret had numbed me to any physical pain.

I cleared my throat when I reached the open bedroom door and tried to speak as loudly as possible. "I don't want to see you, Aric. You need to leave." *And if you don't, you'll die.*

There was so much pain and astonishment in Aric's voice my stomach churned in painful rumbles. "Celia . . . what—"

"I told you, I don't want to see you!" I croaked. The tears that had stopped just moments before returned full force. Being cruel to *anyone*—especially Aric—was unthinkable.

The seconds of stunned silence passed with brutal thumps to my insides until Misha broke through the horrible quiet. "Celia wants nothing to do with you. Go lick your wounds elsewhere, wolf. You are not welcome in our home."

No one spoke. No one moved. No one breathed. For what seemed like an eternity, time stood still. "Come, Aric," Gemini finally said. "Our efforts are better suited in finding Emme."

Liam's growls reverberated against the windows. "You're an asshole, Misha. I know you're influencing her somehow."

Koda sounded more pissed than Liam. "Tim, if you don't wipe that goddamn smirk off your face, I'll tear out your throat and leave it for the crows!"

Shayna rushed past me, pausing only to shoot me a

pained glance over her shoulder. Her presence would help facilitate the wolves' departure, despite the confusion and disappointment shadowing her pixie face.

Taran waited with me with her arms crossed. I couldn't face her. Hell, I couldn't even raise my head. Yet I felt her taking me in and scented the sharp aroma of her shock as it pierced through my damaged nose.

When the last few snarls faded and the roar of the engines disappeared along the lengthy stretch of Misha's driveway, Shayna returned and clasped my hands. "I know Aric doesn't look the same, but he's still the same wolf. He loves you, Ceel. You have to see past his injuries…"

Shayna's voice faded when my sobs overtook me. She thought I was abandoning Aric because of his deformities. And I had to let her believe it was true. Despite how much it pained me, it would keep him, her, and everyone else safe for now.

Taran maneuvered her way between us and led me toward the sink. "Leave her alone, Shayna. Now's not the time. Come on, we need to get this fucking glass out of her back."

Chapter Three

A glimmer of silver light flashed beneath Shayna's white tunic and traveled along her arm. Koda had given her a platinum belly ring for her birthday. Using her special gift, she transferred the alloy into the tweezers she held to lengthen and thin the tips. She hoped the more precise tool would help her remove the shard of glass embedded in my shoulder blade. The pain sucked. I didn't understand how something so small could have pierced so deeply, but then I remembered Anara's show of strength. I'd never encountered magic so powerful.

I gritted my teeth and worked to bury my pain, but Shayna's unrelenting burrowing into my muscles had me writhing beneath her touch. It was all I could do not to *change* and bolt from the room.

Shayna's grip remained firm, despite the shakiness in her voice. "I'm so sorry, Ceel. I'm having a hard time reaching it."

Misha knelt before me and lifted my chin with his fingertips. "My darling, meet my eyes and I can help you endure the pain."

My sisters and I were immune to the hypnotic

power vampires have over humans. Misha alone could connect with me, given he'd pass me his *call* . . . and because he almost killed me once, feeding from me. I nodded. After the day I'd had, I was ready for a "Misha high." The moment our eyes locked, a soothing wave of peace filled me. The last time he'd calmed me I felt mellow and content—similar to when I woke in my warm bed to gentle raindrops pitter-pattering against my window. Not this time. Images appeared in my mind, full of vibrant colors and complete with surround sound.

Yellow finches chirped and flew happily across a vast grassy field where Misha and I sat on a soft brown blanket. A thick white sweater swathed the muscles of his arms and chest. I smiled. He looked amazing, although it was strange to see him in jeans rather than the designer slacks he preferred to wear. A soft breeze blew against his long blond hair, draping it over his shoulder while the blue sky illuminated his gray eyes like pools of melted silver.

A long white cotton dress covered my thin frame, a matching lace wrap draped over my bare shoulders. Misha's gaze wandered down my body, softening when he fixed it on my chest. I glanced down, curious to see what held him so captivated.

My body jerked and I almost dropped the small bundle in my arms. A baby nursed at my breast. A *baby*! He squirmed a little before settling down and cuddling closer against me.

Taran's swearing and Shayna's panicked voice echoed in the distance. "What's wrong with her, dude?"

"Her pain is more than I predicted. I will attempt a stronger hypnosis..."

The scene repeated itself before quickly morphing into another equally mind-blowing image. Misha and I held hands, walking along the same field, wearing the same clothes while three small children ran toward us with open arms. There were two boys and a little girl, their cheeks bright pink from running and laughing. They all appeared happy.

And they all resembled Misha.

Long blond hair swept away from their faces, revealing their twinkling gray eyes. The two boys jumped into Misha's welcoming embrace. The pretty little girl skipped to me with a smile as warm as sunshine. "Mommy!" she cried.

I awoke abruptly, huddled on the bathroom floor with several towels wrapped around me. Cold sweat chilled my body. Misha lay sprawled at the opposite corner. Judging by his pallor and bulging eyes, he'd seen everything.

Okay........ clearly the "Misha high" was the wrong way to go.

For the first time since I met him, Misha's voice actually cracked when he spoke. "What ... happened?"

Shayna and Taran crouched on either side of me. Their attention alternated between us, and confusion angled their small brows. Shayna adjusted the towels around me. "You were holding Celia's face in your hands. Everything was fine at first, but then you started shaking."

Taran's eyes narrowed. "Not just shaking, but freaking glowing. Damnit, I don't know what the hell happened, but it looked like you both went into shock."

Misha said nothing, stunned into silence. So not a good sign.

Thank God Emme arrived . . . although I wasn't thrilled to find Hank at her side. Her eyes brimmed with tears the moment she saw me. "Oh my goodness, Celia."

Shayna's deep blue eyes widened as she took in Hank. "Em . . . where have you been? We left you a bunch of messages telling you Celia was in trouble."

"I know. I'm so sorry." Emme reached her hands out to heal me, encasing my trembling form with her soft yellow light. "We hurried back as soon as we knew."

We?

Every menacing stare shot toward Hank. A spark of white and blue fire sizzled over Taran's head. "Oh, *hell* no."

Hank ignored us and focused solely on Misha. "Emme has been with me, Master. We wanted some privacy so we silenced our phones."

Misha had Hank by the throat before we could blink, dangling him several feet off the ground and shaking him with every word he hissed. "Do you find me so beneath you that you may disregard me at your leisure?"

My larynx may not have been completely crushed, but Hank's sure was. He could barely spit out an apology. "Of course not, Master. Please forgive me."

Misha's eyes flickered to Emme before returning to Hank. "Did you harm her?"

Emme's palms shot up and her fair skin darkened to red. "Of course not. Please let him go, Misha."

Taran rounded on her, blue and white flames sizzling in waves along her arms. "Forget that asshole and worry about your sister. We've just spent the last hour removing glass from her back. Now for shit's sake work your mojo and heal her!"

Emme's soft green eyes glistened with unshed tears. I'd never seen Taran so angry or aggressive toward Emme before.

Hank snarled, a rare feat considering the purple tinge working its way up to his hairline. "Don't talk to her that way."

Misha didn't seem happy Hank could still speak. He gave Hank's throat another squeeze, ignoring Emme's audible gasps.

Air fizzed out of Hank's nose. Shayna glanced nervously at him. "Hank, I'd keep your mouth shut if I were you."

I cleared my throat. "Um, Misha, I'd really like my

face back. Could you stop choking Hank so Emme can concentrate?"

Misha flung Hank out the door. Emme clasped her hand over her mouth as Misha stalked past her. He cranked the hot water into the bath. "I will have clothes and food brought to you. Later this evening, if you are well enough, I would like a word with you."

Sure, can't wait. "Okay, Misha." He kissed my head and left without further incident, although I couldn't fail to notice the hesitancy in his steps.

Emme approached me under Taran's watchful glare. Taran's fire had died down enough so the mansion wouldn't burn to cinders, but the tension around her curvy figure was hot enough to scorch.

Emme bowed her head, her honey-blond hair falling around her face. "I'm sorry, Celia. If I knew you were hurt I never would have—"

"Forget it, Emme. I'm fine." I stared at my injuries in the mirror. "This is going to hurt, isn't it?"

Emme nibbled on her bottom lip. "Since I have to readjust the bones in your face… a little."

Emme lied. It was torture. Pure, unadulterated, beat-me-with-a-battle-axe-and-stab-me-in-the-face torture. We all jumped at the sick, crunching sound my cheekbones made when they realigned. And although I think Emme tried to quickly lead my nose back home, the agonizing pain lingered. My scream woke the dead—or at least every vamp in the house. Snot trickled down my face like a faucet in time for Misha to charge back in.

I smeared all the nasal contents across my face in my failed attempt to wipe. "Hi," I muttered.

Liz gagged. "Is she healed?"

Shayna narrowed her eyes and reached for one of the toothpicks she kept in her pocket, ready to convert it into a long, deadly needle and stab Liz with it. "Well, duh," she said. "Can't you see how much better she looks?"

"No. I can't." Liz made an irritated gesture with her hand. "Wash her. She looks nasty."

As much as Shayna appeared ready to stab her, she managed to clasp Taran's wrists before she shut Liz up permanently. Aside from surrounding herself with blue and white flames, Taran couldn't gather her magic without the use of her hands.

"Now, Liz, is this any way to address your mistress?" Misha remained calm, unlike Taran, who screamed obscenities at the top of her lungs.

Liz, like all vampires, was very tall, slender, and beautiful. She seemed to shrink as she cowered at her master's feet. The slightest narrowing of Misha's lips inspired her to flee.

"You'd better leave, you ignorant bitch!" Taran yelled after her.

Misha bent to face me as I continued to use the towel as a tissue. "You will feel more like yourself after you bathe," he said gently.

Misha's obvious strength and allure intimidated most everyone. He commanded any room he entered—women *and* men fell over themselves to please him. He had power, wealth, and everlasting beauty. He'd grown accustomed to getting what he wanted . . . and then he met me.

I'd turned down his invitations to bed more times than I could count. In spite of my rejections, I'd become something he didn't have, a real friend, and he had absolutely no idea what to do with me. Unlike the vampires he ruled, I was loyal because I wanted to be—not because I had to be. Initially he'd continued to flirt, but when I moved into his guesthouse our relationship changed. Misha developed genuine feelings for me. While I loved him, it wasn't the way he wished. I loved *Aric* and no one could change that.

Misha gazed at me with complete tenderness. It was

a look he never gave anyone—not even his beloved master, Uri, who regarded him as a son. Although not completely my fault, I ruined our moment. I'd been nauseated for days, but the scents of my slathered body fluids overwhelmed me at once. I made it to the toilet just in time. Shayna was a labor nurse, like I was before I joined Team Misha to help him and his vampire allies take down the Tribe. Emme had continued working in hospice. They were both accustomed to vomit. Taran worked in the cardiac catheterization lab. She didn't do puke.

Taran was the perfect blend of a thin figure and voluptuous curves. Out of the four of us, she had inherited the majority of our mother's Latin genes. Her deep olive skin and dark wavy hair drew males to her with a simple bat of her thick lashes. Taran was beautiful. But she wasn't acting beautiful then. "Damnit, Emme, I thought you healed her!"

Emme held back my hair and rubbed my back. "I did!"

"Then why the hell is she puking?"

Emme's voice grew defensive, but tears drifted into every word. "I can't cure everything perfectly. She may still have a concussion."

I wiped my mouth with some tissues. "Enough, Taran. No more fighting. I need a bath. Do you think you could calm down enough to help me?" It was pathetic, but I did need help. The throbbing in my face had stopped, but every part of me ached from being forced to heal so quickly. I had to rest soon. Not just for me, but for our little one, too.

Misha led me to the bath when I stood. "The water contains eucalyptus and special salts that will help remedy your pain."

"Thanks, Misha." He bowed slightly and disappeared from the room.

After I brushed my teeth, my sisters gave me a

thorough washing. Taran, I'll admit, was more than a little rough when she shampooed my hair.

"Son of a bitch, I don't believe this day."

"It's okay, Taran."

"No, Celia. It's not. First you get the shit beaten out of you and then your own sister isn't there to help you."

"Dude, stop already. Emme feels bad. How many times can she apologize?" Taran shot Emme another glare.

"Not enough, Shayna."

Emme added more salt to the water without a word. Taran huffed and dug her nails against my scalp. I jerked my head away. "Taran, stop. You're yanking out my hair."

"Well, if you would just stop moving—"

I lurched away from her. "Just let me do it."

Taran crossed her arms. "Damnit, Emme. You upset Celia."

Shayna threw her hands in the air. "Will you stop blaming her? None of this was intentional!"

Taran opened her mouth to say something, but I silenced her with a growl. "Just zip it, Taran."

I climbed out of the tub and dried off. After moisturizing my skin, I slipped on a clean robe. I tried to appear calm, but no one believed my façade. The day should have been one of the happiest of my life, but instead it toppled into one giant hell hole.

Shayna wrapped her arm around me. "What's wrong, Ceel?"

I pinched the bridge of my nose. "It's been a rough day. I just need some rest. Call Koda, he's probably missing you."

Koda, like Aric, had been burned. And while his scarring was severe, it wasn't as extreme as Aric's.

Shayna shook her head. "I can't leave you like this."

"I'm fine, Shayna. Go to Koda. He needs you." I tried to smile, but there was only so much encouragement I could muster. The great thing about Shayna was that although she knew she should stay, she also realized I didn't want her to.

"Okay, but call me if anything changes."

I paused for a moment, trying to gather my words. "Will you tell Aric that I'm fine . . . and not to worry about me."

She puckered her brows. "Shouldn't you tell him yourself?"

I lowered my head. "It's not a good idea for me to talk to him right now."

Shayna didn't like what I had to say, but didn't push me. She pulled her cellphone out of her back pocket and called her mate. "Hi, puppy. Emme's here. She healed Celia so she's okay now. Could you come get me?"

"Just you, baby?"

Shayna looked over at Taran. I answered for her when she shook her head. "Taran's going, too. I need to rest."

Taran watched me for a beat. "Screw all this vampire shit and come with us."

"I can't. Aric will get in trouble with the Elders for seeing me."

She whispered low in my ear so Koda wouldn't hear. "The Elders' directives haven't stopped either of you for weeks."

I shot her a hard stare. "A lot has changed, Taran."

Taran angled her perfect brows. I let her believe I meant Aric's injuries. It was wrong, but for the moment, it was also easier. "Shayna, tell Koda I'll be joining you."

Shayna didn't tell him right away, she was too busy explaining to Koda where Emme had been. Koda growled upon learning she'd slipped away with Hank. Even Gemini snarled a curse. Emme turned her back, tired, I suppose, of being judged by those she loved.

"Puppy, just don't say anything to Liam. I don't

want him flipping out. How long will it take you to get here?"

"We never left. We're outside the gate."

Taran veered around. "Oh, hell, even Aric?"

"No. He and Liam went back to the house to try to figure out who attacked Celia."

My heartbeat lowered to a dull throb. I'd been so hurtful to my wolf, and there he was, trying to figure out who'd harmed me.

Shayna played with the edges of her ponytail. "Taran and I will be right out."

"We'll be waiting. I love you, baby."

"I love you, too." Shayna smiled into the phone while misery shimmered in her eyes. Koda was no longer in pain, but she was. The scars would be a reminder of how much *weres* suffered protecting the earth.

Taran pulled me into a hug. "Call me later, okay?"

"I'll try."

Normally my answer wouldn't have satisfied Taran, especially when she suspected something amiss. But of all my sisters, she knew me best. She realized there was a reason for my silence. Just like she knew I would talk about it when I was ready.

Shayna's hug was tighter. "I'm glad you're safe— and don't worry, the wolves will figure it out."

My body stiffened against her. *God, I hope not.*

Shayna and Emme also embraced. When Emme released her and stepped toward Taran,

Taran stormed out without another glance. I wasn't in the right frame of mind to talk to Taran about her behavior. Hell, I didn't know how I was still functioning. All I could do was hold Emme against me and try to comfort her.

"I really am sorry, Celia."

I stroked her hair. "I know, sweetie. It's okay." Someone rapped impatiently on the door leading out to the hall. Emme wiped her tears and answered it while I towel dried my hair. The massive granite counter held dozens of hair products. No wonder Misha's hair always appeared perfect. I picked one that I thought would keep my curls smooth and sprayed it on.

Maria's thick Brazilian accent echoed the length of the hall. "Dis is for Celia. De master had Chef prepare her dinner. If Celia is too tired to come down, he would like her to remain in his chambers and de food will be brought to her."

"No, that's okay, we'll be down," I answered quickly. If I stayed in Misha's bedroom, he'd expect more than I could give him.

I passed into the suite when I heard the door shut. Emme perched on the bed next to a beautiful white dress.

The exact same dress from my vision.

Chapter Four

"Is something wrong?" Emme asked.

No, just my life going to hell. I gaped at the dress. "Uh, I'm just going to wear what I have on."

Emme took in my not-so-impressive ensemble. At five foot three, the robe I wore hung to the floor.

Emme lifted the dress and examined it closely. "It looks like it will fit you."

"I have no doubt," I mumbled.

Emme blinked back at me. "Um. There's lingerie, too . . . in case that's what's troubling you."

"I wish going commando was my only problem."

"Huh?"

"Nothing." I sighed, defeated, and yanked on the panties and strapless bra with as much enthusiasm as putting on a funeral shroud. I slipped the dress over my head. The spaghetti straps were thin but comfortable and the soft cotton skirt flowed down to my shins.

Emme smiled softly. "You look beautiful, Celia. Misha must know your love of sundresses, but I'll admit it's unusual attire for spring in Tahoe. Are you warm enough?"

"Yeah."

Emme watched cautiously. "Okay, I guess we should head down, then."

I nodded. Emme gently clasped my elbow and led me out into the hall when I didn't move. Misha waited at the bottom of the sprawling slate and wrought-iron staircase. The adoration in his eyes completely unnerved me. He wasn't Misha then; he resembled a groom meeting his bride at the altar. My breath hammered out of my lungs in time with my rapid heartbeat.

Oh. God. What's he doing? Why is he looking at me like that? What's wrong with him?

I'm pregnant with another male's child, for heaven's sake! I can't give him what he wants, I . . .

The last thing I remembered was Emme screaming my name. I awoke exactly where I didn't want to be—Misha's bed.

"How are you, honey?"

I didn't answer Emme until I was sure I still had clothes on. "What happened?"

"You fainted. I'm pretty sure you have a concussion. I've tried healing you, but it doesn't seem to be working."

I jerked up and scanned the colossal suite. "Why am I here? Why aren't we at the guesthouse?"

Emme placed her hand on my shoulder. "Misha is really worried, and so am I. I'm afraid if we don't wake you every two hours you'll slip into a coma."

I leapt out of the bed. "Good idea. Let's head back to the guesthouse. You can set your cellphone to wake me every two hours."

"Celia, I don't think you should—"

Misha's footsteps approaching the door put me into crazy mode. I shot out to the deck, jumped off . . . and landed on top of Hank.

Hank provided me with a surprisingly cushy

landing. I rolled off him and stood on the cold wet ground. "Sorry, Hank."

Hank stumbled to his feet. "Where the hell did you come from?"

"Ahhh."

His head snapped up. "Did you just jump off the goddamn deck?"

"Well—"

"I always knew you were bats, but this is nutty even for you!"

Considering he was trying to get into my little sister's pants, he had a lot of nerve being pissy with me. "Bats? Did *you* just call *me* bats, Dracula?"

Hank bared his fangs. "You have a lot of goddamn nerve. You land on me and now you're making racist jokes. I oughta—"

I rammed my finger in his face. "You oughta what? I've had a bad day, Hank. If you want a piece of me, just say the word."

"Hank?" Emme peered over the stacked stone deck. "You're making a big mistake by taking on Celia."

Hank flashed her his fangs. "Don't worry about me, baby. I can take her."

"Um, she'll pound you, Hank. But I'm more concerned about Misha."

A breeze blew in from the lake strong enough to chill my bare shoulders . . . and send Misha's aroma downwind. We hadn't noticed him before, but we did then. He emerged from the shadows. Hank and I swallowed hard. Me, because I wasn't ready to face him, and Hank, well, because Misha might just kill him.

Misha stepped between us, sending Hank scurrying back. "You have sorely tried my patience today."

Hank bowed his head. "I apologize, Master."

"Your requests for forgiveness have grown tiresome. *Leave.*" Misha clutched my arm when I tried to bolt. "Not you, Celia. There are matters we need to discuss."

My shoulders slumped. "Fine." I didn't want to do this now, or ever, but it wasn't fair to keep him waiting and wondering.

"Can we talk back at the guesthouse?"

"As you wish." He bent to lift me, but I leapt from his grasp.

"What are you doing?"

"My darling, your feet are bare. Although the rain and sleet have subsided, I can hardly allow you to walk as you are."

No way in hell was I letting him carry me over the damn threshold. I sped ahead of him. "I'm fine, Misha. My inner beast has me covered."

Misha, of course, kept up with ease, chuckling despite my erratic behavior. The frozen slate chilled my soles, but sure enough, my metabolism made it doable. I crossed through the garden and reached the guesthouse in record speed. Misha opened the thick wooden door before I could reach the handle. I never locked the door. Vampire bodyguards with the ability to tear limbs like dry grass were all the supernatural security I needed.

I reached for a kitchen towel and wiped my feet. The moment I tossed it in the laundry room Misha pulled me to him and tried to kiss me. I whipped my head back. He managed to reach my cheek, but not much more.

Misha laughed against my ear. "My darling, at this rate we shall never conceive our children."

I broke from his hold and backed away. "Misha, we're not having children."

Misha crossed his arms, the edges of his lips curving into a patient smile. "You cannot deny the future we saw today. We will have children, and you—you will finally love me."

I buried my face in my hands and willed myself to

calm. I didn't understand the vision— why I'd had it, why he'd seen it. None of it made sense. I loved Aric, and knowing I carried his baby kept my feet firmly placed in reality. I dropped my hands to my sides and took a breath. Misha was my friend, and the last thing I wanted was to cause him pain. But I wouldn't lie to him just to spare his feelings. "Misha, I don't love you. The vision we saw isn't real."

His smile faded, but he refused to admit defeat. "Perhaps now, but in time—"

I shook my head. "Aric is who I love. You've known this from the start."

Misha took my hand in his and brushed his lips over my knuckles. "If that is so, why did you have me send the mongrel away?"

I froze. Misha's smile widened, pleased by my silence. He brushed a curl away from my face. "Will you join me in bed tonight?"

My jaw dropped open. "No, Misha. I told you this isn't real."

Emme's soft footsteps had me turning toward the door. She stilled when she saw us in the kitchen, Misha holding tight to my hand. Her cheeks reddened to a bright pink. "Am I-I interrupting?"

I pulled away from Misha, my own face heating. "Of course not, Emme."

Emme slowly walked in and slipped out of her cream wool coat, keeping her gaze away from mine.

"It's not what you think, Emme," I insisted.

I might as well have been talking to the door. Misha kissed the top of my head. "I will have dinner brought to you. My love, if you decide to join me in bed, call the main house. Otherwise the women who wait to pleasure me will still be present."

"Gee, thanks for the heads-up," I told him.

Misha laughed. "Do not fear, my darling. Once we

marry, I will no longer have need for other bedfellows." He paused and thought about it. "Unless, of course, it's what you desire."

My unamused, perturbed, and partially psycho expression must have told Misha exactly how I felt about his bedfellows.

I laid into the buffet Chef delivered like my life depended on it. I couldn't remember ever being so hungry. Halfway through my meal I caught Emme staring at me. "What's wrong, aren't you going to eat?"

Emme folded her hands on the wooden table. "I would, Celia, but you took my plate."

I waved my fork around. "Chef brought four over, take one of those."

Emme sighed and tried to gather her thoughts. "I did, Celia . . . and I put food on it, except you took it from me and added it to your piles. You're eating from all four plates."

I glanced at the almost empty plates in front of me. "Oh." I polished off the contents on one plate and handed it to her. "Here you go."

She took it to the sink and washed it, but when she returned a frown shadowed her soft features. "Celia, what's happening between you and Misha?"

I shrugged. "He thinks he loves me and is convinced I'll eventually love him back."

"Is there more?"

"No, Emme!" I hissed. Even though I'd already consumed what most linebackers ate in a day, I was strangely irate that she was interrupting my chewing and digesting process. When she reached a hand toward me, I growled and gathered my plates closer.

"I was just reaching for a spoon."

I felt terrible for frightening her, just obviously not

enough to stop eating. "Sorry, Emme," I said through a mouthful of food.

It was only seven at night when I finished devouring everything I could get my hands on, but I thought it best to turn in. I remember brief periods of Emme waking me, otherwise I slept soundly. Perhaps the emotional strain of the day had taken its toll, because I don't remember dreaming. I just remember a wave of nausea hitting me strong enough to jolt me awake.

I raced to the bathroom and was immediately sick. My stomach continued to do flips as I cleaned up. When I exited the bathroom, Emme sat on the bed. Her troubled expression convinced me she suspected my pregnancy. I leaned against the door and tried to assume a relaxed pose. "What is it?"

"Um, Celia. Misha and I are very worried about you. He's asked Chang and Ying-Ying to help relieve your condition by doing a combination of Asian mystical treatments."

My fingers nervously picked through my hair. "When you say 'condition,' what exactly do you mean?"

She puckered her brow. "Well, your concussion, of course."

"Of course." Relief washed over me until I sensed something more was up. Having everyone believe that I had a concussion should have helped to explain my symptoms. I didn't understand why she appeared so frightened. Concussions were common. I was coherent, and God knew I was eating enough. "Don't fret, Emme. I'm fine. I don't need Ying-Ying and Chang's help."

"Celia," Emme said slowly. "You've been asleep for two days."

"*What?*"

"Everyone is worried sick. I've been trying to keep them calm, but it's hard when I'm scared myself."

I shoved away from the frame and sat next to her,

trying my best to smile. "I'm just tired and need to sleep, Emme. That's all. Call the others and tell them there's nothing to worry about."

Emme covered my hand with hers. "Don't you want to talk to them yourself?"

I turned my head to look at the time. Two o'clock. Damn. I'd slept for almost forty-eight hours. "I don't feel like talking to anyone."

"Not even Aric?"

"No." I stood and gave her my back, unable to face her blatant disappointment in me. "Could you give me a moment alone? I'd like to shower."

"Sure, Celia," she mumbled.

I checked my phone messages when Emme shut the door quietly behind her. There were several from our other sisters and a couple from our werewolf BFFs, Bren and Danny. Most were from Aric. His voice was so different, and not just because the scarring to his lips and jaw limited his enunciation. His deep timbre, once so strong, lacked the conviction that made those he led stand and take notice.

In his first message, I could detect his fear for my well-being, yet I also caught an underlying note of rage. "Celia, call me. I need to know you're safe."

The next demonstrated escalating worry. "Look, I don't care what happened between you and the vamp in his room." There was some fumbling and swearing, before he continued. "That's a lie—I do care, but it doesn't change how I feel about you. Call me, love."

Aric's third message broke my heart. "Sweetness . . . I haven't heard from you. I know a lot has changed. But I still love you. Please know that I love you."

There were a few more threatening to disembowel Misha if he was keeping me from him, but those weren't the ones that triggered my tears. I caressed my stomach softly, feeling so alone—and knowing there wasn't a damn thing I could do about it. My hatred for Anara grew, burning deep within me until it pained me physically.

I dropped my head and tried to slow my breathing. No. There wasn't anything I could do.

For now . . . .

Someone knocked on the door. I wiped my eyes as Emme spoke. "Celia? Misha is here with Ying-Ying and Chang."

I groaned, in no mood for company. But when it came down to it, everyone meant well. I stood and marched toward the door. Besides that, how bad could mystical Asian treatments be?

I froze when I saw what awaited me. Apparently, they could be pretty bad. And sticky. "Misha, is this really necessary?"

I lay in my bathtub covered in a paste made from hundred-year-old dried herbs while Ying- Ying floated in lotus pose above my body. Chang sang in Korean, an offbeat ballad I was convinced he made up as he went along.

"My darling, do try to relax so the remedies will help you."

I narrowed my eyes. "How can I relax? I'm covered in glop and it feels like something is crawling on me."

"I think it's just Ying-Ying," Emme offered.

"Chang, I believe Celia is having difficulty calming her spirit. Perhaps she would benefit from some He Huan Hua."

Chang stopped singing and regarded Misha like it was the greatest idea ever. While he mashed up more goo, Ying-Ying assumed entertainment duties. Chang's baritone was as low as a deep bass drum. Ying-Ying's voice was as high as the strike of a triangle. In key, yet sharp enough to cut designs into glass.

Misha and Emme fled in an obvious attempt to save their hearing. I tried to cover my ears, but I inadvertently shoved the Shu Di Huang slime into the canals. It was surprisingly soothing and helped block Ying-Ying's high soprano yodeling. It was not, however, enough to prevent me from hearing what Emme rushed back to tell me.

"Celia, Aric is here to see you."

Chapter Five

In my haste to jump out of the bathtub, I completely forgot about poor Ying-Ying hovering above me. I slammed into her and sent her flying into the tiled wall. The impact broke her concentration and she crash-landed on the floor. Anyone else would be swearing and cursing me, and maybe she did. But after a couple of short phrases in Mandarin, her maniacal laugh bounced off the walls with an echo. Chang pumped his fist triumphantly and said something to her in Korean. Apparently, they both believed they had "cured" me.

I hauled her off the floor. "Sorry, Ying-Ying." She resumed her lotus pose and floated out the door after Chang. My head jerked back and forth from the door to Emme as I completely panicked.

Emme pointed to the door. "Should I have Aric wait in the living room?" "No. I don't want to see him."

Emme crinkled her freckled nose. "It shouldn't take you long to clean up."

My eyes trailed down my slop-dripping form. Was she kidding? I resembled something that had just emerged from the trenches of a Staten Island landfill. I grabbed a towel and wrapped it around me. "I told you, I don't want to see him."

Emme played with her hands nervously. "Celia, Aric is hurting. He needs you."

"Don't you think I know that?!"

I didn't mean to snap at her. And I didn't mean to cause the tears that welled in her soft green eyes. I should have apologized then, except Aric's deep growls had me darting into my room. I grabbed my cellphone off my dresser and hid in my supersized closet. I skimmed through my contacts until I found the Alpha I needed.

Aric's Alpha.

I hated calling Martin, except there was no other choice. Out of the two remaining Elders, Aric was closest to him. He'd been one of his father's Warriors and had helped raise Aric following his father's death. Aric would probably still be reprimanded, but it would spare him from Anara's wrath.

"Hello?" answered a deep baritone voice.

"Martin, it's Celia Wird. Um, you probably heard I was attacked a few days ago."

"Yes. We are looking into the matter. You have my word the wolves responsible will be taken care of—"

"That's not why I'm calling." I took a deep breath, still unsure whether my actions were the right ones. I banged my fist against the door. "Aric is here . . . at Misha's house."

He paused, probably either furious at Aric for disobeying him or questioning why I'd ratted him out. "I see," he finally said.

"He probably only wants to make sure I'm safe," I added quickly. "But since he doesn't get along with Misha, he might need help leaving."

"Indeed, he might," he said quietly. "I'm in the area. I'll be there shortly."

The closet door swung open as Martin disconnected. I jumped. There stood my love, in all his battered glory. He'd shaved what had remained of his hair. His face was unreadable, frozen from the deep scars that crisscrossed his face like reptilian scales. The slit that had allowed his left eye to see through the battered flesh was larger. His right, completely sealed just days before, was now visible. I couldn't see his baby browns well. But I saw they remained intense, healthy, and beautiful.

He inhaled deeply, taking in my scent as he often did when we'd been apart. His nostrils were incapable of flaring, from the severity of the tissue damage, but it didn't matter. It was his subtle way of demonstrating he'd missed me. Aric didn't seem to care that my aroma was masked by an array of Asian herbs; he just wanted to feel close to me.

I reached out and touched his hard, jagged face without thinking. He leaned into my hands and rubbed against them. The show of affection was so strong in such a small gesture, I lost my breath.

My eyes fixed on his as he spoke. "Makawee cut through the skin, in hopes that my eyes had survived." I nodded, but said nothing. He tried to kiss my hands, but what remained of his lips was nothing more than tough and melted flesh. "I can't blink or close them, so I have to moisten them and cover them with wet gauze to sleep. But I can see. I guess that's more important."

He obviously felt the need to explain. I let him as I linked my hands around his neck. God, I'd missed him. Aric fastened his strong arms around my waist. But as I melted against him, the faint song of wolves filled my ears. Something struck me in the shoulder, hard enough to break Aric's hold. I stumbled back. Aric's grip to my arm kept me from falling backward. To my absolute horror, Anara's faint image appeared next to Aric's. My blood turned to ice. He'd arrived to kill Aric.

"Perhaps I didn't make myself clear," Anara's voice echoed in my head.

"No!"

Aric swerved around, growling. He'd scented my fear, but he failed to see Anara. He veered back to me. "Celia, what's wrong?"

Anara examined him closely. "I can kill him now. Perhaps it might end his misery." His glare cut back to me. "The decision is yours."

My body plunged into survival mode, releasing my breath in rapid bursts. "You have to leave Aric...I don't want to see you anymore."

Aric stiffened. "What?"

"Too much has happened to keep us apart. Don't you see? We're not meant for each other."

Aric's anger and hurt masked his ability to scent my lies. "*Don't say that!* You can't just give up on us. I love you."

The song of wolves built into a crescendo. Anara's menacing focus returned full force on Aric. My efforts hadn't impressed him. I bit the inside of my cheek and let loose. "There is no more us, Aric. Get out!"

Aric reached for me. I slapped his hands away. "Get out," I sobbed. "You need to leave. *You need to leave now!*"

I'd expected Aric's fury. Instead he became strangely quiet. "No. I'm not going anywhere."

I shoved Aric hard, over and over again, Anara following us every step of the way. "I can't be with you! I won't be with you!"

My sobs threatened to choke me, but it was my hysterical screams that brought Misha and his vampires sweeping into my room like an avenging army. Martin and Emme rushed in behind them.

Misha covered me with a robe and hauled me away from Aric. I cried into my hands, humiliated and devastated by how I'd treated Aric.

And still Aric wanted me. Once more he reached for me, his head shaking in apparent shock and confusion.

Martin held him back with a simple clasp of his shoulder.

"It's time to go, Aric."

Aric slowly lowered his brutalized hands. "Please don't do this," he begged. "I love you."

I gasped, trying to catch my breath, caught between leaping into his arms and sputtering harsher words to force him away.

"You said you'd never leave me," he whispered.

I dug my claws through the thickness of the robe, digging into my flesh to keep me from collapsing. *I'm sorry. I'm so sorry. . . .*

Martin led Aric away. He didn't resist, but watched me until he disappeared around the corner. Anara's presence lingered long enough to show me a glimpse of his satisfied face before disappearing like a passing breeze.

An Elder, a master vampire, and Aric—a royal among *weres*—in one room. And no one had sensed Anara. My God, how was I going to stop him?

One by one, the vampires left, seemingly bored now that the drama had concluded with no bloodshed. Misha held me close until my cries lessened to mere whimpers.

Emme stood near my bed. I couldn't bear to look at her. It wasn't just how I'd treated Aric, but also the spinelessness I'd shown before Anara. The pain I felt from his physical assault was nothing compared to the ache in my heart. I'd been many things in my young life: an orphan, a foster child, a delinquent, but never a coward.

"I hate you," I hissed aloud.

The viciousness in my voice made both Misha and Emme tense. They exchanged glances. Emme walked slowly toward me. "Who are you talking to?" she asked. When I didn't answer, she stroked my hair with her fingers. "Celia?"

Emme's gentle touch disgusted me. I didn't deserve kindness. I tore away from her and bounded into my bathroom, slamming the door hard enough to crack the frame. Once again, I threw up, although this time it had nothing to do with my pregnancy. It was, however, a reminder that this situation wasn't solely about me. My baby depended on me to keep it together, and I'd be damned before I'd lay down and die.

After spending nearly half an hour getting cleaned up, I walked into the living room. Misha and Emme waited in silence. Misha should have been in his glory now that he believed Aric was out of my life. Instead he sat with his hands clasped in a praying position, something he often did when troubled. Emme kept her head lowered and fiddled nervously with the sleeve of her lavender sweater.

I rubbed at my face. "May I please have something to eat?"

Misha stood. "Whatever you wish," he said softly. He kissed my head. I was grateful for his show of affection. Perhaps I wasn't such a monster after all.

Emme approached me when he left and held tight to my hands. Her sweet face searched mine with sad eyes. "Celia, I don't know what's happening, but please promise me that if I can help, you'll let me."

I didn't promise her anything. Instead I released her and sat on the soft chocolate couch, staring at the unlit fireplace. Emme sighed and ignited it with a flip of a switch then took a seat beside me. She waited with me until Chef arrived with an assortment of finger sandwiches and hot bowls of carrot soup. I ate what I could stomach and went back to sleep.

In my dream, I returned to the same field I'd been in with Misha. This time, I walked through the soft green grass with the Aric of my past. His long dark hair hung slightly over his brown eyes and his five o'clock shadow hugged the strong jaw of his sexy face. My fingertips slid down his cheek. His dark Irish skin was soft and whole once more. He smiled and kissed my hand.

"I love you, Aric."

His smile faded and his dark brows creased into a deep frown. "No, you don't."

He shoved my hand away from him and stepped back. A flicker of fire sparked from his core and spread, engulfing his large form in a blanket of flames.

I screamed over Aric's agonized roars. The heat blistered my face and hands as I shoved him to the ground and swatted the blaze with my palms. The flames eventually died, leaving Aric crouched in a fetal position, naked and shivering. His entire body had been burned, every muscle raw, exposed, and horribly charred. Tears leaked from my eyes. "No, baby, no," I whispered.

I tried to hold him, but he leapt to his feet and bolted away. The field around us erupted into an inferno. I chased him, calling his name, pleading for him to return. My legs grew heavy and weak, I couldn't catch him. "Don't leave me, Aric!" I begged. "Please, let me help you!"

Aric vanished into the thickening cloud of smoke. Behind me children screamed for their mother. I whipped around frantically. Three small children raced toward me with their arms outstretched. They had all been burned, they were all in pain, and they all resembled Aric.

Chapter Six

My screams woke me from my hellish nightmare. Emme's voice called to me over the rising commotion around me. Strong arms grabbed me and held me down as hisses wafted above me. I forced my eyes open, my chest heaving from my attempts to shove away the vampires holding me down.

One by one they released me when I stopped struggling. Sweat stuck the thin fabric of my T-shirt against my skin and dripped from my scalp.

"Celia, can you hear me?" Emme stood about ten feet away, held firmly in place by Misha. She was bleeding from deep gashes to her chest and arms. Misha's vampires licked their lips greedily, turning their attention from me to her. Hank appeared especially ravenous.

Emme blushed before her soft yellow light erased the signs of her embarrassment and knitted her wounds closed. "Let me go to her, Misha." He released her and she approached me slowly. "Celia, do you know where you are, honey?"

Her words were clear and I knew I should answer, but my lack of strength and the numbness wearing me down made it seem like an impossible demand.

Edith slinked toward her, puffing out her chest and lengthening her incisors. "Maybe you should simply ask if she knows her name, sweet one," she cooed. She reached her hand toward Emme's face, but Hank forced his way between them.

"Emme isn't yours to take," he snapped.

Edith smiled sinfully. "Is she yours, then, Hank?"

Emme cleared her throat. "I'm not either of yours to . . . eat."

Edith's sultry eyes made Emme step back toward Misha. "We weren't just talking about feeding from you, little one."

Edith's arrogance vanished at Misha's hard stare. *"Leave!"* He ordered through clenched fangs.

The vamps obviously wanted to stay. While they could live forever, immortality tended to dispel excitement, and they grew restless with the monotony of everyday life. So, they eagerly waited for anything out of the ordinary to spice up their so-called lives. Unfortunately, today I'd been the one to provide the entertainment.

Emme slipped onto the bed and crawled to the center, where I sat unmoving. "Can you hear me, Celia?"

"I didn't mean to scratch you," I responded in way of an answer.

She tried to smile. "It's okay. It's my fault. I should have called for help instead of approaching you in your sleep. You were thrashing around so violently I thought that if I could heal your fear, your panic would cease."

My eyes scanned her blood-soaked sweater. "You were wrong."

Misha suddenly appeared alongside me. "Celia, you need to . . ." He referred to me as Celia only in the direst of situations. ". . . you need to eat," he finished quietly.

It was still daytime. The hazy spring sun shone softly against the window, just as it had before the start of my nap. "I just ate." My stomach growled, insisting otherwise.

Emme shook her head. "That was yesterday, Celia."

I had lost another day. "Oh. Then I guess I should eat."

Once again, I ate enough to feed a legion then returned to bed almost immediately. I didn't sleep. I was afraid to. I wanted to be with Aric. I longed to touch him and have him in bed with me, laughing and wrestling as we'd done countless times before our world fell apart. My new reality was too much to bear. My mind wandered to an intimate moment from our past, the first time I asked to see his wolf form.

"If you show me yours, I'll show you mine," I'd teased.

He adjusted his position above me, tickling me a little with his warm naked body. "I just saw yours, rather closely, I might add. Ohhh . . . you mean your beast form."

I hadn't fully adapted to being naked around him. And despite being in the familiar surroundings of my bedroom, my cheeks flushed and I squirmed beneath him. He smiled and bent his head to kiss me.

I moved his hand away when he cupped my breast and teased the nipple. "Ah, ah, ah. Not until you show me."

Aric groaned and slipped out of my king-sized bed. "Fine. But I'm warning you, I'm rather intimidating."

"I know." My eyes traveled down his muscular torso and fixed on a certain spot before returning to meet his. His face reddened at my grin. Most males would've been rather pleased with themselves. Not Aric. But his modesty was one of the characteristics that made him so sexy. "I'll tell you what, Aric. As soon as I see your big bad wolf, you can intimidate me some more."

Aric's body heated, this time for a different reason. "I'd like that," he murmured gruffly.

He jumped into bed as a magnificent large gray wolf. Silver and black covered his head and back, while snow-white fur encased his underside. He wagged his tail when I stroked him. It felt strange being naked around him while he was a wolf, so I *changed* and licked his face. He rubbed his head against my neck, making me purr. Even as a beast, he felt good, soft . . . perfect. My bed threatened to break when he playfully flipped me onto my back, so we returned to our human forms. His skin was as warm as his fur against me. For a while neither of us moved, we just stared at each other, breathing heavily as the heat continued to rise between us. Slowly, he stroked my hair away from my face. "God, you're beautiful," he'd whispered.

He had kissed me, and within moments had me writhing in pleasure. I rolled onto my stomach and gripped my pillow against me. I missed Aric—not just the intimate moments between us, but how he made me feel. In his arms I'd never known fear.

Celia? Aric's voice whispered in my head.

I scrambled to my feet and stilled, my eyes scanning the room. Through our bond as mates, Aric was communicating. They were more than just words; his feelings attached themselves to his verbiage. I felt his torment, just as I knew he felt my longing and hurt. And yet unlike a phone conversation, it didn't appear as though we could talk back and forth. It was more like our deepest emotions transferred to each other's soul.

The phone rang before I could panic about how much he knew. "Hello?"

Anara snarled on the other line. "Break the bond." My blood pounded through my veins and into my skull. I couldn't speak. Anara, though, had plenty to say. "Aric's yearning for you is so desperate, I can sense it as his Elder. It sickens me to feel your presence. Break the bond."

My claws protruded. "I don't know how."

"You will find a way or you shall suffer. You have two days."

My phone shattered in pieces when I threw it

against the wall. "As if I'm not suffering enough, asshole!"

I unwittingly *changed* into my tigress form and paced for the next half hour. It helped.

My inner animal dealt with stress far better than my human side.

Someone knocked on the door leading out into the garden. Within moments Shayna poked her head into my bedroom. She took in the shattered phone and her sister the golden tigress, but without missing a beat, she skipped in fearlessly.

"How's it going, Ceel?" Shayna hugged my neck and scratched behind my ears. I purred and dropped to the floor. "Koda loves his ears scratched, too—when he's a wolf, I mean." She chatted about her life, the weather, and Taran's plans to set Hank aflame if she caught him near Emme. Gruesome details aside, it was the distraction I needed. I licked her hand in appreciation.

"You're welcome, dude."

She rolled on her back and she used my belly for a pillow. "Celia, we're all meeting at the house tonight for dinner. I'd really love it if you'd join us. Aric won't be there. I promise he won't."

Aric's name made me cringe. Not just because of how I treated him, but also because I didn't know how much Anara suspected. She moved when I stood and *changed* back. "I don't feel much like socializing, Shayna." I yanked on a thong and bra and pulled a stretchy T-shirt over my thick hair. I fastened my skinny jeans and paused, knowing they wouldn't fit me in a few weeks. I was thin and muscular. My pregnancy wouldn't be easy to hide once I began to show.

Shayna flung an arm over my neck. "Then what do you need, Ceel? Tell me. I just want to help."

She was trying. Lord knows they were all trying to reach me. Against my better judgment, I reached back. "A milkshake would be nice."

She smiled. "Can I drive?"

Shayna tore out of Misha's driveway like her tiny butt was on fire. Her excited "woo-hoos" sent Emme into a tizzy. Despite Emme's protests in the form of shrieks, Shayna refused to slow down. She took the curves along the back roads like a band of crazed knife-wielding clowns were on our tail.

Emme screamed at the top of her lungs. My baby didn't like the ride any better. On the last turn out of Tahoe City I stuck my head out the window and threw up. *So much for lunch.*

Shayna pulled the car over. "Oh, Celia! I totally forgot about your concussion. I'm so sorry."

I slumped over the door. "Maybe I should just head back to Misha's."

"No, we finally got you out." She threw her palms out in surrender. "I'll tell you what, Emme can drive."

At that moment, Emme wasn't driving anywhere. She crawled out of our SUV on her hands and knees and puked onto some poor dwarfed bush. Shayna's driving had that effect on people. Shayna yanked old napkins out of the glove compartment and rushed to her side. I stepped out just to breathe in the cool dusky air. Ice cream with Shayna was clearly a bad idea.

Shayna handed Emme the wrinkled bunch of napkins when her *Star Wars* ringtone blasted from her back pocket. She reached for her cellphone. "Hello?"

"Shayna, it's Aric."

My head whipped in her direction. Oh, crap. "Koda said you went to see Celia."

Shayna glanced at me. "Yes. I'm with her now."

My nerves were already shot from the car ride, but when Aric didn't speak right away, I knew he was going to ask for me.

51

"I'm not trying to put you in the middle, but I need to talk to her. Please put her on."

Shayna walked toward me with the phone outstretched in her hand. She slowed to stop at my glare. "Celia, please talk to him," she pleaded. "He's already been hurt enough. Don't add to his pain."

Nothing she could have said would have felt more like a betrayal. I stormed down the main road leading back to Misha's estate. Shayna bolted after me. "Celia, you don't know what he's going through. He and Koda are a mess—"

I whirled around and screamed at her through my protruding fangs. "Damnit, then why aren't you with him? Go to your husband and leave me the hell alone!"

She dropped her hands to her sides. "I want to help you."

"You can't, Shayna. Go home. There's nothing you can do for me."

Shayna grabbed my arm when I turned to leave. Big mistake. I wrenched my arm and flung her across the asphalt on her back. Emme shrieked. Initially Shayna just lay there stunned. But when she stumbled to her feet, tears streamed down her pixie face. "What's wrong with you, Celia?"

What was wrong with me? If Koda hadn't transferred his healing abilities and some of his werewolf strength to Shayna, I could have killed her. I *changed,* guilt-ridden that I'd hurt my kind and perky sister. My paws dug into the ground and launched me into a rapid sprint. I ignored my sisters' pleas to stop and raced forward, back to the land of the undead.

At the speed my tigress propelled us, it didn't take long to return to Misha's estate. The vamps at the gate immediately let me in. Normally I would have jumped the whole thing, but I was going too fast and lacked the focus I needed to land safely. I couldn't risk harming my baby. I needed to keep my little one safe, no matter what.

I threw some clothes on in the guesthouse and crawled back into bed, suddenly weary with exhaustion. I awoke a while later to the aroma of one of my favorite things, Bren.

Danny had introduced us to Bren years ago when my sisters and I were still new to Tahoe. I didn't like him at first, but it didn't take him long to charm his way into my heart and become one of my best friends. He snuggled against me, spooning. "Celia, we've been in bed together so many times, when will you come to your senses and bang me?"

My life sucked, my heart was breaking off in chunks, and the lives of those I loved hung by my fingertips, and yet as always, Bren made me laugh. He turned me around and greeted me with his good-humored face and bright blue eyes.

I stroked his soft beard. "What are you doing here?"

"Everyone thinks you're losing it and they sent me here to gauge your loony meter." He shrugged. "You look fine to me." His eyes wandered down my body. "Hmmm, actually you look pretty damn fine. How about a quickie?"

I climbed out of bed. "How about dinner instead?"

Bren rolled on his back and tucked his hands behind his head. "Your sisters want us to eat back at your old place."

My smile faded. "I'm not going there."

Bren examined me carefully. "You're not going to tell me what's wrong. Are you, kid?"

There was no point in pretending with Bren. "No," I said simply.

He stood and stretched like he didn't care, but I knew he did. "How about Café Fiore, then?"

We exited the restaurant almost three hours later. I didn't speak much, and let Bren do most of the talking. The path

I'd chosen hadn't allowed me to spend much time with him over the past year. So, I'd sat and listened to my friend's stories while he worked to get me to smile.

Bren slung his arm around me as we walked out into the brisk dark night. He scratched his beard. "Ceel, I don't know what's up. Just know whatever shit's going down, you're going to get through it."

I leaned against him. "I hope so." He paused before giving my body a little squeeze. My response had worried him. I didn't need a supernatural nose to realize as much. We crossed into the dimly lit lot several blocks from the restaurant in silence. Bren had managed to take the last spot at the very end. Although it was only eleven, most of the businesses along Ski Run Boulevard had shut down. Springtime didn't generate many tourists, but come summer, the place would be booming with activity.

The quiet around us grew heavier and our steps overtook any other trace of sound. Bren opened the door to his Mustang for me and offered me a small smile. "No matter what, I've got your back, kid."

I opened my mouth to thank him. Anara's scent silenced me and hit my nose like a punch. My body trembled violently at the encroaching howl of wolves.

Bren immediately growled; his inner wolf acute to my fear. The aroma of my terror must have overwhelmed the air, because he didn't immediately detect Anara. I grabbed him and tried to *shift* us into the sewers, but my ability was obstructed.

Bren clasped my shoulders. "What's wrong?" His eyes widened and his head snapped toward the increasing call of the wolves. "Oh, *shit!*"

Anara materialized from the shadows, solidifying from a flimsy apparition to a dark, imposing form. Bren shoved me behind him, his anger surging. He knew what was happening, he recognized the danger, but he didn't know enough to run. I fastened my hand on his wrist and bolted, using the strength of my beast to zigzag us around the remaining cars.

We might as well have waited where we stood.

Something wrapped around my waist and yanked me backward like the tug of a thick rope. I slammed into the wall of a building. Bren's body hit next to mine, cracking and disintegrating the brick.

I coughed and wheezed, struggling for breath. My tigress leapt inside me, arching my back but failing to *change* us. The veins in Bren's throat strained from his effort to break Anara's hold. He swore and spat, barely managing to move.

Anara ignored him and strolled toward me with the ease of a man in complete control. "Out having a good time? Even after I gave you a task to accomplish?" He struck me with his power, raking my face and chest. I grunted from the sting of my flesh being sliced.

"Don't fucking touch her!"

Anara angled his face in Bren's direction. Bren snapped his teeth and growled.

My heart sank when I caught the glimmer burning in Anara's sadistic eyes. He was going to make Bren bleed and he was going to enjoy it. "*No.* Leave him alone. He has nothing to do with this!"

Bren's screams rattled in my head like the roar of a train as Anara twisted Bren's limbs from their sockets. My horror catapulted when Bren's wolf failed to heal him. *Jesus,* Anara could keep him from mending.

Misha, help me! Help me! Anara had blocked Aric's link to me. I only hoped he couldn't block my *call* to Misha.

Bren fired obscenities at Anara. Anara silenced him by ramming the barrel of a gun through his teeth. Cold sweat tore down my spine. I knew what was coming, and I was helpless to stop it.

I smelled the cursed gold bullets before Anara

pulled the trigger. I heard my screams overshadow the blast. And I watched as Bren crashed to the ground next to the remains of his skull.

Chapter Seven

Anara released me. But I still couldn't move. Disbelief and terror held me in place. It was only when his invisible hand smacked me across the cheek that I faced him. He met me with impatience, like I'd somehow inconvenienced him by making him shoot my friend. "You've yet to taste the full wrath of my anger, Celia. Break the bond."

Anara dissolved into the shadows again. The eerie howls of the wolves followed. I pulled Bren's limp form against me and wept into his chest. Misha found me moments later, huddled against him, trying to keep his cooling body warm.

Misha knelt beside me and placed his hand on my shoulder. "Get me the Elder Martin on the phone," he commanded. To Ying-Ying he said something in Mandarin. Ying-Ying answered softly, then bent before me. Her dark almond eyes pooled with tears. She stroked my hair once before squeezing her hand between me and Bren and covering his heart. She hummed then, sweetly, as if somehow calling Bren home.

Ying-Ying whispered something to Misha, who in turn spoke to me. "Your wolf is almost dead. His soul partially remains. If he is important to you, I can attempt to save him." I nodded, unable to speak. He opened his hand. "Give me your wrist."

Numbly, I did as he asked. I barely flinched when his incisors grew and punctured my vein. Ying-Ying opened Bren's mouth while Misha squeezed my blood into him.

"Martin is on the phone, Master," a female vampire told him.

Liz ripped the phone from her grasp and shoved her away. "Fool! Do not interrupt the master during the blood rising."

Misha's lick to my wrist sealed the wound and warmed my body enough to soothe my sobs. Ying-Ying tore open Bren's shirt, exposing his chest, while Misha bit into his own arm with ferocious aggression.

Misha poured his blood over Bren's torso, dripping it directly in the center. "Let the blood of my body and that of my bride return your soul completely. *Corpo. Vivo. Mente. Cuore.*" The droplets of blood swirled around and formed what resembled a lowercase "r."

Misha repeated the process three times more. Each time the symbol he formed grew thicker and darker with his blood. "Uruz," Agnes whispered. "The rune of strength and healing."

Nothing happened for a long while. I wasn't sure how long I lay against the cold asphalt, but an eternity could have passed without my knowledge. No one spoke in the deafening silence until Misha stood and offered me his hand. "My darling, his spirit is beyond my reach." I didn't move. "Celia, he has left the earth."

I clutched Bren's unmoving form as my tears spilled across my cheeks. "You're supposed to stay and make me laugh. Who will do that if you're gone?"

Time marched forward again without my consent. But then the whisper of a soft breeze tickled my skin. Slowly, very slowly, the scent of magic surrounded Bren's body. I blinked, unable to believe what I saw. Fragments of bone lifted from the ground and realigned into his skull. His scalp knitted itself across the wound, closing it shut. Hair follicles grew in twists and lengthened to match his mop of curls. I jumped when his flaccid limbs abruptly snapped back into place. My hold on him tightened. *He's healing. He's coming back.* His lids flickered shut and his chest expanded with one deep breath after another. Still, his body remained terrifyingly cold.

I glanced up at Misha. The Catholic schoolgirls busied themselves licking the trailing blood from his healing wounds. "Consider this a wedding present," he said. "Now come to me so I may tend to you."

There was so much sexual connotation in his voice, it brushed against my face like a lover's touch. Ying-Ying and Chang urged me toward Misha while they took over Bren's care and covered him with a blanket.

Misha had saved Bren's life. I owed him, but I refused to repay him the way he intended.

I stood to face him. The Catholic schoolgirls smiled, pleased that I had seemingly come to my senses. I wiped my tears with the back of my hand, but my nervousness at confronting Misha made my motions overly aggressive. I reopened the large gash in my cheek. The cut was deep. Anara had literally punctured a hole in my face.

Misha took my face in his hands in one motion and began to feast. I don't think his tongue stroked me more than twice before I shoved him away.

Misha's eyes widened with confusion while his breath released in short bursts. The taste of me had aroused him. Perfect timing, seeing how the Elders had finally arrived, with Aric.

Aric broke away from Martin and rushed to my side. His wild eyes took in my injuries and blood-smeared clothing. There was nothing I needed more than to fall into his arms and cry, but when he touched my arms, I shrugged him off.

Makawee stepped forward, her pure white hair blowing in the breeze. "What's happened, Celia?" she asked in her calm voice.

I backed away to where Misha waited. "Bren and I were attacked, by the same wolves that caught me at the house."

They frowned as if they didn't understand. Martin's voice boomed above us. "He's over here."

It was only when Martin spoke that they noticed Bren. Makawee hurried toward him and touched his face. Aric watched me closely before joining his Elders. "Brendan is injured, but not healing," Makawee said. "Celia, please explain what transpired."

Anger slowly dissolved my fear. I lifted my chin. "We were walking to the car when we were attacked. Bren was . . . was shot in the mouth with gold bullets."

Aric bent and lifted Bren's head to examine it. "If he was shot with gold, where's the exit wound?"

Misha closed the distance between us. "It sealed when I mended his soul."

The three wolves exchanged glances. Martin removed the blanket covering Bren's chest, exposing the rune created by Misha's blood and vampiric magic. "You performed a blood rising. . . on a wolf," Martin said slowly. Disbelief shadowed his dark skin. "Why?"

Misha smiled at me. "My love wished it so."

Although Martin held on to Aric's shoulder lightly, there was tremendous power behind his gentle grip. "How many wolves were there?" he asked, keeping Aric in place.

I recalled the echo of all those howls. "It's hard to tell, at least a dozen, maybe more."

Martin rose, the hint of suspicion deepened his voice. "I scent the wolf pack you claim attacked you, but not their blood—only yours and Brendan's. Did you fight back?"

"No. Bren and I were helpless. There was nothing we could do."

Bren and I were tough fighters. The fact that there were no other dead bodies or limbs strewn about fueled their doubts. Yet they knew I spoke the truth when I admitted how powerless we were. I began to ask questions before they could catch me in a lie. "Can you tell me why he's not healing?"

Makawee stroked Bren's head gently. The deep-set wrinkles in her forehead creased further the longer she stared at him. "Tell me what you see, my Omega," Martin said.

Makawee shook her head. "He's not allowing himself to heal. It's as if his wolf wishes to die."

Even if I hadn't been present for the attack, I would have known Makawee was wrong. Bren wasn't suicidal—and neither was his wolf. Anara was restraining his wolf from healing him. Misha's power had only allowed him to live.

I bit my bottom lip and tasted my blood. "What's going to happen to him, Makawee?"

"Until he chooses to heal, he'll remain in this state."

A coma. That bastard Anara had left my friend in a goddamn coma.

Martin picked him up. "Let's get him back to the Den."

"No." My sudden outburst caught everyone by surprise. "Misha, I want Bren to stay with us." I glanced at the Elders. "I'm a nurse. I'll look after him and take care of him."

There was so much anger in Aric's voice I had to avert my gaze. "He's *Pack,* Celia. Bren goes with us."

I dug my heels in and stood my ground. "The attack today was directed at me. Bren got hurt protecting me. I owe it to him to help him now."

Makawee regarded me with patience and with a

voice as gentle as a streaming brook. "Celia, young Brendan is part of our family. We care for our own."

My head snapped toward her. "Since when? Aric had to fight for him for you to allow him into your Pack. Now that he's hurt, you feel sorry enough to claim him as your own?" Makawee had never shown me anything but kindness. I hated disrespecting her, but I couldn't turn Bren over to them. Not when it meant he would be easy pickings for Anara.

Martin held Bren. "Celia, our wolves will watch over him."

"I'm surprised you can spare them, Martin. Shouldn't you be sending them off to breed?" My tone was hideously cold. I wasn't proud, but I couldn't let Bren go. The problem was, I wasn't just picking a fight with the neighborhood kids. I was stepping on the toes of two *Elders*. Martin and Makawee were as formidable as Anara. I knew the patience of their beasts would soon wear thin.

"I-I can try to help him," Emme interrupted.

My sisters and Aric's Warriors had arrived without me knowing. I wasn't sure how long they'd watched me, but it seemed they'd witnessed enough.

Emme knelt by Bren and placed her hands against his chest, careful to avoid touching the symbol. Aric blocked my path when I rushed to stop her. I stood close enough to feel the warmth of his love, so strong it stung my eyes with tears. He tried to catch my gaze, but I looked away. "Just let her help him, Celia," he said softly.

I feared that Bren would wake and explain what happened . . . and that I'd watch everyone I loved die because of it. My frustration made my tears run faster. Aric sniffed the air. "You're still bleeding." His voice was different then, he'd always hated seeing me cry.

I nodded.

"Are you in pain?"

"Yes," I mumbled.

Aric moved closer. The heat rose between us. Sweet heavens, I just needed him to hold me.

"Something is terribly wrong," Emme said. "It feels like I'm touching. . ." She scrambled away from Bren with her hands clasped over her mouth.

I wasn't sure what had happened until Liam loomed over him and said, "Shit. Bren just popped a tent."

Liam was right. Bren might have been in a coma, but he still managed an erection. He even smiled. Emme must have "touched" him in more ways than one.

Taran sighed with relief. "Thank Christ. That's a good sign, right?"

Makawee stroked Bren's moppy curls. The smile on her face faded. "No. His wolf still refuses to mend him."

"I'd like to take him home now." My eyes stayed fixed on the ground, not wanting to face the judgmental stares bearing down on me.

Aric took my hand in his. "Celia, have Emme heal you first and we'll talk—"

Moving so abruptly from Aric's body heat was actually physically painful. "Misha, I want Bren with me." Misha furrowed his perfect brows. The last thing he wanted was a werewolf living in his home. My eyes implored him. "Please, Misha."

He nodded slowly. "Very well, if that is what you desire."

"No," Aric growled.

"I want to take care of him, Aric. I need to, it's my fault he's hurt!" No one moved. Instead they regarded me like someone juggling grenades. They thought I was losing it. I reinforced their belief when I threw a ridiculous tantrum in my desperation to save Bren. "Give him to me, I want him now!"

Martin stood, I thought, to attack me. Instead his teak-colored eyes watched me with pity. "Celia, the events in recent days have left you in an extremely fragile state. I don't feel you're the best person to care for Brendan—"

"Or for any one of your wolves, right? Goddamn you, Martin—"

Aric placed his hand over my mouth and grabbed me tight. Although I was Aric's mate, that didn't give me free rein to say what I pleased or to disrespect Martin. Despite my anger, the familiarity of Aric's arms abruptly unleashed my misery. I sobbed. Worse yet, I began to bleed when I attempted to break free from his hold.

Aric lifted me and carried me to Koda's SUV. "Emme, get over here! Her wounds are opening." The other wolves quickly stowed the seats so everything lay flat. It was hard to struggle against Aric, but I panicked that Anara would know of our contact. "Stop fighting me," he whispered in my ear. "Let me help you, baby." I stopped thrashing, but the moment Aric released me, I tried to escape. Aric yanked me back and restrained my arms behind me. "Shayna, hold her legs—Taran, get her sweater off."

I yelped when Taran pulled at my clothing "Damnit, Aric. I'm hurting her. You'll have to rip it off."

Aric tore off my clothes and growled hard enough to shake me. My sisters gasped in horror. "What's happening?" Koda asked over his shoulder. He and Liam guarded the back of the vehicle.

Fire sparked in Taran's eyes. "Those assholes clawed her to shreds!"

Gemini shoved a bottle of water and towels through the front. "Here. Take these." Shayna slowly released my legs and began to wipe off the blood with the wet towels Taran handed her. "Ceel," she said, her voice trembling. "Did they . . . ?"

"No, Shayna. I wasn't raped."

Although I could still sense Aric's anger, he relaxed slightly at the news.

I followed Shayna's movements. Deep gashes

marred my breasts, chest, and neck. Misha would have had a field day. Emme touched me with tremulous hands. Her warm tears fell against my bare skin as she closed the gaping lacerations. If not for Aric's gentle murmuring, I might have joined her.

"Rest, sweetness. I'm here."

I allowed his words to melt against my battered soul. *You're here.*

"Trust me."

I trust you.

"You're safe now, no one can hurt you."

I stiffened. *You're wrong.*

Aric released my arms when Emme finished. I cringed and dressed in the sweats Gemini tossed to me. "I have to go get Bren," I mumbled.

I kept my arms crossed over my breasts, feeling violated. My breasts were emblematic of my womanhood. They were intimate body parts. And they'd been defiled by a monster.

Aric and my sisters followed behind me. They kept speaking and asking me questions. I ignored them. Misha scowled at Aric when he saw him so close to me, but when he returned to his conversation with the Elders, his voice was calm. "You have my word as a master that no harm shall come to your wolf. My family will keep their distance and Ying-Ying and Chang will assist in his care."

I sighed with relief. *Fantastic. Bring on the Gan Mao Ling.* "Can we go, Misha?"

"As you wish, my love. Hank?"

Hank lifted Bren in his arms using great care, probably because his master and the Elders were watching. Aric's glare followed him, but it wasn't until Misha placed his arm around me that the growls that accompanied his glare turned challenging.

"Let her go, Aric," Makawee said softly.

My sisters tried to say their goodbyes. I hurried

away from them and chased down Hank. I was emotionally beaten and incapable of dealing with more questions. My prime concern was getting Bren to safety and finding a way out of this ever-worsening nightmare.

Emme ran full out to catch us. "I'll go back with them."

The vampires had formed a perimeter around the lot, using their mojo to alter the memories of the few humans walking the streets. They abandoned their posts as soon we appeared, exchanging annoyed glances when they caught sight of Bren.

Hank usually drove Misha's Hummer limo, but this time he asked Tim to drive us back. It wasn't until we were seated that I realized why. Bren's head rested across Emme's lap and she stroked his hair with easy affection. Hank was not at all pleased. He watched her, grinding his fangs. I leaned forward. "This might be a good time to remind you that you aren't allowed to hurt my friend. And if you do, I'll skewer your liver and feed you the chunks." Hank clenched his teeth to hiss, but something in my face told him that now was not the time to mess with me. I leaned back when he turned his focus elsewhere.

Emme's fingertips slid over the new section of Bren's scalp. "Misha, how did you help Bren?"

"Masters at my level can often heal those near death. It's referred to as a *blood rising*."

Emme smiled at him. "What a wonderful gift. You could help so many—"

"No, he could not," Hank snapped. "My master risked demonic possession by helping your mutt."

I straightened. "Is that true?"

Misha casually shrugged off my question. "The soul you returned to me combined with my immortality affords me unimaginable power. Yet it's not without its weaknesses. During the *blood rising* my body became vulnerable to the Dark Ones. However, the close proximity to Tahoe's magic was likely enough to deter their presence."

"But there was still a risk."

Misha nodded. "There is always a risk."

I clutched Misha's hand in mine. My vision blurred with tears when he squeezed back. "Thank you, Misha." I swallowed hard. "Thank you for helping Bren."

I rested my head against him when he wrapped his arm around my shoulders. I was so tired; it felt good to drop my guard for a moment. Emme didn't understand. Her crinkled brow made it clear she didn't approve of my relationship with Misha. Especially given how I'd dismissed Aric.

Danny arrived shortly after we'd settled Bren into the living room of the guesthouse. He embraced me at once. "How are you holding up?"

I motioned to the pull-out couch. "Better than Bren."

Danny left me and squatted beside Bren. "Can you hear me, buddy?" He waited patiently for a response. It was sad to watch them. They were the best of friends, and the connection they shared was more like that of brothers. Bren failed to react, crushing the hope we had that Danny could reach him.

Danny turned back to us. "I'm sorry I couldn't get here sooner. Heidi and I took off for a few days. We were on our way home from Sacramento when Liam called."

Emme drew back the sheer curtains and peered out into the garden. "Where is she?"

Danny lowered his head. "She's waiting outside the gate. She's not a fan of vampires and I didn't want any more problems."

More problems? The sadness in Danny's tone made me think he meant something besides Bren's state. I ran my fingers through my curls, still damp from my shower. "What's going on?"

"It's not anything worth mentioning now." He stood and rubbed his hands together. "I'll stay here tonight, if that's okay."

Emme released the curtain and moved to stand by Danny. "You don't have to. Celia and I will both be here. And I'm sure Heidi would rather have you with her."

Danny shook his head. "I'm sure she'd prefer the company of another male." Emme and I gawked at him. Heidi had quite the reputation. But I'd hoped her relationship with Danny had changed all that. He walked across the hardwood floors and toward the kitchen. "My bags are in the car. I'll go grab them."

I shoved my feet into a pair of UGGs and followed him out the door. "I'll go with you so Misha's family doesn't give you any problems." It really wasn't necessary for me to escort Danny. The vamps never bothered him. Mostly because he was passive and respectful, and since he hadn't been a wolf that long, they seemed to continue to regard him as human.

My pulse raced as my anxiety grew. Aside from my sisters, Danny and Bren were my closest friends. I always thought I could trust Danny with my life. But as I stopped him in the garden, I realized I had to entrust him with the lives of everyone I loved.

"Danny," I whispered, my voice trembling. "I need you to break my mate bond with Aric."

Chapter Eight

Danny's brows shot up to his hairline. He couldn't believe what I'd asked any more than I could. "Celia, I-I can't break your mate bond. I'm one of Aric's Warriors!"

"Hush!" I scanned the darkness and gripped his hands. "Danny, please. I'm begging you to help me."

Danny gaped, from my hands tightening around his, to my face. "Celia, I know things are strained between you, but he loves you. You're emotionally frail right now. As soon as you work through your trauma, you'll be able to think more rationally."

My muffled sobs stopped his rant. I composed myself enough to speak. "Danny, I'm in so much trouble. People I love will be hurt if I don't break my bond with Aric."

Danny's face split with shock and confusion. "How will sacrificing your relationship keep the Tribe from attacking you . . ." His voice trailed off and his eyes widened. "Oh crap," he whispered. "This has nothing to do with the Tribe, does it?" My blank expression answered for me. "Then who? Who's hurting you, Celia?"

I rushed toward the gate. "Danny, you already know too much. If you don't want to end up like Bren—or worse—you won't question me. Just please help me. It has to be done by tomorrow or someone will die."

"There has to be another way, Celia."

It hurt to swallow the lump in my throat. "I wish there was, Danny." "We can fight this somehow, I know we can."

In the past, I'd always seen Danny's optimism as rousing, but now I recognized it as only naïveté. "Danny, at first I might have believed you, but tonight Bren was with me and we both had the shit knocked out of us. For God's sake, did you see him? We're lucky he's alive!"

Danny seemed to sense my desperation, but wasn't totally convinced. "Celia, the only reason Aric has been able to defy the Elders' order to stay away from you is because of your mate bond. Do you realize if you break it, he'll no longer be able to contact you? You may never see him again. Are you prepared for that?"

The image of that small beating heart appeared in my mind. Never once, since first learning of my pregnancy, did I believe my baby would grow up without a father. No matter our circumstances, I always knew Aric would be there for us. Now I couldn't allow him to be.

"If I could see any other way out, I'd take it. I can't stand the thought . . ." I took a calming breath. It did nothing. I was going to shatter into a thousand pieces. "I can't stand the thought of losing Aric. But if I don't do this he'll die. Do you understand me? *Aric will die.*"

As a new werewolf, Danny had worked hard to determine his place in the Pack. As a blue merle werewolf—a rare entity and a symbol of power—we'd waited to see what special ability he'd acquired. So far, nothing had manifested. He struggled despite his best efforts. Much younger *weres* surpassed him in strength, agility, and tracking. But one thing Danny had to his advantage was his incredible intellect—that, and he'd quickly learned how to sniff out lies. My scent, my posture, the tone of my words—everything told him I spoke the truth.

We stopped a few feet from the gate. He sighed. "As one of Aric's Warriors, I am duty bound to protect his life, and yours, as his mate, at any cost. If ending your bond will do that, I guess I have no choice."

He was giving me what I wanted. It should have made me happy or at least granted me some relief, but my despair only worsened. It was going to happen. Aric and I would no longer be one.

Heidi's car door opened and she stepped out. Two vampires descended from the thick cluster of the trees and blocked her path. Heidi resembled an adult film actress— big blond hair, full pouty lips, and boobs the size of Rhode Island. But she was as tough as sin and had become one of the few female *weres* ever granted the title of Warrior. Her speaking voice was cute and bubbly, yet the growl that rumbled from her throat thundered across the stone pavers.

I stepped between them. "Michael, Clara, stop."

"She doesn't have permission to be here, Celia," Clara hissed. "Do you, bitch?"

Heidi smiled. "We'll see who the bitch is when I'm wearing your fangs as earrings."

"Back off, Clara. Heidi was just leaving."

Heidi seemed hurt when I made it clear she couldn't stay. "Did Danny tell you?" she asked.

I ignored her to watch Michael lead Clara away. "Come, Clara. Celia gave you a direct order." I waited until they left before addressing Heidi, but she was busy watching Danny unload his belongings.

"I'll be staying with Celia," he said without meeting her face.

Her high heels clicked against the pavers as she rushed to his side. "You're not coming back with me?"

"No." He wouldn't glance in her direction as he passed. She lurched forward and clutched his arm. "Heidi, not now."

"Will you ever come back to me?" Tears dropped from her eyes and his.

"I don't know." Danny wasn't cruel. He could never leave someone in Heidi's state.

They were almost the same height, so he easily turned to kiss her forehead.

Aric had to practically bend in half to kiss me. "I love you," she whispered.

Danny's face crumbled. "No. I don't think you do."

I was intruding on their moment and quickly hauled ass back to the guesthouse. Danny raced after me. "Celia, wait."

"I'm sorry, Danny!" Heidi yelled behind us. "I'm so sorry!"

Danny scrunched his face and focused ahead, struggling to maintain control. "Do you want to talk about it?" I asked quietly.

"Don't worry about me. We need to deal with your situation."

I wasn't the only one in need of a friend tonight. I caught his arm. "Tell me what happened."

He dropped his bags onto the slick wet slate of the garden path and rubbed his eyes. "Heidi hasn't been faithful to me. Since we've been together, she's had sex with several *weres* and a couple of humans."

My mouth popped opened. They'd only been together a few months. "How did you find out?"

"She told me over dinner tonight. She said she couldn't help herself. That it was something she'd always done so that others, specifically men, would like her."

"I'm not trying to minimize what's happened, but you told me yourself she was new to dating. She seems to genuinely care about you. Maybe she just needs time to adjust to being with one person."

"I know what you're saying—and part of me does

pity her. At the same time, I'm humiliated." He sighed. "She's slept with *weres* from the Alliance with whom I've worked closely. Since Aric brought me into the Pack, *weres* have openly laughed at me. I used to blame it on my lack of skill. I realize now it was because they were banging my girlfriend."

What could I say? I wouldn't put it past some of those idiots. Especially since Aric had chosen Danny as his Warrior over them. "I'm sorry, Danny. I know how much you liked her."

A single tear ran down his face. "I'm in love with her, Celia."

My heart sank a little lower and I joined him in his grief. "Then I truly am sorry."

We paused outside the door to the guesthouse. Danny couldn't talk about Heidi anymore.

So instead he returned his focus to me. "Are you sure you want to go through with this?"

My head pounded just thinking about it. "I don't have a choice."

Danny hugged me. "I'll drop off my stuff and then go to my apartment to do some research. As soon as I locate the spell, I'll call you. Can I borrow your car?"

I handed him my keys, but I snatched his wrist before he could walk inside. "Promise me you won't say anything to anyone—*especially* that you helped me break the bond. I don't want anyone to hurt you."

The color drained from Danny's face. "Celia, if Aric finds out I helped you, you won't have to worry about anyone else. He'll kill me himself."

Emme and I spent the rest of the evening using the supplies the vampires had brought us to care for Bren. I laid out a fresh pair of sweats and boxers and stared at my grubby friend. Dried blood caked his beard and moppy curls. "We should bathe him, Emme."

"Do you think he'll mind?"

Despite my night, I let out a laugh. "Are you kidding? He'd probably like us to record it and put it on YouTube."

Emme filled the bath while I cut through Bren's clothes with my claws. I hoisted him into my arms and carried him into the bathroom. His weight didn't bother me. I could probably lift three of him without breaking a sweat. But his floppy limbs were a stern reminder of his precarious state.

I gently placed him in the warm bathwater and scrubbed his hair while Emme lathered his body. We washed everything . . . except what he affectionately referred to as "Little Bren."

"You do it," we both said at the same time.

Normally I'm the stubborn one. This time Emme wouldn't budge. We settled our dilemma in rock, papers, scissors style. Emme lost and Bren won. Once again, Little Bren perked up in her presence. Bless her heart, Emme accomplished her task with her eyes averted, even though we'd seen his bare ass more times than I could count. Her deep blush diminished slightly once we yanked on his sweatpants. Except the thick cotton fabric wasn't enough to keep the not- so-little guy down.

"Why does he keep doing that?" Emme might have been embarrassed yet she couldn't hide her smile.

"Consider it a compliment. He doesn't react that way with me." *Thank goodness.*

"I kind of do." I angled my head in her direction. "I mean it's nice that I can still have that effect on someone."

"You miss Liam, don't you?"

"Of course I do. I love him, Celia." She shrugged. "But it is what it is. Unlike you and Aric, we're not meant to be."

My limbs froze and another piece of my heart broke

off. *How am I going to get through this?*

Emme reached for me. "Did I say something to upset you?"

I wriggled my hands nervously. "No, I'm just tired. What's left to do?"

"Just to start an IV for hydration, but I can do that. Why don't you go to bed? I'll sleep on the couch tonight and Ying-Ying and Chang will relieve me in the morning."

"Yeah, okay. Good night."

Emme embraced me warmly. I found myself unable to release her. She was patient with me, she didn't move, and she didn't speak. She knew I needed it, though she didn't know exactly what *it* was. It was my moment to feel loved—to know I wasn't so horrible—because the next day things would be different. I would be horrible and awful and hated. I would be the one to crush Aric's heart.

Danny never called.

I spent the night throwing up, worried Anara had targeted him and sick from my baby growing inside me. My stomach finally settled around dawn.

Emme and I were finishing breakfast when I noticed Bren's nostrils flare. I pushed out of my chair and hurried to him. "Emme, grab that plate of pancakes. I think Bren's hungry."

I sat Bren up and leaned his limp form against my chest. Emme held the plate of pancakes apprehensively.

"Celia, how can we feed him without him choking?"

I supported his head with my hand. "I'm not planning on feeding him. I'm just trying to see how aware he is. Move the plate closer to his nose."

She did and I accidentally dropped Bren's face on top of the pancakes. Or so I thought. It wasn't until Bren devoured the food like a starving animal that I realized he'd intentionally slipped from my grasp.

Syrup and whipped cream covered Bren's face, but he'd eaten. Emme wiped his beard with a damp cloth. "Do you think he wants more?"

A low growl from his stomach answered her question. After some bacon, eggs, sausage, and more pancakes, Bren finally seemed satisfied. I turned up his IV to give him more fluid while Emme busied herself washing his face. He smiled at her with his eyes closed . . . and raised another flag.

Emme's jaw dropped. "Do you think he's doing it on purpose?"

"Maybe he can't help himself." My cell phone rang, stirring my already sensitive nerves. "Hello?"

"Everything is ready," Danny said. "I'll meet you on the west corner of Misha's compound."

Sweat slid between my breasts. I worked my throat, but couldn't swallow. "O-okay."

Emme stopped adjusting the pillow behind Bren's head when she caught the misery etching its way across my features. "Celia, you don't look well. What's wrong?"

"I feel sick. I need some air. I'll be back later." Almost robotically, I grabbed my jacket and dashed through the kitchen door. Raindrops splashed against my nose. I wanted to turn around and rush back inside. Instead, I started toward the lake. "Hello, Michael," I said when I scented him.

Michael's dark mocha skin glistened from the rain. He'd been standing by the boathouse for a while. "Where are you going, Celia? The master doesn't want you to leave the premises without escorts."

"I'm going for a walk." *Then a ride.* "I'm not feeling well."

"I'll accompany you."

"No. I can't have anyone with me right now." Michael raised his chin, already suspicious.

"What I mean is, I need time alone."

Michael hadn't been a vampire long. In fact, he was probably only twenty-six, like me. And yet his maturity and wisdom far surpassed that of the other vampires. So did his kindness. "Will you stay on the grounds?"

I nodded. *For the next few minutes I will.* I ambled onto the dock and stared at the lake for a long while. Waves splashed against the smooth boulders, one after the other. I counted to a hundred before I finally forced myself away and into the large patch of woods covering Misha's thirty-acre estate. *God, give me the strength to keep Aric safe.*

I sprinted through the thick trees as soon as I lost Michael's scent, using my powerful legs to leap over the great stone wall. I landed almost atop where Danny idled my car and hurried inside it, taking care to avoid his stare. He drove off without a word. Perhaps he hoped I'd change my mind.

"Where do you want to do this?" he asked when we turned off the road leading to the compound.

"There's a small estate nearby that has been on the market for a while. Misha thought about buying it to house his mistresses, but decided against it."

"What made him change his mind?"

I blew out some air; this was just another burden I carried. "His vamps told me it was his way of committing to me." I tried not to react when Danny cringed. "Turn right here. It's just up this street."

Danny parked in front of the large metal gate just as the rain dwindled to a halt and the sun broke through the clouds. The house, although about five thousand square feet, was minute compared to some of the opulent mansions circling Lake Tahoe. Hell, Misha's house alone was six times that size.

Danny's gaze scanned the exterior. "What about security?"

"From what I remember, the house has an alarm

system, but the detached garage doesn't. Come on." I scaled the gate and leapt over in a graceful flip. I landed in a crouch, rising smoothly.

Danny crashed next to me with a loud thud and a pained grunt. I helped him to his feet. "I'm okay," he mumbled. His face reddened, but he didn't pull away until he steadied himself.

"You're just off balance because of the backpack you're carrying."

He bowed his head, clearly humiliated. His struggles to master the strength and powers of his beast deeply affected his self-esteem. I patted his back, wishing I could help him, before leading him forward.

I *shifted* underground when we reached the detached garage and let Danny in through the side door. The vast empty space was big enough to house four SUVs, and although well-kept and relatively new, it carried an eerie vibe. I wiped my sweaty palms against my jeans. "Will this do?"

He nodded slowly and pursed his lips. "I have to ask you one last time. Are you sure? I mean, is there no other way?"

Tears filled my tired eyes. I sniffled, trying to keep my nose from running. "What do I have to do, Danny?"

Danny knelt on the floor and removed his supplies from the bulky navy pack. "According to the book, breaking the bond is emotionally and physically painful. You're . . . *destroying* the spiritual link that connects you as mates. I'll have to bind your hands and legs to keep your body from turning against you. You'll also be opening your soul to the Native American *weres* who used to inhabit the area. The ring of salt I'll surround you with will keep those spirits from entering your body and speaking through you."

At that point, I was having a hard time worrying about me. "Will this cause any permanent injury?" *God, what if I hurt our child?*

Danny examined the pages of the book carefully. "You won't be physically harmed, Celia. It'll just feel like you are."

I nodded. "If that's the case, I want to take the brunt of the pain. I don't want Aric to suffer."

Danny met my eyes. "Celia, that's not possible. You're severing his connection to you. I'm afraid there's no way around it."

I buried my face in my hands. "What about his soul? Can spirits possess him?"

Danny's voice shook and I could taste his fear. "Aric will be spared. Only the one who breaks the bond is vulnerable."

I sat on the floor and hugged my knees. Danny riffled through the pages. "It took me a long time to find the right book because mated couples just don't do this. In ancient times, when a pureblood and a non-pure were discovered to have mated in secret, the Elders would use this to force them apart. The spell was written in a rough form of Latin. I translated it into English as best I could."

Danny handed me an old weathered book. The worn and yellow-stained pages had already begun to disintegrate at the edges. He pointed to a handwritten passage. The illustration beside it was less than encouraging. Two naked beings reached out to each other, unable to touch. Their asexual faces contorted with agony and desperation so gut-wrenching I almost wept for them.

"I'll say the verses in English first and then you'll read them aloud in Latin. This way you'll understand what you're saying."

"I don't want to understand." It was cowardly of me to say it, but a future without Aric seemed unbearable.

"Celia, you'll have to. Otherwise they're just words and the spell won't work."

I pressed the book against my chest and squeezed my lids tight. *They are just words. I'll find a way back to you, Aric. I swear it.*

When I opened my eyes again, Danny's face was shadowed with dread. His voice cracked. "Are you ready?"

I placed the book down on the floor and knelt so Danny could bind my hands behind my back then fasten the ties to my ankles. When he was done, I crouched on my heels and he encircled me with salt. "Keep her safe, keep her strong," he muttered over and over.

I stared at the open book in front of me. *God, I don't want to do this.* Some time passed and my legs fell asleep. The sun moved across the room and still I did nothing. As if on cue, Anara's hateful glare blazed across my mind like the flare of a match. I startled, realizing my time was up. Anara made it clear he'd soon choose his next victim if I didn't act. I gritted my teeth and bowed my head. *Aric . . . I love you. Forgive me.*

Celia?

I forced myself to ignore Aric's voice and nodded to Danny. His shoulders drooped. He'd likely hoped I'd change my mind. He reached into his pocket and pulled out a folded sheet of paper. "I ask you, Great Protector, to break our bond."

I bit into my lip so hard it bled. Tears blurred my vision making it hard to read the words on the page. *"Ego scisco . . . vos valde . . . patronus ut . . . effrego nostrum . . . vinculum."*

"By my blood break our bond."

"Per meus . . .cruor effrego . . . nostrum vinculum."

"By my spirit break our bond."

"Per . . . meus . . . phasmatis . . . effrego nostrum . . . vinculum."

"By my will break our bond."

"Per meus . . . mos effrego . . . nostrum vinculum."

"Let the love of my love inhabit me no more."

My cries ripened into painful sobs. Every word, every syllable hurt to say. *"Permissum . .*

. diligo of meus . . . diligo . . . commoror mihi . . . haud . . . magis."

"Let our spirits go their separate ways."

"Permissum . . . nostrum . . . phasmatis . . . vado . . . nostrum . . . separate . . . mores."

"Let our love no longer be one."

"P-p-p-p-ermissum . . . nostrum diligo . . . exsisto . . . haud . . . diutius . . . unus."

Lightning flashed in the garage. My flesh ripped away in one vicious pull and my world exploded in pain. Every nerve in my body screamed. And so did Aric.

Celia! Celia! Nooooooo!

His screams echoed in my head and morphed into the pained howl of a wolf. My tigress roared in agony. Needles, ablaze with fire, punctured my form, searing and piercing my organs. My muscles ripped from my body, piece by torturous piece.

My screeching burned my ears, yet Aric's anguished cries thundered above my wailing. A chill wind whipped around me, lifting me off the ground and thrashing me against the floor.

The pain was unbearable. I couldn't endure it and yet I did, until my rib cage was cracked open and my heart was clawed from my chest.

Darkness covered me. It lifted in time for me to see the sun set against the garage wall.

My face rested in Danny's lap. I was crying, cold, shaking, and alone. "Aric's dead."

Chapter Nine

Danny stroked my soaked hair. "No, Celia. He's not."

"He is. I . . . *killed him.*"

Danny sat me up. My bindings had been cut, but I couldn't support myself. He held me tight. "The bond broke and you felt the effects of losing him. As his Warrior, I can still sense his presence."

He lifted me and carried me outside. His body was warm, while I remained unbelievably cold. I felt lighter—hollow—as if only my skeleton remained. Yet the loneliness was worse. It scratched at my decrepit bones, searching for where my heart had once beaten only to discover a gaping cavity of emptiness. I shuddered, mourning my loss and fearing I'd never again be whole.

Danny's eyes took me in. "My God, Celia. What have I done?"

We reached the gate and he sighed. "Celia, I don't think I can jump us both over without hurting you. Can you manage?"

My mind wandered back to my baby. "Can I manage?" I repeated aloud. "I guess I'll have to for both of us."

Danny answered me, believing I meant him. "Don't

worry about me, Celia. I'll get over." He placed me on the ground and graciously hung on to me. My legs wobbled like rubbery strands and it took me a few moments to straighten. I lacked the breath and energy to *shift*, so I moved a few steps back and leapt over.

My jump lacked grace and I had to roll to break my fall, unable to stay on my feet. Danny crashed next to me with a loud grunt. I scrambled to his side, my voice trembling. "Are you okay?"

He held on to his side. "I broke a couple of ribs, but I'll be fine by the time we reach Misha's."

"Danny, you're not taking me back to Misha's. I can't risk anyone seeing us together— including the vamps." I searched my pockets. Misha always snuck money into my clothes. Usually I snuck it back into his house, but I hadn't worn this jacket in a few days. Sure enough, there were several hundred-dollar bills. I shoved them into Danny's hand. "Here. Go to a hotel, shower, and buy some new clothes."

He shook his head. "I can't leave you, Celia. You look . . . *terrible*."

A couple of tears leaked out. "Believe it or not, I feel worse. But I have to go on, Danny...*I have to*." The talk was for both of us except neither of us seemed very encouraged.

Danny pulled me tight against his side and kissed the top of my head. "Be careful, Celia." I nodded numbly and backed away, forcing my legs into a sprint. My movements were awkward at best, like a newborn foal rising to stand. My limbs no longer felt like my own, more like strange appendages on a foreign body.

I tried to focus. My tigress had always made me light on my feet. This time I felt as if I trekked on air, sensing nothing but the breeze against my cold cheeks. I forced myself to hit the ground harder so I would feel something besides the implausible emptiness. It didn't work, and I feared nothing would.

My speed and all the grace of my inner beast remained. It took me mere minutes to reach the stone wall surrounding Misha's compound. I didn't slow down, using my speed to propel me. I landed and kept going, maintaining my pace until the excruciating cries of my sisters ground me to a stumbling halt.

Oh, God.

I staggered toward the guesthouse, terror stabbing my skull with each step closer to the door. *I was too late. Someone was dead. Anara had struck again.*

My hand shook violently as I reached for the knob and threw open the heavy door. I lurched forward, gripping the granite counter to keep me on my feet. Koda sat on the chocolate- covered love seat, his face shiny with tears, holding Shayna, who was beyond hysterical. Taran and Emme clutched each other on the opposite couch, where Bren continued to lie in a comatose state, crying so hard their bodies heaved with each wretched sob.

My sisters and Koda looked up, their eyes widening when they saw me. For a moment no one moved. They just stared. Shayna was the first to react, rising slowly before rushing to me and throwing her arms around my neck. "Oh my God. We thought you were dead!" She kissed my face and bawled against me. Taran and Emme encircled me, speaking and screaming through their choked moans.

I couldn't cry with them. Their tears didn't make sense. One by one they released me, smiling despite their blotchy faces and smeared makeup. Taran clasped her hand over her mouth. "Shit." She glanced over her shoulder at Koda. "Call Gemini. They have to let Aric know Celia's alive before he hurts someone."

They led me toward the couch and sat me near Bren's feet. Koda didn't move. He stood in front of the love seat, staring at me. "You died," he said. "I felt you leave Aric's soul."

"How is he . . .?" I couldn't finish the words.

Shayna wiped her eyes. "Not well, Ceel. We were with him when he thought you'd been killed. He started howling—freaking *howling* that you were dead."

Taran blew her nose on a tissue. "Aric went berserk. No one could control him. Koda grabbed me and Shayna and raced us out of the Den. Gemini and Liam stayed to help the others trying to restrain him." She lowered her head and shook it. "It was *awful*. I could hear and feel his pain."

"I was at the main house with Misha when they arrived. He didn't believe you were gone, but he was worried you might have been attacked, since no one knew where you were. He and his family are out searching for you." She reached for her cellphone on the coffee table. "I'll let him know you're okay. "

Emme froze at the sight of Koda. He held his phone at his side, his nose flaring with rage. "Goddamnit Celia. You broke your mate bond, didn't you? You severed your sacred bond!" He stormed toward me. "How the *fuck* could you do that to Aric!"

Koda had appeared dark and menacing long before the deep-set burns riddled his face with scars. But at that moment, his vehemence threatened to devour me.

Shayna pushed herself between us. "Koda, stop it. Celia would never do such a thing!"

I clasped my hands over my eyes. *But I had.*

Everyone seemed to stop breathing. The drizzling rain against the windows was the only sound. I forced my hands from my eyes and faced my family, knowing there was no way to defend my actions.

Shayna carefully turned away from her mate, her cheeks wet with fresh fallen tears. "Celia, tell Koda you didn't break your bond. Please tell him," she asked, but she knew then that he was right.

The silence while they waited for me to answer was

deafening.

Taran covered her mouth with her hands and gaped at me like she didn't know me. "Why the hell would you do this?"

I wouldn't answer. Koda let out a string of swearwords and tapped the screen on his cellphone. Aric's dreadful howls filled the room the moment the call connected. I covered my ears, unable to stand his mournful ire.

Gemini spoke urgently. "I can't talk. We're hitting Aric with tranquilizers. It's not working—"

"Celia's alive. She's with me now."

There was a pause on the other end. "That's not possible."

"She broke their mate bond."

"Why?"

Koda glared at me. "I don't know. She won't speak of it." Gemini's voice tightened.

"Is she hurt?"

"She looks like hell, but no, she's not harmed."

"There's no blood or—"

"There's nothing wrong with her, Gem. Goddamnit, she's just sitting here looking at me!"

A brief stretch of time passed on the other end. This time when Gemini spoke, his voice lowered with anger. "I'll tell Aric."

Koda disconnected. Everyone watched me, waiting for me to scream, cry, laugh—*something*. But I couldn't. I could barely stay upright.

Shayna stood over me. I lifted my chin. And she slapped me hard across the face.

Koda shoved his way between us to protect her from me. It wasn't necessary. My tigress didn't so much as growl. After what I'd done to Aric, I deserved far worse.

Bolts of lightning sizzled from Taran's perfectly manicured fingertips. "Son of a *bitch*. What the hell,

Shayna?"

Koda growled, deep and challenging. His wolf sensed Taran threatening his mate and readied himself to attack.

I couldn't move from the shame overtaking me. I had caused all this hate. All of it.

Shayna gaped from her hand to my swelling face, her voice trembling. "I-I didn't mean to hit her. I . . ."

Koda's growls surged at the sight of the blue and white flames flickering above Taran's head.

"Everyone, calm down." Emme gripped Taran and Koda's wrists and bathed their forms with pale yellow light. Her healing touch soothed them only enough to prevent a brawl, but their anger remained.

Time stretched on in the tension-filled quiet.

Then Koda's phone rang. It rang six times before he finally answered it. Aric growled on the other end, his snarls mixed with tortured sobs. "How could you do this to me?" He knew I could hear. "I thought you were dead. Are you listening to me, Celia? *I thought you were dead!*"

I curled into a ball, saturating the couch with my tears as he continued to shout.

"Don't you dare cry. You did this to us. Goddamnit, why? Just tell me why!"

I shook from the force of my misery. There was nothing I could say. I couldn't explain my actions. I couldn't beg him to forgive me. I couldn't do anything but weep. Emme rested her head against me and slung her arms around my waist. She cried, too. I heard her even above my own hysteria.

Aric eventually disconnected. But it failed to diminish my sadness. If anything, his absence, however aggrieved, made my tears run faster. It was a reminder that he was no longer a part of my life. And that I had forced him out.

I stared blankly at the wall. Only Misha's arrival

finally caused me to stir. Koda lunged at him. "You goddamn leech!"

Tim tackled him in midair, forcing him away from Misha. They fought viciously, striking each other with blow after blow and barreling through the living room wall. My sisters screamed, begging them to stop. I rose and staggered outside, trailing behind them and the mob of hissing vampires. My mind reeled with exhaustion and my weak muscles failed to sustain me. I nosedived onto the slate walkway. Michael barely caught me before my body smacked down.

"Master," he said. "Something's wrong with Celia."

Misha gathered me in his arms. I could barely speak. "End the fight. End it now."

"As you wish."

A rush of vampiric energy swept against my battered nerves. I blinked my eyes open. Tim writhed against the grass. His severed right leg lay behind him. Shayna yanked on Koda's arm while Emme pushed him with her *force*. Taran followed closely. Her focus and that of my sisters were fixed on the vampires shadowing them.

Koda bled from the chunk of muscle missing from his arm and the deep gashes raked across his chest. He locked eyes with Misha before my sisters hauled him away. "I'm going to find out what you did to her and you're going to pay! You piece of *filth*, I'll get you back for what you did to them!"

He blamed Misha for my actions. They all did.

My head spun and my vision wavered. I remembered the cold rain splashing across my nose . . . and then I was floating in a sea of warm water that smelled like lavender and jasmine. Soft and slippery hands lovingly stroked my body before finally wrapping me in a lavish blanket and laying me on a sprawling surface.

Something sensual and delicious slicked over my lips. I licked them. The taste filled the emptiness inside me.

More was offered and I took it willingly.

My subconscious eventually nudged me awake. It was hard for me to abandon this dream. I didn't want to leave the warmth and security. The alluring scent surrounding me insisted I relax and enjoy the euphoria. But I wasn't completely myself. My arms held something. No, *someone*. My eyes immediately shot open.

Misha stared back at me. He was naked. And so was I.

Chapter Ten

"Good morning," he said.

I didn't normally swear much, but I did then. Like the offspring of a sailor and a trucker, obscenities shot out of my mouth like machine-gun fire. This only made Misha's smile widen. He looked happy—too happy. I scrambled out of bed so quickly the sheets tangled around my ankle and I crash-landed on the wood floor. I snatched the corner of a blanket and pulled. Misha yanked it out of my grasp and patted the space next to him.

"Come back to bed, my love, so that we may continue to pleasure each other."

"Continue?" My stomach dropped to my ankles "We like, *did it?*"

I traced my hands over my body, trying desperately to figure out what the hell had happened between us.

Misha groaned. "It pleases me to watch you touch yourself."

"I'm not touching myself!" I screamed defensively. "Well, not like *that*." I caught sight of a blanket left abandoned on the floor and wrapped it around me. I froze as the familiar scents of lavender and jasmine wafted into my nose and triggered my scattered memories: the warm water, the massage, and the . . . *tasting*.

I clutched the blanket against me. "Oh my God. I'm a slut."

"Yes, you are, you bad girl." Maria and the good Catholics sashayed into the room with an extra spring to their stiletto-clad steps.

And that's when I recalled the slippery hands. Fantastic. I'd been felt up by the Catholic schoolgirls. Because my life just wasn't entertaining enough.

Liz embraced me and kissed both sides of my face. "It's so nice to see you're still having sex. Would you like us to join you?"

Edith smiled and unzipped her thigh-high leather boots. "Oh, yes! Can we join you, Master?"

When I pinched myself and still couldn't snap out of Bizarro Land I protested— vehemently. It was too late. Maria had stripped down to nothing and her tongue was already visiting with Misha's tonsils. The others were busy tugging off their uniforms.

"What the hell? Put the plaid skirts back on!"

Misha stopped kissing Maria *and* Edith and frowned in my direction. "Would you prefer they did not join us?"

"I don't want them to join us!"

He shrugged indifferently. "As you wish. Leave, my precious ones, so that Celia and I may commence our lovemaking."

Edith zipped up her boots and scowled. "You suck."

My eyes narrowed. "I know. You've mentioned it more than once. Don't let the door hit your unholy ass."

I fixed my gaze on Misha when the last of the girls had disappeared from the suite. He sat in bed with his hands crossed behind his head. A sheet barely covered his waist. Strands of his long blond hair grazed his erect nipples.

I sighed. More than once I'd compared Misha to a

Greek god. Like most anyone with a pulse, his physical beauty gave me pause. And for a vampire, Misha possessed the heart of a lion. Yet even now, my body failed to respond to his. Only guilt bored its way to the surface. I wanted to be in Aric's arms—Aric, who was scarred beyond recognition, who no doubt hated me, and who most likely would never want me again.

"Why do you look so sad, kitten?"

"What we did is wrong, Misha."

He walked to the chaise lounge where I sat. I averted my eyes when he knelt before me and brushed my hair away from my face. "I know why you broke your bond with the wolf."

Perspiration trickled from my pores. If he knew about Anara, he was now in danger, too. "I don't know what you're talking about." A slow, amused smile lit his gray eyes. Of course, he knew I was lying.

"Yes, you do, my darling kitten," he replied. "It stems from your desire to be mine."

It felt like he had slapped me. I took a second to absorb his words. "Misha, what happened between Aric and me has nothing to do with us."

He smiled. "Really? Tell me then why you would break such a sacred connection."

I couldn't tell him squat, but I had to say something. "Aric and I just shouldn't be together."

That was so the wrong thing to say. Happiness radiated from his features. "I know."

His joy crushed my already battered heart. I could never love Misha. And it was time for him to accept it. My hard stare met his. "Misha, you need to let me go. We don't have a future together."

"You're wrong. Tell me what you desire and it shall be yours."

"The only thing I want is what's best for you. And I'm not her." I shook my head.

"Misha, one day you're going to fall in love. And it will be an incredible selfless love with someone you can give yourself completely to. Someone you can be vulnerable with. Someone you can't live without."

Misha gritted his perfect teeth. "I have already found her within you."

"If that was the case, you wouldn't have made out with your naughty little girlfriends." My eyes stung with tears. "I'm not who you really want. If I was, you'd abandon your thirst for multiple women and commit. *Really* commit."

"I just did." His arm waved around the room. "Do you see anyone here but you?"

"It's not the same thing, Misha." I adjusted the blanket around me. "No one you're devoted to should have to ask you to tell your hoochies to leave. It goes to show you don't love me as much as you think." I stood and left his room. I was halfway through the open corridor when the aroma of familiar scents slammed into me like a shopping cart. I stopped short, almost falling.

Maria smiled. "Oh, I forgot to tell you, your sisters are here."

Emme's lips parted with surprise. Taran crossed her arms. I could scent her disappointment, just as I could Shayna's anger. Her fists were clenched and she refused to look at me.

I don't know which reaction hurt me more.

Misha leaned against the railing. The wrought-iron bars weren't wide enough to hide his naked form. He nodded to my sisters in way of a greeting. "Kitten," he called casually. "The coordinator will arrive on the premises immediately following lunch. Take this time to be with your family. We have many decisions to make."

"Coordinator?" I asked like an idiot.

"Why, yes. A wedding of this magnitude requires the flair of an expert."

Shayna's head snapped up. "What wedding?"

"Ours, of course. Celia and I are getting married."

It didn't matter that I screamed at Misha in front of my sisters that we weren't getting married. Nor did anyone care for my dramatic, breaking-down-the-doors exit. My sisters saw what they wanted. The broken bond, my naked figure wrapped in a blanket, and Misha's smile when he asked them to be bridesmaids. *Bastard.*

My sisters and I sat in the kitchen of the guest house's second-floor apartment. Chang and Ying-Ying had already moved Bren so the contractors could repair the damage from Koda and Tim's smackdown. We'd spoken very little during our care of Bren. Not even Taran had commented on Little Bren's elation when Emme wished his bigger half a good morning.

It was awful. Normally when we sat drinking chai, we talked a lot, whether to discuss our lives, seek advice, or simply laugh between jokes. But no one laughed, joked, or even spoke. My actions had confused them. They wanted answers, but I had none to give.

"So, she chose Misha," Taran finally said. Everyone's gaze shot toward her. She shrugged and took a sip of her tea. "You're a big girl, Celia. You know what's best for you."

Shayna scowled. "No, she doesn't. What she did to Aric was low."

My eyes closed firmly and I took a breath. When I opened them, Shayna continued to frown my way. Emme set down her cup. "Leave her alone, Shayna. Celia is not a hateful person and you know it."

"You're wrong." Shayna scoffed, "I don't even know who she is anymore."

A spark of blue and white lit above Taran's head. "*Stop it*, Shayna."

Shayna slammed her palms down and rose, the werewolf essence Koda had given her surging her anger. "Why couldn't you just tell Aric to his face? Why did you have to be so brutal? You humiliated him—"

The crashing sound when I tipped the table stopped Shayna's anger from building. Hell, it stopped everything. I couldn't even hear the birds outside anymore. Deep fury heated my body and my tigress's eyes replaced my own. All my beast wanted was to lash out. She was ready to fight, to maim, or kill, and so was I.

Emme slipped out of her seat and backed away. "Oh, God . . . Celia."

My sisters' terror incited my beast. She was done being caged by those who sought to hurt us, and rushed forth to protect me.

Even if it meant charging those she had always looked after.

I took a step forward without realizing. The speck of humanity that remained within me forced me to stop and close my eyes again. I thought of my baby, that little peanut whose heart beat because I lived. I had to keep it together. I had to get us through this. My fury slowly abated and I wiped the two tears that escaped without my permission. When I regained enough control, I gathered the garbage pail and broom and began to sweep. At first no one moved, but then they knelt on the floor and helped gather the broken pieces of ceramic.

My grip on the broom handle cracked the wood in two. Shayna clasped my wrist and slid the handle from my hands. Her eyes reddened and she wept. It seemed her fear and sadness were enough to manage the wolf Koda had passed her. "What's happening to you, Ceel?"

Taran and Emme whimpered as their own grief unfolded. They were frightened for me.

God, what *was* happening to me? "I have to leave," I croaked.

Taran wiped her mascara-streaked face. "Where are you going?"

I pushed the hair out of my eyes. "I mean I'm leaving . . . and not coming back." A sense of relief washed over me. *That's it. That's the answer. I have to get as far away from here as possible. It will please Anara and keep everyone safe.*

Emme knelt over the mess with a cracked mug in her hand. "Celia, honey, you can't just leave us."

Taran slammed a chipped saucer into the garbage pail. "Shit, Ceel. I don't know what the hell is happening, but there's no way you're going anywhere!"

I ignored them. The more I thought about my plan, the more it made sense. I had money saved from years of working and from the missions I'd accomplished for the vampires. I could rent something small and work as a nurse until the baby was born.

Shayna dropped the pieces of broken broom and gripped my arm. "Dude, you're sick. You can't be alone in your condition."

I looked from the skinny arms that held me to her imploring expression. *Great, they think I need meds. I was better off when they thought I was a bitch.*

I shrugged her off. "I'm not sick. I just don't belong here anymore."

They exchanged glances, unsure of what to do next. In her desperation, Emme threw down the Catholic guilt. "What about Bren? You promised you'd take care of him."

Bren slept peacefully on the couch, blissfully unaware of the horrors surrounding us in the conscious world. "You're right." They all sighed with apparent relief. "I'll take him with me."

"No, honey, that's not what I meant!"

"Screw that, Celia."

Shayna approached me with her palms out like I was going to catapult off a building and take them with me.

"Don't panic, Ceel. You need help—but that's okay. We're going to get you through it."

She jumped when her cellphone rang. I appreciated their attempts to be supportive, but their idea of "help" involved me, a straitjacket, and a trip to the funny farm. I was surprisingly calm, finally feeling like I had made a good decision.

"Puppy, I can't talk right now."

Koda's voice boomed on the other line. "Did Danny help Celia break the bond?" Shayna's gaze slowly traveled up to meet mine. Emme and Taran fell silent. "Baby, it's important. Ask her—"

"She's right here, Koda." Shayna put him on speaker. "She heard you."

Taran slowly walked toward Shayna's outstretched hand. "What's happening?"

Koda took a breath. "Heidi was upset and wanted to speak to Danny about a fight they'd had. She tracked him to Harrah's in Stateline. She told us when she kissed Danny, she could taste Celia on his lips."

There was an audible pop when my sisters' jaws fell open.

Koda snarled. "Now, that was last night. The same goddamn night the bond was broken. So, Celia, I ask you this: Did Danny help you break the bond?"

My heart shouldn't have been beating so hard, seeing how all the color had drained from my face. "Koda . . . where's Aric?"

"He went to find Danny to ask him himself."

Chapter Eleven

Never in my life did I believe I'd say these words: "Shayna, drive faster."

My hands shook. Danny was smart—too smart. He'd hidden his tracks by using a different name when he'd checked into the hotel. I couldn't reach him at Harrah's and he wasn't answering his phone.

"Do you think Aric will hurt Danny?"

Emme wasn't asking, she was begging us to tell her Danny would be fine. None of us answered. We didn't want to admit that Aric would probably do more than hurt him.

If he dies . . . it's my fault.

Koda and the other wolves were already hightailing it to Harrah's when he'd called. But they were coming from Squaw Valley and they didn't have Shayna at the wheel. She sped into the Nevada side of Tahoe, slamming down on the accelerator until we screeched to a halt in front of Harrah's.

We rushed out and stopped short, staring at the eighteen-story giant. Shayna's eyes bulged. "How the heck are we going to find him?"

I urged them forward. "Taran, use your charm to get

the staff to tell you where he is."

Glass shattered with a scream as we bolted toward the building. A king-sized bed followed by a set of table and chairs flew out a sixth-floor window. The bed landed in the lake. The chairs punctured the lawn like tombstones while the table slammed into the sidewalk, cracking the concrete into large chunks.

Oh no. Aric.

Taran and Shayna charged into the hotel. I grabbed Emme before she could follow. "Toss me up."

Emme jumped from my grasp. "Celia, my aim is terrible. I might hurt you."

"Just do it!"

Emme threw me with her *force*. I rocketed through the air with flailing limbs. She was right, her aim was awful. She stopped just short of ramming me into the side of the building. I scrambled along the brick and through the broken window while she kept me suspended. My claws dug into the thick carpet and I dragged my body forward, rolling aside in time to avoid the giant dresser hurtling toward me. It plummeted toward the sidewalk and exploded with a splintering crash.

Aric loomed over Danny, snarling. "All this time, you've wanted her for yourself. *Didn't you?*" Danny cowered on the floor, his face varnished with bruises and his mouth gushing blood from his missing teeth.

In his rage, Aric had failed to notice me. I shot forward and rammed myself between them. He glared back at me with vicious eyes. "Did you come to save your lover, Celia?" There was nothing left of my wolf behind that malicious and hateful stare. Only a beast bent on destruction remained.

"Don't hurt him, Aric. None of this is his fault. Please, love. Just let him go." A strange stillness gathered around us.

"All right," he said.

I didn't have time to blink. I didn't have time to breathe. Aric moved around me with dizzying speed and pitched Danny out of the window. Emme screamed from below as I sprinted forward and dove after Danny. The wind whipped at my face and hair. I reached for the tip of his shoe moments before his skull smacked the concrete.

I *shifted* us through the sidewalk and resurfaced. Aric vaulted down, swinging off a lamppost and landing in a crouch, mere feet in front of us. "You betrayed your Leader, Daniel. Now you will die."

My body froze in horror. Aric's wolf had shoved aside his humanity, transforming him into the merciless killing machine he'd been bred to be. He stalked forward, a hungry beast who'd found his meal. I snapped out of my terror and shoved Danny behind me. I wouldn't let Aric hurt him. He'd have to go through me first.

My heart thundered in my chest as I crouched and readied myself to take on my mate. He didn't even see me; his gaze stayed fixed on his prey. I almost buckled with relief when I heard the pounding footsteps behind me. The Warriors had arrived.

Gemini tackled Aric onto the sprawling lawn and the others leapt on top of him. Sirens blasted behind me where a large crowd had gathered. Women screamed as Aric broke loose with swinging fists, exposing his ravaged and scarred face.

I shoved Danny farther away. "Get out of here! *Get out of here now!*"

Danny tried to haul me with him. "Celia, you have to come with me. Aric is in shock. If his wolf fails to recognize you, he'll kill you."

In the few breaths Danny had spoken, Aric's murderous rampage had been unleashed. Liam and Koda sprawled against the demolished turf, unconscious. Gemini thrashed in agony his legs broken. Emme hurried forward, trying futilely to hold Aric back with her *force*. He broke through as if bursting through paper and stormed past her.

Shayna rushed to Koda's side. She wouldn't risk stabbing Aric unless there was no other choice. Only one sister stood between us and Aric.

Taran gathered her magic and blasted him with a jolt of lightning. I screamed when he collapsed to the ground. He rose almost immediately, growling, his glare just as piercing and still targeted on Danny.

I gave Danny one last shove and lurched forward. My anger at Aric's actions and my fear for Danny's safety propelled me onward with my claws out. I meant to hurt him. I meant to make him bleed. Yet my love for him beat my wrath into submission.

I flung my arms around his neck. In breaking the bond, I thought the glorious warmth between us would cease to exist. I was wrong. Heat immediately encased us, soothing my tattered soul with unbelievable reverence. My breaths released in sobs. Everything inside me had missed Aric and failed to live without him.

"Baby, don't," I begged when he took another step toward Danny.

Aric stopped, as if the current charging his monstrous demeanor had been cut. Slowly, his body relaxed and his head fell against my shoulder. The rough and sharp textures of his damaged skin scratched at my face, but I didn't care. I just needed him.

His arms encircled my waist. "Why?" he choked. "I love you so much. Just tell me why." My cries turned to hysterics. We dropped to our knees, tightening our hold.

Taran released a blue and white mist to hypnotize and calm the panic-stricken crowd. I barely felt her magic as it passed over my skin. The world around me ceased to exist, except for Aric. I knew only him and his beautiful scent. He kissed my head and ran his fingers through my hair. My hands swept over the hard muscles of his back. He felt so right. I couldn't fathom how I'd abandoned him. I was going to confess everything. But before my lips could part, I was silenced by the deafening sound of howling wolves.

Anara's translucent form charged toward me. "You *bitch*!"

I jerked away from Aric, falling backward on my hands. Anara shoved his face in mine. "I will kill him if you don't force him from your life!" I sat there, held in place by the Pack magic swirling around him. "Need I remind you of my strength?"

He motioned to where Shayna knelt over Koda and flicked his hand. Her head was wrenched to the side as if yanked and her limp form slumped against the pavement. Koda awoke abruptly and pulled her into his arms. Emme shrieked and raced to her side.

Taran started toward them only to suddenly still. Slowly she turned and stared at me with irises that had bleached to white. "Something's here," she said in a hollow voice.

She'd felt Anara's presence.

My gaze darted around. Anara was gone. Aric rose, his blue shirt saturated with my tears. He didn't glance at Shayna, Taran, or anyone else. His light brown eyes fixed on me. He sensed my fear, but he failed to understand it. "Celia, tell me what's happening."

Anara's voice whispered savagely in my head. "Make him hate you." Shayna screamed again. He was hurting her just to be sure I was listening. My head whipped from her to Aric. "Make him hate you or they both die!"

I clenched my teeth. "Misha is planning our wedding." Aric froze.

"He wants to be with me."

Aric fell silent, but his anger tore forth like a raging bull. My voice quivered. "I can never see you again."

Aric's large form trembled with uncomprehending

fury. "This is why you broke our bond—so you can be with *Misha*?"

"I . . ."

"Answer him, Celia!" Anara growled.

"Forget about me, Aric. Forget you ever knew me. You deserve better."

Aric loomed over me, his deep timbre thick with anger. "You're right. You're no good for me. You're no good for anyone—except maybe that *fucking* leech!"

My heart stopped as I watched Aric disappear. Danny's cold hand on my shoulder kept me from falling over. When I faced him, his skin was ashen.

"God, Celia," he said. "How long has Anara been hurting you?'

Chapter Twelve

"Shut up, Danny," I hissed.

The desperation in my face instantly silenced him. I stumbled forward to Shayna's side.

Koda sat her up. She rubbed her neck. "I'm fine, puppy," she told him.

Koda didn't appear convinced. "What happened?"

"I don't know. It felt like someone tried to break my neck." Her slender fingers swept over her sternum. "And my heart kept trying to stop."

Koda glared at me.

Danny's hand returned to my shoulder. "Celia was over by me."

Blue and white fire crackled around Taran. "Damnit, Koda, don't look at her that way. Something was here. I *felt* it."

"What was it?" he asked. Taran didn't say anything.

"If something was here, tell me what it was!"

She jerked a flaming finger in his face. "I don't know what it was. All I know is that it was dark and sinister and strong. Like *ungodly* strong."

Koda rose, lifting Shayna to her feet. "That's because evil deeds attract evil beings." Emme's eyes widened. She knew he meant me.

"Celia isn't evil."

She reached for my hand, but Liam pulled her away. "What Celia intentionally did to Aric follows the path of evil. The dark ones enjoy that level of torture. If any were present when she broke the bond, they might have followed her, waiting to strike."

Out of Aric's best friends, I was closest to Liam. His scrutiny crippled my already tattered emotions.

Koda stalked over to me. "Your selfish acts could have cost me my mate."

Gemini clasped Koda's shoulder and pulled him back. Good for him, because the way I felt I would have nailed him in the face. "Enough, Koda. You're jumping to conclusions. We need to take care of this mess."

Taran had charmed the crowd into dispersing and ignoring the destruction around us.

Danny took in the demolished furniture. "I have some money I can contribute toward the cost."

Gemini's dark almond-shaped eyes shimmered with barely controlled rage. "You're not doing anything. You're no longer one of us." His hands tightened to fists. "Daniel Matagrano, as Beta to Aric Connor, pureblood and Leader of the Squaw Valley Den Pack, I hereby strip you of your title as Warrior. Step foot on our land, and I will personally end your life."

My sisters and I gasped. Danny bowed his head. The title of Warrior had been his crowning achievement— more than his doctoral degree, more than his academic accomplishments. This had been the honor that made him feel like he finally belonged.

Taran stomped toward Gemini. "Damnit, you can't freaking do this to him!"

Taran was Gemini's kryptonite. His resolve typically melted like ice in her presence. Not this time. He righted himself and met her with equal force. "This isn't up for discussion. Dan's actions are inexcusable. As his Leader, Aric has a right to kill him for his betrayal. Dismissing him from our Pack will spare him so long as he keeps his distance."

Taran rammed her finger in Gemini's chest. "This isn't his fault!"

Gemini leaned back on his heels. "He has free will, Taran. He made a choice. Are you suggesting Celia forced him to break the bond?"

My sisters turned to me, I guess with the expectation I'd save Danny and make things right. The wolves didn't have such hopes. Their anger surged as they continued to regard me as their enemy.

Danny knelt before Gemini in acknowledgment of guilt. "He's right. I could have refused Celia, but I chose not to." Tears dripped down his long nose. "I accept the conditions of my exile and the penalty placed upon my life."

Taran lurched away. "For a pack of wolves you spew a lot of horseshit!" she screamed over her shoulder. Emme wiped her eyes and helped Shayna lead Danny to a nearby bench.

I begged the earth to swallow me whole. All my actions—every last one of them—had caused nothing but harm. "I'll pay for the damages," I mumbled.

Gemini rubbed his goatee and huffed, "No, Celia. You've done enough."

It stung to have him speak to me that way. He was the most reasonable and patient werewolf I'd ever met. But even he hated me for what I'd done.

Taran influenced the manager to send the bill to the Den and to believe college coeds had destroyed the hotel room. As we waited for the wolves to wrap up with damage control, my hatred for Anara grew more heated. I'd done as he asked and severed the bond, and still it hadn't been enough. He'd forced me to hurt Aric yet again.

And he wasn't going to stop. No. That twisted bastard was having too much fun. My only choice was to distance myself. The events of the day had taught me as much. I took in Danny's despondent state. Maybe he'd like to come with me. Then my baby and I wouldn't have to be alone.

Taran left the bench when Gemini appeared, stormed to our light blue Legacy, and slammed the door shut behind her. Gemini watched her before addressing me. "Celia, we will take you back to the vampire's estate. There is much we need to discuss with you."

The last thing I wanted was the lupine express back to the mansion. Emme grasped my hands, her voice trembling. "Everyone's fighting, Celia. Please go and try to make amends."

I couldn't say no to her or to Shayna, who hugged her body tight. I knew nothing I could say would appease the wolves, I'd let enough people down that day. I followed the wolves back to Koda's mammoth Yukon.

Koda drove with Gemini next to him. Liam and I sat in the back. Koda took the long way back to Misha's, along the Nevada side of the lake. I supposed he felt we needed more quality time. No one spoke until we reached the Zephyr Cove–Round Hill Village area.

Liam twisted his body and leaned toward me. "You haven't been yourself. Tell us what's happening, Celia."

In loving my sisters and standing by Aric, the wolves had become my family. But like Aric, they were safer hating me, too. I crossed my arms. "If Aric's been ordered to stay away from me, why do you have a problem with what I did?"

Koda looked over his shoulder and grinned. "Actually, we're happy you're finally out of his life." His eyes blazed gold and he backhanded me across the face.

Koda's strike broke my nose and launched me into Liam's chest. Liam wrenched my arms back, leaving me open for Gemini's attack. Gemini's eyes fired with gold as he hurtled his way into the back and punched me in the head. My tigress went ballistic. I kicked Gemini away and butted Liam with the back of my skull. Liam released me. I sliced at the seat belt, but Liam yanked my left arm and snapped it before I finished cutting through.

I roared with agony and raked my claws across Liam's eyes. The move gave me time to rip through the strap just as Koda caught one of my thrashing feet. He crushed my instep within his grip. I ignored the excruciating pain and kicked him in the face and thrust my other foot into Gemini's throat. Koda lost control of the car and smashed into a utility pole. I threw open the door and rolled onto the street. A passing car swerved to avoid me and slammed into the side of Koda's SUV. Screams echoed behind me and cars screeched to a halt. I didn't look back. I clambered onto the sidewalk, using my knees and right arm to slide myself across the concrete.

An elderly man on the corner yelled at me to stay down and stop moving. I pulled myself up and ran for my life, cradling my limp arm and dragging my injured foot.

Human reasoning had abandoned me completely. I was nothing more than a desperate and frightened animal whose only thought was to flee with her baby. I cut through one alleyway and then another, only to hit a dead end.

My claws extended and I tried to scale the wall. My feet had barely left the ground when I fell backward onto my spine. Jolts of anguish reverberated across my useless limbs. It was impossible. I couldn't climb.

The hammering of approaching footsteps grew louder. The wolves had found me. I could smell their blood. I spun from my back and forced myself upright. No way could I take them on. My only choice was to *shift* into the sewers, but I didn't know where I'd land and feared the fall would exacerbate my injuries. I tried to slow my breath and waited. If I made contact, I could *shift* them and make my escape.

That is, if they didn't kill me first.

A hideous growl exploded from deep within me, bred from fear and desperation to protect the child within me. The hulking form of the wolves appeared and their urgent steps slowed. Their eyes no longer glowed in that horrible, angry gold. To my shock, they appeared solemn and completely freaked out.

Gemini softened the intensity of his stare as he took in my injuries. "Celia, it's okay. No one is going to hurt you."

"Stay away from us!"

They scanned the alley, expecting the presence of another. I'd impulsively referred to me and my baby. Except they didn't know that, and my comment only deepened their unease.

"Celia, it's me. Your buddy, Liam."

"You're not my buddy," I said through clenched teeth.

Koda took a step, but stopped when I unleashed another ferocious growl. "She must have injured herself when she jumped from the car," he murmured to the others.

My breath came out in quick frantic bursts. Either they were losing their minds or I was.

More footsteps approached. My sisters screamed when they saw me.

Taran tried to shove her way forward. "What the hell did you do to her?"

Gemini snatched her around the waist and hauled her back. "She attacked us while we were driving. I'm not sure what provoked her."

Furious tears leaked from my eyes. "I did *not*. You attacked me!"

Liam's eyes widened. "Oh shit. She believes what she's saying."

Gemini released Taran and spoke with a soft but

level voice. "We didn't attack you, Celia. We merely attempted to restrain you when you assaulted us."

My sisters drew back, absolutely sickened. "I didn't," I cried. "You have to believe me."

My sisters exchanged glances. The wolves' crimson-splattered shirts hung in tatters from where my claws had struck, and blood coated their hair and faces. Hell, I guess I wouldn't have believed me either.

Gemini inched forward. "Let's take her back to the Den. Perhaps the Elders can help—"

"*No!* I'm not going anywhere with you!" My instinct to run took over. I made the mistake of trying to barrel through the wolves. Koda immediately seized my waist. My fangs shot out and dug into his shoulder.

"Shit. Get her legs!"

I *changed,* only to collapse on my damaged limbs. My sisters shrieked. The wolves wrestled me onto the ground, struggling to restrain my 370-pound form. My roars of pain echoed out of the alleyway and into the darkening sky as my damaged bones snapped beneath me.

"Put her out, Taran!" Gemini hollered. "She's going to kill herself."

You know it's going to be a bad day when you wake up crying.

My sisters surrounded me, their faces grim. Blotches smeared Emme's fair skin and puffy eyes. Misha waited in the corner, standing perfectly still. If it weren't for his scent of sex and chocolate, I'd never have noticed him. Emme moved when he approached, so he could sit beside me. He pulled me into an embrace. I let my head fall against him, comforted by the knowledge that he could never hurt me.

Unlike the wolves.

"How long have I been out?"

"Just a few hours, dude. You woke up when it started to rain."

Taran swore and paced in front of the bed. "We've called a psychologist. She'll be evaluating you in the morning."

I stared at the wall of my room. It was a soft sage, such a pretty color . . . peaceful.

"That's not necessary. I'm leaving tomorrow and taking Bren with me."

Misha's arms tightened around me. "No."

Emme leaned forward. "You're sick, sweetheart. You need help."

I stood abruptly and went to the window. "The only thing I need is to get out of this cursed state."

"Damnit, Celia. You can't just run away from your problems!"

Shayna's voice broke. "And what about us, Ceel? We always promised to be together."

I began to hum. It no doubt reinforced their belief that I was loony, but it helped soothe me and kept me from having to explain myself. One by one, everyone left.

I stepped into the family room sometime later. Emme sat alongside Bren, combing through his thickened beard and trimming it with long, sharp scissors. He grinned at her and so did Little Bren.

I smiled softly. "You have quite the effect on him."

Emme blushed without skipping a beat. "We bathed him after I healed your fractures. I think Taran was a little jealous she couldn't, you know, get him to react like this."

"Are you serious?"

Emme nodded. "Yes, but after all, she's always been the man-eater." She placed the scissors on the table and stopped smiling. "Celia, when you leave, I'd like to go with you."

As far as I was concerned, everyone was better off without me. "You need to stay with Taran and Shayna."

She shook her head. "They have their wolves. I'll only be in the way."

"No, Emme."

She maneuvered her way around the sofa and gripped my hands. "Please, Celia. I can take care of you and Bren. Maybe you won't need Haldol if I try healing you every day."

My laugh bordered on fanatical and probably frightened her. She thought I needed antipsychotic medication. In my attempts to deal with my problems, all I'd managed was to convince everyone I was nuts.

Emme's sweet expression held all the world's hope. She didn't want me to leave her behind. I squeezed her hands. It would be nice to have her with me. In time, I could tell her about the baby. "Okay, Emme. You can come with me."

She threw her arms around me. I hugged her back. The way she loved, I knew she'd make a perfect aunt.

Emme drove us to Dollar Point in the morning to gather our belongings. I'd spent most of the night trying to reach Danny. He failed to answer my calls, texts, and emails. I prayed he was just lying low and off Anara's radar. Knowing Anara would have rubbed Danny's death in my face gave me hope he was still alive.

Our horrible neighbor, Mrs. Mancuso, watched us unload the empty boxes from our Tribeca. All it took was a simple glance her way and out came her middle finger. She stood behind her hummingbird curtains, keeping her finger erect until we stepped onto our porch. I sighed. Mrs. Mancuso's sunny disposition was just another reminder that I needed to get the hell out of California.

Emme had called our sisters to tell them we were leaving. Taran flipped out and demanded to speak to me. I refused. They thought I was crazy. Nothing I could have said would've changed their minds. Emme also explained she would be leaving with me. Needless to say, they weren't happy campers. Taran swore bloody murder into the phone until Emme eventually hung up. So, there I was, packing like the dickens, before they could show up and drag me off to the nearest psych ward.

Misha refused to accept I was leaving. I contemplated my goodbye with him while I boxed a few kitchen appliances. My sisters were one thing. It would kill me to leave them, but they had their mates and their happily-ever-afters. Who did Misha have? The horny Catholic schoolgirls, that's who.

I finished sealing the box and realized why Misha thought he loved me. I'd shown him kindness and devotion with no strings attached. Gifts that didn't come easily, I imagined, when you were a god among vampires. Maybe that was his interpretation of love.

I opened another box to pack our bread maker. It gave me pause. I used to bake bread every day to pack in Aric's lunch. My hand swept over the machine but then I stopped. The terms we were leaving on couldn't have been any more horrid, and the direness of our situation threatened to cripple me. I didn't know how I'd function without him. And yet there I stood, with the hope that one day I'd be able to reunite him with our child.

I quickly boxed up the last few items when the doorbell rang. My hackles immediately rose, knowing who had arrived. "Emme, no!"

"Hi, Liam," she said just before he sent her flying into the wall.

Chapter Thirteen

Koda and Gemini stampeded through the door directly behind Liam, their eyes blazing like molten gold. I lunged at Emme to *shift* her unmoving form out. But the wolves were ready for me.

They tackled me and forced me against the wall. Liam's fingertip swept beneath my jaw. "Here, kitty, kitty."

I jerked from his touch. Koda licked his lips. "What's the matter, little cat? Don't you want to play?"

My panic had me hyperventilating. The first time they'd hurt me, I failed to hear the dreadful call of howling wolves. But I heard them now.

Anara was coming.

Gemini tangled his fingers into my long tresses. "Is this how Aric used to touch you?" He yanked out a chunk of hair, making me screech.

I couldn't *shift* or *change*. Piece by piece they ripped strands from my scalp and berated me with insults.

"Whore."

"Freak."

"Spic."

My struggles were worthless and my screams were silenced by a large hand. I couldn't breathe. I couldn't

114

fight.

The front door flew open. And Danny stumbled in.

I bit down on Koda's hand, forcing him off my mouth. "Run!"

Danny didn't flee. He *charged,* throwing his weight against Koda and Gemini. It was suicide. He was going to die.

Then something bizarre occurred. The moment his lean form smacked against their more formidable weight, the wolves closed their eyes and staggered back, swaying as if working to keep their balance. Liam dropped me on the floor and seized Danny by the throat.

Liam's hand loosened when Danny clasped his wrist. Like the other Warriors, his lids drooped and he rocked in place. The howling wolves abruptly stopped their song. For a moment, no one moved.

I rose on trembling legs. Danny circled the wolves, carefully examining their swaying figures, his expression reeling with shock. We jumped when their eyes whipped open. The frightening glow from their irises was gone, replaced by revulsion as they gaped from me to the locks of torn hair littering the hardwood floor.

Dismay filled the room like a storm cloud. Gemini swallowed hard. "Celia . . . what have you done?"

Koda approached me. I flinched when he reached to touch me. He pulled back his hand and let it drop to his side. "It's self-mutilation and hatred," he muttered. "I'm not sure we can stop it."

They were putting all this back on me. Just like Anara had likely intended.

Liam sniffed the air, his muscles tensing. "Where's Emme?" His head snapped to where she lay near the fireplace. "No!" He ran to her, sweeping her into his arms. "Angel, can you hear me?"

Koda's sadness turned to horror. "You *hit* her?"

"No. I . . . *no!*"

I started toward her. "Stay away from her!" Liam growled.

Koda and Gemini blocked my path. "Don't move," Koda warned. "We don't want to hurt you."

Danny opened his mouth to defend me, but I silenced him with a glare. He nodded slowly and inched his way to Emme just as she began to glow. I sighed with relief. She was healing herself; she would be all right.

Liam seemed surprised to see Danny. "Did you see what happened?" I put my hand out. "No. He came after you arrived."

"I came after you," Danny repeated numbly.

Gemini watched me carefully. "We have to figure out what to do with her."

My fingertips itched with the need to protrude my claws. He didn't mean Emme. "I'll take her back to Misha's," Danny said quickly. "He'll look after her."

Koda snarled. "She doesn't belong with him. Damnit, don't you see? He's part of the problem." He stomped to my side. "Tell me what he's done to you!"

Danny grabbed my arm and tugged me toward the door at the sound of my growl. Koda rushed forward, blocking our way with his Rock of Gibraltar physique. With as much courage as he could muster, Danny met his gaze. "You have no right to hold us, Miakoda."

Gemini held his ground next to Koda. "You're wrong. She's a danger to herself and those around her."

"But she's not *were,* therefore she doesn't fall under your jurisdiction. Let's go, Celia."

Gemini hardened his stare. "As a supernatural being she does fall under our jurisdiction."

Danny tried to sound assertive, but his voice cracked like a prepubescent boy. "Technically, we're not sure what Celia is. She was born human, so if you want her arrested, you'll have to call the human police."

Danny hooked my arm under his and raced us to his

car. He started the engine and floored it. "Holy crap! Holy crap! Holy crap!"

Danny's mother died from leukemia when he was young. Before her death he promised to always be a gentleman and never swear in front of a lady. Under the psycho-werewolf-Elder-coming-to-getcha circumstance though, I think she'd say, "It's okay, son, you can say, 'Fuck me!'" But no, there he was, saying "crap" while he drove the car like he was blindfolded.

I ran my fingers through what remained of my hair. The bald spots stung and blood oozed from my scalp. I stared at my hands. Small broken strands mixed with tiny chunks of skin laid against my palms.

"Holy crap!" Danny yelled again. I sighed. "Yup."

Danny drove faster, breathing in rapid bursts and teetering on the verge of a breakdown. I didn't say anything. I knew he'd pull it together. We had reached Tahoe City when he finally collected himself enough to speak.

"Anara is using Pack magic to control the wolves."

I could barely respond. "Yes."

"And they can't remember their actions."

"No. They can't."

"Celia, he forced you to break your bond with Aric, didn't he?"

I nodded, shuddering slightly. "He told me if I had any contact with Aric, he would know and he would kill him. When Aric kept trying to reach me, Anara gave me two days to break our connection or he'd kill someone I loved."

"Holy crap!"

"I know."

"That's how Bren got hurt, wasn't it? Anara's the one who attacked you."

I sighed and wiped my hands on my jeans, smearing them with blood and hair. "He'd grown impatient when I didn't immediately bend to his request. He came after me the night I went out with Bren."

"That's why Bren's with you. You're protecting him against Anara."

"Yes . . . and I think he's keeping Bren's wolf from healing him."

"We have to tell Aric!"

"No, Danny. We can't." My voice shook. "Anara is capable of killing anyone from miles away. He said if I told anyone, my sisters would die."

Danny's eyes swept around the car like he half expected Anara to appear. "Okay . . . okay. We have to get you someplace safe."

"No. *We* have to get someplace safe. I was thinking Bermuda."

"Celia, we can't go there. There's only one place we'll be safe—Misha's."

"What?"

"Misha's place is fortified with vampire power, strengthened by the mysticism of the lake. It should be enough to interfere with Anara's *were* magic. He can't reach you there."

"But Anara appeared to me the day Aric broke into Misha's compound."

I could almost see the wheels turning in Danny's head. "He probably managed through his link to Aric as his Elder. Aric's emotions likely boosted his power and therefore strengthened the connection. Otherwise, I don't think he could have presented himself."

"What if you're wrong?"

Danny wiped the sweat off his face. "Then we're probably all going to die."

We drove in silence for a while. It was a lot to take in, and I was trying to give Danny more time to calm. "How did you stop the wolves from hurting me?" I finally asked.

"I don't know. They just sort of stopped when I touched them."

I thought about what he said. "Maybe that's your power." "Huh?"

"Your gift as a blue merle werewolf, maybe you can somehow block magic or reverse it."

"If that's the case how come Bren is still in a coma?"

I wiped my eyes. "I don't know, Danny. I don't know much of anything anymore." Danny slipped an arm around me. "Maybe I can't help Bren, but I'm definitely aware of Anara. I saw him appear before you yesterday and I heard what he said to you—even after his image vanished."

This information did little to ease my worries. "Do you think he knows about you?"

"If he did . . . I wouldn't be here now."

"Then what happened to you last night?"

Danny's face turned bright pink. He slinked his arm from my shoulders and returned to focusing hard on the road.

"Danny . . . where were you last night?"

"Um. Heidi tracked me down again. She heard about me getting kicked out of the Pack and, er, tried to cheer me up."

I raised my eyebrows. "Did she now?"

"Uh, yeah."

"So, let me get this straight. While I was up thinking you'd been tortured, killed, and possibly castrated, you were actuality getting laid?"

"Yes, but you should feel sorry for me."

"And why is that?"

"Because sex is still the only way she's able to communicate her feelings."

"I see. Pull over, please."

"Huh?"

"I think I have to vomit."

"Because of me and Heidi?"

"No. Because I'm pregnant with Aric's baby."

Danny almost lost control of the car. "HOLY CRAP!"

"Holy crap indeed, Danny."

Danny stopped a mile or so from Misha's house so I could hurl. The moment I was done, he embraced me. "Does anyone else know?"

"No one but you."

It felt good to tell someone my secret. And although Aric was the wolf I first wanted to tell, Danny was sure as hell a close second.

"How long have you known?"

"I found out the day after we arrived from Chaitén."

Danny shook his head, his expression heavy with worry. "The same day you were attacked in your house."

"Yes."

"Also by Anara."

"Yes, Danny."

He hugged me tighter. "You've been dealing with so much on your own. How the heck are you even functioning?"

I'm not really. "No one can know about the baby." I started trembling and almost broke down. "Anara told me he'd rather see Aric dead than have an abomination like me curse his bloodline."

Danny tensed against me. I could scent his anger and his fright and yet he tried to comfort me. "I swear I won't tell anyone."

Danny stopped the car in Misha's driveway moments later. The Catholic schoolgirls immediately pounced on me like a ravenous dog on a chunky squirrel. They crinkled their noses and Maria huffed, her Brazilian accent seething with annoyance. "Celia, dis whole attention thing is getting old. And what de hell did you do to your hair? Honestly, you look dreadful."

Before I could smack her into the middle of next week, Liz shoved a bunch of fabric swatches in my face. "Pick your goddamn colors."

"For what?" I shoved them back and started toward the guesthouse. And look at that, they followed right behind me.

"For the bridesmaids' dresses. I look better in the lavender, so that's the one you need to go with."

"Liz, I'm not getting married."

Everyone ignored me and then Agnes started in on me. "Regardless of the color, we've decided we want platinum necklaces as your gift to us."

Maria agreed, of course. "It's de least you can do. We'd also like them to have added bling. I was thinking colored diamonds."

That perked up Edith in more ways than one. "I want pink diamonds. The same color as my nipples." She tried to pull down her push-up bra. "Want to see?"

"*No,*" I growled.

Maria elbowed her away. "We also want hair jewelry. Just because you're bald, don't expect de rest of us to follow suit."

Sympathy was a term completely unfamiliar to the good Catholics. My temper flared. "Step away from the tigress, before she knocks you on your butt implants."

Agnes played with one of her long pigtails. "Celia, let me be perfectly blunt. You've been a real pain in the ass. If you want us in your wedding party, you'll have to work for it."

They ranted about what a bitch I was after I slammed the guesthouse door in their faces. Danny stared at the closed door. "Wow. They're convinced you're marrying Misha." Ying-Ying had been watching some kind of Asian game show with Bren. She took a good look at me and hugged me. When she swung open the door, the naughty Catholics scattered. She winked my way and lotus-pose floated down the steps. No one messed with Ying-Ying. Ever.

Danny bent over Bren, closed his eyes, and touched his bare arm. We waited but nothing happened. He failed to block Anara's power like he'd done with the other wolves. Bren didn't so much as stir. "What do you think we can do to save him?"

Danny shook his head. "I don't know. For Anara to manipulate the wolves and trap Bren's wolf in this state, he must be even more powerful than we think. Especially if none of his Pack suspect what's happening." He paused and took a seat next to me on the lounge. "I don't know how to fight him, Celia. And I'm not sure if we can. Pack Elders . . . they just don't do this."

"Well, this one does and has had fun doing it." My attention fell to the thick binder on the wooden coffee table. The sticky on top read: *Guest List for Bride's Approval.*

I groaned. On to problem number two. "Danny, there's something else I need to talk to you about...I had this dream—a vision actually—that Misha and I had children. It was right after Anara first attacked me. Misha was trying to soothe me with his vamp mojo. When he attempted a stronger hypnosis, he saw the image, too." I pointed to the binder. "I think that's why he's convinced we're getting married. Despite my protests."

Danny's eyes darted nervously. My voice turned from Demi Moore husky to shit-has-hit-the-fan high-pitched. "This is the part where you tell me it's nothing to worry about. That it was just some freaky thing that happened." He remained silent. "Danny!"

"Celia, I don't know what's happening. Seeing as you're pregnant, you could be developing the ability to have visions of what is to come."

I stood abruptly. "Why would I, all of a sudden, develop a new power?"

"You told me the first time you *changed* into a tigress, you had just gone through a growth spurt."

"Yeah, so?"

"Growth is hormone-related and so is pregnancy. Your body is producing tremendous amounts of hormones to maintain the fetus. They could have given your gifts an extra boost."

"But Danny, Aric is my baby's father. In my vision, I had three children and they all resembled Misha."

Danny touched his chin thoughtfully. "That does add to the confusion. Have you had any other images involving Aric?"

I hesitated. "There was one. But it was more like a nightmare." I explained the dream involving Aric burning and the scarred children.

Despite the gruesome accounts, he surprised me by smiling. "That was likely a result of your guilt over hurting Aric. I wouldn't worry about that one coming true."

"But at least that involved children where Aric was the father."

Danny stopped smiling. "Yeah. Well, I guess you're right about that."

Not exactly what I wanted to hear. But as much as Danny always tried to make me feel better, he'd never lie or give me false hope. He excused himself and went into the hall bathroom. He returned with a bottle of antiseptic and a wet towel. Very carefully, he wiped saturated cotton balls across my bleeding bald spots, and then covered my head with a nice cool towel. My sensitive scalp throbbed at first, but the coolness of the thick cotton soothed the sting.

"Thanks, Danny."

His face remained unusually pale. "Celia, I'm concerned about your baby's life. If Anara, the remaining Tribesmen, or heck, even the shape-shifters find out, they'll want your child dead."

My claws splintered the wood as they protruded across the heavy table and my words released with a growl. "Anara considers me an atrocity. I recognize that any child of mine and Aric's would be perceived the same way. But why should the Tribe or those damn shape-shifters care?"

"Celia, you're an extraordinary and powerful being, whose powers are yet to be fully tested. Aric is believed to be the strongest *were* in history. That makes you both dangerous and a threat. Any child from your union will be perceived as a force to be reckoned with."

I stood, my chest rising and falling quickly. "But what if the baby is human? A human couldn't possibly harm them."

He placed a hand on my shoulder. "The dark ones likely won't wait to find out."

All of my concerns lately had revolved around Anara, but Danny was right. I'd made multiple enemies and none would be jumping for joy at the news of my pregnancy. The shape- shifters especially frightened me. They were born witches, murdering countless in exchange for the ability to transform into any creature they wished. They were hard to detect, hard to kill, and carried the power of hell within them. I'd met one briefly a while back. News that I'd conceived a child with Aric Connor might renew his interest in killing me.

My vision blurred with tears. *Damnit.*

Danny took my hand. "Celia, I promise to do anything to protect you and your baby." If he was trying not to make me cry, it wasn't working. Without saying the words, Danny had just vowed to die for me if he had to. He sat me back down. "I was thinking there has to be a way to get everyone together and tell them about Anara."

"So we can all die in one shot?"

Danny chuckled. I wasn't trying to be funny. "I mean someplace safe where Anara's magic could be blocked—like here at Misha's. The problem is, the presence of so many *weres* will diminish the amount of vampiric power and provide multiple links for Anara to reach you. Aric's presence especially will tip the scales toward Anara's advantage. *But,* if we can manage to recruit extra vampires—including multiple masters—I think it will be enough to override Anara's power."

"Danny, this all sounds great in theory, but how are we possibly going to get all these beings together at one time?"

"Simple: invite them to your wedding to Misha."

Chapter Fourteen

"Are you crazy? I'm not marrying Misha!"

"Celia, think about it. Your sisters will come to support you whether they like what you're doing or not. And the elite of the vampire community will also be in attendance." Danny's excitement grew the more he contemplated his idea. "There are only five master vampires in the entire world who match Misha's and Uri's power. They'd all be dying—well, you know what I mean—to attend. But even if only two of them came, it would diminish Anara's magic."

"He'll still have access to Aric."

"Not if Aric is here, too."

"Oh. You're right. I'm sure Aric will just be thrilled to death to get an invitation. Maybe we could ask him to be the ring bearer—or better yet, the best man. Do you think he'll give me away if I ask nicely?"

Danny watched me pace the room. "Celia, your bond with Aric is severed, but his love for you remains. He won't let you marry Misha. He'll crash the wedding and his Warriors will try to stop him. As soon as everyone arrives, we reveal Anara's actions. This way no one gets hurt."

"No one, except Misha." I stopped pacing. "He's

my friend, Danny. I won't hurt or humiliate him to save my own ass."

Danny crossed his arms. "I know it's a lousy thing to do to someone, but I don't see another option. Anara must be stopped. His actions aren't those of a sane *were*."

Logically, everything Danny said made sense. Regardless, I knew I was incapable of such a ruse. Yes, my loved ones would be spared. But Misha would be disgraced before his peers and inferiors. I could never use anyone like that. Especially Misha. "I won't do it, Danny. There has to be another way."

Emme rapped on the door before opening it slowly. She'd changed into a long ivory sweater dress and brown boots. Her other clothes must have had blood on them. "Are you all right?" I asked her.

She nodded as Shayna and Taran slipped in behind her. They seemed surprised to see Danny alive. I'm sure they'd expected to find him partially eaten and me flossing. I tried to push away my hurt and adjusted Bren's position.

Shayna angled her way around the couch to see Bren, likely to make sure I wouldn't hurt him. She fixed the sheet to cover his bare arms and cleared her throat. "Koda and the others say you knocked Emme out. Is it true?"

My heart clenched just having her ask. "No. I would never hurt Emme."

Emme fidgeted with her hands. "The last thing I remember was answering the door before I blacked out—and I remember you screaming. What happened?"

I shrugged. "I couldn't tell you."

Taran pursed her lips and scowled. "Damn, Ceel. What if Liam's right and evil things are following you around? Do you think you might be possessed or something?"

I shrugged again, unsure how to answer. She was trying to come up with a plausible solution instead of simply assuming I'd lost my mind.

Danny hooked his thumbs through the belt loops of his jeans. "She's been herself around me."

My sisters exchanged glances. They took that little bit of hope Danny gave them and ran with it. Shayna grinned. "Awesome! I bet this whole thing is just temporary."

My other sisters nodded, excited by the possibility I might not need shock therapy. Emme approached me slowly. "Can we see your hair, sweetie? Taran and I think we can fix it if we work together."

I carefully unwrapped the towel. "Okay. But I have to warn you, it's not pretty."

"How bad can it—*son of a bitch!*" Taran screamed once, twice, and yeah, a third time. And just like that, they were back to thinking I was screwy again.

Shayna jumped up and down, pointing at my head. "Ceel! You have like, three hairs left."

"Son of a bitch!"

Emme circled me. "Y-you're missing pieces of your scalp!"

"Son of a bitch!"

"Um, I put antiseptic on it," Danny offered.

Emme stumbled forward, urging me to sit. She closed her eyes and touched my face.

Almost instantly, the throbbing around my scalp diminished.

Taran took a small bottle from her designer purse. "It's Tahoe water." She unscrewed the cap with shaky fingers. "I'm going to try to manipulate the magic to grow back your hair." She sighed and took in my condition. "I'm not sure it's going to work."

It took a long while before anything happened. Taran wasn't a witch and she'd only dabbled with Tahoe's magic. After several long minutes and many a swear word on Taran's part, my scalp buzzed.

"Whoa," Shayna whispered.

Long, loose spirals blossomed from my scalp until they once again hung past my shoulder blades. I ran my fingers through my curls as I walked to the bathroom to take a peek. The texture had thinned slightly. When I ran my fingers through my waves, they stayed out of my eyes instead of falling forward from the weight. I thought of Aric and wondered if he'd still like it. I quickly dismissed the thought. Aric probably didn't like anything about me anymore.

Shayna rested her head on my shoulder as I continued to take in my reflection. My hair, although somewhat thinner, was still bulky enough to hide me. I didn't want anyone to see me. It was silly. I knew covering my face wouldn't make me disappear, but I longed to be invisible. More than anything, I wanted to fade away from the likes of Anara, the Tribe, and the scary shape-shifters.

Since first learning about my baby, my maternal instincts to protect had radically kicked in. I was strong. I had powers. But I knew I wasn't enough to keep my child safe forever. If only Aric and I were still together. Although only two against thousands, there was something sacred about a pair of beings protecting what they'd created together. We would love our baby like no one else could and give each other strength to survive.

My heart had broken a million times when it came to Aric, but as I continued to stare at my reflection, it broke once more. Shayna's voice shook. "What's wrong with you, Ceel?"

I wiped my eyes. Without my knowing, I'd begun to cry. The last few weeks had left me so emotionally battered, my impulse to cry had become as automatic as breathing.

Emme squeezed her way into the hall bathroom with us. She broke down the moment she saw me. She wrapped her arms around my waist and buried her face in my chest while Shayna wept against my shoulder.

"Oh shit." Taran clasped her hand over her mouth and let loose.

We were pathetic, clutching each other and sobbing like the girly-girls we were. Poor Danny didn't stand a chance. He handed Taran a box of tissues, but not before taking one for himself.

Taran blew her nose and swore. "Ssspa day."

"What?" the rest of us asked.

"Spa day. That's what we all need, a spa day."

It wasn't a suggestion. She dragged me out of the bathroom with my sisters and Danny trailing behind us.

Aric hated me. Bren lay in a coma. And a twisted asshole prick Elder basked in the blood of my suffering. My first thought with regard to spa day was no. My second, *hell no*. I'd never felt so alone and helpless. I didn't need my nails done. I needed a damn battle-axe to tuck under my pillow at night. And still I agreed, if only to escape my troubles and spend one last moment with my sisters. I was leaving Tahoe and my family. The way things stood, I couldn't be sure I'd ever see them again.

Danny's face reddened the minute we entered the day spa in South Tahoe. He probably thought a day of pampering was unbecoming to a werewolf, but still wouldn't risk leaving me.

Taran led me to the counter and slapped down her credit card. "Five Spa Adventures, please, three Tranquilities, one Gentleman's Favorite." She put her arm around me and smiled. "And for this little lady, the Beauty and Bliss package."

Taran must have been spending a small fortune. The women attendants couldn't move fast enough. They escorted us down a hallway decorated in beautiful shades of green and blue and a floor resembling a lovely pier set over sand. The mural before us was so realistic, it was as if we were about to dive into paradise.

One by one we were ushered into rooms with massage tables. The smells of tropical flowers and sounds of trickling falls suggested nothing but peace and deep relaxation. My startled nerves and tense muscles began to relax even before reaching my destination. *Good idea, Taran.*

My room was the largest. A multitiered fountain of glass dribbled lazily in the corner while the delicate scent of jasmine tickled my nose and a sweet bird whistled above the soft sounds of the rain forest. Peach candles lit the dark room. This wasn't a spa. It was heaven.

The attendant escorting me handed me a pink cotton gown. She stood a few inches taller than me. Her dark hair was pinned in a chignon, revealing her perfectly fair skin and flawless makeup. "Hello. I'm Mindy. Please undress and lie on the bed so we may begin your journey into serenity."

Mindy's voice dripped of soothing comfort and harmony—an angel welcoming me through the pearly gates.

I quickly discovered she was the devil himself.

She positioned me onto my side and had me hug my knees. "What are you doing?" I asked, wondering what she could possibly massage in this position.

Mindy spoke sweetly. "Beginning the cleansing part of your 'Beauty and Bliss' experience."

I should have read the damn brochure. Then I could have stopped her before she lubed my ass.

As it was, I jumped in the nick of time. If it wasn't for my horror upon seeing that nutcase holding a hose in one hand and a giant tube of KY in the other, I might have cracked her spine in half. "What the *hell* is wrong with you, Mindy?"

I had to give it to "Little Miss Stepford." She continued to smile in that delicate way of hers before politely requesting I release my viselike grip on her wrists. She then snapped off her thick rubber gloves and excused herself. I was trying to wipe the lube off with a towel when Mindy returned with a rather irate Taran.

Taran adjusted the belt on her robe. "What's the problem?"

"She tried to stick a hose in my bat cave!" I answered, pointing.

"So?"

"What do you mean, 'so'? Mine's an exit only!"

"Celia, it's a cleansing. No different than getting a facial. Your body will thank you for it, trust me."

For a minute, I just scowled and wondered how to tactfully dispose of Taran's and Mindy's bodies. Then guilt rushed in to haunt me. Taran had spent a lot of money and I knew she meant well. And maybe she was right. Maybe it would benefit my health, and therefore my baby's. Against my better judgment, I turned myself over to Mindy.

Damn, was I an idiot.

The experience was many things: humiliating, creepy, and downright uncomfortable. Yet as unpleasant as the experience was for me, Mindy earned my deepest condolences. I'd been a labor nurse. I'd seen the most intimate parts of a woman as I focused on helping her through one of life's most incredible journeys and, in the end, the woman was able to hold a precious baby in her arms. All Mindy got to hold were my butt cheeks.

When she finally finished, I was ready to haul what remained of my ass. Mindy insisted it was time to start the "bliss" part of my day. I supposed the facial and the hot stone massage would have been relaxing if my intestines weren't screaming that something had gone horribly wrong.

An hour later, I found my sisters and Danny lounging on velour couches enjoying champagne, cheese, and fruit. Danny leapt up the moment he saw me and raced out the door. "I'll wait for you outside."

He must have heard the deets about my jolly good time with Mindy. I was mortified yet grateful Bren wasn't waiting in his place. Bren would have taken a pic and mailed it out as his Christmas card.

My sisters' nails and toes were freshly manicured. They were in brighter moods, laughing and smiling, having enjoyed their spa adventures.

Another no doubt crazed colonic expert approached me smiling and started working on my hands and feet. I squirmed, unable to sit still and convinced Mindy forgotten to remove the hose.

Taran admired her French manicure. "What's with you?"

I grimaced. "I'm in pain."

"Do you want me to heal your butt?" Emme offered.

Taran interrupted before I could take Emme up on her generous offer. "Why? Because of the colonic?"

My voice was less than Mindy-like. "*Of course* it's the colonic—it feels like things are hanging out!"

"You're probably passing a seed," Mindy's minion answered. She buffed my nails and blew off the dust. "We use only organic herbs in our colonics."

"See, Celia." Taran patted my arm like she'd done me a big favor. "That shit's all natural."

I'd wished then that Taran had picked a better choice of words. I also wished I could squash the vision of vines sprouting out of my emergency exit.

Misha stroked my hair. "You seem in better spirits."

I smiled. Despite the dim lighting inside his Hummer limo, his gray eyes sparkled with humor. "Why wouldn't I be? You were willing to take me to dinner despite my fragile and slightly psychotic state. If that's not true friendship, I don't know what is."

Misha placed his arm around me. I leaned against him, content to hear the rhythmic beating of his heart. "Why do you continue to believe that what exists between us is nothing more than companionship? Your vision has clearly shown us our future. We will be married and you will be the mother to my children."

I pulled away, no longer content. "Misha, I don't know exactly what we saw, but it wasn't real."

"How do you know?"

Well, for starters, I'm already pregnant with Aric's baby. "There's too much that doesn't make sense."

"Such as?"

He smiled when I stared at him wordlessly. "Jeans?" I finally offered.

"I beg your pardon?"

"In my vision you wore denim. You never dress in jeans."

His smile widened and that scary and familiar twinkle filled his eyes. "Would you prefer I wear nothing at all, just as we did the other night?"

I scrambled to the other side of the Hummer with Misha hot on my tail. His aroused scent proclaimed, *Hey, is it me or is it hot in here? Let's get naked and cool off.*

Misha pounced and pinned me to the sprawling leather seat.

"Misha, what are you doing?"

He tugged off his tie. "Preparing to make you scream."

I flipped him over and held him, trying to steady my heart. Except the party in Misha's pants announced it was New Year's. His tongue flicked over my jugular.

"If you want to be on top, you need only say so."

I shoved my hands over his mouth before he could kiss me. "Misha, stop. I don't want to do this."

The corners of his eyes crinkled in amusement. He mumbled something I couldn't understand, so like a moron

I loosened my hands over his mouth.

"What did you say?"

"I said your nipples tell a different tale."

I didn't have to look down to realize that once again, my areolas were saluting their leader. The night the Powers that Be created the vampire, some drunk asshole among them must've decided their super mojo wouldn't be complete without the power to stiffen tips. Misha especially had received an extra helping.

My body temperature soared. "Will you stop looking at my breasts and—*I said stop looking at my breasts!*"

"It is my only alternative while you remain clothed. Now, once I remove your panties, however—"

I covered his mouth again and growled. It was time to get serious. "Misha, I don't love you. And I won't marry you. I'm sorry I led you on by having sex with you."

I removed my hand. A slow, wicked smile spread across his face. He laughed, hard and strong. He glanced at my stupefied expression and laughed harder yet. "Why are you laughing? This isn't a joke!"

He tried to control himself. "You can't recall the evening we spent together, can you?"

"Well, no." *And hell, I've tried not to.*

Misha tossed me over and was suddenly on top again. He ran a finger down my throat and played with the neckline of my blue dress. "My darling, we didn't have sex. If we had, my expertise and superior manhood would have assured you'd never forget it."

I jumped when I realized what he said. "We didn't do it?"

He chuckled again. "No."

"Then why were we in bed naked?"

"You went into shock in the garden and failed to respond despite your open eyes. My lovelies bathed you and brought you to my bed as they should have."

"Of course, God forbid they put me in my own bed."

Misha's grin widened as he teased my skin with his chin. "Mine was warmer, I assure you."

I cleared my throat. "Just tell me what happened."

"When you failed to wake into a more conscious state, I pricked my finger and offered you my blood. As you drank, your delicate condition dissolved itself. Ultimately you relaxed and fell into a deep slumber."

I gripped his collar. "Swear to me, Misha, that you're telling me the truth. Please. It's important."

"My darling, taking an unconscious woman, even one as desirable as you, would be distasteful." His smile faded. "I would never hurt anyone, especially you, in such a way."

Despite his flaws, Misha was honorable, an attribute I deeply admired and one that cemented our friendship. My body perspired with relief while my heart screamed with joy. I'd remained faithful to Aric.

"Thank you, Misha." He smiled, but remained fixed against my body. I let out a sigh. "You know, fragile state or not, that still doesn't explain why you allowed us to sleep together naked."

"My darling, I am a vampire, not a saint. Now, at the moment, you are very alert, as are those lovely nipples. So, let's not waste another moment speaking."

I twisted beneath him. "Misha, we're not having sex!"

Something large and heavy landed on top of the limo and ripped the roof away so forcibly, Misha and I fell on the limo floor. I couldn't believe my eyes when a giant pterodactyl peered down its long beak at me.

"Celia Wird!" it screeched.

Chapter Fifteen

I rolled to the side just before I would have been impaled by a gargantuan beak. The impact jolted the car like a missile strike. I scrambled toward the warped door behind Misha. Misha kicked it open and we crawled out. We backed away slowly in disbelief, a prehistoric raptor hovered overhead, flapping his long, leathery wings and stinking of reptile and copper.

Copper? Oh hell—shape-shifter!

The giant creature watched us carefully.

Misha led me farther back. "Do not fear; my guards shall protect us."

Screaming, guzzling, and crunching sounds made me glance toward my right. Three of Misha's decapitated bodyguards flopped around like fish out of water while a giant saber-toothed tiger slurped a fourth like spaghetti. If I had wanted to meet a similar fate, I'd have taken a moment to bang my head against a tree.

"Master, run!" some vamp's head yelled from the woods.

Ten miles remained to Misha's estate—close enough that his entire family would sense their master in danger, but too far for them to reach us quickly. I knew shape-shifters could assume the form of any creature, alive or dead, but this was beyond eff'd up and so totally unfair.

I took in the prehistoric mob bosses and moved forward. "I'll take the cat," I muttered right before *changing*.

"Cat" was a loose term. This thing was more bearlike and about two hundred pounds heavier than my tigress. Six-inch fangs hung from her blood-soaked mouth. One bite from those jaws would kill me, so I thought better of challenging her. My tigress equally thought we could kick her ass. I pounced on the saber-tooth's face, clawed at her eyes, and then bolted like a thoroughbred on crack.

She was faster, but not used to this form. I was in my second skin. I dodged and whipped around trees. She barreled through them, sending strips of bark to pelt my back and sleeping birds jetting out of the branches in a frightened scurry. All I was doing was buying some time. I wasn't stupid. No way I could beat her on my own. *Shifting* her was also out of the question. I needed to be able to hold her for a few seconds, and she didn't strike me as the type to stand still. I cut through the woods and doubled back to return to Misha when the thundering of massive paws stopped. That would have been a good thing had it not suddenly been replaced by the beating of powerful wings. The shifter had transformed into a pterodactyl. Unlike in her other form, this one allowed her to move with ease, grace, and unholy speed.

The trees around me blurred as I dodged and leapt, and still I wasn't fast enough. I dove the last thirty feet to the road and *shifted* through the pavement. The earth above me rattled with the force of a massive quake. I surfaced a hundred feet away, still feeling the ground rumble beneath me. The pterodactyl had crashed into the road, temporarily stunned from the impact. I leapt onto her back and *shifted* her far below before I lost my breath. My body resurfaced through the pavement and barely avoided the stampeding feet of a giant woolly mammoth.

The shifter that had attacked the limo had taken on a new form—one that could attack on the ground. Misha and a horde of his vampires rode the beast, stripping chunks of flesh from his back. The deafening trumpet sounds signaled his agony, but the damn pachyderm wouldn't die! He snatched two vampires with his trunk and stomped them into bloody ash. I jumped on his nose and hacked into the muscle until he swatted me away like a pesky fly. I landed hard on my paws, moments before he charged.

"Celia Wird. Celia Wird. Celia Wird," he shrieked in a demonic voice.

I was already freaked out that a nine-ton, supposedly extinct creature was barreling at me, but throw in the psycho voice and I just about passed another seed.

My claws raked against the tendons of his legs while I tried to avoid his sweeping, bloody trunk. I'd managed to sever one of his hind legs when deep, angry hisses cut through the cold night. The rest of Misha's keep had arrived.

We skewered and dug our fangs through the leathery skin, beating the shifter into submission with more brute force than grace. We brought him down just as the earth erupted beneath me.

Pebbles and chunks of asphalt smacked our faces. The road cracked and the shifter I'd buried reemerged. And, damnit all to hell, wasn't prehistoric predator the flavor of the evening? The former saber-toothed tiger turned pterodactyl morphed into a tyrannosaurus. This couldn't be happening. To transform with such ease and hold so much power took scary-ass evil to a whole new dimension. I jerked out of the way of her snapping jaws when a silver Yukon slammed into her side and rode over the top of her.

Anyone else driving would have hit the gas and kept going, but then again Shayna was behind the wheel.

The wheels squealed in protest as she thrust the SUV in reverse and parked it over the T-Rex's throat.

Shayna leapt out with a prima ballerina's poise, converting her sword into an axe as she twirled it in her wrist. Taran stumbled out behind her, tripping in her high heels. "Son of a bitch!"

I trained my efforts on blinding the dinosaur to help protect my sisters. If she couldn't see us, she couldn't eat us, right?

The creature's furious eardrum-shattering shrieks mixed with wails of agony. Above it, all I heard was Shayna chopping away, and I smelled the burning flesh as Taran set it ablaze. A few vampires abandoned the mammoth to help us, puncturing where the T-Rex's jugular pulsed.

"Celia, look out!" Emme's face deepened to purple as she suspended a jagged boulder in the air. I moved—*fast*. She crushed the gargantuan skull, and still she couldn't kill it. The T-Rex writhed, taking out a couple of vamps with her tail like a cluster of bowling pins.

I pounced on her head and pulverized her cracked skull, anchoring my body with my hind claws while my front burrowed into her head. Slime and blood soaked through my fur. I just about retched when I reached the brain and mashed it with my paws.

The T-Rex collapsed. Shayna jumped up and down and cheered . . . until the last hunk of brain fell in a wet splatter between her and Emme. They hurled. Not wanting to feel left out, I leapt off the shifter and joined them.

Cries of horror erupted behind us. The vamps had failed to finish the other shape-shifter. He morphed again into another giant pterodactyl, staking anyone within reach with his long beak. The vamps scattered like marbles to avoid him. They screamed, unable to escape the jabs of his pointed beak. The shifter screeched with triumph and spread his wings, lifting into the air before diving at Misha and spearing him with its talons.

Pandemonium erupted through Misha's tortured hollering. I leapt onto the pterodactyl's narrow torso while the remaining vampires worked to bring the shifter down. Except his wings were too strong and they couldn't hang on. Emme launched an array of sharp stones like bullets. They bounced off his leathery skin. I tore an opening in his chest, trying to break through the rib cage to reach for the heart. I never made it. He snapped my front right leg with his beak and yanked me back, holding tight so I couldn't wrench free. The pain was blinding. I *changed* back to human, unable to maintain my tigress.

Shayna launched four knives at the creature as a strong wind chilled my bare skin. The shape-shifter took flight while my sisters and Misha's family yelled below.

Pain and weakness kept me from *changing,* but not from acting. I tugged one of Shayna's knives free from the creature's neck and jammed it into his eye. His clamp on my wrist released and I plummeted to the ground, landing on what felt like a giant hand.

Emme had caught me with her *force*. She lowered me as the shape-shifter flew toward the rising full moon with Misha.

"I'll find you, Celia Wird. I'll find you!"

"Master!" Tim yelled. "Master!"

The Catholic schoolgirls collapsed against one another, bawling hysterically. Tears escaped my eyes as I watched Misha's writhing form disappear into the moonlight. The bad guys had my guardian angel—my *friend*—and there wasn't a damn thing anyone could do.

Hank solemnly draped his cashmere coat over my shoulders as I broke down. Emme hurried to heal me. I jerked violently when her light enveloped me. The bastard shape-shifter had crushed my arm in two places. The pain receded, but my tears did not. For whatever reason, the shifter had come for me. In my place, he'd taken Misha and my last defense against Anara's wrath. There would be nothing to keep Anara from killing me now.

Emme's healing touch kept me from falling into a state of despair, but just barely. If Misha died, it would be my fault. He could have escaped with his family. Instead he'd stayed and fought to protect me.

Emme released me and rushed to where Taran lay across Shayna's lap. I hadn't realized she'd been hurt. "What happened to Taran?" I managed.

Emme held Taran's face. "She was drawing lightning when the pterodactyl smacked one of the vampires into her."

Taran awoke—in a really bad mood. She took in the carnage and sorrow around her. "For shit's sake, did we at least win?"

Tim kicked the bits of asphalt near his feet. "No. We killed one shape-shifter, but the other abducted the master." His shoulders slumped, and he was unusually pale. It was more than the need to feed from blood loss; Tim was frightened. What he did next, though, scared the bejeebers out of me. He knelt at my feet and bowed his head. If that wasn't bad enough, the remaining vampires followed his lead. "Celia Wird," he said, his voice grim, "mistress of the House of Aleksandr, we pledge our devotion to you."

"Our devotion," repeated the vampires.

"We will serve only you, until our destruction or your death." "With our existence we serve only you," echoed the others.

My jaw fell open, unable to comprehend the vampires' actions. Tim lifted my hand to his lips and tried to kiss it. I yanked it from his grasp. "What the hell, Tim?"

Tim scowled at me. It was more of how he usually treated me, so I relaxed ever so slightly. "Give me a break, Celia. I'm trying here!"

"Trying to do what?"

"Swear our allegiance to you. With the master gone,

we belong to you now."

I really had to work on my language. It wouldn't be appropriate for me to curse like I did then in front of my baby. But the pleading expressions of the surviving vampires proved their sincerity and desperation.

"Everyone on the ground now!" Dozens of deputy sheriffs spread out around us.

My sisters fell to the ground. They were smart. The deputies appeared jumpy and ready to shoot the crowd of blood-smeared suspects standing amid scattered limbs and demolished vehicles. I let out a sigh. "Okay, everyone. Time to convince Tahoe City's finest there's been an earthquake."

The vampires' heads snapped up, instantly entrancing the deputies. My sisters followed me quietly when I left them to approach the dead shape-shifter. Her T-Rex form had dissolved. In the street lay a naked woman, surrounded by sections of her broken skull. She couldn't have been older than forty, and despite her broken body, I was left with the impression she was once beautiful. It sickened me to think what she'd sacrificed for power. She'd hurt so many and gained nothing, as far as I was concerned.

Agnes walked slowly to my side, tugging nervously on her pigtails. "Will she stay dead or do we need to do something special with her body?" I asked, knowing her expertise on the supernatural.

"She can't come back, Mistress. She surrendered her soul long ago to her deity in order to gain her ability to transform. We need only to dispose of the body."

I touched the corpse with my finger, wanting to have as little contact with it as possible. She might have been dead, but I could still sense evil permeating from her skin. I *shifted* her deep into the ground and returned to the vampires.

Liz bowed before me so deeply, the strands of her

ice-blond hair brushed against the asphalt. "The deputies believe an earthquake took place as you requested, Mistress. They're helping to locate eyewitnesses so we may influence their memories as well. Do you desire anything else of us?"

Liz was so solemn then, and so sad. I would have preferred her bitchy and self-centered disposition rather than seeing the level of gloom she carried like a casket. I closed my eyes and willed myself to be strong. "Yes. Stop calling me Mistress, find me some pants, and get someone here to tow what remains of the cars."

Though Liz remained close to tears, she smiled a little. "As you wish, Celia."

Taran muttered a few swears. "I don't like this, Ceel. You can't adopt the damn bloodsucking prom squad. You're not one of them." Her comment earned her a few hisses from the surrounding vamps. She rolled her eyes and flipped them off.

I rubbed my face. "I know, Taran. But for the moment I'm all they have."

Shayna threw her hands in the air. "Ceel, you're a mess. How can you possibly take care of a family when you can't even take care of yourself?"

Shayna's question made me defensive, especially given my pregnancy. Like Misha's vampires, I was all my baby had. "I owe it to Misha to watch over them until his return."

Emme stared at the ground. "What if he doesn't return, Celia?"

I couldn't think about life without Misha. He was my friend. "I'll phone Uri when we return to the house and figure things out. For the time being, I have to assume the role of head of his family."

A cellphone rang from inside the overturned Yukon. Shayna crawled in to retrieve it. It was Koda, and guess what? He was pissed. "Baby, where have you been? I've been trying to reach you all night."

"I'm sorry, puppy. Emme called Taran and me at the store to tell us Celia was in trouble." There was a pause.

"Did she hurt herself again?"

I caught traces of movement in the background. Wherever Koda was, he wasn't alone. I swore under my breath, hating that everyone believed I'd fallen over the edge into masochistic territory.

Shayna dug a wood chip from her hair and continued unaffected. "Oh, no, nothing like that. She and Misha were attacked by shape-shifters."

"What?"

"Now, puppy, calm down. I hit the one with your ride twice when she was a T-Rex and Taran set her on fire. I have to tell you, dinosaurs are hardy things. Each time I stabbed it—"

"You fought a shape-shifter?"

Shayna sighed. "No, honey. I fought two. The problem was, we couldn't bring the other one down once it became a pterodactyl."

"Are you trying to give me a heart attack?"

She grinned into the phone. "Now, puppy, you know perfectly well that *weres* don't get heart attacks."

"You know what I mean! What were you thinking, taking on something so powerful?"

Koda's growls thundered through the line, but Shayna remained calm and spoke to him like they were discussing a TV show, not my eff'd-up life. "Well, I couldn't exactly let her eat Celia. Anyway, we're safe now. Emme cracked the shifter's head with a rock and Celia squashed the brain. The problem is, the other one flew away with Misha, and now the vampires have adopted Celia as, like, their mom."

More growls rumbled from Koda and the other wolves with him. Aric's voice boomed over the snarls. "Find out exactly where they are and tell Shayna we're on our way."

I gritted my teeth. For his safety, he couldn't come down here. "No. The matter has already been taken care of. There's no need to come."

The ferocity in Aric's voice made Emme step back from the phone. "This isn't your decision, Celia. A shape-shifter has attacked in our territory. As guardians of the earth we're required to investigate the matter."

I stormed to where Shayna held out the phone. "The destruction has been blamed on an earthquake. We're safe. The only crisis at hand is that Misha has been taken."

"I'm only coming to ensure no human has or will be harmed. Don't fool yourself into thinking I care about you or your damn fiancé!"

Aric's hostile tone and words were a punch to my gut that robbed me of my breath. I paused and stared stupidly at the touch screen. "Don't worry, Aric," I told him quietly. "I realize my safety is no longer your concern."

Emme reached out to me. I stepped away and started rounding up the vampires. If I stood there I would cry, from frustration, hurt, fear, and anger—mostly anger. I was trying, damnit. And nothing was working in my favor.

Taran yanked the cellphone from Shayna's grasp. "You're an asshole, Aric. Don't you ever talk to my sister like that again!"

Aric growled. "Wake up, Taran. She's not your sister anymore. She's turned into some goddamn vampiress."

Shayna's head whipped back and forth between me and the phone. "Dude, cut it out. She can hear you!"

"Do you think I care? Do yourself a favor, forget the Mistress of the Night and tell me where you are!"

I tried to ignore the arguments that ensued, an impossible task since it involved me. Taran and Koda were both upset at Aric for yelling at Shayna. Koda made it clear, Leader or not, that Shayna was his mate and he would defend her. Taran swore at him for snapping at Shayna and ripped him a new one for the way he'd treated me.

Hank's approach gave me an excuse to focus elsewhere. "The vehicles have been removed, Celia. All of the witnesses have been located and their memories altered. Are you ready to return to the manor?"

"I'd like a group of vampires to stay here and guard my sisters. Tell them to return to the house as soon as the *weres* arrive. I don't want any problems between them."

"Very well." Hank led me to a town car and opened the door before walking back to give the vamps their orders and returning with Emme. She slipped into the front with him. Maria and Agnes placed themselves on either side of me, assuming their role as my bodyguards.

I took in Maria's and Edith's tense stances. "How many vampires did we lose?"

Hank huffed. "Including the master? Seventeen."

Emme gasped. "Sixteen vampires lost—and we only stopped one shape-shifter?"

I leaned my head back and tried not to beg God to kill me. "Agnes, how many shape-shifters are there?"

Agnes adjusted her librarian glasses, falling into academic mode. "Seven are known by name. But it's rumored there are as many as twenty."

My voice squeaked. "Do they often fight together?"

"Only if they share a common goal."

I looked at her then. "Like killing me?"

Agnes stared straight ahead, refusing to meet my gaze. So, not a good sign. "For the most part, they rule their territories independently of each other."

Emme swiveled to face me. "They came for you. Didn't they, Celia?"

"I guess, but I'm not sure why."

Hank watched me through the rearview mirror. "It

seems they want a blood sacrifice for one or more of their deities."

There was no masking the terror in Emme's face. "Why Celia?"

Maria grew impatient with Emme's naïveté. "Isn't it obvious? Celia is strong. In killing her de shape-shifter will leech her power. Since de shape-shifter failed to take her, he'll sacrifice our master instead."

"But they'll continue to hunt Celia, won't they?"

Hank nodded. "Especially now that they've seen the depth of her strength."

A few tears rolled down Emme's cheeks. She wiped them with her hand and then turned back toward the front. It must have really sucked having me for a sister.

I rubbed my arms, feeling cold. "Misha is still alive." I don't know how I knew, I just did.

Agnes lowered her head. "Yes. We still feel him, too."

Hank tightened his grip on the steering wheel. "Can you sense where he is?" I shook my head. "Celia, use the *call* he gave you to find him. You've done it before. You can do it again."

I hadn't mastered the reverse speed dial. The few times it worked was more by chance than skill. I closed my eyes and tried to focus on Misha, but only darkness shadowed my mind.

Maria touched my shoulder. "Do you see anything?"

"Not a thing."

She wiped her face irritably. "He's probably in too much pain to contact you. De bastards will pay for our master's suffering."

Hank sped through the opening metal gates and over the stone bridge. Danny and Chang raced down the steps, with Ying-Ying floating in lotus pose behind them. I sprinted past them and toward Misha's office with Agnes and Maria at my heels.

"Get me Uri on the phone. We have to get Misha back."

Chapter Sixteen

Uri took Misha's kidnapping as badly as I knew he would. Fury and agony accentuated every syllable of his words. *"My son! The evil ones have my son!"*

His anguish was heartbreaking and caused the Catholic schoolgirls to break down. Except that wouldn't help Misha, I needed him to focus. "Tell me how to get him back."

He worked to rein in his sorrow. "With the shapeshifters involved, we need the Alliance behind us. I'm in Sweden, but I shall contact the current leaders." He sighed. "In the meantime, I need to entrust you with Misha's family."

"Yes, Uri. I'll look after them."

"And his home."

"Yes, I know. I'll take care of the house."

"And all of his real estate."

"Er, okay."

"And the companies."

"Companies?"

"Of course. You cannot allow the bankruptcy of a twenty-billion-dollar empire in Misha's absence."

I waited for Uri to laugh and tell me he was only

joking. He didn't. Of course, I flipped out. "You're putting me in charge of a twenty-*billion*-dollar business? Are you nuts? I can't keep track of my ATM receipts!"

Uri's contemptuousness quickly pimp-punched his misery. "Celia, my son chose you as his bride for many reasons. If your strength and intelligence failed to rival his, he wouldn't have bothered to entertain your company."

I screamed into the speakerphone. "But why do I have to run his entire domain? Can't you handle that?"

"Celia, as head of the House of Aleksandr, it is important that you assume complete charge, if for nothing else, for the sake of appearances. Once Misha's rivals become aware of his absence, they will plot to take control of his family and his empire. The sooner they sense weakness, the sooner they shall strike. Do not fail him."

"Thanks for the pep talk, Uri," I grumbled, but he'd already hung up.

Emme and Danny had sat in on my phone call with Uri. I thought their eyes would literally launch out of their heads and little people would climb out waving white flags. They were scared stupid and none of this was even their problem. The Catholic schoolgirls, Tim, and Hank remained unusually tight-lipped. I pinched the bridge of my nose. "What exactly did Uri mean when he said Misha's rivals will plot to take control of his family?"

Hank stepped forward, his jaw clenched tight enough to snap bone. "It means the current masters will conspire to kill you so we, and all that's his, will become theirs."

My expression must have been priceless, because Hank stepped back. "That's fantastic, because, you see, not enough supernatural predators want me dead!"

Emme rose slowly. "I'll call Shayna and Taran. We'll protect you, Celia. Don't worry."

Liz shoved her hands on her hips and loomed over her. "That's *our* job. She may be your sister, but she's our mistress now. We're strong. We'll handle it!"

Emme's face reddened, but my little sister met Liz with equal force. "If you're all so strong, then why can't one of you take over as head of the family?"

Good point. Why the hell did it have to be me?

Liz hissed at her. And although she knew better than to attack Emme, both Hank and Danny moved to her side. I held a hand out. "Liz, back off. She's not familiar with your ways."

Liz withdrew her fangs, but it did nothing to squelch her temper. "It's not that we couldn't fight a master, it's that we couldn't win. It takes a master or another powerful being to kill one. That's why ours selected Celia to take his place. Only she can protect us."

I drummed my fingers against the desk. "Does Misha have any masters under his control?"

The vamps all shook their heads. Hank furrowed his brows. "Why?"

Maria answered for me. "She's worried someone in de family will turn against her."

"Yup." I leaned back in the leather seat that was more like a throne than an office chair.

The thought of the vampires betraying me had crossed my mind. "Still, if something does happen to me, I'd want one of Misha's own to take over—one strong enough to face another master."

"There are no other masters," Hank answered. "Once a vampire is created, his or her status is immediately known. The elder master then either kills the newer one for power or releases him to begin his own dynasty. Either way, they don't continue on in the same household."

Interesting. "So technically Uri could have killed Misha upon recognizing his master status."

Tim ran his hand over his shaved head. "Yes, like he had so many others before him. However, Grandmaster Uri was always fond of our master, even before he *turned* him vampire. He saw his potential and gifted him a small piece of his fortune. Our master in turn transformed his, and the Grand Master's businesses, into a vast empire."

Danny stood and paced, unable to remain still. "What about the age of the vampire? Doesn't that factor into his strength? If there are no masters available, maybe Celia can appoint the oldest in Misha's keep."

Liz whipped out the file she kept tucked into her tiny plaid skirt and passed it over her claws. "Age adds to our strength and makes us harder to kill. That's why a vampire older than two hundred years requires both a stake through the heart and decapitation. Otherwise she could still regenerate. Despite age, no mere vamp can match the strength of a master." She shrugged. "Besides, the oldest among us were devoured by the shifters."

I looked across the vast expanse of Misha's office to the closed door. "Edith, go get Michael. I'd like him here." She stood there as if she hadn't understood my request. "Edith, get Michael." She didn't move. *"Edith."*

Before I could ding her in the head with a paperweight, Michael knocked and poked his head in. "You wish to see me, Celia?"

Okay . . . "Did you hear me call you?"

Michael crossed the room and stood at parade rest before the desk. "No. But as our mistress, whatever you desire of us is merely a thought away."

Someone else knocked. Chef entered, pushing a rolling tray filled with Philly cheesesteaks and onion rings. He set a plate in front of me and poured me a tall glass of ice water. "Here iz the meal you desired," he said in his thick French accent. "I shall return with your milkshakes. Did you decide on cherry vanilla or blackberry?"

"Uh, cherry, please." I pushed a curl behind my ear nervously and stared at the mountain of food. "Can you, um, hear all of my thoughts?"

A hungry and sinful smile split the expanse of

Edith's face. "Only if you want us to."

"I don't, actually." I took a few gulps of water before speaking. "Okay, look. There's no way I'm qualified to run a dynasty. Therefore, you're going to do it." Funny enough, the vamps lacked the enthusiasm I was hoping for.

"Why us?" Hank asked.

"Because young vamps or not, you're the strongest and most trusted in Misha's keep and have firsthand knowledge of his business ventures." I pointed to Maria. "I know for a fact you advise him on his financial affairs and that you sit in on meetings."

"Only when his business involves Portugal and my native Brazil."

I slammed my palm on the desk. "Good to know. You're in charge of Misha's European empire with the exception of France. Liz, you're originally from Iceland, right?" She nodded. "Then you help Maria. Hank, do you want Asia? You've traveled there with Misha the most."

"Ummm."

"Excellent, it's yours. Michael, you studied business while human, correct?"

Michael nodded. "Finance at Howard. You wish me to assist Hank?"

"No. I want you to handle the American companies—all of them. Ying-Ying and Chang can help Hank. Agnes, since you and Tim both speak French, I'll put you in charge of the Canadian companies and France."

Tim raised his palms. "Celia, slow down. There's no need for this. The master has appointed board members to handle each company."

I dipped an onion ring in ketchup and took a bite. "That's nice. But it will be your jobs to keep them in line. If there's even a hint of corruption I want you to—"

"Kill dem?" Maria offered.

"I was thinking you could fire them, but I guess that could work, too. Now, Edith, as for you . . ."

Edith bounced in her thigh-high boots, eager with anticipation. "I'll do whatever you want, Celia. You're really turning me on right now."

"Er, thanks, but why don't I just put you in charge of all of Misha's homes. Make sure they're maintained and don't fall into disarray. I want this empire to function like a well-oiled machine—even if it's only on the surface."

Emme walked around the desk and held my hand. "What about us, Celia? How can Danny and I help?"

"You can keep me from tearing my hair out." Emme's face paled to chalk. Perhaps I could have picked a better choice of words.

The vampires dispersed, ready to set my plan in motion. Emme called our sisters to update them on the latest threat to my life while Danny and I tore into the food like it was our damn job.

We'd almost finished when Edith sashayed back into the office. "Your room is ready, Celia."

I wiped my hands on the cloth napkin. "The contractors are done repairing the guesthouse?"

It probably took everything Edith had not to ram the last onion ring up my nose. She swallowed hard and tried to smile. "I meant your room upstairs. As head of our family, you can't possibly reside in the guesthouse. I've prepared the master's room to fit your tastes so you'll be more comfortable."

Edith was taking her assignment seriously, so I felt bad refusing. "Thanks anyway, but I need to stay near Bren to look after him."

She pursed her lips tightly before forcing another smile. "We'll place the mongrel in the suite next to yours."

"What about Danny and Emme?"

Her protruding fangs made it difficult for her to speak. *"They can sleep here as well."*

Danny eyed her warily. "Just do it, Celia. It will be safer if everyone stays close."

I stood and stretched. "Fine."

Edith rushed around the desk and clamped on to my wrist. "Wait until you see your room!"

I let her lead me up the grand staircase. Danny followed close behind. With the assault by the wolves, the invasion of the psycho shape-shifters, Aric's hideous behavior, and Misha's kidnapping, I couldn't wait to lie down and put the day behind me. And yet when Edith threw open the double doors to Misha's suite, I wasn't sure how I'd manage to sleep. Let's just say Edith had a different take on what I liked.

Dark wood furniture and different tones of brown, white, and gold made up the décor of my Dollar Point bedroom—pretty, but not overly feminine. Misha's room was the epitome of Mountain Craftsman elegance—high beamed wood ceilings, slate stone fireplace, tones of brown and red, heavy dark mahogany furniture, and a bed roughly the size of Vermont.

I don't know how Edith did it, but she'd somehow painted all the furniture white. Instead of the more traditional and classic colors there were about seven different shades of pink. Yes, *pink*. Girly, lacey, and frilly fabrics covered the bed and floor-to-ceiling glass doors leading out to the terrace. Yet what threw me over the edge were the unicorns. Yes, *unicorns*. A dozen or so stuffed unicorns fought for space amid the lip- and heart-shaped giant pink pillows. Not to mention the immense velvet painting of a unicorn at full canter, hanging over the bed.

Edith clapped her hands together. "Do you love it?"

Danny gnawed on his lip, appearing more unnerved than amused.

"I appreciate all your hard work, Edith." It was a lame response, but it was all I could manage.

Edith pulled me into a tight embrace before skipping off in her thigh-high stiletto boots.

Danny nudged me toward the bathroom. "Why

don't you get a shower? It might help you relax."

I opened the doors to more pink. Edith had redecorated the entire suite. As I pushed soap out of the pink unicorn dispenser I began to think I'd put the wrong vampire in charge of maintaining Misha's homes.

I went to help with Bren's care following my shower. Emme had already taken care of him, just not in the way he would have preferred. He slept in a king-sized bed wearing blue silk pajamas. And although he was in adult diapers, it was damn obvious he'd missed Emme.

A twin bed had been brought in and set up on the opposite side of the room. Emme and Danny argued over who should sleep with Bren. For a moment, I thought the matter might come down to blows. Emme crinkled her nose at him. "He's your best friend!"

Danny pointed to where Bren lay snoring. "He has an erection—we're not that close!"

Hank entered and flashed Emme a panty-dropping smile. "Forget the wolf. Spend the night with me."

Emme's entire face reddened. "That's not something I do with someone I barely know."

Before you could say "There's a virgin in the house," all of the Catholic schoolgirls were ringside. Maria eyed Emme like she was the freak. "You can't be serious."

Emme sidestepped her way closer to me. "*Yes,* I am."

Edith turned to me. "So, does that make you the whore of the family?" she asked with a little too much enthusiasm.

Danny clasped my arm while Emme defended my honor. "Celia's only slept with two men."

"At the same time?" Liz asked, confused.

My cheeks burned. *"Of course not!"*

"Don't worry, Celia," Agnes said. "Sexual incompetence is nothing to be ashamed of."

"Yes, it is," Maria muttered.

"I never claimed to be bad in bed!"

Liz ignored me. "But we can fix that—Tim, get up here!"

Tim appeared before I could blink. "What?"

Liz yanked off his skin-tight T-shirt. "Celia wants to be better in bed. Be a dear and help her, would you?"

I backed away when his jeans hit the floor. "What the hell are you doing?" I smacked his hands away when he reached for me. "Tim, stop! I'm not having sex with you."

Tim shrugged and left with his clothes wadded up in his arms. "Fine. Call me if you change your mind."

"Would you prefer a human?" Edith asked.

"No. I prefer you get the hell out of here."

I slammed the door behind them. It did little to silence Liz. "She'll be in a better mood once we get her some."

Emme's expression split between horror and worry. "Celia, you can't assume the care of them—you're nothing like them."

Danny, who had been at a loss for words, finally spoke. "They're trying, Emme. In their own way they're trying to be kind to her."

"But Danny, they're all so . . . *bizarre*. What if she's stuck with them for the rest of her life?"

"The way things are going, that won't be much longer." Emme's sweet face creased with sadness. I didn't mean to sound so melodramatic. Embarrassed by what I said, I left them and went to cuddle with a stuffed unicorn.

Danny entered the room a few minutes later and crawled into bed with me. He knew I was awake. "You're not giving up, are you, Celia?"

I gripped the fluffy pink monstrosity against me. "No, it's just that things seem so bleak. Every time I manage some degree of peace, it's robbed from me."

Danny pushed my hair from my face. "Tell me what you're thinking."

I turned and stared into the soft dark eyes of my friend, whose messy curls always made his hair appear unkempt. Danny's face was so different now that he no longer needed glasses, but his expression carried the same compassion it always had. He didn't want me to suffer in silence. I took a breath and told him exactly what I was thinking. "I want Misha not to die. I want the scary things to stop finding me and trying to kill me. I want my baby to be safe and grow up happy." I tried to stop my tears, but they fell anyway. "I want Aric to hold me and tell me he doesn't hate me. I just want everything to be all right."

Danny hugged me tightly and kissed my forehead. He didn't tell me things were going to get better. He only gave me the comfort I needed to get through one more night.

Chapter Seventeen

The vampires I assigned to handle Misha's affairs took turns traveling the world to keep things in order. Or at least that's what I hoped they did during their long periods away. To add to my stress, they constantly bombarded me with requests to contact Misha. I tried to reach him through our *call*. Yet despite my best efforts to focus and connect with him, I failed to sense anything. Still, I remained certain he was alive—tortured and no doubt suffering, but alive.

Uri hit a wall everywhere he turned. The European Alliance Leaders refused to meet with him to discuss Misha. The collective thought was that now that the Tribe numbers had dwindled, it was time to strike and eliminate every last threat. No Alliance members would be spared to help find one master vampire.

Even with my constant worrying about Misha, Anara, and the things that went bump in the night, my thoughts always returned to Aric. It hurt to know he despised me. But he was alive, and that gave me hope that should I survive, maybe one day Aric would meet our son.

Son? I touched my belly and smiled. *Are you a boy, little one? Will you look like your daddy?*

Danny staggered into the suite, interrupting my

thoughts. "Hey. Do you mind if I crash in here again tonight? Bren went into full salute the moment he heard Emme's voice."

His bleary eyes blinked back at me and he clutched a pillow, ready to keel over. He'd spent another day researching shifters and trying to locate their strongholds.

"Sure, but if you want more privacy Emme could sleep here and you can take the other bed in Bren's room." His shoulders drooped slightly. "What's wrong?"

"Celia, Liam pitched a major fit when Emme decided to live here with you. He's worried about her safety and made her promise she wouldn't sleep with you in case . . ."

My entire body stiffened. "In case I tried to kill her."

Danny held out his hand. "Don't be mad. He still considers you a friend, but he's convinced you knocked Emme out that day at the house."

I let out a frustrated sigh. "I know. I just wish I could tell them."

Danny wrapped his arm around me. "Someday, you will. Someday they'll all know what Anara has done to you."

My stomach tightened. "Not if I want to keep them alive."

Although I remained on edge, Danny's presence and calm demeanor settled my nerves.

We both slipped beneath the polka-dot pink covers and fell asleep.

Pounding on the door and the sound of music in the distance jerked me awake less than an hour later. I flipped on the unicorn lamp next to me. "Yes?"

Liz stormed in, ice-blond hair mussed from sleep, fingernail file pointed right at me. "Celia, I'm a patient vampire."

"No, you're not, Liz."

"Okay, fine, I'm not. But your freaky friends are getting out of control."

Danny sat up and rubbed his eyes. I didn't know what the hell Liz was bitching about.

Emme was asleep and Bren lay in a coma.

Edith stomped into the room next, wearing an itsy-bitsy nightie and her damn boots. "Did you ask her if we could kill her?"

I yawned. "Who do you want to kill this time?"

"The *were* doing the really bad John Cusack impression." Tim strolled in with a naked woman riding piggyback as his only accessory. She bit his earlobe and couldn't give a fig that Danny and I sat there gawking at her.

Agnes bolted in with binoculars. "Follow me. You're not going to believe this." She swept past me and threw open the doors leading out to the terrace. Tim and his snack were kind enough to pull back the pink heart curtains so I could pass. I gave them ample space. Agnes shoved the binoculars into my hands and pointed out to the lake. *"Look."*

There, standing on a rowboat in the rain, holding an old boom box over her head, waited Heidi while Peter Gabriel blasted away on the gigantic speakers. I put the binoculars down, blinked a few times, and then looked again.

Emme poked her head through the drapes. "Is something wrong?" I ignored her and addressed Danny.

"Has Heidi been calling you?"

"Yes, why?"

"Have you been returning her phone calls?"

He watched me carefully. "No. I told her we needed time apart."

"I think you should reconsider." I handed him the binoculars and moved aside.

"Holy crap!"

Danny thought it best to "talk" with Heidi in the guesthouse. I returned to Misha's room, ready for some much-needed and uninterrupted sleep.

Someday scientists may discover a cure for my delusions of hope.

Frantic knocking woke me around 3:00 A.M. "Come in?" I croaked. The Catholic schoolgirls raced in with Hank, Tim, and Chef. Their terrified scent struck me down to my toes. Suddenly I was wide awake. "What happened?"

Thunder boomed in the distance. They crouched like the roof was caving in. When the noise settled, they glanced around at one another and shoved Hank forward to speak on their behalf. "We need to sleep with you," he muttered.

"Excuse me?"

"Not in that way, Celia." Edith winked. "Although you look really cute in that nightie."

"It's a tank top."

She hurried forward and sat at the edge of the bed. "Are you wearing panties?"

"Of course I am."

"The lacy ones that look like thongs?"

I gave up on Edith and focused on Hank. "What's going on?"

Hank straightened and puffed his chest out . . . a little too much. "Celia, our master's absence has weakened our bond and temporarily robbed us of our courage. There's only one way to get it back." Again, with the puffy chest. "We must get close to you because you are so close to him."

"Meaning . . . ?"

"We must spend the night with you."

The vamps met me with eager if not lecherous grins. "If you're telling me I have to have sex with you, you're out of your damn minds!"

Tim moved toward me. "Perhaps I should explain."

"Uh, yeah, please do."

"Of all the family, we are the closest to the master. Hank and I, because we guard him; Chef, because he interacts with him several times a day; and the girls . . . well, because of the multitude of times they've had sex with him."

"I can give you some pointers," Maria offered.

Tim continued unaffected, unlike me. I was ready to run out of there screaming. "By spending the night in your presence, we will be reenergized by your aura, given your link to the master."

"How will it affect me?" I asked, more for my baby's sake than my own.

Edith sighed. "Celia, don't worry. If we munch on you, we'll only screw ourselves. You're the only one keeping us together."

Liz sensed my growing apprehension and tried to sweeten the deal. "Let us in bed and we'll give you tips to please the master. There's this one thing I do with my thumb that—"

"Uh, thanks, Liz, but I'm good." I pulled the sheet up to my chin. "Tim, will this weaken me at all? I need my strength to . . . keep things running."

"Nah, the worst that'll happen is that our dreams will invade yours."

Terrific. The thunder blasted and everyone jumped into bed with me. "Are you guys normally afraid of thunder?"

Maria answered with her head buried beneath a unicorn. "No. But like Hank said, de distance from our master has left us weakened."

I took in the trembling bodies huddled around me. "In other words, if we're attacked, you'll be too scared to fight and I'm on my own."

"Yes," the bastards answered without so much as a

hesitation.

Maria poked her head from beneath the fuchsia bedspread. "We'll watch helplessly while some evil creature plays with your intestines."

Awesome.

Edith patted my hand. "Don't worry. The other vampires are still fine and we should regain our strength come sunrise. However . . ."

"Yes?"

Edith yawned and snuggled closer. "The rest of the family will probably join you tomorrow night."

Why does the universe hate me?

Misha would laugh if he knew his gigantic bed had come in handy for something other than an orgy. As the vampires settled around me, I was reminded of that scene from *The Sound of Music.* Except I was no Julie Andrews, and I'd bet my life none of the von Trapp children ever tried to cop a feel.

"Edith?"

"Yes, Celia?"

"Get your hand off my butt."

I was afraid to fall asleep, worried how the vamps would affect my dreams. Eventually exhaustion won and I drifted off. My mind wandered to that same open field from my visions. A high noon sun shone in the beautiful deep blue sky. Flowers surrounded the brass bed I lay in with Aric. He rested beneath a soft white sheet with his hands clasped behind his head, naked. Scars marred his face, arms, and chest, yet all I cared about was that he was with me. He watched me closely. I reached out to him with my fingertips, smiling when he allowed my touch.

"I'm sorry for how I've treated you," I whispered.

He sat up and leaned toward me. "So am I," he added quietly. His lips met mine. The dream was so real.

That wonderful heat that bound us took away my pain, grief, and fear; only our passion remained. His sweet tongue tickled mine as he pulled me against him and unzipped my long white dress. My breasts fell against his chest. He deepened our kiss and rolled on top of me. "I want to make love," he murmured between kisses.

"I do, too," I moaned.

He pushed himself inside me and flipped me over, allowing me to take control. I arched my back, moving quickly, desperate for my release. Aric groaned and reached for my breasts. His rough hands scratched against my nipples. I didn't care, I wanted him so much.

"You're doing it all wrong," Liz said from out of nowhere. "I told you, I can give you pointers," Maria chimed in.

I froze. They were leaning against the brass rails at the head of the bed. I yanked at the sheets, trying to cover us. *"What are you doing here?"*

Liz rolled her eyes. "Trying to help you."

"Your technique needs serious work," Maria said, pointing.

Aric moaned beneath me and spun me onto my back. "Just ignore them, they're only vampires."

"It's no wonder you've only had sex twice." Agnes stood before a fire pit roasting huge sausages. She lifted one in my direction. "I like to pretend they're penises," she admitted.

Aric continued to make love to me, but the presence of the schoolgirls freaked me out too much to enjoy it. "Aric, I can't do this now…"

A horse whinnied from atop a grassy knoll. Coming at us full dash was Edith riding a giant pink unicorn. "Bear down, Celia. Bear down!" she yelled as she galloped past us.

Looming darkness and the smell of rot replaced the breathtaking sunshine. The only light flickered from a single burning candle. I walked toward it. Against its subtle glow, I found Misha, naked and dirty, kneeling on the cold stone floor. Thick, matted strands of dirty hair hung over his face. Except it wasn't enough to camouflage his glowing eyes, shining bright green with bloodlust. Fear kept me from drawing too close, but I recognized his need to communicate. He pointed to the tequila bottle gripped in his hand, and I immediately woke up.

The vampires surrounded me protectively, crouching to attack and charged by my terror. "What is it, Celia?" Hank asked.

I tried to catch my breath. "It's Misha…He's in Mexico."

Chapter Eighteen

The digital unicorn alarm clock told me it was only 6:30. "Liz, call Uri. Agnes, I need a map of Mexico and all the countries to the south of it."

Tim moved closer to me. "Where is he, exactly?"

I closed my eyes. Words, thoughts, and images swarmed my brain in a mad rush. "In Palenque, but they're planning to move him to Guatemala."

"The shape-shifters?"

"No. There's someone else involved . . . a witch and some vampires. *Weres* are there, too—" My lids flew open, stirring the tension and excitement around the room. "The Tribe! The Tribe is responsible."

Hank leapt off the bed. "This means the Alliance has to help retrieve the master."

Liz bolted back into the room with Emme right behind her. She handed me the phone. "The Grandmaster is on the phone."

Agnes returned with several maps in her arms and spread the largest one on the bed. I scanned it quickly before taking the phone.

"Have you found my son?" Uri asked anxiously.

"Sort of. Right now, he's in Palenque. They're

moving him sometime this morning to Panajachel in Guatemala." I passed my finger down one of the highways. "Their ultimate destination seems to be somewhere in El Salvador." I paused. "Uri, I saw Misha in my dreams. He has bloodlust."

Everyone held their breaths, waiting for Uri to speak. "They are not fools Celia," he said. "They will feed my son if they expect to control him." Uri was right; the more they starved Misha, the more dangerous he'd become. "Celia, I shall arrive in Tahoe by nightfall, but this matter cannot wait. Go to the Den and plead your case before the Elders. The sooner the Alliance assembles, the quicker we will retrieve my son."

All the color drained from my face. Uri was literally asking me to throw myself to the wolves.

"Celia? Are you there, my sweet?"

Hank held me and kept me from falling over. "Celia doesn't appear to be well, Grandmaster." Like all the other vampires, he probably wondered what the hell was wrong with me.

I fought the urge to vomit. "It's not a good idea for me to go, Uri. I'm not welcome at the Den."

"Celia, it is my understanding that you and the Elders have had your differences as of late. Nevertheless, you should not fear. As members of the Alliance they are forbidden to harm you."

Yeah, right.

Danny hurried into the room in full intellectual bullshit mode. "Uri, Celia's emotions have been extremely fragile and unpredictable. I'm afraid if she has another outburst in front of the Elders, she may ruin your chances of getting Misha back. She'll hold up better with you at her side and together you can present a united front."

Uri and I weren't close. He'd shown me respect only out of love for Misha and because he considered me a strong ally. While he appeared the charming and dashing gentleman in public, he still remained a grandmaster vampire—one of the world's most lethal predators, and one who didn't appreciate a werewolf telling him what to do. I suspected some major fuming on the other end of the phone.

"Excuse me, Grandmaster?"

"What is it, Agnes?" Uri snapped.

"While our mistress has led us well, she does appear to be stunned by the master's current state. I have no doubt that your greatness will aid in strengthening her. Perhaps it is in the master's best interest to wait until your arrival?"

"I'll go for her." All heads turned toward Emme.

Uri's terse response didn't go over well with me. "How will your presence be better than Celia's, my dear?"

Emme clutched my hand. "Being her sister, I'm the next closest thing."

"Emme has been a guest in our home, Grandmaster," Hank interrupted. "It will give the impression the Wird sisters stand with the vampires."

Nothing else Hank could have said would have pleased Uri more. The undead lived to drop names. The pleasant tone returned to Uri's voice. "Very well, dear Emme. I shall arrange a meeting between you and the Elders. Celia, when I arrive, we will attend the wolves together."

Danny nodded, giving me the okay to run with it. "Okay, Uri. I'll go with you when you arrive."

The vamps prepared for Uri's arrival while I met with Danny and Emme in Bren's room. "Thanks for doing this, Emme."

She hugged me tight. "It's okay, Celia. It'll give me an excuse to talk to Liam in person."

Her cheeks turned a pretty pink as they often did when she spoke of him. "You're going to ask him to get back together. Aren't you?"

Emme played with her hands. "I love him, Celia.

My life hasn't been the same without him."

Liam was the best thing to come Emme's way. They'd made the perfect couple. Or so I'd thought. This time, I took her hands in mine. "Emme, your relationship ended when you came to terms that you weren't his mate. What happens if he meets her while you're with him?"

Emme shrugged. "I want to take the chance, he's worth it. There's no one else for me."

Danny elbowed me slightly. Based on the rising bedsheet over Bren's pants, he disagreed.

I worried about Emme facing the wolves alone and sent Michael along to accompany her. I paced the whole time she was gone, unable to remain still. She returned an hour later, crying. I rushed to the foyer, where the vampires had gathered around her. "What happened?"

"Anara told me he wouldn't help Misha."

I clenched my teeth while the vampires swore and hissed. "What about Martin and Makawee, were you able to gain their support?"

"I asked to meet with them. Anara refused and told me to leave. I sought Aric, hoping he could at least arrange an audience with the Elders, but the only wolf I found was Liam." Her voice shook and her tears ran faster. "He's engaged. You were right, he found his mate. She's one of the *weres* who fought in Chaitén."

I froze. "Oh, God, Emme . . . I'm so sorry."

Edith stomped her foot. "Who gives a shit? What about our master?"

I glared at her. "Back off, Edith. Can't you see she's hurt?"

Liz rammed her file into a small wooden table. "You don't get it, Celia. If our master dies, one of the others will kill you and claim us."

My growls had her backing away. "Do you honestly

think I'm not trying here? Contrary to popular belief, I want to live, too!"

Liz dropped her gaze, but angry tears welled in her eyes. For a moment, no one said anything.

Agnes inched her way toward me. Like the other schoolgirls, she'd begun to cry. "You don't understand the peril of our situation, Celia. Most masters aren't as kind as ours."

Her words surprised me. Misha could be unbelievably sweet—to me. The way he ruled his vampires, though, was harsh at times. They feared him, and rightfully so.

Tim put his arm around her as she wept, a feat of compassion I'd never seen. "There are some who will kill us just for sport."

"And others who will force us to commit unthinkable acts," Edith added.

I blinked back at her. For Edith to consider something unthinkable was scary as hell.

Michael stepped forward. "I used to belong to Petro. Power had made him cruel, as it often does most masters. He would . . ." Michael shuddered and stared at the blue slate floor, unable to continue.

I sensed the vampires' anger, but their growing fear masked their fury. Shit. What would happen to them if we couldn't get Misha back? "Would Uri be able to take you on as his?"

The girls kept their heads down. Hank and Tim exchanged glances. "To do so he'd have to kill you," Hank said.

I swallowed a few times. I supposed I should've started making a list of all my potential murderers so I could keep track.

Tim released Agnes. "Don't worry. Out of respect for our master he won't kill you . . . maybe."

"Maybe?"

Edith bit her bottom lip. "Though he might force us to kill you."

"Uri can force you to kill me?"

It was Michael who answered. "As the master to our master, yes."

Liz nodded. "But we would feel terrible about it, wouldn't we, everyone?" The vamps all muttered in agreement.

"Gee, thanks. I feel better now."

Emme stopped crying. Being scared out of her mind for my life sobered her right up.

Danny didn't look much better. He knew, like I did, that my only hope for survival was Misha.

"How the hell did you wind up involved in this horseshit?"

Needless to say, Taran didn't take my latest news well when I phoned her and Shayna. I fell back into the bed. "What can I say, I'm on a roll."

"Dude, leave them."

I draped an arm over my eyes. "I can't, Shayna. Whether I live with them or not they still belong to me."

Danny sat next to me. "Besides, where else would she go? At least with the vampires she's protected from everything that's after her."

Taran huffed. "Oh, yeah, until another master challenges her or Uri makes them kill her. Celia, this is total shit!"

I sat up on my elbows. "I'm counting on Uri to take them should another master take me out."

"What if he doesn't want them, Ceel?" I could hear Taran pace. "Hell, he has his own family to care for and he's never struck me as the daddy type. Didn't he stop *turning* vamps years ago because they got on his nerves?"

"He may not love them. But he loves Misha. He knows he'd hurt Misha by turning his back on them."

"I think you should ask Aric for help," Emme said quietly. "He would protect you against the other masters if he knew your life was at stake."

Aric by my side wasn't an option . . . no matter how badly I wanted it to be. "Aric wants nothing to do with me."

Taran swore a few times. "Ceel, he's being an ass. But he still loves you—despite what he claims."

I turned away from the phone, feeling more hurt. Several weeks had passed since Aric and I had spoken, but his words still stung. Danny lifted the phone from the bed. "It's better if we don't involve Aric."

Liz marched in then with a garment bag. "The grandmaster's plane has landed in Tahoe. He'll be here shortly."

"I'll see you guys soon." I disconnected the call and addressed Liz. "What's in the bag?" "It's your attire for the evening. The grandmaster wants us all to dress alike to signify a cohesive group."

Emme unzipped the bag, revealing a sexy black business suit—short skirt, and a jacket with plunging neckline, designed to be worn without a blouse. Four-inch black heels were tucked at the bottom. I rose and walked to the giant closet, where I selected a soft silver cashmere sweater and a long, flowing white skirt. I slipped into them and a pair of silver ballet flats. My ensemble was casual, comfortable, but most important, me. I wasn't a vamp or a *were*. And despite my faults, and how tumultuous my life had become, I still maintained my sense of worth. I needed to hang on to what I was . . . weird as I might be.

Emme and Danny smiled when I returned to the bedroom. "You look pretty," Danny said.

The vampires didn't agree and neither did Uri. "Did you not approve of the garment I ordered?" he asked when he arrived.

"It's important that others see me as a leader, not a

follower. Choosing to dress as I please demonstrates my strength, don't you think?"

Uri surprised me by nodding, seemingly won over by my reasoning. I had to watch it though; my bullshit meter had maxed out its limit.

Emme and Danny rode with me in the limo, along with Uri and his guards. Emme didn't want to return to the Den, having been humiliated. I didn't want to return because of my fear of torture and dying.

Uri patted my knee. "I won't allow the mongrels to harm you."

Would you prefer to do it yourself? "Thank you, Uri," I said cautiously.

We didn't speak much on the way to Squaw Valley. Uri was angry at Anara's dismissive behavior toward Emme and took it as a personal insult, given she'd been acting on the vampires' behalf. My tigress paced restlessly within me. She sensed there would be bloodshed tonight and so did I. We just didn't know whose it would be.

My pulse was racing by the time we passed through the front gate. I willed myself to relax. If it came down to fighting for my life, I needed to remain calm. Two *weres* greeted us when we arrived at the monstrous château that served as the main building—Liam, and a coyote I didn't know. She was slender and small boned, and just about my height. Deep scars marred her face. Like many of the *weres* who fought in Chaitén, she'd suffered irreparable damage from the demon's fire. Two flaps of dry leather sealed her eyes shut and her auburn hair was missing along her crown. But she smiled, and that made her pretty. Liam beamed as he led her down the steps.

"Celia, it's me, Li-am." He spoke to me like I was two years old.

"I know who you are, Liam."

"Oh good, she's still with us," Liam explained to the *were* like we weren't even standing there. He then turned back to us. "I'd like to introduce you to Allie, my mate."

My hand gripped Emme's when she tensed. Allie sniffed the air. "Hello, Celia. It's nice to meet you." Her head angled toward Emme and she smiled gently. "Hello again, Emme."

I was supposed to hate her. That's just what sisters do for each other. It's written in stone somewhere that we have to hate our sisters' ex-boyfriend's new girlfriends. But I couldn't. She seemed sweet and unthreatening. And leave it to Liam's huge heart to fall for someone who was disfigured. "Hi, Allie," we both said, and smiled politely.

Liam lit up. "Hey. I've got a great idea! How would you two like to be bridesmaids?" Everyone, including Allie, stopped smiling then.

"Liam, I don't think that's a good idea," I said.

"I know it's short notice—"

Uri's guard interrupted. "If you don't mind, we're here to see your Elders."

Liam seemed unaffected by the guard's tone. He punched me affectionately in the arm. "We'll discuss the wedding later," he said.

We swept past him and into the foyer. Aric's aroma of water crashing over stones overpowered the large space, hitting my nose like a reprimanding swat. He was angry. I could feel it. My God, I could feel *him*. My tigress bashed against my rib cage, ready to seek out his wolf. I barely managed to rein her in and keep from *changing*. Her impulsiveness worsened my nerves and exacerbated my need to find Aric. My body trembled violently. I couldn't keep it together. I was falling apart.

Tim nudged me hard. "Get a hold of yourself," he muttered.

Uri peered down his nose at me. "Is something the matter?"

Danny shoved me down the long wooden corridor.

"Go to the bathroom," he urged. "I'll wait for you here."

"I have to go to the bathroom," I repeated numbly and sprinted down the hall. Emme and the Catholic schoolgirls raced after me. I fell against the emerald green granite counter. My claws shot out, scratching the surface. It hurt to withdraw them.

Emme gaped at the deep scrapes and the tinges of blood I'd left behind. She blotted my fingers with a paper towel and quickly tended to my damaged nails with her magic. "Celia, what's wrong?"

"Aric's scent is everywhere—I can't think straight." My chest tightened. "*Shit*. I can't even breathe."

Liz fastened her hands on my shoulders and shook me hard. "Damnit, Celia—snap out of it. You have to get us through this or we're all going to die. Do you hear me? We're all going to die!"

Blood coursed through my veins like lava. I'd felt this relentless pull once before, when Aric first left me and we were forced to remain apart. I recognized it now for what it was—our souls' need to merge and bond. *Damnit*. I lowered my lids and concentrated on my baby. Liz was right: I had to get us through this. I took several calming breaths and managed to steady myself. "Okay. Okay. I'm ready." It was a total and complete lie and they all knew it, except I couldn't exactly hide in the bathroom forever.

We hurried back toward the foyer. Uri and his guards were already in the meeting room. I could hear him arguing with Anara. I forced myself forward, only to be intercepted by a she- wolf. She was taller than me, with olive skin and jet-black hair. In my distress, I failed to realize she was challenging me. I tried to sidestep around her. Again, she blocked my path. *"No,"* I told the vamps when they hissed. I frowned, confused as to why she was picking a fight with me. Her eyes didn't glow gold and no song of wolves accompanied her presence.

I moved toward the right. This time she hit me hard

in the shoulder. "What—?"

"Get away from my mate," Aric growled. But it wasn't until he snaked his arm around the she-wolf that I realized he didn't mean me.

Chapter Nineteen

Mate. Aric had called *her* his *mate*. My breath came out so hard my chest threatened to collapse inward. Emme and Danny whispered tightly in my ear and the vamps urged me forward, except no one made sense. My entire focus remained on Aric and the she-wolf he held in his arms. A smug smile inched across her face as she leaned her body against his. But it was what she said that slammed me back into reality. "Aric promised to give me a child."

I didn't think. I reacted, yanking her from his grasp and embedding her in the back wall. The she-wolf grunted from the impact. I thought Aric would rip into me for attacking her, or rush to her side. After all, he did call her his damn *mate*. Instead he froze, watching me while I fought the rage and hurt that burned my eyes with tears.

"How could you do that to me?" I demanded. "How could you *fucking* do that to me?"

Aric leaned back on his heels. "You left me," he answered quietly.

A single tear dripped down my cheek. "No . . . I didn't."

The wall behind me cracked. The she-wolf dislodged her body and charged. Aric snatched her up in his arms and hauled her back before she could reach me. "Go back to the room, Diane," he told her, continuing to scrutinize me closely. "I'm needed inside."

"I'm going to kill you, you stupid freak!" she growled at me.

"I'll be sure to add you to the list," I shot back.

Emme had to run to keep up. I threw open the doors to the meeting room with the vamps hot on my trail and marched across the polished wood floor to the end of the room.

The Elders sat on a raised platform. Uri stood before them; they hadn't even offered him a chair. My sisters waited at a nearby table with their wolves. Their brows shot up to the moon upon catching the fury burning its way across my face. "She must have met Diane," Koda murmured to Shayna. Next to them lounged Tye, a werelion with whom some crazy clairvoyant named Destiny claimed I'd make babies—babies who'd apparently rid the world of evil. He greeted me with a lazy grin and a flash of a dimple. I didn't smile back, but if he needed something dead, I'd gladly oblige.

Three master vampires and their families lined the opposite wall, including Angelo Cusamano. Angelo was the most powerful vampire on the East Coast. He was also an evil bastard who'd come close to killing me, Danny, and my sisters. Danny tensed beside me. Angelo chuckled and tipped his glass of red wine my way. He appeared pleased to see me, but in a way that clearly meant trouble.

Anara and Uri didn't react to my arrival, too wrapped up in their argument to pay attention to little ol' pissed-off me. Anara sneered. "We will not waste valuable resources on the hunch of an unstable woman. If you want your property back retrieve him yourself."

Uri seethed hard enough to burn a hole in the floor. "My position in the European Alliance does not permit me to fight, nor use my resources for personal issues."

Anara waved him off. "Then I suggest you step down from your position."

Uri clenched his fists. "You have never held more than the position of Elder. What do you understand of the responsibilities I would be walking away from?"

Anara leaned forward. "I will know soon enough. My efforts to ensure the survival of our species have impressed the members of the North American Were Council—so much so, I've been elected prime advisor to our president." He stole a glance my way. "Soon I'll be everywhere, with power so immense it will crush the trivial amount I currently possess."

Martin stiffened, seemingly furious at Anara's disrespect. Makawee raised her chin, more embarrassed than insulted. Neither spoke up, but I did.

"I'll go after Misha."

Suddenly all eyes were on me. Anara laughed. "What did you say?"

"You heard me." I didn't bother masking my resentment or hatred then. "I'll take a group of vampires with me and we'll find Misha ourselves."

Uri's shoulders slumped with relief. He hurried to my side and kissed my cheeks. "My son has chosen well."

Shayna rose from her table. "Ceel, you can't be serious."

Aric leaned against the wall and crossed his arms, his anger toward me returning now that I'd volunteered to find Misha. "Of course she's serious," he responded stiffly. "After all, he is her lover."

"Oh, shut up!" I snapped. Despite his immobile expression, Aric regarded me like I'd slapped him across the face. I didn't care. His freaking *mate* would help him get over it. "We'll leave tonight," I told Uri.

I barreled toward the exit. Angelo and his family swept in front of us like a breeze, his vampires blocking mine and crouched to attack. Guttural hisses echoed along the vast room, promising to smear the walls with death.

Angelo's glare bore into me like a slow-twisting screw. "I challenge you, Celia Wird, for your family. I—"

Word to the wise: Don't mess with a hormonal pregnant woman at the end of her rope.

My jumping, spinning back kick completely shut him up. There was a collective gasp when his head left his shoulders and landed somewhere near the Elders. My sisters, friends, and—to my surprise—*Aric* had all raced forward to help me.

I ignored them and followed the stream of blood to where Angelo's head lay, careful not to soil my skirt. This time it was my turn to glare. "You ever threaten me or Misha's family again, I'll ram a stake through your goddamn heart—you got me?"

"Yes," he muttered.

I addressed the other masters. "Anyone else want to challenge me?" Funny, they all found somewhere else to look. *"I didn't think so."* I bowed my head slightly at Makawee. "Sorry about the mess." It was a stupid thing to say, but it was my way of showing her some respect. She tilted her chin slightly and tried her best to squelch her grin. With that I turned on my heel and left, but not before Misha's vampires shoved Angelo's body aside in another show of strength.

Tye dashed after me. "Oh, *shit*. I can't believe you took down a master in one strike." He followed me to the limo and jumped in ahead of me.

I dropped my arms to my sides. "Tye, what are you doing?"

"You're my destiny, dovie. I'm going with you."

"That's a great idea. Isn't it, Celia?" Danny's insistence told me not to argue.

I wanted to tell them both they were nuts, except that chaos then blasted behind me like a siren. Leave it to Hank to escort Emme out with his arm around her waist.

And leave it to him to then taunt Liam, the wolf, Warrior, and Emme's ex-boyfriend.

Liam stepped between them, forcing them apart. His upper lip curled in a snarl. "Emme, tell me you're not with this damn parasite."

Emme clutched Liam's arm. "Lee, don't."

He reeled on her. "Just because we're not together doesn't mean you should settle for a vampire!"

Hank swung, aiming for Liam's face. Liam sidestepped, gripped his wrist, and they both toppled down the stone steps, punching and landing hard blows. I grabbed Emme and shoved her into Shayna and Taran's arms to keep her back. The wolves leapt from the large porch and charged to where Liam and Hank pounded each other like sledgehammers meeting rock.

Emme screamed at them to stop, tugging them with *force,* unable to pry them apart. Misha's vamps jetted to the rolling mound, their claws and fangs out. To say I was in no mood for a *were*-vamp smackdown was an understatement. Gravel flew up around me with how fast I moved. "Back," I hissed to the oncoming vamps. They grounded to a halt. "Hank, *stop.*"

Hank did as he was told, like a good little vampire. Liam wouldn't stop and ripped off Hank's arm before Koda and Gemini could haul him away.

Aric broke from the crowd and stalked toward me. "I want to talk to you," he said under his breath.

I couldn't hide the hurt in my voice. "I wouldn't want to keep you from your mate." He didn't follow me when I gave him my back, but I felt him watching me.

Liam spat blood on the ground. "I don't want you with him, Emme. You deserve better than him."

"Go back to your coyote, mutt," Hank snapped. "Tonight, when you're with her, Emme will be begging me not to stop."

And with that one statement, Hank completely

ruined his chances with Emme. Her cheeks burned red and she edged away from him.

"Nice one, Hank." I yanked the dismembered limb out of his hand and smacked him upside the head with it. "Get in the damn car!"

Hank grumbled but took his arm back and obeyed. Liam continued to struggle. "You *asshole,* don't ever talk about her that way again!"

Gemini dragged him farther back. "Settle down, Liam. It's over."

Liam wouldn't listen. I didn't want any more trouble and neither did Emme.

"Go get Allie," she said quietly. "She's Liam's mate. She'll be able to soothe him."

Emme's reaction tore at my heart. In her soft, simple words she'd given Liam her blessing. He broke away from the wolves and lifted her in an embrace. "Thank you for understanding, angel," he whispered.

"I'm happy for you," she said as tears trickled down her small face. "But please don't invite me to your wedding...I can't watch you marry someone else."

Liam released Emme and bowed his head. For the first time, he realized just how much his upcoming marriage had hurt her. I placed my arm around Emme and ushered her into the limo and into Danny's arms.

I meant to leave then. Not just for Emme's sake, but for mine as well. Shayna's voice kept me in place.

"Don't go after Misha, Ceel. If you do, you won't come back." She stood behind me, clenching the hilt of the dagger at her hip. She didn't understand what Misha meant to me or that he was my only chance of surviving, especially now that Anara's power would soar into something unstoppable.

"I can't abandon him," I told her. "He's my friend."

I tried to hug her, but she wrenched away from me. "You're going to die—don't you get it? What you're doing is suicide!"

She fell against Koda's chest, sobbing. I expected him to explode at me for upsetting her. Instead his solemn expression revealed his worry and disappointment. Once again, I'd managed to kick everyone in the emotional gut without even trying.

I paused, sensing Aric's attention fixed solely on me. Instead of acknowledging him, I addressed my remaining sister. Taran's eyes glistened with tears before narrowing sharply. "This isn't your problem, Celia. Let it go."

"I can't."

She muttered a bunch of swearwords and kicked at the pebbles at her feet. "*Fine.* But I'm going with you!"

"No," Gemini and I both said at once.

Taran's anger charged the magic around her. "For shit's sake, what the hell happened? It used to be all of us, or none of us!"

"Not this time," I told her quietly.

Gemini slipped his arm around Taran's waist and gripped her hip, holding her protectively and lovingly all at once. It was hard for me to watch them, realizing Aric used to hold me the same way.

Gemini spoke calmly. "Celia, your decisions lately have been irrational at best. Give yourself time to think things through before running after what is evidently the source of your problems."

My shoulders crumbled and my body wasn't far behind. I was so tired of fighting with those I loved. "I have to go," I said, my voice cracking. "Take care of each other."

I hurried into the limo and slammed the door. Taran pounded on the glass. "Celia. Don't do this!"

The limo thundered away at my nod. Emme grappled with her misery all the way back to the mansion. I'd moved past misery and cuddled up with anger. Given a choice, anger always made a better lover than heartbreak.

Of all the things Aric could have said, how could he call Diane his mate? And how could he promise to give her a child when ours grew inside me with every breath?

Tye cleared his throat. "What are you thinking, dovie?"

"That I'm probably going to die, and so will you if you come with me."

Tye tucked his hands behind his neck and spread his long legs across Agnes and Edith's laps. They let him, obviously charmed by his white-blond hair, smooth tanned skin, and light blue eyes that cut through the darkness of the limo. "You know what your problem is?"

I groaned. "No, Tye, but I'm sure you're going to tell me."

Tye reached out to me. In a blink, I lay across his lap and his mouth was tickling my ear. "You don't believe in Destiny," he whispered.

I pressed my fingers against his lips before he could kiss me. My thoughts at that moment remained with Aric. "I did believe in destiny once. I don't anymore." The tone in my voice wasn't harsh like I'd intended. It betrayed every last trickle of emotion I'd fought to suppress.

Tye backed off and placed his hand gently on my knee. "Hell, Aric really did a number on you, didn't he?"

Tye's comment surprised me. He must have heard I'd broken our bond. And yet instead of blaming me, he held Aric responsible. I shrugged and moved back to my seat, just in time for the limo to roll to a stop.

I abandoned the Hummer at the same time Uri emerged from his. "I have arranged for a plane. Where do you intend to fly?"

I rubbed my hands, chilled from the sudden drop in temperature. "Panajachel. That's the Tribe's first destination. I'll need cars and access to another plane in case we don't stop them before they reach El Salvador."

Uri nodded to his vampires. They dispersed to set my plans in motion. Tim bowed to us. "Who do you want to come with us, Celia?"

"The strongest vampires we have. Make sure they eat, we leave in an hour—oh, and tell Hank to pop his arm back in place. He doesn't have time to regenerate a new limb."

I urged Emme, Danny, and Tye upstairs to check on Bren. They left without question, realizing my need to speak with Uri alone. "There's something I need to discuss with you. If anything happens to me—"

"You wish me to care for Misha's keep." He scoffed when I said nothing. "Celia, as this family's grandmaster my subordinates apprise me of everything. I see and know all through them. You'd be a fool to think otherwise."

It amazed me. The last few weeks and just now at the Den, I'd been Uri's hero. Despite my fears, I'd stepped up to the plate and ensured the survival of his family. And now he felt the need to flex his supernatural muscles in my face. He'd never disrespected me before, but I found his arrogance offensive. "Whatever, Uri," I snapped. It was a cocky response, and one that could have been perceived as a challenge. But I'd be damned if I allowed him to treat me as he pleased and kill me if it suited him.

He watched me for a beat, not speaking, not moving. I watched him too, certain he'd attack. When he spoke again, his tone was softer, but by no means apologetic. If anything, he resumed the role of the gentleman he pretended to be. "I will take custody of Misha's family should you die. However . . ."

I rammed my hands onto my hips. "Yes?"

"Just return with my son and there will be no need to worry." Uri stared at me closely, in a way that made me want to bite. I should have expected his greatest concern, like that of most vampires, was meeting his own needs. He

187

didn't care who perished if it meant getting Misha back. Hell, for all I knew he'd probably told the vampires to exchange me for Misha if it came down to it.

My anger rose, and I cursed myself for thinking I could rely on Uri. Would he keep Misha's family safe if I died? As we continued to eye each other, I wasn't so sure. He was nothing like Misha. He may have respected me to a degree because of my abilities, but to expect him to show me any compassion or weep at my graveside would be absurd.

Tim returned and bowed once more. "Excuse me, Grandmaster. Here is the meal you requested."

Uri's dinner consisted of two strapping young males that couldn't have been older than twenty-three. Like most of the men Uri preferred, they carried a feminine beauty. He nodded approvingly and beckoned the tallest one forward. Lust glimmered in the young man's eyes as he reached to stroke Uri's neatly trimmed beard. Their arousal hit me almost immediately. "If you will excuse me, dear Celia, I need to dine before I turn in. I expect to hear from you regarding your progress."

"I'm sure the vampires will keep you informed." I started up the stairs. I knew what was coming, and yet I still cringed when Uri's fangs punctured his dinner's jugular.

Chapter Twenty

Emme perched on the bed next to Bren. To my joy, Bren's bugle wasn't blasting away, though it could have been out of respect for her sorrow. Tye leaned her against him. "Emme, don't cry. Liam may have found his mate, but in time, you will, too."

She rubbed her red swollen eyes. "I hope you're right," she said quietly.

He rubbed her back, but winked my way. "Don't be jealous, Celia. I'm just trying to make my future sister-in-law feel better."

I let out an exasperated laugh and sat next to them. Danny rubbed my shoulders. "How are you holding up?"

"About as good as always," I muttered.

I examined my sister closely. Emme was born premature and had always been small. Her stature and her sensitive nature granted her a free pass to be vulnerable.

I was denied that pass—stereotyped instead as a strong and fierce protector who couldn't show weakness. So, when I broke down, it made others uneasy. It was as if I wasn't allowed to hurt. But I did, especially then.

I smoothed my sister's hair and tried to smile. "Emme, I want you and Danny to take over Bren's care while I'm gone."

She wrinkled her brow. "Celia, I'm going with you."

"No, sweetie, you're not." I sighed and tried to force the words out. "I need you to watch over Bren in case I don't come back."

Emme's tears started all over again. "Don't say that, Celia. I don't want to lose you, too." The lump building in my throat made it hard to speak. "Emme, someday you'll understand why you can't come with me, but now is not the time to explain." I didn't want to cry; I had told myself I wouldn't. But how could I help it? I was saying goodbye to my sweet baby sister, the one I'd protected most.

Danny placed his hand on her shoulder. "Just do what she asks, Emme."

Emme glanced back and forth between us, realizing Danny knew what was happening and that, despite her reservations, she needed to trust me. "Okay, Celia. I promise to take care of Bren."

And just like that, "Reveille" played in Bren's pants.

Maria knocked on the door. "Celia, I have de items you requested."

She crossed the room and handed me a briefcase and a large envelope. I brought Danny into the unicorn room and opened the case. "Holy crap," he whispered when he saw it stuffed with cash. I dumped the contents of the envelope on the bed. There were two sets of passports, birth certificates, and driver's licenses, for him and Bren.

"The briefcase has been magicked. Anyone who opens it besides you will see only folders and paperwork. Once you take the money out the spell will be broken. So, try not to use it unless you have to."

"Celia, this is a ton of money. Where did it come from?"

He was probably worried I'd stolen it from the vampires. "Most of it I've saved throughout the years. Some of it is from the work I've done for Misha. The war has been profitable for him and the other masters."

Danny's eyes darted over the wads of bills. "What were you saving it for?" he asked quietly.

I stared at the contents on the bed, but said nothing. "Celia?"

It was humiliating, but I told him anyway. "I always knew that I'd end up alone, and that my sisters would marry and move on without me. This money was going to help me start a new life on my own."

Danny shook his head. "My God, Celia. You really believed that?"

I closed my lids tight and tried to swallow the ache building in my throat. "If I'd never met Aric, I would have been fine—I wouldn't have liked it, but I was prepared, you know?"

He squeezed my arm. "Celia, it doesn't have to be like this."

"You're right, it doesn't. If I can get Misha back, I know he'll help me disappear." I hugged my belly and managed a weak smile. "My baby and I will be safe, and I'll never be alone."

Tim rapped on the door. "We're ready to go, Celia."

"I'll be right down." I waited until I heard him leave, then grabbed my backpack and threw it over my shoulder.

Danny handed me a tissue from the unicorn tissue dispenser and then took one for himself. The unicorn whinnied and the horn lit up. "Keep Tye with you at all times," he whispered. "Anara can't control him, he's not Pack. And if the vampires turn against you, he'll help keep you safe."

I took his hand in mine. "If I don't come back, take Bren and run. You won't be able to keep him safe without the vampires. You have all the papers, including forged medical records, that will allow you to travel with him."

Danny nodded and stared hard at the floor. "Celia, about Aric—"

"Aric will be fine. He has his mate and he'll have his own family soon enough." I wasn't Emme. I didn't have it in me to be happy for him.

Danny held my face in his hands and blinked back more tears. "You're wrong, Celia . . . about everything. Come back safely and I'll prove it."

We hugged, but neither of us could say goodbye. Danny was the first friend I'd ever made.

Now he was my family.

As Emme and I embraced, her tears poured out like rain. I fought to keep it together, finally breaking away from her before I lost my nerve. I kissed Bren's forehead and raced out of the house with Tye, only to be stopped by one of the vampires staying behind. He handed me a large cream-colored envelope. "This just arrived for you by courier, Mistress."

I opened it and couldn't believe my eyes. My stare was so intense I thought my anger would set the expensive paper on fire.

Tye leaned over me. "What is it?"

"An invitation to a luncheon at the Den, in honor of Anara's appointment to the North American Were Council," I bit out. My hands crumpled the paper into a ball. Had Anara delivered it himself I would have rammed it down his goddamn throat.

My phone buzzed as we barreled onto the landing strip. I checked the screen . . . and time stood still. The text was brief, but hit me like an eighteen-wheeler sliding over ice.

Don't go. Aric

I deleted the message at once, and tried not to think about why he'd sent it. It was better to think he considered Misha unworthy of being saved, and not—definitely not—because he still cared for me.

"He likes playing games, doesn't he?"

Tye lounged beside me in the limo. I wasn't surprised he saw the message nor was I shocked by the annoyed bark to his tone. I shoved the phone deep into my pack. "It doesn't matter."

I practically kicked the door open and dashed toward the luxurious jet. The vampires chasing me hissed, their growing anxiety and anticipation making them restless. My anxiety and anticipation churned my stomach. I raced to the rear of the plane and hurled in the bathroom. Stunned silence greeted me when I finally rejoined the vamps in the cabin. Once again, my leadership and stability were in question.

Maria shoved a bottle of water in my hand. "For mercy's sake, take a sip."

"And a Valium," Tim muttered.

The water bottle bounced off his bald head when I threw it at him. Maria flashed me some fang, seemingly impressed, and passed me another bottle. I grabbed it and searched for the closest window seat. Edith and Agnes had strategically positioned themselves on either side of Tye. He left them to sit with me. The moment I buckled in, Hank whistled and the plane readied for takeoff.

I closed my eyes and tried to breathe slowly. I had to rest, if only for a short while. No sooner did we reach altitude than a sharp image of Misha appeared in my mind. I jolted upright. "Shit. They're moving him again. Get me a map of Guatemala."

Agnes opened the map and spread it out on the wide table in front of me. I looked around at all the names of the cities until one grabbed my attention. I pointed. "There. They'll be in Escuintla by morning."

Hank rubbed his arm and examined the map. "That's near a seaport. Are they planning to ship the master somewhere?"

"I don't know."

Edith tugged on my long-sleeved T-shirt. "How does the master look?"

The image of Misha had not been a pretty one. His once sleek and shimmering hair lay in greasy clumps mixed with dirt. Deep gashes covered his filthy arms and chest. His wounds told me two things: his captors whipped him regularly, and that they weren't feeding him enough blood.

Edith tugged harder. "Well?"

"Hungry." I didn't lie. Misha was falling further into bloodlust.

"You have to tell us more than that!" Edith demanded to know what I'd seen, yet I wasn't sure she could handle it.

"Just tell us," Tim asked. "Please, Celia."

I sighed. "He's lying in filth . . . and they're whipping him."

The fury that filled the plane incited my tigress to growl. The vampires bowed their heads out of respect for me as their current mistress. Had they held me responsible for Misha's suffering, they'd have torn me to pieces and played volleyball with my liver. In a strange way, perhaps it was the pep talk they needed. If they weren't ready to slaughter before, they certainly were then.

"You need to contact him." Tye's voice was calm, but he'd leapt to his feet in attack stance when he sensed the vamps' rage unleash.

"I don't think I can do that." I looked around. "You forget, we're not mates—we're not bonded."

"It's not about being mates." Tye raised my arm and traced a line down with his finger. "It's about a master vampire passing you his *call*. That's like an indestructible cellphone with unlimited service, dovie. If he can contact you, you sure as hell can reach him."

"It hasn't worked in the past, Tye."

Maria stood. "Take a nap. Make certain your very last thought is of de master. You'll be sure to reach him then."

Tye lifted me to my feet when I hesitated. "Celia, you have to try. Your presence will help him to fight the bloodlust. There's no sense in rescuing him if he's going to try to eat us."

Though I had my doubts, a nap sounded good. I walked into the rear of the plane to the ultramodern suite and spread out on the bed. Tye rolled next to me. I punched the pillow beneath my head and tried to settle. "Is this really necessary?"

He flashed me one of his more lionlike smiles. "I'm just here to keep the scary leeches away."

My lids drooped. "Oh, is that all?"

"That, and to brag to my friends that I finally got you in bed."

I laughed. "Just don't write anything on the bathroom wall about me."

I flipped to my side. Exhaustion weighed on me like a brick in water. I drifted away, but it wasn't into sleep. Instead I appeared outside an old barn. Humidity slicked my skin despite the late-night hour and neglected palm trees grew like weeds along the garbage-strewn yard. *Where am I?*

The barn door was thrown open and an old woman hurried out, dragging a young teen by her long dark hair. I dove behind a rusted pickup truck before they could see me. *"Estupida,"* the woman admonished in a low voice. *"No le hagas caso a lo que te prometen esos diablos."*

Deep-throated laughter echoed from within the barn. The males inside were either *weres* or vampires to have heard the woman scolding the girl for believing their promises. But even if their keen sense of hearing hadn't given them away, I knew only preternaturals could imprison a master vamp. Misha *called* to me, luring me forward with a tangible pull.

I snuck through the crack of the open door. Dirt mixed with dry grass and old cow manure made up the floor. Pigs squealed with fright from their pen in the corner. Darkness concealed most of the dilapidated structure, except for a small dim bulb hanging from the rafters. My tigress eyes came forward, permitting me to see while I hid behind a splintered stall.

Three were oxen stood facing Misha where he'd been staked to the wall. At first it didn't make sense why he didn't yank his limbs free. While his muscles and bones would be damaged, in a bloodlust state, a vampire was stronger. He could feast on his captors, mend, and then easily escape.

Misha raised his head and hissed through his fangs. The three *weres* answered him by lifting their guns and firing. My heart resumed beating only after I realized he'd been struck with tranquilizers instead of bullets. His head and shoulders slumped. One by one, his muscles ejected the darts. They clinked as they fell against the pile at his feet.

My plan was simple: break the neck of the *were* closest to me and *shift* the other two underground before they realized what had happened. I crept behind the were ox and attacked, falling when my arms went right through his body. I landed in a crouch, growling and ready to fight. No one reacted. That's when I realized I was nothing more than an apparition despite my ability to sense my surroundings. My mind worked through how I could use my invisibility to my advantage until the *were* reaching for a whip ground my thoughts to a halt.

The whip soared through my chest, striking Misha's face, chest, and groin and inciting laughter from the group. I wrenched my body away, unable to watch. The *were* closest to me backed away into a stall and lifted a half-empty bottle of tequila from an old plastic table. He took a few swigs, filling his mouth before spitting the rank fluid on Misha's open wounds.

They each took turns lashing Misha, until the last grew bored and dropped the blood- smeared whip on the ground. The tip shimmered. It had been dipped in cursed gold. *Shit.* No wonder the strikes had been so effective.

The group returned to the table and resumed their card game, passing what remained of the tequila. I didn't want to see the damage they'd inflicted yet I realized Misha had summoned me for a reason. I cringed. The gashes dug deep enough to expose his ribs. His head slumped lifelessly against his chest, and he wheezed with every breath.

Without thinking, I reached to touch him. I couldn't feel his skin directly, but I did sense a twinge of something, like skimming the surface of water.

"Celia," he rasped.

"Yes, Misha. I'm here." I tried to push his hair back. And while I felt that strange sensation, I failed to move the matted strands from his face.

He spoke between harsh gasps. "I fear . . . my time . . . has come."

My tears moistened the dirty barn floor. "Don't say that. We're close. You have to stay strong."

His eyes shot open, illuminating in that horrible shade of green. *"Tell me you love me."*

I barely recognized his voice. When I didn't answer he winked and bared his famously wicked grin. "Please," he added, a little less psychotically.

Under the circumstances, I shouldn't have laughed, but I did as I continued to weep. The hint of humor proved he wasn't too far gone. "I love you, Misha."

He smiled again. And although his eyes continued to shine in that sickly green, they held the same tenderness he'd often demonstrated in my presence. "Tell me you'll be my bride."

My arms encircled his neck. Dirt and salt from his sweat masked his normal scent of sex and chocolate. "Don't push it, Misha."

Misha chuckled and rubbed his face against my hair. "Will you join me soon?"

"Yes, your family and I are coming for you."

His body trembled. "Will there be blood?"

I glanced from the whip lying carelessly on the filthy floor to the *weres,* who kept their guns close to their sides. "Yes, Misha. There will be blood."

Chapter Twenty-one

The doors crashed open. The woman who stomped in brought the *weres* scrambling to their feet. She stood about my height, with curly brown hair down to her shoulders, eyes as black as midnight, and dark olive skin marred by years of sun exposure. A soiled T-shirt and cotton skirt covered her stout figure over bare legs. Varicosities raked her shins like old tree roots, and worn flip-flops encased her dirty feet. Anyone human would have mistaken her for an average peasant woman, but I wasn't human and neither was Misha.

I released Misha and swerved to face her, only to tense from the vile odor of magic seeping from her pores. The *weres* rushed to bow before her. It might have seemed comical for someone like her to intimidate such cruel-looking males. Yet I recognized this woman was nothing to laugh at.

Her voice was gruff and her lips pursed in displeasure. *"¿Porque no le han dado de comer al vampiro?"*

"Lo siento, Lucinda."

Rather than explaining why Misha hadn't been fed, the largest were ox apologized and raced toward the pigpen. He snatched a medium-sized hog by his hind leg and dragged the shrieking creature across the dirt floor.

My head jerked toward Misha. "They're feeding you pig's blood?"

Degradation hollowed Misha's stare. "Go."

"¿Quien esta aqui?" Lucinda scanned the area surrounding Misha, demanding to know who was there.

She'd sensed me and stalked to where I waited.

While she didn't know precisely where I stood, she was close enough. She glowered at me, just slightly to the left. My tigress already hated her. The growl that escaped me was meant to challenge and frighten.

It failed to have the effect I wanted. The edges of Lucinda's mouth curved into a sadistic smile. *"Te veo luego, puta,"* she said right before jabbing her finger into my sternum.

I gasped for breath, clutching my chest as a strong hand seized my lung. Tye shook me and yelled my name. It took a few more coughs before I could breathe again. His eyes fired with anger. "What the hell happened? You stopped breathing!"

The vampires around us stilled, waiting for my response, seemingly more furious than
ever. "She squeezed the air out of my lung," I answered, thinking aloud. "She told me she'd see me soon."

"Who?"

"Lucinda—a witch. She knew I was there, but she couldn't see me."

Tye swore and paced the room. "I was hoping she wouldn't be involved."

"You know her?"

"Not personally, but she's bad news. She was one of the thirteen strongest dark witches in Central and South America."

"What do you mean *was*?"

Agnes adjusted her tiny librarian glasses. "She's

one of only four who still reign. The others have been killed, captured, or gone into hiding. Her daughter—who was almost as powerful—died recently."

I continued to rub my chest. "Really? How'd she die?"

"Your sister Taran killed her."

I stopped rubbing my chest. "Oh, this can't be good."

Agnes worked on rebraiding her hair, something she often did when agitated. "Her daughter was Veronica, the witch who helped the Tribe raise Ihuaivulu."

I suddenly felt nauseated. "And you're telling me Veronica—who was strong enough to awaken a seven-headed fire-breathing demon after it had been asleep for a millennium—was still not as powerful as her mother?"

Agnes started on her other braid. "Mmm-hmm."

Hank leaned forward. "You saw the master, didn't you?"

I tried to relax my breathing. "Yes . . . he's really sick. We have to get to him fast or he may not make it."

"Who has him?" Tye asked.

"A few *weres,* but I could also scent traces of vampires." I shook my head thinking back to their torture of Misha. "Lucinda seems to be the one in charge. The wereoxen guarding Misha are scared to death of her."

Edith tugged the edges of her plaid skirt. "But they're feeding the master, aren't they?"

She wanted me to give her hope. They all did. I debated whether I should tell them, but ultimately it wasn't fair to keep information from them. "They're forcing him to drink pig's blood."

The she-vamps screamed and collapsed to their knees, clawing at their faces and wailing.

The males locked arms and shook each other violently, hollering with fury and sinking their fangs into their arms.

Okay . . . maybe honesty wasn't the best way to go.

Tye escorted me away from them and to the doorway, watching them cautiously. The only vampire who didn't completely lose it was Michael. He merely stood with his arms crossed, grimacing with disgust. "Michael, what are they doing?"

"They're mourning our master's disgrace, Celia. To be forced to drink the blood of an animal is the ultimate insult, specifically if it involves the blood from a swine."

I gaped at Edith, jabbing herself in the eyes. "Is it really that bad?"

Michael knitted his brows tight. "It would be like someone forcing you to eat feces to survive."

I tried not to gag. "Okay. I get it now." I took in the state of the other vampires. Their grief was so dramatic, it was difficult to watch. "How long will they continue to mourn?"

"Not much longer. They will take the offense and transfer it into anger, to fuel our vengeance."

Tye brought me out to the cabin and encouraged me to lie on the long velvet couch. "Let them do what they have to. In the meantime, try to rest. We have a hell of a fight ahead of us . . . especially if Lucinda knows we're coming."

We reached Guatemala in six hours. Misha's latest message jolted me awake just before we began our descent. "Change in plans. We need to land in El Salvador and double back to Guatemala."

Hank peeked over the seat in front of me. "Shit, Celia. Are you sure? We're going to lose hours if you're wrong."

"It's what Misha wants us to do." That was all I needed to say. Hank rushed to speak to the pilots.

Liz watched him disappear into the cockpit.

"Why do you think they changed the plan?"

"It doesn't matter," Tim hissed. "Wherever they are we'll find them and destroy them for shaming our master."

I thought back to the smile Lucinda gave me. She didn't fear us. If anything, she couldn't wait to get her psycho hands on us. "Agnes, do you know if El Salvador holds any significance to Lucinda?"

Agnes thought about it. "It's where she was born. All the whackos are from there."

I narrowed my eyes. "My mother was El Salvadoran."

"Oh. Sorry." Although she apologized, I had the feeling she didn't really mean it.

Tye frowned at her, but it wasn't because of the slight against my mother. "Agnes, do you know if she's one of those witches who are stronger on her home turf?"

"Technically it's not where the witch is from, but where she made the most sacrifices. That's why dark witches tend to stay in one area, rather than migrating to different regions," she replied.

I dragged my fingers through my hair and swore. "But if she was born there, and she spent her life there, it's likely that's where she's murdered most of her victims."

Everyone exchanged glances. Tye's fist knocked on the table. "Celia's right. We need to stop her before she returns to El Salvador. We don't want her stronger than she already is."

Soldiers with machine guns the length of my body served as our welcoming committee when we landed in San Salvador. Thankfully none of the imposing males were immune to the vampires' charms. After Misha's family enjoyed their breakfast, we jumped into three awaiting SUVs constructed roughly around the First World War.

The worthless shocks jostled, shook, and rattled us

down the highway. The humidity sky- rocketed the temperature to over one hundred degrees and none of the vehicles had working air conditioners. Good thing I wasn't nauseated and dehydrated from puking or anything.

Tye had handed me a bottle of water upon landing, but I managed only a few sips at a time.

"You don't look well. Do you have motion sickness?"

I caught a sign indicating our arrival in Santa Ana. "I haven't been the same since we arrived back from Chaitén. But I'll admit traveling this much isn't helping."

Edith handed me her hair tie. "Here, Celia."

Next to setting up the unicorn bedroom, that was probably the nicest thing Edith had ever done for me. "Thank you." I pulled back my mess of curls and welcomed the air against my sweat-soaked body. "That was really kind of you."

Edith smiled and fixed her gaze on my throat. "You're welcome. Now I have a full view of your neck! I love how your jugular dances against your hot skin, glistening with sweat and begging me to pierce its yummy goodness—"

"That's enough, Edith."

She frowned. "I'm trying to give you a compliment."

"No. You're not. You're talking about eating me."

"But—"

"Just turn around before I hurt you."

Edith pouted her outrageously plump lips before turning to face the window. Her long black hair blew majestically in the breeze in true photo-shoot perfection. Like all of the good Catholics she had probably always been beautiful, even before being *turned*.

I admired her exotic looks and yet not much more. Of the four naughty schoolgirls she remained the wildest and her antics were disturbing, at best. Still, she had a heart and was completely devoted to Misha. She glanced back, likely sensing me watching her and smiled with perfect teeth . . . perfect teeth that elongated when she focused back on my throat. I sighed, knowing one day I might have to kill her.

Thankfully, she turned away at my glare, allowing me to take in my mother's homeland in peace. Like in most third world countries, the poverty level was extremely high. None of the women risked walking in public with handbags. The ever-escalating gang violence and crime rate made everyone a potential victim despite their threadbare skirts and faded jeans.

Bright colors decorated the rows of cinder-block homes we passed, bars protected the windows and doors, and broken bottles ran along the edges of the high walls to keep intruders out. It was sad. These people probably didn't have much, but all they had they'd fight to protect.

Hank pulled over when he noticed a woman selling food on the street. He and Tye climbed out and approached the old lady, completely intimidating her. Beside each other they were night and day. Hank with his dark hair and fair skin, dressed in a polo and khaki shorts, and Tye with his white blond hair, T-shirt, and cut-off jeans. Their long, muscular legs, arms, and torsos, combined with their scorching level of hotness, drew a crowd who watched them with cautious awe.

Hank and Tye bought all the food the woman had. She shoved the bills Tye handed her into her shirt and dashed down the street with her cart before Hank and Tye finished piling in.

"How much did you give her?"

Tye handed me a bundle of leaves wrapped together. "Six hundred."

I tugged on the tie holding the leaves together. "That was generous of you."

Tye shrugged. "Someone like her deserves a day

off."

Or the year, given what he'd tipped her. I smiled softly. "You're not so bad, you know that?"

Tye answered with that infamous dimple. "Nice to see you're finally warming up to me."

He motioned to the food on my lap. "I take it you know what that is?"

I pulled open the leaves. "It's *yuca con chicharrón*. Yuca is a root, like a potato. The *chicharrón* is fried pork mixed with a tomato sauce. It's topped with a sort of coleslaw. My mom used to make it when we were kids. It's one of the few dishes she made that I remember well."

The starch from the yuca and its delicious flavor soothed my nausea, so much so I ate my fill. Tye handed me the last package and insisted I eat. I devoured it and finished what remained of my water. "Thank you. I feel better."

Tye placed his hand on my knee. "I could make you feel better in a lot of ways, Celia."

I inched my leg away and blinked back at him in surprise. He smiled at me sweetly—too sweetly. I turned to face the front only to spot Hank's glare in the rearview mirror. "Watch it, beast. She belongs to our master."

My jaw clenched. "I don't belong to anyone."

Hank and Edith responded by grinding their fangs. Michael remained observantly quiet, as usual, making me wonder what he really thought. My attention returned to Tye. "Believe me when I say, you don't want me."

"Celia, I could help you get over Aric. Just give me a chance." My eyes brimmed with tears just hearing his name. Tye's lips parted. "Okay . . . then again, maybe you need some time."

I crossed my arms and leaned back against the sticky leather seat. "What I need is to find Misha and leave California."

Tye furrowed his brows. "You don't plan on

marrying him?"

Why was friendship with a master vampire such a foreign concept? "No. I just want him safe."

Tye leaned against the door and examined me closely, trying to figure out the Sudoku puzzle with the curly brown hair. "You're risking your life to rescue him. If he means that much to you, why won't you marry him?"

"I've never had many friends. Those I have, I'd do anything for."

Edith slipped her hand over my other knee and beamed. "I find it so sexy that you're willing to bleed for us," she whispered. "Don't tell the other girls, but you're my best friend, Celia."

Sweet heaven, please stop me from killing her. I slapped Edith's wrist away when her fingertips skimmed up my thigh toward my happy place. "Pull over, Hank. Edith needs to switch seats with Michael."

Edith angled her chin, confused by my request. Tye and the others coughed in their attempts to hold back their laughter. Michael lost it the moment he sat next to me. The big guy with the deep voice giggled like a Munchkin from *The Wizard of Oz.*

Thirty miles remained to the border of Guatemala when dread and fear marched from my throat into the pit of my stomach. "They're in El Salvador."

"Oh, hell," Tye said. "Where exactly?"

Michael handed me the map. I stared at the damn thing and searched the surrounding villages. "Misha thinks somewhere outside of Ahuachapán, but he's not sure."

Hank punched the dash. "Screw it. We'll just hit its center and ask around. How far away are we?"

Tye examined the map, our navigation apps were useless here. "Twenty miles, southwest. Take a left at the next highway."

Michael updated the others via text. Hank floored it, leading the other two vehicles. Even at the speed we raced, it took us almost forty minutes to reach Ahuachapán. Potholes battered the road and we got lost twice. When we finally reached the marketplace, the sun had begun to set.

The vamps parked in an alley reeking of urine and littered with waste, but our haste and need to go unnoticed didn't leave us many options. We scrambled out. There were fifteen of us. We divided into five groups of three. Tye was with me, and yippee-skippy, so was Edith. Both tried to take my hand. Both were denied.

I walked ahead of them, hurrying through the marketplace as shop owners closed down. An elderly woman struggled to secure the rusted lock protecting her stall. Pieces of plastic bags tied her long graying hair and the braids of her little granddaughter. The little girl pointed when she saw us coming and whispered to her grandmother in Spanish. "Look at the pretty Americans."

I slowed my steps and spoke softly to the woman in Spanish. "Good evening, ma'am."

Her face carried the wrinkles of a woman who'd lived a harsh life yet she smiled kindly through her missing teeth. "Hello. Would you like to buy some platanos?"

I removed the hair tie Edith had given me and combed through the little girl's hair with my fingers. "No, thank you. We're trying to find someone. It's important, her name is Lucinda."

The woman shook her head frantically and pulled her granddaughter away just as I finished fastening the hair tie. "No. No, no, no. I can't help you."

I pleaded with her with my palms out. "Please, she has my friend."

Her eyes, deeply veiled with cataracts, welled with tears. "If the witch has him, your friend is already dead."

Edith didn't understand a lick of Spanish, but she read the woman's resistance in her cowering stance. "Would you like me to make her talk?" Her tone sounded innocent except there was nothing innocent about her intentions.

I blocked her path. "Let her be. She's already frightened enough."

We abandoned the terrified woman and bolted out of the marketplace and into the street. The sun vanished from the sky. The last few stragglers hurried to their destinations as night descended like a thick cloak. The only signs of life rang from a run-down bar on the corner. Tye took a sniff just as the smell of *were* and vampire reached my nose. "How about a drink?"

Edith sashayed through the open doorway like she owned the place and the party couldn't possibly start without her. With her tiny plaid skirt and neck-breaking boots, she'd have stood out anywhere. It didn't take long for the bar patrons to take interest. A *were* rose from his stool and slinked his way to her. At five feet ten inches, she towered over him. He grabbed her ass. Edith grinned back with her fangs and bit his nose right off his face. The *were* collapsed on the floor with his hand over the opening, screaming and writhing. Edith spat out a chunk of skin and wiped her mouth with the back of her hand. She waved at the onlookers, who—funny enough— didn't find her so appealing anymore.

The level of violence apparently wasn't anything new. Everyone returned to their beers and conversation as Vicente Fernández blasted his sorrowful tune on the beat-up jukebox.

Humans sauntered through the mounting crowd of preternaturals, offering their bodies in exchange for a few bills. Most were teens, provocatively dressed and trying in vain to shield their bare flesh with their hands. I could smell their shame . . . and fear. Some were fondled for show before ultimately being shoved away. It was all I could do not to kill every male there.

One of the youngest prostitutes approached Tye. She lifted her chin and smiled to express confidence, but the indignity in her childlike face when she rubbed her body against his was as obvious as his disgust. He withdrew from her and pulled me close. "Ask her if she wants to make money."

I stumbled over my words when a familiar scent cut through the mob. I whirled around, recognizing the lingering aroma of vampire I'd caught during my meet-and-greet with Lucinda. Tye and Edith shadowed me as I pushed my way to a vamp tucked in a corner with a young girl. The vamp teased her jugular with his tongue. Her right eye was bruised shut and she bled from the fresh scratches on her shoulders. She cringed, begging him to stop when he ruthlessly squeezed her breasts. I hauled him away from her and ripped off his shirt.

"Hey, baby," he said in Spanish. His smile faded when I took a whiff of the cloth and scented the pale aroma of my favorite vampire.

My claws dug into his throat. "He's been with Misha."

My new friend must have held a leadership role. The patrons abandoned their booze and idle chatter and swarmed us. The young girls sprinted out screaming, sensing the escalating thirst for blood. I clenched the vamp's throat tighter and shouted over their shrieks. "Get out of our way and no one will get hurt!"

They stalked forward, vicious hisses competing with lustful snarls. I didn't like the odds and neither did Tye. "Can you *shift* us out?" he muttered.

"No. I'm blind when I *shift* and don't know what's beneath us."

Edith perceived our dire situation as similar to finding a truckload of stranded virgins.

She clapped excitedly. "I get to eat now, right?"

Tye roared, and everyone attacked. Chairs and beer bottles soared at my head. The moment I ducked, the vamp spun out of my grasp and jetted from the bar.

A were mule tackled me when I tried to chase after him. Michael wrenched the mule off before my fists could connect with his face. The vampires had heard Tye's *call*. They flooded the bar, kicking ass and chowing down. I barreled my way through the mass of sweat-soaked bodies and out the door, stopping the minute I reached the cobblestone street. I closed my eyes. In the far distance, my ears tracked the quick feet of the fleeing vampire. I shot toward the sound. Vamps were outrageously fast. I was faster. Within a few minutes, I'd picked up his scent and was almost upon him.

The footsteps suddenly stopped and he disappeared. I scanned the neighborhood he'd led me to. Pathways and sidewalks separated the houses instead of streets and branched into different developments. I'd wandered into a maze, sniffing out my rat. *Where are you?*

A scream from a nearby home alerted me to his presence. "Shut up," he mumbled in Spanish.

I snuck up the concrete steps to a single-story home and peeked through a window. A terrified woman clutched a child in her lap. Five more children gathered around her, the oldest one no more than ten.

A petite little girl cried against her mother's shoulder. "I'm sorry I let him in, Mami."

The woman pulled her around to shield her from the vamp. "Please don't hurt my children," she begged. "I'll do anything."

"You speak again and I'll cut their throats," he hissed.

The woman covered her mouth, her eyes wide with terror. I took a breath to relax. If I didn't calm myself, I'd kill him for threatening the family. I needed him alive— well, at least long enough to find Misha.

The house rested on a small hill. It seemed solid enough so I *shifted* underground and across. My guess to where the vampire stood was slightly off. Instead of surfacing behind him like I'd planned, I popped up in front of him. I scared the crap out of everyone there, including the vamp.

He fell back into a chair. When he realized it was just tiny ol' me he laughed. "I'm going to kill you, little bitch," he told me in Spanish. "But first we're going to have some fun." He lunged at me at full vampire speed. I used his momentum to flip him over and slam him to the floor. He kipped up. I kicked him in the face and knocked him back to the floor with a second shot to his knees.

Tye leapt through the door and pinned the vamp against the wall with his forearm. "Sorry I'm late, dovie. Is there something you'd like to ask him?"

"Where's Misha?" I yelled at him in Spanish. "Who?"

"The vampire Lucinda holds."

The family gasped behind me. *"Go to hell,"* the vamp said, then spat in Tye's face. Tye forced his fist into the vamp's mouth, tore out his jaw, and tossed it over his shoulder.

The poor woman fainted, dropping to the floor with a loud thump. One of the older girls caught the baby before their mother rolled on top of her. I hurried to them, speaking softly. "Don't worry. I won't let anything happen to you," I assured them. I lifted their mother carefully in my arms. They followed me into a small bedroom, holding hands and watching me as I lay her across the bed. "Stay here with your mami," I told them.

The girls listened. The oldest, a little boy, followed me out. "You may not want to see this," I warned.

He jutted his chin. "I'm not afraid."

I smiled. I couldn't help it. He reminded me so much of Taran. I picked the vamp's nasty jaw off the floor and passed it to Tye. "He can't tell us anything if he can't speak."

"Good point." He rammed it back in the vampire's

face. The jaw cracked and popped into place. As the muscles knitted together the little boy charged forward and staked him in the heart with a broken wooden spoon.

Tye and I gaped at him in shock. The kid sprinted toward the bathroom, but he never made it. He hurled all over the kitchen floor. I guessed he hadn't realized how much blood would squirt before the vamp turned into ash.

Tye swore and paced the room. We'd lost our only lead. I knelt near the kid, trying to maintain my composure. "Are you all right?"

He took a few deep breaths, obviously working hard not to vomit again. "I will be once I take you to Lucinda."

Chapter Twenty-two

My lips parted. "You know where Lucinda is?"

He nodded and reached for an old rag to clean the floor. "You're strong," he said.

"Yes."

He stopped wiping. "Will you be strong enough to kill the witch if I take you to her?"

I thought about how she'd almost suffocated me with just one touch. "I don't know."

He threw the rag into a bucket. "But will you try? Or how about your friend?" He motioned to Tye. "Could he kill her?" He did a double take. "What is he doing?"

Tye took the ashes of the dead vamp and smeared them across the threshold. "He's warning all supernatural predators that if they try to harm those who reside here, they'll meet the same fate. But forget that, you're safe. Tell me why you want Lucinda dead."

"The witch wanted my baby sister for a sacrifice. She sent her devils to take her. She killed Papi for trying to protect her."

The other children poked their heads out of the bedroom door. The baby watched me with huge brown eyes. "Your papi sacrificed himself so she would live," I said quietly.

The little boy shook his head. "No. Mami was pregnant at the time. That's my new baby sister. Lucinda got her intended sacrifice after she killed Papi." He averted his gaze and rose to wash his hands.

The little boy who was trying to be a man had lost both his father and infant sister. I tried my best to keep my voice soft. "What's your name?"

"Armando."

"I'm Celia."

His small round face pleaded to me. "Promise me you'll kill the witch, Celia."

"I promise I'll do all I can to stop her."

Tye came to stand by me. "What did he say about Lucinda?"

We had a little talk with Armando after I explained. He insisted Lucinda's home was in an obscure location and we wouldn't be able to find it unless he led us there. He said his sister Conchi could look after his younger siblings, as she often did when their mother worked. I didn't want the vamps to influence him. Little minds were too fragile to mess with. So Tye left to retrieve the others when it became clear we couldn't ditch Armando.

"Why can't we go with him now?" Armando asked me.

"We're sneaking you out of the house. I don't want your neighbors to know you helped us in case things don't go our way."

Armando jutted his chin again. "I'm not afraid to die."

I crouched down to face him. "You should be, Armando. I know I am." He frowned.

"But you're strong."

"That doesn't mean I don't get scared."

I stepped out into the dirt garden where a giant mango tree expanded its thick branches over Armando's house. I'd only been gone a day and yet I missed my family like I'd been gone a year. My first thought was to phone my sisters, but I didn't want to risk a fight. So instead, I called Danny. The phone rang only once. He'd been waiting for my call. His voice shook and I could sense his anxiety with each word. "They know. I told them."

A cold wash of sweat dripped down my back. "What?" I asked, although the fear pulsing through my veins told me I knew exactly what he meant.

"Aric, the Elders, your sisters—*everyone*. They all know Anara hurt you, Celia."

My back fell against the trunk of the tree. I jerked away from it when the thick bark scratched my back. "Oh my God, Danny. You don't realize what you've done! Everyone I love is in danger—"

"Celia, Anara must be stopped. He can't get away with what he's done to you."

My head pounded. "How did you even manage this?"

"Heidi told me about a luncheon celebrating Anara's new position. She let me into the Den . . . and I sort of interrupted the party by announcing he's the one who attacked you."

I was shaking so violently I could barely speak. "What . . . happened?"

"At first there was a deafening silence, as you might expect." He swallowed hard. "And then Anara charged."

I couldn't believe what I was hearing. "How are you still alive?"

"Aric and Martin intercepted him. Don't you see, Celia? Anara couldn't use his *were* power there, there were too many witnesses—including your sisters. And those in attendance— Aric, Makawee, Martin—they could stop him." He paused. "The *weres* could scent I was telling the truth, just like they knew he was lying when he denied it."

I resumed my pacing. "What happened after that?"

"Aric went ballistic and attacked, but . . ."

"Oh, God—did he kill Aric?"

"No! No, of course not. There was a large explosion and Anara disappeared. Makawee and Martin issued *were* protections for all of us and now Anara is wanted by the entire North American Were Council. The whole situation is worse than we thought. The Elders are distressed and suspect he's involved in more than just the plot against you."

"Danny, he's still an Elder, he still has power. He'll come after us."

"He can't. Not anymore. Martin and Makawee conducted a sacred ceremony and stripped him of his Elder power. And from what Gemini says, any *were* who finds him has been ordered to kill him on sight."

Danny expected his news to grant me the relief I'd long sought. And yet as much as I wanted to believe Anara was weakened and wouldn't waste his time on me, I knew better. "What does Aric think . . . about everything?"

"No one knows. He took off soon after Anara disappeared." Danny's voice grew soft. "He's gone to find you, Celia, to bring you home and keep you safe."

My ears heard what Danny said, but my heart warned against believing him. "But Aric hates me."

"No, honey. He loves you."

I choked back a sob and wiped my tears with the bottom of my tank top. "Are the others with him?"

"No. Makawee asked the Warriors to stay and protect your sisters."

"But they're Aric's guards. How can they leave him by himself?"

"Celia, remember how angry Aric was when he found out I helped you break your bond?"

I shuddered at the thought. "Yes."

Danny paused. "It doesn't compare to what he's like now. He doesn't know Anara used the power of the

Pack against you. All he knows is that Anara has been the one hurting you. He's blind with rage. Martin thinks you're the only one capable of settling him—once he knows you're safe, I mean."

I pictured Aric on a crowded airplane in his temperamental state. It wasn't a pretty picture. "How is he traveling?"

"An old friend of his is flying him down on a private plane."

"Okay." I said it, although I didn't know why. Everything was far from "okay." I shook all thoughts of Aric away. He distracted me too easily and there was more I needed to know. "Does anyone know about our baby?"

"No one—and the Warriors don't know they were used as vessels against you. I did tell Martin and Makawee since it was important. Both were furious. Makawee especially felt betrayed."

My head hammered so hard my eyes hurt. Anara would come for me and wouldn't stop until I was dead. I was sure of it.

Danny continued, completely oblivious to my terror. "The Warriors couldn't understand why you didn't come to them. I explained Anara had threatened to kill your sisters if you told anyone. Liam, who's not even mated to Emme, freaked out. Gemini and Koda were incensed, only Taran and Shayna could calm them. That's why I couldn't bring myself to tell them what they'd done."

"Where is everyone now?"

"I'm in Aric's old quarters. They've moved Bren here, too. Since Anara was stripped of his power, Bren has started to heal."

"Are you serious?"

"Yes, but he still has a way to go. Makawee says his body is literally rebuilding his brain and pushing out the magic Anara imprisoned him with. Emme's tried to help, except Anara's residual power blocked her efforts."

My voice continued to tremble. "He's going to be okay?"

"Both Elders believe so. They credit you with saving his life; we all do."

Someone knocked in the background. I held my breath, half expecting Anara to arrive and kill him. I slumped to the ground when I heard my sisters' voices. "Celia's on the phone. It's okay, it's okay. She's safe."

My God, I clearly heard them sobbing. Taran hurried to the line. "Why didn't you tell us that son of a bitch was hurting you? We could have stopped him together!"

"He would have killed you if I had."

"Do you hate me, dude?" Shayna whimpered.

I buried my face in my hand. "Of course not. I could never hate you."

Shayna could barely speak with how hard she wept. "But I've been awful to you. I even hit you! I'm so sorry, Ceel."

"It's okay, Shayna. Calm down, honey." I was telling her to calm down, meanwhile I was battling my own fit of hysterics. They were safe. I'd succeeded in keeping everyone safe, and now because of Danny they all knew the truth.

Emme cried into the phone. "Please come home. We don't want you in any more danger."

I rose from the ground and swatted the dirt off my shorts. "Not until I find Misha."

"Damnit, Celia!" Taran snapped. "Get your ass back here now!"

Shayna sniffed. "The Elders have promised to protect you. After what Anara's done, they feel it's the least they can do."

I steadied myself. "It's not just about me being safe. Misha protected me when no one else could. I have to help him now if I can."

For a few moments, all I heard was their sniffling. Finally, Taran pulled it together enough for all of them. "If anything happens to you, I'll kill you myself."

I smiled into the phone. "I love you, too." I disconnected. The scent of the Serengeti and sensual musk made me turn toward the house. Tye stood with his arms crossed, a deep-set scowl darkening his electric blue eyes. Armando appeared confused and a little frightened by the last few tears to trickle down my cheeks. You'd think with a house full of women he'd be used to hysterical females.

"Is there something you'd like to tell me?" Tye asked.

I wiped my face. "We'll talk in the car. It's time to get Misha back."

I *shifted* Armando and Tye through several backyards until we reached the vampires. Michael snatched Armando quickly while the others kept watch. Hank shut the car door. "Don't worry, Celia. No one saw him."

Armando directed us out and away from the town, into a forest laden mostly with dead trees and wringing vines. "The witch's presence has choked our land," he said quietly.

And hurt those you love.

I told the others about Anara. The vampires became unusually quiet. They seemed focused on finding their master. That is, except for Edith. Her eyes locked on Armando's increasingly pulsating jugular. Vampires didn't typically snack on children, because they provided only nourishment. Adults, however, afforded an orgasmic experience during a feed. They'd been ordered not to bite him, but that didn't mean I'd trust them to babysit.

Tye drummed on the armrest. "If Anara's smart he'll take his own life. It'll be more merciful than what we'll do to him." His eyes skimmed the length of my body.

"How the hell did you survive all this shit? Liam went into detail about how badly you were hurt the day he found you."

I didn't like remembering and tried to shrug off his comment. "What other choice did I have?"

Tye curled his arm around me and played with my hair. When I tried to push his hand away, he instantly found a spot behind my ear that made me purr. My cheeks flushed from my unintentional reaction. He smirked, seemingly pleased with himself. "You're going to make a hell of a wife, Celia. Damn shame you won't be mine."

My blush deepened. "I'm glad you finally realize that I'm not the one for you."

Tye touched my chin gently and his smile vanished. "I never said that. What I meant was, it's clear where your heart is, and it's not with me."

I passed my hand over my belly. *No. It's not.*

Armando pointed to an opening among the dying palm trees. "Turn here." Hank doubled back and maneuvered the SUV through the narrow space. We followed the trail for a few minutes until it widened into a field of an old plantain farm. The lingering presence of pestilent magic curdled around us. Everyone tensed briefly then rushed to unbuckle their seat belts and leap out.

"Is this Lucinda's place?" I asked Armando quickly.

"No. Her home is in Izalco, but her devils stay here." He glanced at the soiled ground staining my white canvas sneakers red. "She's poisoned the earth with the blood of innocents."

I backed away from the spongy surface only to splatter my shoes more. The essence of her kills was everywhere. *Jesus. How powerful is she?*

Armando marched forward with more nerve than I'd expected. "There's a path behind the barn that leads up the mountain and to an ancient Mayan structure. If your friend is here, that's where you'll find him."

I gripped Armando's arm while Hank translated his words. "Thank you for your help. You've been really brave, but it's time for you to return to your family." I needed to ensure his safety, but wasn't sure which vamp to send back with him. With the exception of possibly Agnes, the schoolgirls were out of the question. But then I remembered the dream I had where she'd roasted those sausages and thought better of it. I picked Michael, feeling I could trust him to keep him safe. Armando squirmed in my grasp when Michael approached.

Michael covered Armando's mouth and raced with him to the last car. "I'll return soon."

Tye took the lead. "Watch out for booby traps, magical or otherwise. And remember, no one gets left behind."

Tim rushed to block his path. "We're not of your kind, lion. We remain our master's humble servants. Our priority is to get him to safety even if it means our destruction."

Tye growled. "*We're* not his goddamn servants. I swear if you double-cross us Lucinda will be the least of your worries."

The vamps weren't the kind of species who took threats well. They hissed. I hissed back. "Stop it. All of you. We've come to save Misha. Let's not waste time fighting."

We divided in half and cut through the woods on either side of the path. My tigress and Tye's lion gifted us with the silent stealth of predators. The girls slithered among the decaying trees in high heels. I couldn't fathom why the hell they hadn't brought camouflage clothes, sneakers, shorts—*anything* but the same ridiculous getups they wore every day. They knew we'd be trekking through the freaking jungle. Still, stilettos or not, they barely made a sound as we scaled the mountain. Adrenaline coursed through my veins, and every cell of my being poised on high alert. I stopped and smiled when we'd climbed more than halfway.

"What is it?" Hank asked.

"It's Misha. He knows we're here." Our presence had renewed his energy, but then my inner beast whispered a warning. "Something's wrong."

"What do you mean?"

"We haven't hit any traps. Doesn't that seem strange to you?"

Hank shrugged. "Lucinda is arrogant. She might not have used them, thinking she could take on any threat." The other group opposite us continued ahead in their haste to reach Misha. A high-pitched squeal followed two short-lived screams. Sharpened stakes launched from the ground and impaled the vamps. Hank gritted his fangs. "*Shit.* Come on, they know we're here!"

We sprinted forward as sharp whistling sounds sliced through the air. A vamp in front of us pointed ahead. "Arrows!" None of us had human eyes. We saw the damn arrows tearing through the night like a blizzard of mini-spears. The yelling vamp splattered my legs with his blood as I dove behind a tree. Tye landed in a heap behind a boulder next to me, ash caked on his chest. I kept my back against the bark and scanned the area. More blood splashed around me, the vampires continued to charge despite the danger.

Hank ducked behind a tree across from mine and yanked an arrow out of his thigh. "We lost Jonas and Nadum. We need to get in now!"

I didn't respond. I sensed Misha's restlessness. He was close to losing it.

A few hundred feet stood between us and the fortress. A huge stone wall constituted what remained of the original Mayan ruin. The rest was a makeshift stronghold composed of old trees. There was only one door that I could see—narrow and built to prevent more than one being from entering at a time. It was perfect for them, that way they could slaughter us individually. "I can *shift* three of us in and return for more, but we need to get closer. If enough of you create a distraction, the others will be able to jump the wall."

The surviving vamps quickly relayed my plan. Everyone crouched low and waited for my command. "Now!" I let Tye and Hank race ahead of me. When only a few feet remained to the wall, I tackled them and *shifted* us underground. Luck was on my side for once. We surfaced behind a group of *weres* passing arrows to the archers on the landing. They never knew what hit them. In the time Tye and I tore the heads off two, Hank mutilated three on his own. His insatiable appetite to avenge amplified his strength and speed.

"Get the others," Tye urged.

I *shifted* only one more set of vamps. They, along with Hank, were enough to distract Lucinda's charge so the others could rocket over the wall and attack. The schoolgirls used their stilettos to stake anything with a heart and whipped and choked their enemies with their long, thick necklaces. I hadn't understood why they'd dressed that way, but leave it to the good Catholics to use their accessories as lethal weapons. If Misha didn't know we were here before, he certainly did now. Their banshee-like shrieking became the official battle cry. But even through their wretched screams, one voice rose above them all.

"CELIA!"

The roar was that of a monstrous and extremely hungry Misha. It scared the unholy hell out of me and froze me and the vampire I fought into a stupefied state. I recovered first and severed his head with my claws. Tim, saturated with sweat, blood, and ash, urged me forward. "Go to him. Our master beckons you."

No shit.

Tye clasped my wrist when I failed to move and

thundered forth, stopping only to drag an unconscious *were* along with us. "Come on, this is what we came for!"

We jogged toward the opening of a cave where we'd heard Misha call. Tye released me and lifted a torch from the cavern wall. "I can see in the dark without *changing*," I reminded him.

"Misha is out of his mind, Celia. I'm bringing this along in case we have to set him on fire."

If Tye was trying to somehow reassure me, it didn't work. I didn't want to set Misha on fire. That said, I also didn't want to be eaten. "Master vampires are immune to fire," I managed.

"Not when they've feasted on animal blood to survive," Tye muttered.

The more we advanced, the louder Misha's voracious growls clamored. At every corner we rounded, I expected to find Misha. But it wasn't until I scented the decaying corpses of pigs that I knew we were almost upon him.

We found him at the cave's end. I gasped when I saw him. Misha no longer resembled the vampire I knew. He'd grown at least six inches and his fangs had morphed to those of a snake. His bright green and bloodthirsty stare trained on me, piercing through the greasy knots of hair falling around his face. He was caged and chained by his neck, but despite his confines, he seemed ready to break free. My tigress chuffed within me, insisting we run. My stupid human side took two steps closer.

Tye yanked me back at the same moment Misha lunged for me.

"Celia." Misha licked his lips greedily.

"Here, Misha, are you hungry?" Tye grabbed the *were* and threw him toward the cage. The *were's* lifeless body slumped against the bars.

"Tye, Misha can't reach him—"

In one pull, Misha wrenched the *were*—or what was

225

left of him—into the cage with him. I'd always hated watching a vamp feed. This was way worse. I whipped around and covered my ears yet couldn't muffle the slobbering, munching, and slurping as Misha feasted. Tye spun around. It was too much for him, too. We faced the wall. My growing nausea receded when Misha finished, except then Maria and Edith appeared with the next few courses. They hadn't bothered knocking their prey unconscious, choosing instead to sever their arms so they wouldn't be as much trouble.

The blood dripping from the *weres'* empty sockets sent Misha into a salivating frenzy. Tye tucked his arm beneath mine and led me out, but not before I heard Edith's voice echo behind us. "Open wide, Master. Here comes the choo-choo train."

The dreadful howls from the *weres* made us pick up our pace. When we reached the opening of the cave, Michael and the rest of the vampires waited amid clumps of ash and mounds of dead bodies. We'd beaten the enemy to a nasty pulp and still they remained eager to continue their rampage. Tye straightened to his full height. "Celia and I are leaving," he told them.

Hank snarled. "You can leave if you want, but she stays. Our master needs her."

I cut off Tye's growl with a squeeze to his arm. "Let's all leave. I don't want to be around when Lu—"

Tye clasped his hand over my mouth. "Don't speak a witch's name aloud in her domain, unless you wish to summon her."

I nodded. That wasn't a lesson I needed to learn the hard way.

Tye released me as the vampires advanced, their sharp gazes locked on Tye in challenge.

"Stand down." They ignored my command. My hackles rose. Now that they had Misha, it was pretty damn obvious I was no longer in charge.

CECY ROBSON

The door to the fortress blasted off its hinges. My heart stopped when I saw Aric storm in, leading one of the were oxen by a chain of gold. The *were* was gagged and his eyes wild in fear of Aric. I couldn't blame him. Aric's facial features remained immobile yet the fury permeating his aura promised to butcher anyone in his path. *"Where's Celia?"*

Aric released the *were* when he caught sight of me and, from one breath to the next, stood before me. Thick and wretched humidity coated my skin with perspiration in defiance of the dark night sky. And yet the heat that spread between us was as gentle and welcoming as a warm bath. I inhaled his aroma just once before he snatched me into a tight embrace. My body quivered from the emotion behind his hold and my head fell against his broad chest. All I wanted to do was beg him to make the last few weeks disappear.

Aric rubbed his face against my hair and kissed my crown so softly I barely felt it. His voice held a strange mixture of ire and gentleness, like the power of thunder with the softness of a mist. "Why didn't you tell me Anara had hurt you?"

I clung to his neck and sobbed. Throughout my entire time away from him, I'd tried to be so tough, but as usual he unleashed my vulnerability like a caged beast. The strain and burden I'd carried for so long spilled out of me like a cascade of falling timbers. Within seconds, his sweat-soaked shirt became newly drenched with my tears.

Aric pulled me closer while I rubbed my cheek against the side of his face. His skin felt like hard, crumpled paper, but his tenderness, warmth, and scent tightened my embrace. I'd missed my love so much and now he was finally here.

"Aric, now is not the time," Tye said tightly. "We have to get Celia out of here."

The vampires had circled us in the time it had taken

Aric to reach me. Aric and Tye positioned themselves in front of and behind me, growling.

Maria's claws protruded. "You're not taking her anywhere. Our master needs her!"

"Do you think I give a shit what your goddamn master needs?" Aric shouted. "I came for Celia and there's no way in hell any of you are going to stop me!"

I wiped off my face with my hands and stepped out from between Tye and Aric. "Everyone, calm down. Liz, go check on Misha and see how he's doing. If he's well enough we can all leave together."

Liz didn't like me telling her what to do. *"Fine."* She hoisted the were ox by his torn collar and dragged him into the cave. He bucked and tried screaming, but Aric's gag held.

"I don't like this," Aric muttered to me. He and Tye watched the vamps, their stances affirming their inner beasts would soon emerge.

I linked my arm around his. "It's all right, love. They're not going to hurt me." It seemed like such an absurd thing to say, given the way the vampires lurked, ready to pounce, but I believed they wouldn't attack me.

The oxen must have served as dessert because moments later Misha exited the cave with the good Catholics nuzzling against him. The tranquilizer guns that had been used to sedate Misha dangled at their sides. Misha sported pants, leftover from one of his appetizers. His brutish size had diminished and he seemed a hell of a lot better, but his irises continued to flicker with a touch of insanity.

Misha bounded to me, completely ignoring Aric's and Tye's menacing snarls. When I moved closer to him, Aric hauled me back into his arms. I touched his face and, notwithstanding my nervousness, tried to speak calmly. "It's okay, Aric. Please don't be afraid." Aric tightened his grip. He'd seen straight through me and knew I was scared.

I gently nudged him away. Aric was a lot stronger than me. If he didn't want to let me go, I couldn't have made him. All the same, he released me. He didn't want me anywhere near Misha, but I had to say a peaceful goodbye to avoid any further carnage.

Misha took my hands. "You came for me."

I smiled although I remained very much afraid of him, and just wanted to leave with Aric. "I told you I would, but now it's time for me to go."

Misha's smile faded and his eyes flashed green. "No. You cannot leave me."

Aric let out a sadistic growl and rammed his face into Misha's. Misha gave Aric an inhuman stare, but refused to relinquish his hold. Misha still needed to eat, but Aric was the wrong wolf to take a bite of. The increasing hisses from the vampires and Tye's own vicious growls made my words come out panicked rather than reasonable. "Please let me go, Misha. You're safe now, we all are."

But I was very wrong.

From a back entrance a *were* towing a large crate of supplies strolled into the compound. His pace slowed as he took in the devastation around him. Tye and two vampires charged him, but they were too late. *"Lucinda!"* he screamed before Tye severed his head.

Chapter Twenty-three

The ground shook as a furious scream blasted from all directions. We searched frantically, trying to place the source of the screeching until the fortress exploded around us. Aric shoved me to the ground and shielded me with his body. His entire form rattled against mine as falling debris pummeled his back.

Then everything stopped. I lifted my head. Pieces of the ruin and chunks of wood littered the area and a cloud of thick dust swirled in the still air. Aric leapt to his feet. I pushed up my hands, still shaken by the sudden eruption of chaos when a skeleton's hand broke through the ground and grabbed me by the throat. I broke off its fingers while Aric yanked the rest from the dirt and crumbled the bones to powder. "*Shit*. She's raising the dead—stay close to me."

I didn't really pay attention to the "stay close to me" part, I was still stuck on the "she's raising the dead." Dozens of skeletons ripped through the earth in all directions, bombarding our small unit with flinging arms and furious jaws that could still bite. But the skeletal remains of the Mayans weren't the only things that frightened me. Lucinda had materialized—and damnit all, she was *pissed*. She screamed incantations and swore in

Spanish, only to halt the moment she spotted me. A black film spread over her eyes and her mouth hollowed into a dark pit. *"Te mato, puta,"* she told me.

Great. One more evil darling who wanted to kill me.

Her jaw unhinged from her face to tap against her chest. She retched, spewing a colossal serpent that slithered with preternatural speed in my direction. Hank leapt in front of it, baring fangs and slashing at it with his claws. A noble effort; too bad it had little effect. The snake punched holes into Hank's body like large speeding bullets. No one could help him. We were all busy busting up the skeletons that continued to erupt through the ground. It wasn't easy. If we failed to pulverize the bones to dust, they'd reassemble, seeming more determined to take us down.

Hank stumbled back, crashing near my feet and resembling a bloody Connect Four board with legs. The barrage of swears that accompanied his wobbly rise assured me he'd live if fed. The next vampire, named Jackie, wasn't so lucky. The snake shot straight through her sternum and into her heart. Bloody ash rained upon Aric and me as we fought our way through the destruction and down the mountain. Misha and his family followed, all the while fighting off Lucinda's hexes.

I'd just caught sight of the barn when two hands shot from the ground and gripped my ankles. I fell hard. Dead limbs hooked on to my legs. Decaying fingers raked my body and tugged on my clothes and hair. The smell of rot enveloped me, adding to my terror and making me scream. My fright alerted the snake to my presence. It fired toward me. But before it could strike, Aric attacked.

Tye broke me free from the sea of appendages as Aric tore into the snake in his wolf form. I scrambled to my feet, panting from fear and exhaustion. The only vamp still in one piece was Misha. I fought my way to help Aric only for someone to reward me with a slap to the face—or so I thought. Edith's hand had flown through the air. Unfortunately, Edith was no longer attached. Lucinda's magic had severed it along with most of her arm.

Lucinda cackled through her gaping black mouth and, being the wicked witch from El Salvador she was, formed a tornado around herself. Because flying hexes and an army of fleshless dead aboriginals clearly weren't enough. She whirled toward us, sending Tye slamming into a tree. I bolted away from the pulling force of her vortex and into the forest of dead trees, digging my claws into a thick palm to keep the blustering whirlwind from jerking me back. My efforts were worthless. She ripped me away like Velcro and sent me spinning toward her.

A knife flashed in the dense cluster of debris churning around her. I flipped my body, landing at her feet and away from the blade. Lucinda shrieked as my claws punctured through my sneakers and jutted into her thighs.

She dove at me, clutching her knife. I barely caught her wrist before she stabbed me. The blade arced an inch away from my right eye. It should have been impossible for her strength to match mine. She must have invoked additional power— that grew with every breath she took.

Aric shouted through the howling wind, urging me to fight and yelling that he was coming. He never made it to me. The funnel encircling us launched him into the old barn. I heard him yelp as it collapsed on top of him.

I tried to *change,* but my ability was blocked within the eye of the tornado. Lucinda and I thrashed and rolled over the remains of her Mayan warriors. She must have grown up fighting in the streets, but hell, so had I. And I'd be damned if I'd let her beat me. I twisted her wrist and head-butted her in the face, catching the hilt of her knife and forcing it into her left eye. Her screams were low and evil, calling forth more power and making me want to kill her that much faster.

Lucinda's injured eye squirted a tarlike fluid that

stank of venom. I bored the knife deeper into her skull. Although I hurt her, she kept waving the massive blade dangerously close to my face. I narrowly missed getting gouged in the cheek when I flipped her onto her back. That's when I used my 110 pounds to hold her down and pummel her with my knees. We both hollered, Lucinda from pain and me with ferocity.

"Matare tu bebe, puta!"

I don't how the crazy witch knew I was pregnant, but for her to threaten to kill my baby gave me one last burst of strength. I rammed her with an elbow, flipped the knife, and drove it deep into her chest.

A loud blast deafened me before an eerie silence crept across the land. My body dripped with sweat and I could barely catch my breath. Below me, Lucinda lay perfectly still, her hands clenching the long white handle of the knife.

The blade creeped me out. It had been fashioned from a large bone, with images of skulls etched into the hilt. Old, evil magic seeped from it, so thick I could taste it. I scrambled away, disgusted by all the malice and suffering it had caused.

The black film veiling Lucinda's eyes faded in time with the torrential winds. Her head lolled in my direction and she stared at me with unblinking eyes. Dark blood pooled in her mouth, leaking past her lips and settling into the deep wrinkles of her face.

Everyone watched me as they slowly advanced. Liz casually brushed off the skeleton still clinging to her shoulders. It landed like broken glass against the muddy ground. I stood on weak legs and stumbled toward Aric's outstretched hands. "Come on, sweetness," he whispered. "I'm taking you home."

He gathered me tightly in his arms. I looked up to smile at him, only to catch his eyes sparking with fear. Aric spun me in a rapid blur, once more shielding me with his body. A bolt of lightning struck his back as we fell, followed by another that made his body shudder.

Aric slumped above me. From where I lay, I saw Lucinda. She sat with the knife still embedded in her sternum and smiled, before evaporating in a cloud of smoke. Tye wrenched Aric off me and hurled him in the direction of the demolished barn. Misha fastened his arms around my waist and hauled me away.

"No. Stop. What are you doing? Aric needs me!"

Tye rushed us, but instead of breaking Misha's hold, he grabbed my legs and helped drag me toward the awaiting SUVs. I kicked and fought them, confused by their actions and ready to *shift* them underground when Aric lifted his head. My body sagged with relief when he rose to his knees. But my joy was short-lived.

He *changed* into a wolf and locked his gaze on mine. Except his eyes weren't the soft brown of my love. They flashed bright green—the eyes of a cursed wolf.

Chapter Twenty-four

"No!"

Aric thundered toward us, tackling Tye. The vampires hit him with a storm of darts and still he secured a chunk of Tye's throat. Michael kicked him off. Aric landed about thirty feet away and staggered to his feet, rearing to attack. His massive paws pounded the earth until his powerful form buckled and surrendered to the sedatives.

Tye wheezed and thrashed in pain as he covered the enormous hole in his neck. Blood squirted from his carotid artery like a geyser, beguiling the thirst of the injured vampires. They gathered around him, breathing heavily and gazing at him with primal hunger. I couldn't move to help him. Terror left me paralyzed where I stood.

"Kill the wolf," Misha ordered. He clasped my arm and hauled me away. I didn't fight him. It was only when he tried to lift me into the SUV that I gathered my senses.

My voice shook hysterically. "You can't kill him, Misha."

"He is cursed with moon sickness. It must be done."

"No," I sobbed.

"Celia—"

I clutched his arms with all my strength. "I'm

pregnant." He stared back at me, bewildered by my words. "It's Aric's, Misha. I'm carrying Aric's child."

The betrayal in Misha's face forced me to loosen my grip. His entire demeanor crumbled in unfathomable misery, yet his devastation was quickly replaced with unimaginable fury. He yanked himself away from me only to seize me painfully by the shoulders and glower. His breath came out in threatening bursts. I thought he was going to strike me. But Misha's blows never came. He dropped me and stormed back toward Aric. I struggled to regain my balance and sprinted after him.

Although he said nothing, the vamps who carried Aric's limp form quickly released him. "But, Master," Tim said.

Tim averted his gaze, then he and the remaining vampires discarded their guns and shuffled toward the vehicles. They were all in bad shape; most were missing portions of their bodies or entire limbs. I clutched Misha's hand when he tried to follow. "Thank you, Misha. I—"

Misha tore himself from my grasp, his irises reflecting back in that dreadful green. Every part of him was poised to attack. But instead he closed his eyes tightly. When he opened them again, they were gray, cold, and ominous.

He spoke with guttural rage. "My debt to you is repaid. I owe you *nothing*. You are no longer allowed in my presence. Do not even *dare* to speak my name."

Misha stalked away. He didn't look back. He said nothing more . . . and he didn't have to.

Our friendship was over, but I didn't have time to mourn its loss. I lifted the tranquilizer gun near my feet, shoved it into the waistband of my shorts, then tore a section of fabric from my tank top. Tye's artery had sealed and his trachea had begun to reform, except chunks of flesh remained exposed. He needed help. I wrapped the stretchy fabric of my shirt around his neck and tied it tightly.

He watched my careful movement and swiped at his pale, clammy skin. "I have to kill him."

My tigress eyes replaced my own. "You'll have to kill me first."

Tye clenched his teeth and glared. "You're a fool, Celia."

I stilled. "Maybe I am. But I won't allow Aric to die."

"Damnit, Celia. You don't get it. He's not Aric anymore. The moon sickness has claimed him."

Tye became a blur as my tears blinded me. I blinked, allowing the large drops to streak down my face. "Don't ever tell me what he is or he isn't. You don't know him and you have no idea what he's capable of."

We veered toward the sound of approaching footsteps. Michael limped to us. His right calf muscle had been stripped from the bone, exposing his tibia to the hungry flies gathering to feast. His grimace expressed his obvious pain. He bent and with his only arm gathered the remaining guns. "I'm going to help you," he told me before I could ask.

"Did Misha send you?"

Michael paused. "No. The master wants nothing to do with you."

"Then why?"

"Because you helped us."

I sniffed. "Michael, Misha will interpret your actions as a betrayal and kill you for it. You have to go back."

Michael continued about his task. "You helped us" was all he said.

Our cellphones were damaged during our fight with Lucinda. But even if we could call for help, Aric's condition couldn't wait. We needed to get him home. I left Michael and returned to the cave. Michael was in no condition to assist me in moving the cage that had housed his master, but that's not why I asked him to stay behind. Tye would try to kill Aric in my absence. I knew that. With Michael there, he would think twice.

My fingers stuck to the remains of Misha's victims when I gripped the bars. I dragged the cage out as quickly as possible, slamming it multiple times against the sharp cavern walls. I tried not to gag from the festering smells of death, but it was hard. My head pounded and my stomach lurched, yet it wasn't until I slipped over something that slithered with maggots that I finally vomited. I leaned against the wall just outside the cave and tried to steady myself. It didn't work. I lost what remained of my composure and broke down.

"*Shit*. Goddamnit!"

Never in my life had my faith been challenged more. I was so tired. Tired of fighting, tired of feeling, tired of pretending to be stronger than I was. I was tired of living. It was just too damn hard. I thought about my only other option. I could let Tye kill Aric. We were mates, right? If he died, I'd soon join him, and we'd be together . . . and wouldn't that son of a bitch Anara just love to be rid of me? And the nasty little shape-shifters? Oh hell, they might even throw a party.

I purposely struck my shin against the jagged stone. It hurt. Oh, *damn*, did it hurt! But I deserved it for entertaining thoughts about dying. No. If I died, it would be at God's hands or at the hands of my enemies as I fought them until my very last breath—and not because I was a coward.

Screw that.

I returned to the cave and dragged out the cage, heaving it through the demolition left by Lucinda's cyclone. *Bitch.* Even in her absence she made everything harder for me. Despite my urgency and my frantic tugs, it took an exceptionally long time to return to the base of the mountain.

Tye sat on the trunk of an uprooted palm tree. He seemed a little better, furious at me, but physically more improved. In contrast, Michael's dark skin had turned ashen and sweat slicked his brow. He leaned against a palm for support, swatting the bugs that sought to gorge on the flesh dangling from his knee. If he didn't feed, I'd have more than one bloodlust victim to worry about.

Empty tranq darts lay scattered near Aric's giant chest. Michael motioned to him with the rifle. "He woke up again."

"I figured." I counted the number of darts. There were eight. And I hadn't been gone that long. "How many darts are left?"

"If you're thinking about taking him back to Tahoe . . . not enough."

"Then we'd better get going." I shuffled toward Aric. I didn't want to be stuck in a cage with him, but the only way to lug him inside was to drag him by his hind legs.

Tye scoffed. "The bars and the chain won't hold him long."

I wanted to throw a rock at him. "They're reinforced with magic. I can smell it."

Tye stomped over to me. "It doesn't matter, Celia! Nothing you're doing matters. The moon sickness will continue to drive him to kill while razing his neurological system! You're a nurse, you know what that means— unendurable pain and brain damage. Is that what you want? Do you want him to suffer? Do you want him to kill—?"

My screams came out like choked sobs. "Shut up. I'm not giving up on him!" I snagged Aric's legs and wrenched him inside the cage. "He needs to live—he *has* to live, and that's all there is to it!"

There was more I wanted to say, but it would have meant more tears, and I couldn't waste the energy. Michael shot him with tranquilizers even though Aric hadn't moved.

He bowed his head when I stared back at him in shock. "Sorry," he muttered. "But you won't be able to chain him on your own and there's no way I want him waking up while I'm trapped in there with him."

The collar wouldn't fit around Aric's gargantuan neck. We ended up tying it, limiting his movements. Given his lust to kill, we reasoned it was a good thing.

The cage was monstrous, heavy, and too wide to fit through the rear of the vehicle. Our only choice was to secure it to the roof with rope Michael had found in the remains of the barn. Michael and I struggled to lift it. He had only one hand and I was too short to be of much use. After a round or two of massive swearing, Tye stood and helped. I raced us back to town with Michael in the passenger seat and Tye sprawled across the back, although I doubted he would sleep with a volatile wolf just above his head.

I slowed our speed when we reached town and came upon a group of drunks, singing and stumbling their way home. Michael raised his brows. I nodded and rolled to a stop. My heavy lids lowered as I watched him approach the humans. I didn't realize I'd fallen asleep until the sound of him shutting the door woke me when he returned.

I rubbed my face. "You look better."

"Humph."

I started the engine and floored it. "What's wrong?"

Michael shot me a sour look. "I don't normally feed on men."

"Oh . . . right." Vampires didn't physically orgasm when they fed. It just felt that way psychologically. "Sorry."

Michael grimaced. "I tried to pretend they were ugly women . . . really, really ugly women."

He tried to make me laugh at his own expense, but nothing was funny when Aric's torturous roars drowned the sounds of the engine. Michael lowered the window, sat on the rim, and shot several rounds into Aric until he finally stilled. I flinched with every squeeze of the trigger.

Michael's expression lacked all humor when he slipped back into the seat. "We need to get back to Tahoe, quickly."

I stomped on the accelerator. The weight from Aric and the cage pushed the engine to its limits. Each time we rounded a corner or hit a curb I fought to keep the SUV from tipping. Considering my hands wouldn't stop shaking, it was one hell of an accomplishment.

We arrived at the San Salvador airport close to dawn. I didn't bother telling Michael to influence the minds of everyone we passed. We didn't have the time, he didn't have the energy, and at that point I couldn't care less who saw the giant wolf strapped to our roof.

My eyes cut Michael's way. Poor guy. His feeding allowed his leg wound to heal and prevented bloodlust, but not much more than that. He'd have to nourish a lot more to regenerate his arm. And still he managed to invade enough minds to permit our entry onto the runway and find us a ride home.

Tye and I waited for him in silence, mostly because I refused to speak to him. He leaned against the hangar wall, alternating between scowling at me and watching Aric. "What do you expect will happen when you return to the Den?"

"I expect his Elders to cure him. Or maybe Emme can heal him. If not, perhaps Tahoe's head witch can counteract the spell or something. Genevieve's strong, she—"

"Can't," Tye finished for me.

"What?"

Tye's voice slowly rose with anger. "Genevieve *can't* reverse the spell. Emme *can't* heal him. The Elders *can't* cure him. There is no cure!" He pushed off the wall and shoved his face in mine. "They will kill him, and you,

you will watch him die."

The heat from my anger surged fast enough to suffocate. "Why are you here?" I shoved him away. "If this is what you really believe, why do you stay?"

Tye's thick brows angled in frustration. "Because I don't want him to kill you and I don't want you to watch him die!"

Michael returned, his pace slowing when he caught Tye and me facing off. "I located a U.S. cargo plane here to deliver goodwill medical supplies. They're scheduled to fly back to San Diego sometime tomorrow. I convinced them to leave for Tahoe right away. We can fake an emergency landing if we have to."

I rushed forward to retrieve Aric, just as he woke up. He threw his body against the cage, hard enough to tip the SUV over.

The huge vehicle and cage rattled against the concrete and Aric still wouldn't stop. He slammed into the bars, hard enough to bend them and snap his ribs. Tye shot him with four tranquilizers—and that only partially doped him. He tried to shoot him again and ran out of darts. Michael fired six more times before finally knocking Aric out. I couldn't believe it. The cage and chain barely held him despite being reinforced with magic.

Michael reloaded his gun. "The moon sickness makes him increasingly strong and violent. We're running out of time."

I dropped my hands to my sides. I hadn't realized I'd clasped them against my mouth. "How soon can we leave?"

"As soon as the pilots are done refueling, we're out of here." Michael took in the crowd that had gathered from the commotion. "I'll be right back."

The group of pilots and ground crew walked away smiling after Michael was done with them. Among them were two women. Michael used the opportunity to eat, again. When he had finished, I'd already cut the ropes binding the cage to the SUV. He helped me push the cage into the cargo plane. Tye didn't help. His only contribution was to swear.

Michael nudged me a few hours into our flight. "You should sleep, you don't look well."

I could have slept for a week, but my worry for Aric kept my lids wide open and my heart thumping. He lay with his back to me. I'd been watching him breathe for a long while, agonizing over the spasmodic rise and fall of his chest. His ribs were slow to slide beneath his fur and reattach, taking close to an hour rather than mere moments.

The moon sickness was interfering with his ability to mend. I shuddered, wondering how else it ravaged his body.

I forced myself to rise rather than taking Michael up on his offer and pushed my sweaty hair away my face. "Shouldn't we give him some water or feed him?"

"The only thing he wants to eat is us," Tye answered irritably.

I ignored him and went to find something I could use as a bowl. A helmet stuffed into a storage compartment seemed like my best bet. I filled it with a bottle of water from a cooler we'd found, and grabbed a pack of dehydrated meat the pilots had purchased. I ripped open the pack with my teeth and shoved it into the cage. As I worked to position the water close to the bars, something about Aric's eyes caught my attention. They rolled from side to side, but they no longer glimmered green. I smiled. "Michael, Aric is getting better. He's—"

Tye launched himself on me and slammed me against the rear of the plane. Aric had awoken in a vicious state. He crashed his body furiously against the metal bars like a battering ram, shaking the whole plane. Michael shot him repeatedly, but it didn't slow him. His snarls rumbled with menace despite the blood that soaked his snout.

"I'm out of darts!" Michael yelled.

Aric's thrashing moved the cage directly over the two rifles that remained. Tye and Michael kept trying to snag them, but Aric's snapping jowls held them to a standstill.

I tried to sound as soothing is possible. "Aric, stop it." He beat himself against the bars, jolting the cage forcibly against Michael and knocking him aside. I raised my voice. "Aric, no!"

He fixed his gaze on me. I thought he recognized me, but his menacing stare and the increasing growls said otherwise. If any other predator had stared at me that way, my tigress would demand we snap its vertebrae. But this wasn't some unknown aggressor. It was Aric. "Baby. It's me. Please don't look at me like that."

In one jump, Aric forced the cage toward me, cornering me near the entrance to the cockpit. His snout protruded through the bars, mere inches from my throat. The metal creaked and bent as his mangled face advanced through. His oozing nose scraped against my skin. He was almost to me.

The sound of rapid fire reverberated from the rear of the plane. Michael had reached the gun.

One of the pilots burst into the cargo area. He seemed confused, but unafraid. "I don't know what the hell that was," he called over his shoulder. "Everything seems in order."

"Turbulence," sputtered Michael. He sprawled on the floor breathing heavily.

"It must have been turbulence," the pilot repeated before returning to his seat.

Michael continued to pant. "I'd told them not to notice us or the cage."

I slumped to the floor. "Good . . . good thinking, Michael."

Tye shoved the cage away from me. I couldn't look

at him. The last thing I needed was his sanctimonious needling. "I thought he was getting better," I mumbled. "His eyes weren't green anymore."

Tye sat next to me. "A cursed *were's* eyes won't persistently stay green."

"Okay." I avoided his gaze.

Tye continued. "When a vampire has bloodlust, he constantly needs to feed to suppress his insatiable hunger. When a *were* is cursed with bloodlust, he's compelled to kill to combat his pain." He sighed. "Aric's violence will continue to escalate . . . and so will his hurting. You have to accept that he's getting worse, Celia."

I listened to Tye. Really, I did. And I wasn't stupid. Aric was growing sicker—I could see and scent it. But that didn't mean I'd admit defeat. I stood and made like I was dusting myself off. Now that was a joke. My clothes lay in shreds and nothing short of a thorough Clorox soaking would remove all the blood, dirt, and vampire ash. "Well, then. I guess we'd better get him cured quick."

Michael's normally composed demeanor collapsed like the Mayan ruin. In his alarm, I realized he, too, had begun to doubt my sanity. I was done with everyone thinking I was unstable and felt compelled to defend my actions. "Aric managed his first *change* at less than two months of age—an incredible feat, considering that even the strongest *weres* can't *change* before six months. He's from a long line of pures that have saved the world time and time again— overcoming astronomical odds. Aric isn't like anyone I've ever met. He can fight this, I know he can."

Tye dug his fingers into his chin-length hair. "Celia, no one doubts Aric's strength. That first hex Lucinda struck him with was a death curse meant for you. It would have killed you if he hadn't shielded you from it—hell, it would have killed most anyone I know."

"See, this is what I mean. Aric's strength is

unparalleled…"

My voice trailed off as Tye shook his head. He ambled toward me and took my hands in his. "Celia, when a witch launches a death curse she instantly knows if it works. She knew it had failed, so she hit him with the only other hex that would seal his fate. Lucinda is crazy and evil, but she's also smart. She knew we'd have to kill him—" I jerked away from Tye and walked to the opposite end of the plane, but it wasn't far enough to keep from hearing his next words. "Sweetheart, don't you think if there was a cure, we would have discovered it by now?"

I ignored his question. "Why didn't Lucinda die when I stabbed her?"

Tye watched me for a while before answering. He didn't want to stop hounding me about Aric, but he also realized it wasn't getting him anywhere. "Lucinda is powerful. If you had stabbed her with any other blade, all you would have done was piss her off."

I recalled the creepy dagger. "The hilt had skulls on it."

"The skulls signify death. It's likely the weapon she used to kill her sacrifices. If so, dark magic is attached to it."

"Celia used her own magic against her," Michael said.

Tye nodded. "If the Alliance is smart, they'll finish her now that she's weakened."

Michael rolled onto his knees. "She won't die on her own?"

"She will, eventually, considering what Celia did to her. Problem is, 'eventually' could be a long damn time. That nutcase is still dangerous on her deathbed. She has to be destroyed."

Aric stirred, causing us to tense and forcing Michael to his feet. He leveled his gun at him. Thank God, Aric slumped back to the floor. I looked to Michael. "How much longer to Tahoe?"

He glanced at the clock on the wall. "Two hours. Celia . . . we only have eight darts left."

Two hours of flying and another forty minutes to the Den. "Michael, can you see if the pilots can arrange for a moving truck when we arrive—something with metal walls and a full tank of gas?" He nodded and hurried to speak to the pilots. Aric stirred again, lifting his paw. "And Michael . . . can you see if they can fly any faster?"

Chapter Twenty-five

We ran out of tranquilizers an hour later. Michael was forced to beat Aric with giant bolt cutters any time he stirred. I covered my ears to muffle Aric's growls and yelps. It didn't help, and I became faint more than once. The only reason I didn't pass out was my fear that Tye would try to kill Aric. He hadn't spoken to me, and I worried he was plotting against us.

A rental truck was waiting when we landed in Tahoe. Tye helped me position the cage so the door rested against a metal wall. It was a tight fit, and one that served to better contain Aric. Michael influenced the memories of the landing crew and set to work on creating a diversion. A loud explosion signaled he'd completed his task. He'd set fire to one of the plane's engines, making our emergency landing appear believable. It was the distraction we needed to tear out of the airport.

Michael and his giant bolt cutter rode in the back with Aric. Tye sat in front with me. He still wouldn't talk and continued to watch me carefully. The damn truck wouldn't go faster than seventy and it slowed considerably once we started to ascend Granite Chief Peak.

As eager as I'd been to reach the Den, my entire

body trembled the closer we drew. Tye finally spoke as we reached the main gates. "I'll take care of you." It wasn't a threat. His voice held a great deal of compassion. Yet I didn't welcome his offer, nor the words that followed. "With your mate bond severed, there's a good chance you'll survive no matter what happens to him."

"I can take care of myself. And nothing is going to happen to him!" I tried to growl, but didn't manage. Terror licked my skin and pulsed hot through my veins.

Heidi stepped out of the guard station, ready to tear heads until she saw us. She smiled, until she caught the traces of my fear. "Celia—"

I reached out my hand to her. "Aric is in the back. He's hurt. I need my sisters and the Elders right away."

Her lips parted. She was likely shocked that anything could hurt Aric enough to keep him down. "Your sisters are at their jobs. Go to the main building—I'll summon the Elders."

"Heidi!" Tye called to her before she could run off. "*Everyone* needs to be there."

I didn't like the look Tye shot her and neither did she. She nodded slowly before opening the large metal gates. I stomped the accelerator, passing a group of young *weres* playing football in a large open field. A howl from a wolf sent them, and another band headed for the library, racing toward the main building.

The truck thundered down the road as *weres* emerged from the chateaus that served as dormitories and classrooms. Martin and Makawee waited at the end, standing at the foot of the stacked stone porch, their expressions tight and distraught.

I skidded to a stop. Michael kicked the back doors open and leapt out before I cut the engine, clutching the giant bolt cutters against him.

Aric was waking up.

I raced toward the back of the truck and so did the

Elders. Martin took in Aric's state. "Celia, what's happened? Why is Aric caged?"

Like a hound from hell, a deep menacing growl rattled from Aric's throat. "He's cursed with moon sickness," Tye said before I could answer.

Everyone stilled. "My *God*," Martin whispered.

Aric struggled to his feet, falling more than once. His growls worsened each time he fought to stand. I veered to face Martin. "It's okay. He's going to be all right. Emme can help him. I know she can."

Strong hands fastened around my arms. Koda, Liam, and Gemini had arrived, their faces ashen with shock. I hadn't noticed them until Koda attempted to lead me away. I jerked out of his hold. He reached for me again. "Celia, get away from the truck."

Aric rammed his body from side to side, rocking the giant vehicle. He was now completely awake and rabid with fury.

Gemini yanked me back. "Celia, you have to move *now!*"

I struggled against his strength. "No! We need to—"

Aric tipped the truck over. It slammed against the gravel, scattering the stones and coating the air with a large cloud of dust. He collided against the bars, bending the metal.

Gemini and Koda restrained each of my arms, keeping me in place as Makawee approached. Her wise eyes darkened as they met mine. "Child," she said quietly. She stroked my hair away from my face. To my absolute horror, the faint howl of wolves erupted around me. She was using the power of the Pack against me.

Tye's arms circled my waist and hauled me backward. "I've got her!"

"No. No. No!" I screamed as he dragged me inside the building, trying to *change* and *shift*—anything to break free. But like Anara, Makawee had robbed me of my abilities. I kicked and clawed. Tye wrestled to control my upper body while another wolf hugged my legs. Michael followed, except he did nothing to help. I couldn't fault him. He stood as a lone vampire on *were* territory.

We reached the door in time for Aric to burst free.

Tye dragged me to a large study on the second floor where a grand piano sat in the corner and a large shelving unit took up an entire wall behind a mahogany desk. Michael shut the door to deaden the chaos and uproar outside. I still heard it, even through all my struggles and swears.

Pain sharpened Gemini's commands. "Herd him toward the back, but keep your distance."

"*Jason,* you're getting too close!" Liam's tone was off, as if fighting back cries of anguish.

I started to hyperventilate and grew limp in my captors' arms. They relaxed their hold. And I attacked.

I head-butted Tye and slammed my right elbow into his stomach. The other *were* dropped with a single kick to the head. I scrambled under the piano and out the other side before Tye could grab me again. Michael stayed put by the door. He couldn't help me any further, but he sure as hell wasn't going to help Tye.

Tye and I circled around the piano. He clenched his jaw. "Celia, listen to me."

The baby grand weighed about five hundred pounds. I grunted as I lifted it over my head and propelled it forward. Tye dove across the wood floor, thinking I meant to launch it at him. But it was meant for the window and that's where it headed.

Glass shattered in a melodious shower. I leapt outside before he could stop me, landing hard atop a thick layer of slivers. I dug in my heels, kicked back the shards, and sprinted toward Aric's snarls.

Tye bolted behind me, stopping short when the Elders halted my steps with their magic. Their power weighted down my muscles like hundreds of sandbags. I could barely move. Tye's hand touched my face. "Celia, *please*. Come back with me, you don't want to see this."

He was right; I didn't want to watch. But I did. The entire pack closed in as they surrounded Aric. He bared his fangs and scanned the crowd, seeking the weakest to kill first. Except among a throng of thickly muscled *weres* trained to fight, trained to slaughter, no one looked weak.

I turned desperately toward Martin. "Please don't do this. You raised him as your own— like a *son*. My sister can help him. I know she can!"

Martin shuddered. His head slumped and his entire body seemed on the verge of collapsing. The Alpha male I'd always known vanished, in his place stood a dispirited old man.

"Makawee . . . give the order," he said. Then, almost silently, he murmured, "Forgive me."

Makawee held up her head. "Members of the Squaw Valley Pack, your honorable Leader, Aric Connor, suffers. As his loyal supporters it is your duty to send him to his final resting place." Makawee's voice remained soft, but the might of her command was unmistakable.

"No!" Animal-like screams tore from my throat. "No, *no*. You can't do this!"

Aric growled. Thick white foam slid down his mouth, drenching the damaged muscles of his torso. His eyes twitched, and his head jerked as if convulsing. He was so sick, but the tension in his back legs demonstrated he stood mere moments from attacking.

No one moved despite Makawee's order. Gemini, Koda, Liam, and the other *weres* exchanged apprehensive looks, torn between obeying their Elder and sparing the Leader they loved. And while they openly feared Aric, sorrow was the prominent emotion they collectively shared. It hunched their shoulders and smeared their expressions with grief. Heidi and some of the younger students openly wept.

Their trepidation gave me hope. I thought they were incapable of hurting him. I thought wrong.

One by one, they *changed* into their formidable beast forms and stalked closer toward Aric. "*No!* Please don't do this, it's still Aric!" I sobbed.

Makawee pursed her lips. "There is no choice, child. He's already gone." She and Martin maintained their hold. My anguish did nothing to relax their grip; their power remained, obstinate and absolute. My heart threatened to stop. I didn't want the Pack to tear him to pieces or to hear his anguished howls before he was silenced forever. I didn't want to watch my baby's father die.

My eyes burned with how hard I cried. "I brought him here so you could help him. You can't kill him. There has to be another way!" Martin turned his face away from mine. Makawee's expression stayed fixed on the Pack.

Aric whipped around in circles, ready to strike. I cursed, screamed, and struggled, but my efforts were in vain. Even if I broke free, how could I possibly take on a pack of wolves?

I looked up to the sky. For a moment, everything turned quiet and eerily still. A cool breeze gently hit my face. I didn't understand what was happening until my body convulsed violently and I *changed.*

I didn't become the formidable tigress that would fight to the death to protect her mate. In her place wiggled a rabbit. A rabbit small enough to slip through the stunned Elders' hold.

I dashed toward Aric, dodging the astonished *weres* who were oblivious to what had happened.

Martin's voice boomed across the yard. "It's Celia! Stop her before Aric kills her!"

They were too late. I reached Aric and leapt at him in a burst of feathers. I dug my talons into his flesh and took flight . . . as an eagle.

Chapter Twenty-six

The element of surprise saved us.

I was a bad swimmer, but I positively sucked at flying. My cursed-with-bloodlust mate didn't help. He growled, writhed, and tried to bite.

Ingrate.

I flapped my wings and continued upward. The Pack snapped out of its shock and gave chase, sprinting at full speed, scurrying up tree trunks and ricocheting off branches. Some didn't appear to try very hard. Others drew close, determined to bring us down. I flapped harder and faster. It made a huge difference. The wolves below me became smaller and soon we left the Den behind us.

My new form was tremendous, easily four times as large as an average eagle. And, more importantly, strong enough to carry a distressed werewolf. I carried us north toward Canada, searching for solace despite my doubts that we'd make it that far. My eagle form didn't come naturally. I had to concentrate to maintain it. It wouldn't be long before my body would surrender to exhaustion and *change* back—and I really didn't want to do it midair.

I focused on how the wind blew and ruffled my feathers and swept over my magnificent wings. I looked to the heavens, determined to join them as one. Aric lunged and threw off my balance more than once. And still I worked to keep my form.

We soared for what seemed like hours. Aric had either fallen asleep or collapsed from his illness. He hung limp from my talons, but his heavy breath proved he still lived.

The sun set deep into the mountains. I descended into the sprawling forest below, trying to slow my pace as I dove down, alternating between not flapping and flapping. It worked— well, sort of. I released Aric a little too far from the ground. He banged into a thick pine, smacked against a large branch, and crashed to the ground.

Oops.

I tried to land smoothly. I might have managed had a pissed-off Aric not tackled me just as my talons skimmed across the earth. He struck me hard enough to knock out feathers. I tried not to fight him, but he didn't make it easy. He buried his front claws into my wings and growled in my face. I *changed* back, hoping to appear less threatening as a human.

It didn't work. He growled louder, appearing more angered by my sudden transformation. Drool dripped on my face. It would've grossed out me out had I not been terrified he was about to eat me. "It's okay, Aric. No one's going to hurt you."

Nothing of my Aric reflected in those ferocious brown eyes. He was all rabid wolf— volatile and incapable of reasoning. My primal instincts implored me to fight. But I couldn't. If we fought, it would be to the death, and no way could I kill him.

I realized I shouldn't have met his eyes. Aric had always welcomed my gaze, but he wasn't himself and perceived my stare as a challenge. I played the submissive and glanced away, lying before him with my throat exposed, praying the man I loved wouldn't hurt me. His snarls intensified and panic twitched along my spine.

I broke away, but not fast enough. Aric's fangs dug into my shoulder. I thought for sure he'd kill me, but at the sound of my screams he released me and kept his jaws from clamping down.

He backed away, stopping suddenly when his light brown eyes fixed on me. His stare softened and he whined, his attention bouncing from my face to my damaged shoulder.

I rolled onto my knees, watching him. Tears filled my eyes as he continued to whine. He wasn't attacking. He wasn't aggressive. He was simply sorry for hurting me.

Aric knew me. By some miracle, he'd recognized who I was.

I reached to touch his face. "It's okay, love. I know you didn't mean it."

Aric sniffed my hand and wagged his tail, then slowly leaned forward to lick my wound. It tickled a little and made me laugh. He stopped and cocked his head to the side before continuing until the site was free of blood.

He sat next to me, nuzzling my neck. I stroked his head and absorbed his scent, taking a moment to gather my strength.

Finally, I rose. "Come on. We need to find a place to sleep."

Instead of following me, Aric collapsed into a massive seizure—the convulsions so violent, they flipped his hulking form in the air. He howled with every brutal strike against the ground. I stood, petrified with fear, watching helplessly until his head slammed with a sickening crunch against a boulder.

I raced to his side when he fell limp. Blood dribbled down his scars from the deep gash on his head, and his jaw hung slack and twisted. He'd broken it, and cracked his skull. For the first time, I began to doubt whether I could save him. I knelt and buried my face in my hands, taking several calming breaths until I erased all thoughts of defeat from my mind.

"No, Aric. You won't leave me. Not like this."

I lifted him in a fireman's carry. My strength made hauling him manageable but awkward. His limbs draped past my ankles, forcing me to drag them along. I tried to avoid stepping on sharp rocks and debris, but wasn't very successful. The added weight caused the tiny shards to embed deep in my soles. I *changed* into a tigress from the waist down, hoping the thick pads of my paws would provide some cushion.

Balancing became impossible. I toppled over with Aric and landed hard on my chest. Every swear word I knew flew out of me. Our situation sucked. I had absolutely no camping skills and no money to lodge us somewhere in civilization. I didn't even have clothes! But Aric needed me. And our baby needed him. I dissolved my paws and forced myself to my feet, lifting him once more.

I walked for a long while, until the sweet sound of running water beckoned me forward. A small waterfall emptied into a large pool of clear water. I lowered Aric near the edge. His breath remained ragged and his face oozed with foam and drying blood. Thankfully, though, his wound and jaw had healed.

The cold water soothed my bare feet when I stepped into the pool. I cupped a small amount in my palms and sniffed, welcoming its pure scent. I moved Aric closer and washed his face and chest. After a couple of splashes he woke, confused by his surroundings.

His angry barks and growls made me back away. He stopped when he realized who I was and waded into the water to rub against me.

I bent to wrap my arms around his neck. "Hello, love," I cooed.

His head jerked and his eyes twitched, and yet he sweetly licked my chin. My hands passed over his face and

chest. His deformities were more severe in his wolf form—
likely since he'd been burned as a beast. The leathery skin
scrunched together forming deep, sharp ridges and
indentations. I took my time touching him, trailing my
fingertips over every last imperfection. God, his body had
been through so much.

And still I loved him.

I kissed his head, needing to feel close to him.
"Have a drink with me."

He didn't move. I wondered whether he understood
or if the moon sickness had damaged his ability to
comprehend language. My muscles relaxed slightly when
he touched his nose to the water and drank like the poor
dehydrated wolf he was. I maneuvered my way to the
waterfall and sipped as much as I could then washed my
face and hands.

My inner tigress usually kept me warm. Not this
time. My teeth chattered and my muscles shivered from the
frigid mountain water. I hurried out behind Aric. He
stumbled at the edge of the pool and collapsed yet again. I
stroked his head and whispered words of comfort. His sleek
and beautiful fur was missing from his head, chest, and
front legs. I worried about keeping him warm, and how in
the world I was going to save him.

A single tear streamed down my cheek, but it was
all I would allow. It wouldn't do any good to keep crying,
so instead I decided to find us somewhere to sleep.

"I'll be right back, Aric. I'm going to look around."

I *changed* into my tigress form and circled the area
near the waterfall. I found shelter a small distance away. A
huge tree had fallen against a large slab of rocks. I jumped
on top of the pseudo-cave and was relieved to see it held. I
used my paws to clean the debris beneath and to soften the
earth before returning for Aric. Although his eyes were
incapable of closing, I knew he slept. I *changed* to human
and carried him back to our new home.

When I wrapped myself around him to keep us warm, I resumed my tigress form. I'd worry about food tomorrow. For now, I just wanted to sleep with my mate.

Our night together was long and torturous. I barely slept. Aric's seizures and pained howls returned in spurts throughout the night. I held him during the convulsions to keep him safe. He was strong and the process exhausted us both. When I did manage to sleep, I wasn't able to keep my tigress form. I'd wake up shaking, cold, and forced to *change* back.

Morning finally arrived. I rose on my paws and shook the dirt cloaking my fur. I didn't return to sleep following Aric's last seizure. There was simply no point now that the bright sun cut through the tall line of firs and into our tired eyes.

Aric's stomach growled. I scratched at the earth irritably, knowing I could no longer avoid the inevitable. I needed to hunt. We wouldn't survive without food. My insides clenched from hunger and from regret of needing to take an innocent creature's life. I paced around Aric, using his hunger and mine to encourage my inner predator to track. When I was as ready as I could possibly be, I licked his head and sped off, not wanting to leave him for long.

My tigress sniffed, searching for game. The sun brought the clear spring day, raising the temperature to about sixty degrees, but within the darkness of the forest it dropped significantly. I trampled through the cold mossy floor, grateful May had arrived to put an end to April's torrential downpours.

I traveled deeper within the woods. Aric's outbursts must have frightened the animals away. It took several miles to catch the scent of deer. I latched on to the aroma and it led me to a grassy knoll where a herd of females munched lazily while the bucks rammed their antlers to win their mates. I crouched, using the thick ferns, the shadows of the mighty trees, and scattered boulders littering the forest floor to camouflage my movements. I worked to bolster my courage with every step. I'd never killed an animal nor had I ever desired to. I reminded myself it was for our survival and to ease Aric's suffering. But none of it lifted the guilt from the pit of my stomach.

I singled out the oldest buck in the group, reasoning he'd lived a good life here in the pretty forest and would likely die soon anyway. My body trembled, unsure whether I could snap his neck. I swallowed hard and stalked closer. When I was almost on top of the herd, I roared to stimulate my tigress and to frighten the other deer away so they wouldn't see me kill their grandpa. They all bounded off sure and swift—except my prey. His eyes flew open and he keeled over. *Plop.* Just like that.

I sniffed and poked him with my right paw. *Okay . . . he must have had a heart attack.* I guessed I'd been right about his time being up. While I still felt bad, I felt less guilty knowing he'd died of almost natural causes. Almost.

I *changed* to carry the deer and hurried back to Aric. When I returned to our cave, I found him covered in dirt and saliva and panting heavily. He lay on the opposite side of our camp with leaves scattered everywhere. He'd suffered another seizure. I wiped my tears before he saw them. Pity wouldn't help either of us. I dropped Grandpa Bambi and carried my wolf to the falls for a much-needed drink. After washing him as best I could, I laid him on a patch of soft grass to dry in the sun and returned to deal with the buck.

I skinned the hide with my claws, using quick motions and trying hard to ignore the details of my task. Aric watched me with his twitching eyes, but didn't approach. I tore off a piece of meat—still warm, bleeding meat—and brought it to him in my hands.

"Please eat, love."

Aric licked my hands apprehensively. As soon as he got a taste, he swallowed the piece whole. He stood on wobbly legs and lumbered toward the deer. My jaw fell open. Aric tore into the kill with a ferocious appetite. It had probably been several days since he had eaten. I *changed* to join him, unable to stand eating raw meat in my human form.

At first, I had to concentrate hard on chewing and swallowing. Soon the blood enticed my beast and I devoured large chunks of the venison. Aric ate long after I had had my fill. I watched him while I waded into the water to cleanse my furry face and paws. I shook off the excess water, knowing I couldn't save him alone. I needed help.

I needed my sisters.

I *changed* to explain to Aric. "I'm going to leave for a while." He swallowed the piece in his mouth and abandoned the buck. I shook my head. "No, Aric. You stay here. Your job is to eat and rest. Don't worry. I'll be back as soon as I can." I gave him a smile I didn't know I had in me. "I love you."

That earned me a whine and a small tail wag.

When I tried to *change* into an eagle form, all I managed was wings for arms. It sucked, but I couldn't wait for more.

I soared into the air, hoping no one would notice a naked woman with eagle wings flying around. I used the brook that snaked out of the waterfall as a landmark and found it eventually turned into a river, perfect for finding my way back to Aric.

I flew for about half an hour before spotting an abandoned truck stop and landing near a cluster of trees. I shook off the *change* to regain my human form and arms, and then poked my head around a thick trunk, using my senses to detect anyone on the road or near the old store. I bolted to the pay phone by the side of the building. Thick rust coated the face. I was shocked when it actually worked. I called collect to my home in Dollar Point. After everything that had transpired at the Den, I knew my family would refuse to stay there. They'd wait for me in our home.

"Dude! Are you all right?" Shayna asked when the operator put me through. My voice cracked upon hearing her voice.

"Yes. I'm fine."

"No, you're not." She screamed for my sisters. "Celia's on the phone!"

I heard her racing down the steps. The phone tapped and I was placed on speaker. My sisters and Danny bombarded me with questions. I quickly cut them off. "Listen, I don't have time to talk. I need to get back to Aric."

Danny fumbled onto the line. "He's still *alive*?"

"Yes, but he's really sick. He's seizing and is in constant pain." I leaned my forehead against the dirty glass of the booth. I took a breath, but my words came out faster than I wanted. "I need you to find the witch who cursed Aric with moon sickness. Her name is Lucinda. She lives in the village of Izalco in El Salvador." I swallowed back my sudden nausea. I couldn't believe what I was asking them to do. "Find her and do whatever it takes to get her to rescind the curse."

I sensed their apprehension in the silence that followed. "Celia," Danny finally said. "Moon sickness is a one-way curse. There's no cure. There's no taking it back."

So not the response I wanted to hear. "I don't believe that, Danny."

He sighed and I could almost picture his grim face. "Celia, the *weres* infected are irrational and deadly. There's no choice, they have to be . . . destroyed before they worsen."

I punched through the booth door and knocked it off its hinges. The few panes of glass that had survived the past decades shattered. "Then explain to me how Aric is still in control!"

It was Emme who spoke. "He hasn't tried to hurt you?"

I almost lied to them, but decided against it. "He bit me—once, but he remembers me now."

Her voice shook. "He *bit* you?"

"It's okay—"

"For shit's sake. This is so not okay," Taran shot back. "You need to get away from him before he kills you!"

"He won't hurt me again. I'm sure of it."

"Damnit, what if you're wrong? All we keep hearing is that no *were* in history has ever been cured—"

"That's because none are given the opportunity! Everyone is so damn quick to put them out of their misery. I swear he knows me and understands what I'm saying. Doesn't that tell you anything?"

Taran began to argue with me, but Danny interrupted her. "That is rather unusual. Celia, when he bit you, did he break through the skin?"

I absentmindedly rubbed my fingers over the puncture wounds. "Yes," I muttered.

"Hmmm. It could be that the magic in your blood could be clashing with Lucinda's. Did you hurt her?"

"I stabbed her with the knife she made sacrifices with."

Danny took his time answering, likely disturbed by the ease of my response. "To weaken a witch with her own power gives you strength over her magic," he said.

I stopped moving. "So *I* can cure Aric?"

"Perhaps, but I don't know how. Celia, these are unusual circumstances. But then again, you're an unusual being. My other theory is that our essence runs in our blood. That's how vamps keep their beauty and power. They nourish themselves by taking portions of the soul mortals carry in their bloodstream. Maybe Aric's spirit recognized yours through your blood and your bond as mates. Combine that with your strength over Lucinda's magic and it could have been enough to help Aric recognize you."

Emme interrupted quietly. "But Celia broke their bond."

Danny's voice softened. "Celia and Aric remain mates. The only thing she severed was the bond they created when he claimed her during their, um, lovemaking."

Hope filled me until Taran interrupted. "Okay, say that's true, but what if Aric continues to get worse? Will their connection and her strength over Lucinda's magic be enough to stop him from hurting Celia?"

"I don't know," Danny answered.

"Then you have to get Lucinda to rescind the curse," I said.

When no one said anything, I fell apart. "Please," I sobbed. "I can't lose him again. He's my life."

"It's okay, Ceel." Shayna's voice was surprisingly soothing and calm. "We're going to help you." There was a short pause before she continued. "Celia almost died because we didn't believe in her," she told the others. "I'm not going to let that happen again. I'll find Lucinda myself if I have to."

"We'll all help you, Celia," Emme said. "We'll call the wolves and—"

"No." My voice shook as my panic rose. "I can't trust the wolves not to hurt Aric. Makawee ordered them to put him down. They were trying to kill him when I flew him out of the Den."

A truck thundered by while I waited for everyone to take in my words. Taran's swears punched through the line like hailstones. "Really? Well, they left that little tidbit out. All they said was they needed to find you before Aric killed you."

Panicked shuffling ensued. "Don't worry, Ceel," Shayna said. "We'll pack now and catch the next flight out."

Emme's sadness seeped through the receiver. "I'm sorry for what you're going through, Celia. Just . . . stay strong and I promise we'll help you through this."

"Thank you," I whispered. "Just be careful. Lucinda may be weak, but she's still deadly."

The darkness in Taran's tone wafted through the receiver. "Don't worry, Celia. That bitch doesn't stand a chance against us."

My family would help us. I had to keep it together . . . just a little longer. "I'll call you at this same time in exactly seven days."

I hung up the phone and raced back to the forest and tried to *change*. The first time I only managed a beak, then talons, then feathers on my ass. I swore, frustrated. I didn't comprehend how I'd managed those other *changes*. I continued to focus until I finally formed wings. On my return flight, I spotted an old cabin. Overgrown grass and tall weeds circled the tiny structure and thick moss carpeted the roof. It rested just a few yards from the river. It surprised me that I'd failed to notice it before.

This will be a good place to bring Aric.

I found my wolf resting in the sun. He'd devoured the entire buck—including the bones. His eyes continued to twitch and his head jerked, and still he wagged his tail upon seeing me land. I shrugged my shoulders to shake off the *change* and lay next to him. "Hi, baby. Did you get enough to eat?"

My arms wrapped around his bloated stomach to feel his soft warm fur against my body.

Before I knew it, I dozed off to sleep.

My morning sickness worsened over the next few days,

completely freaking out my companion. Aric paced back and forth until I finished, nudging me with his head. I tried to reassure him yet I found it challenging to settle his distress. He thought I hurt, except he was the one in pain. Aric's seizures increased in duration and intensity, as did his howls of torment. The twitches in his head were so severe, he could barely walk straight.

I tried not to let our misfortunes affect me. I continued to scare old deer into meeting their Maker and cared for Aric as if he was on the mend, despite realizing his condition deteriorated with each passing day. Our one blessing was the old cabin.

One room and an outhouse made up our new home, just enough to suit our needs. It seemed the owners had planned to return, but never did. Sheets and blankets were tucked into an old trunk. I washed them in the river and hung them to dry on a clothesline and used a broom to sweep the windows, walls, floors, and ceiling. Much to my delight, the old-fashioned water pump in the small kitchen worked and a full box of matches lay next to the fireplace. The owners had even left a couple of pots and plastic tumblers.

Three thick sleeping bags lay against the cabin wall, and I spread them in front of the fireplace to make us a bed. The sheets and blankets remained stiff following my river wash and air-drying, but they were a welcome comfort after sleeping outside. And, score! I uncovered a duffel bag filled with men's clothes and toiletries. I greeted the disposable razors, toothbrushes, toothpaste, and soaps like the tiny treasures they were, rejoicing that they remained in their original packaging.

Much to Aric's annoyance, I made good use of my discoveries to scrub and rinse his fur at the river. I also brushed his fangs with the extra toothbrush. He hated the taste, and kept flicking out his tongue to spit out the foam. After I finished with him, I concentrated fully on me—

washing my long hair, brushing my teeth, and oh, yeah, shaving my legs.

I emerged from the freezing water shaking and desperate to put on the extra-large cotton shorts and T-shirt I'd found. Aric sprawled in the sun to dry his fur. He abruptly sat up and wobbled over, twitching and shivering, and proceeded to yank on my shorts with his fangs.

"Aric, cut it out!" He ignored my protests and pulled harder. I gripped the edge and tugged. "Come on. I've been walking around naked for almost three days!" My comment had little effect on him. Instead of backing off, his efforts became more urgent until he tore them off.

"*Fine*. Keep the damn shorts. But my shirt stays on." He wagged his tail, apparently happy with the compromise.

Later that afternoon, Aric had a particularly violent seizure, one that lasted longer than the rest. His yelps and moans brought tears to my eyes. I knew his agony remained between seizures, and still he'd push through. This time, he continued to whine from the hurt eating away at his body long after the convulsions had stopped. Unable to stand, he lay where he'd collapsed. It killed me to see him giving up. My morning sickness and fatigue made caring for him challenging, and yet I did my best. I hunted and kept us clean and cared for. I did so because I still had hope, but his defeatist attitude would claim us if I didn't stop it.

I spread out in front of him and tried to distract him. "I've missed cooking for you." His whines continued, but he turned his head toward my face. "Remember when you'd find me in the kitchen making you dinner?" He quieted, then slowly wagged his tail. He remembered. "You'd come up behind me and wrap your arms around my waist." I smiled, recalling the memories. "And then you'd ask, 'What are you making me, sweetness?' Every time, you'd kiss me before I could tell you. Every time."

Aric's tail thumped against the ground. He moved closer and poked me in the nose with his. I grinned. "Sometimes I hadn't finished cooking before you'd whisk us upstairs." I stroked the side of his face. I'd meant my words to be uplifting, but my voice cracked as I continued to speak. "Even if you don't stay with me and choose"— I couldn't say Diane's name— "someone else, I need you to live. I need to know you're okay." Aric rose to his haunches and whined. I wiped my tears on my shirt. "Please don't give up, baby."

Behind the hard slits on his face, Aric's eyes rolled and darted. I knew he heard me, but I didn't know if my words alone would be enough to save him.

Chapter Twenty-seven

On our fourth night in the cabin, my exhaustion levels reached an all-time high. After managing to build a fire, I immediately crawled into bed. Aric was already asleep, his long body draped across two of the sleeping bags. I kissed his head and cuddled next to him. Although I tensed in anticipation of another long night of seizures, I drifted off almost immediately.

Sometime during the night, I awoke to an explosion of light and a strong wind blowing against my back. I sat up and glanced around. Everything appeared unchanged. Outside the forest was still. No wind or rain rattled the trees. The only sounds came from the river and a couple of noisy owls in the distance. I dismissed the experience as a dream and rose to add another log to the fire.

I checked on Aric and adjusted the sheet over his back. The wet cloths I'd applied over his eyes had slipped off. As I replaced them, I noticed his eyes stared ahead, devoid of any awkward movements. His trembling and twitching had also ceased and his muscles and breath appeared more relaxed. He seemed . . . at peace.

I wrapped my arm around him. "Are you feeling better, love?" Aric didn't respond.

My fear was that he'd grown too weak. I watched him for a long while wondering if I should try to wake him. When his condition didn't deteriorate, I decided it was safe to return to sleep. Lying close to his fur made me too hot. I removed my shirt and snuggled against his back.

I awoke not long afterward to Aric sniffing my neck. Instead of feeling the rough texture of his scarred face, soft fur stroked against my skin. I turned and scrambled away when I saw what he'd become.

Aric blinked back at me in his human form. His dark Irish skin glowed against the firelight, smooth and absent of scars. Short, thick dark hair covered his head and beautiful brown eyes glistened back at me. I crawled forward, my eyes widening and my breath quickening with each movement. "Oh my God."

What I initially mistook for soft fur was actually a full beard, the length of his short hair. I reached out, skimming my fingertips over his face. Aric's gaze followed my hands as I traced them down his neck, chest, and arms. Silky, unmarred skin stretched over dense bulging muscles. He was . . . *perfect.*

I could see and feel his metamorphosis, and still I couldn't believe it. After several passes over his skin, I finally accepted his body had mended. My words broke through my tears. "Baby, you're *cured.*"

Aric tilted his head, as if working to understand. He may have resembled his former healthy self, yet something about him seemed off.

Using extreme care so as not to scare him, I returned my hands to his face. His beard mimicked the soft whisper of newborn hair. To my relief, he continued to welcome my touch. He rubbed his jaw against my hands and caressed my face—mirroring my movements. I kissed his lips as tears streamed down my cheeks. Aric didn't kiss me back; instead he watched me with curiosity while I stroked his hair and took in his magnificent scent.

My hands slipped down to his chest. Aric leaned forward to sniff my neck once more. I laughed. He stopped just to smile at me. My heart soared at that familiar grin . . . only to stop when he pushed me down into our bed and climbed on top of me. He ran his tongue over my throat and across my jawline. His licks were unwolflike—sensual, with enough heat to make me quiver. Goose bumps spread the length of my body. But he wasn't well—not completely—so I thought it best to discourage his behavior.

"Um, Aric. I don't know if you should—"

I started when his tongue found my left nipple. Aric stopped to stare at it, deeply fascinated and evidently impressed with how the tip responded to his affections. He continued to experiment until it hardened to his satisfaction, then he moved to the other. Arousal shot through me like blazing bullets, stiffening body parts that made me ache and groan. It had been a long time since he'd touched me that way.

Aric's nostrils flared. He'd scented my passion. His excitement built, knocking hard against my thigh. He abandoned my nipple and searched for the source of my heat. I screamed when he found it with his tongue.

My back bowed. *Okay, I officially like the beard.*

My moans grew as he continued. Still I questioned whether our lovemaking was appropriate in his given state. I tried to squirm away. Aric wouldn't allow it. He hauled me back and spread my legs further. Suddenly, our roles were reversed. He held me as I convulsed out of control. I screamed and thrashed, my hands searching blindly for something to grasp as ecstasy ripped through my core.

I reached for him, but Aric refused to relinquish control. He flipped me over and placed me on my hands and knees. Even after all the times we'd made love, he still had trouble penetrating. His moans of pleasure resonated over mine as he pushed his way inside me. His rhythm was slow at first, but then became quick and needy. I turned my head to see the perfect outlines of our shadows against the wall. Watching made the moment sexier. I rocked my hips, driving him crazy. He thrust faster and faster until we reached a very loud and enjoyable end.

Aric and I collapsed in a sweating mess on our sides. He pulled me close, nuzzling my neck. *"Celia,"* he moaned before I succumbed to sleep.

I'm not sure how late I slept the next day. A strange scent forced me to open my eyes. Aric had gone grocery shopping in the woods. Under one arm, he carried about five dead pheasants. In the other, he held a large pot from the kitchen shelf. I peeked inside. Mushrooms, chives, and dandelions lined the entire bottom. In his teeth, he carried a mouthful of cattails by the stems. He grinned, thoroughly impressed with himself. His good humor abandoned his strong features when I ran to the sink and proceeded to vomit.

I leaned against the edge. *Freaking morning sickness.*

Aric dropped everything and alternated between pacing and nudging me with his head— just as he'd done as a wolf, this time appearing more distressed. Crap. You'd think he'd be used to it by now.

"It's okay, love . . . don't be scared. I'm all right."

He didn't believe me, but why should he? Sweat dripped over my cold and clammy skin.

I brushed my teeth and rinsed my face. I turned to meet Aric's deep furrowed brows. His hands touched my face, demonstrating the same adoration he'd shown me last night. I kissed his palms. "I'm fine, baby. Just tired."

Aric cocked his head. Even in his state of mind, he knew I was lying. But now wasn't the time to tell him about our baby. His demeanor softened the more I stared. He linked our hands and led me back to bed. I wouldn't release him. "Stay with me."

Aric smiled and joined me in bed, covering us with the blanket. I closed my eyes, content in having him so close to me. Initially I thought I'd rest until my nausea faded. Instead I once more drifted to sleep.

Hard knuckles lightly stroked my cheek. I opened my eyes to find Aric spread out beside me.

"Hello, wolf," I whispered.

He lowered his lids and rubbed my nose with his, then sat me up and presented the feast he'd prepared. He'd roasted all but one of the pheasants using the fire poker. With the remaining bird, he'd made me soup. He placed the pot between us and tore pieces of pheasant to feed to me. In turn, I fed him the mushrooms, chives, dandelions, and what remained of the cattails with a wooden spoon. The pheasant was the best I'd ever enjoyed and the soup, while bitter and minty, completely settled my stomach.

As physically healthy as Aric seemed, I was still worried. He seemed better in many ways, but in others, he remained more like his inner wolf.

Could this be permanent?

We ate everything; our empty stomachs made us ravenous. I escorted him to the sink and washed our hands and faces. He rubbed his wet beard against me, making me laugh. I was still giggling when he pulled me to him and led me outside.

Aric *changed* the moment we left the shadows of the house. He pulled a Lassie on me and proceeded to whine, gesturing me to follow. When I tried, he *changed* back to human and then back to wolf again.

"What's that, girl? Timmy fell in the well?"

He bared his teeth playfully and took off running as soon as I *changed*. I chased him through the woods and tackled him. We wrestled and then he darted off, making me chase him once more. Our play continued until we returned to the waterfall with the small pool.

Aric *changed* back to human and skidded to a halt near the water. I didn't stop. I tackled him one last time as a tigress. He grinned as I lay on top of him, and yet even as a human he managed to flip my almost four-hundred-pound self onto my back.

I resumed my human form. Aric moved aside, helping me to stand. I leaned into him, offering my mouth. Rather than kissing my lips as I so wanted, he licked my face. I laughed, so he did it again. When he wouldn't stop, I grabbed him by the shoulders and pressed my lips against his. I kissed him softly at first then pushed my tongue slowly to meet his.

I spent several minutes teaching Aric how to kiss, loving every moment and relishing feeling so close to him. Aric's lips were soft and greedy. They left mine to whisper words against my neck and shoulder. I didn't understand their meaning, nor did I care, choosing to welcome the affection I for so long was denied.

He caressed my back. The more he moaned, the more I knew he wanted more. Once again, he placed me on my hands and knees. And once again, we reached a very loud and enjoyable end.

When we managed to catch our breath, Aric helped me to my feet and led me to the pool for a drink. I waded into the frigid water. He stayed fixed by the edge. I didn't understand why until I finished quenching my thirst.

Aric stared at his reflection, running his fingers over his face and chest in stunned silence. He examined his arms and hands. For the first time, he realized his body had healed. He grabbed my hands when I hurried to his side and swept them over his face and body, focusing on the areas where the scarring had been the most severe. He pointed at the water then back to himself, unsure whether to believe what he was seeing.

I wrapped my arms around him and held him close. "I don't understand what happened, Aric. I'm just glad you're safe. It's all I've wanted."

We stayed by the falls for the remainder of the day, savoring the deep intimacy we shared in being alone. As the dim sun moved westward, we made our way back to the little cabin.

Aric *changed* into a wolf and charged when he caught the scent of a large elk. I covered my face, unable to watch and cringing when I heard the elk's neck snap. Pocahontas I wasn't. Aric beckoned me forward, chortling in his wolf body when he found me with my eyes clamped shut.

"Yes, this whole thing is just hilarious," I quipped. And yeah, he laughed harder yet.

I *changed*, knowing I needed to eat and hoping to keep down the meal. We'd finished half of the large animal when Aric resumed his human form and howled. His wolf song serenaded like a tender lullaby. I followed his lead and returned to human. He gathered me close, his arms anchored around my waist and his fingers caressing the small of my back. I lifted my head, to find him staring past me.

I followed the direction of his gaze. A small pack of wolves approached warily. I smiled. That explained the wolf song: Aric had invited company for dinner. They varied in shades of black and brown with three small pups trotting among them. I wanted to stay and watch them, but Aric lifted me and carried me away. At first, I thought he meant for the pack to eat in peace, but when he placed me on our bed upon our return to the cabin, I realized he desired to make up for our time apart.

Sunlight cascaded into the small cabin. Another day had arrived. Aric caressed my belly, now plump from where our child grew. I covered his hand with mine and faced him as his lips grazed across my jawline to meet mine. He smiled. "Good morning, sweetness."

I bolted upright. He gently urged me back down. "Shhh. It's okay. Don't be afraid."

"Are you . . . all right?" I asked.

He took me in. "I am, but only because of you."

"You remember," I whispered.

Aric rubbed the healing fang marks on my shoulder, his expression riddled with sadness and guilt. "I wasn't completely in control at times, but yes, I remember everything."

I flung my arms around his neck, crying. Aric held me and smoothed my hair, his voice tight. "You still love me . . . despite how I've treated you and how badly I've hurt you."

I spoke through my sobs. "I never stopped, Aric."

He clutched me tighter. "I don't deserve you or your love." He kissed me, deeply and passionately. I pulled away, suddenly terrified Anara would reach us. In his illness, no one could connect with Aric except for me. Now that he was well, I wasn't so sure.

"It's too dangerous for us to be together," I told him. "For the time being, we need to stay part."

Aric yanked me to him when I tried to stand. "*No.* I'm not abandoning you again." He kissed his way down my neck, burying his face between my breasts.

I squirmed beneath him, my thick lashes fluttering. "Aric, stop." I really didn't want him to, but I feared Anara's link to Aric remained.

"Sweetness, please. We made love when I was more wolf. Don't deny me now that I'm more man."

I gripped his shoulders. "You don't understand. Anara will find us, and when he does, I'll watch you die."

Aric's hatred fired his light brown irises. "Anara has been stripped of his power. He can't hurt me and he sure as hell won't touch you."

Something in Aric's words, be it rage or brute

strength, made me believe him and expunged my fear. As I relaxed, he dipped his head and pulled my nipple into his mouth. My heart pounded like a slew of angry fists. "Please, sweetness, please," he murmured against my skin. "Let me make love to you."

I responded with a moan and by pulling his lips to mine. Aric climbed on top of me, running his fingertips down my body and slipping them between my legs. My gasp broke our kiss. He returned his mouth to the tips of my breasts, latching and tugging with his teeth.

My arousal grew too much for him to manage. He pushed himself inside me, thrusting hard and groaning with increasing hunger. We climaxed quickly, and yet I couldn't bring myself to stop. I rolled him on his back and began to move. His stare held mine, beseeching me with longing and need. He surged to life with each pass of my hips, his thick knuckles skimming and teasing my nipples, encouraging me to move faster. A sultry charge radiated from within me, electrifying my body and clenching it tightly around him.

My heart threatened to explode. Aric intertwined his fingers with mine, helping me through the multiple crashes rocking through me. "I love you, Celia," he panted. "*No one* will keep me from you again."

Chapter Twenty-eight

"Tell me about Anara."

My body and mind basked in the aftermath of our lovemaking. Hearing that bastard's name shattered the tender moment and left me shaking.

I sat up, burying my face in my hands. Terror and fury warred when I thought of him, with terror always emerging as the victor. Anara could rob me of those I loved. No matter what anyone claimed, he was still strong and he still had power.

My fear set off Aric's growls. He tucked me against him until my trembling finally subsided.

Aric swept my hair away from my eyes. "What did he do to you, Celia?" He kept his voice soft yet there was no masking his fury.

I couldn't initially answer. With his mind cleansed of the moon sickness, any of the Elders could link through Aric's mind, including Anara. So, I listened hard, searching for any trace of howling wolves while scanning the area around us. Aric followed my gaze, scowling with more confusion than anger.

"Celia, please tell me what happened."

When Anara failed to present himself, I took a

breath. My wolf was right, I had to tell him everything. "Aric . . . since our return from South America, Anara has been using the power of the Pack against me."

Fury pulsed from Aric's skin in tangible waves, bending the air like heat rippling off asphalt. "What do you mean he used the Pack?"

I knew that deadly tone, and delaying would only escalate his anger. "He used his link to you and your packmates to multiply his power. Every time I saw you, he materialized and forced me to tell you things so that you'd hate me. He . . ." I swallowed hard and couldn't finish.

Aric's voice was unrecognizable. *"What else?"*

I tried not to cry—God, I really did. But revealing meant reliving everything Anara had put me through. "He possessed the wolves and turned them against me."

"My wolves?"

I couldn't look at him. "They didn't have a choice, Aric. With our bond broken, their collective instinct to protect me was severed, too."

Aric held my shoulders, angry tears leaking from his eyes. "Why didn't you tell me? I would've stopped him. I would've kept you safe."

His pain lodged the words in my throat. But there was no going back. By not telling him, I'd betrayed his trust. He needed to understand I hadn't made that choice lightly. "Anara swore to kill you if I didn't keep my distance and threatened to kill my sisters if I told anyone what was happening. He can hurt anyone from miles away, Aric. I've seen it. I had no choice but to obey."

Aric tried to steady himself. His eyes wandered to my neck, breasts, and stomach. "He's the one who attacked you and Bren. There were no rogue Tribe wolves. It was all him, wasn't it?"

I nodded, cringing as the memories bombarded me with ruthless hands. I didn't want to remember where Anara had clawed me and how Bren had almost died in my arms.

Aric gently held my face, his voice dripping with ire. "Anara has taken our *were* magic and harnessed it into something evil. But even if he hadn't, he *will* die. I swear, I'll kill him for touching you."

It wasn't what I wanted him to say. "Aric, please don't go after him. All this time, I've struggled to keep everyone safe. Don't let my efforts be in vain."

He gathered me to him. The scent and warmth of his skin helped alleviate some of the horrible experiences seared into my mind while my body helped to ease his wrath. We held each other for a long while until he abruptly pulled away, the anger he held replaced by a sudden understanding. "Anara made you break our bond."

It surprised me he hadn't figured out that little tidbit sooner. "Well, *yes*."

"It wasn't about my scars?"

The fact that he had to ask really pissed me off. I grabbed his left nipple and twisted.

"Ouch!"

"Aric Connor, when the hell are you going to realize that if you were nothing more than an eye and a foot, I'd still love you?"

Aric laughed despite himself. "But sweetness, if I was just an eye and a foot, I couldn't do this."

I yanked his hands off my backside. "You know what I mean. Are you saying that if I'd been the one burned, you'd have left me for someone who wasn't scarred?"

Aric's brows furrowed tight. Apparently, I'd insulted my big badass wolf. "*You* will always be beautiful to me no matter what—" He stopped upon catching my smirk. "You don't understand. I was going through a lot then and felt you deserved more than…"

I angled my head. "More than what?"

He released a sigh. "More than half a man."

That earned him another nipple twist.

"Damn, baby," he said over his laughter. "Will you knock it off?"

"You deserve it for believing I'd be so shallow—and for yelling at me and . . . for calling Diane your . . . mate." I no longer laughed and neither did he. I sat and hugged my knees. Aric tried to curl his arm around me. I shrugged him off. Now that he was healthy, I could allow myself to be mad at him.

"Celia."

"You could have called her your girlfriend, your fiancée, or even your wife. All those terms would have hurt me less. But to refer to her as something so sacred—something only I was supposed to mean to you—Aric, nothing you could have said would've hurt me more."

I wiped my tears with the backs of my hands. While I knew I should forget that moment, I couldn't. Not then.

"Celia, the anger and hurt I experienced clouded my judgment. But in no way does that excuse how I've treated you." His eyes brimmed with tears. "*You* are my one and only mate. I'll never know love or happiness without you, and I'm nothing without your smile." He clasped my hands and knelt on one knee. "I love you, sweetness Will you marry me?"

I covered my hand over my mouth to silence my sob. I'd convinced myself I'd never hear these words. And yet there was my love, asking me, and waiting for me to answer.

I smiled at him through my tears. "How can I marry a *were* I'm not officially mated to?"

Aric's eyes widened before fixing on mine. "You're right," he murmured. "I guess we should fix that."

He hauled me on top of him. I licked him in places that made him growl, jerk, and beg for more while he made me scream and thrash. We were practically out of our minds, yet he managed to focus enough to reclaim me.

"Do you want me, my love?" "Always."

"Can I have you?" he grunted.

"Yes."

Aric struggled for breath. "Then you're mine…forever."

The aroma of a burning fire stirred me from sleep and beckoned me to the small window. Aric knelt over a fire he'd built by the river, grilling fish on a spit constructed from twigs. I had to laugh. *Show-off.* The ripped pair of shorts he'd torn off me hung low on his hips. On anyone else, they'd have looked ridiculous. But my mate made everything look good. I tugged on a shirt and a pair of extra shorts I'd found and joined him. He glanced up from turning the fish and grinned.

I paused, overpowered by the stench of fish guts he'd dumped in the river. I raced downstream and vomited. Aric held back my hair. I rinsed my mouth and washed my face, embarrassed. "We have to get you back to Emme." He sounded worried. "The wound I caused may be infected and the mountain water isn't safe for you to drink."

My hands skimmed over my belly. "Aric, that's not the only reason I'm sick."

He lifted me in his arms. "I know, sweetness. Your stomach wasn't meant to handle the raw meat we've consumed. I'm taking you back to bed. You need to rest."

"No, I'm fine—really. I just need to brush my teeth."

He stroked my hair. "I'll get you whatever you need. It's my turn to care for you."

I managed to eat a little after brushing my teeth. As Aric extinguished the fire I paced and wrestled with how best to tell him about our baby. But then something else occurred to me, causing dread to stir deep within my stomach. "Aric, is it possible Diane is pregnant?"

He stilled. Instead of telling me no, as I hoped, he walked to me slowly. He bent to cup my face, his expression bleak. "Celia, in my anger at you I didn't remain faithful."

I felt the color drain from my face. "Oh, God."

"I didn't have sex with her," he added quickly. "My wolf denied her . . . but we did share moments alone."

It was better than the alternative, and that's what I told myself. And still the pain in my heart spread throughout my body. Aric, *my* Aric, had been intimate with someone else.

"I'm sorry," he said quietly.

The betrayal searing through my veins kept me from meeting his eyes. He said nothing more, knowing I needed time to work through the wounds his confession had inflicted. He busied himself cleaning the camp, stopping only to glance my way. When he finished, he joined me on a thick piece of driftwood where I sat. He waited, before slipping a cautious arm around my shoulders. I leaned against his broad chest, unable to fight my need to feel close to him. His response was to envelop me with his body. "Please, don't leave me," he whispered. "I don't want to know a life without you."

We stared at the river for a time, losing ourselves to the splash of the water against the stony bank and the call of birds soaring without a care above. I forced the anger and jealousy from my being, shoving it deep where it couldn't poke and prod at my insecurities. Aric wasn't perfect, but hell, neither was I. We'd messed up. A lot. We'd destroyed each other with words and actions until our souls bled. But the hurt was deep only because our love was, too.

Roses couldn't grow without the rain, and we'd had our share of thorns and storms. Instead I snuggled closer against him, resolved to abandon our past and concentrate on our future, one that would allow us to marry and be with our child. It was then I decided to tell him my news. It was then a horde of familiar scents hit us at once.

We leapt to our feet to find Gemini, Koda, and Liam. They dropped the backpacks they carried, clearly surprised to find us. I couldn't believe they were there, but what surprised me more was Koda's smooth and healthy reddish skin beaming against the background of the deep blue sky. Long midnight hair swept past his shoulders like a yard of pure black silk. Like Aric, his scars had vanished and his mutilated skin was whole once more. "Aric?" he gasped.

Gemini carefully stepped forward. "You're *cured*."

"And Celia, you're . . . alive!" Liam charged and swept me in his arms. I caught sight of the others embracing Aric while he spun me in circles. The moment he put me down, I kicked him hard in the groin. He crashed to the ground, curling into his body.

"Celia, what are you—"

Koda never finished. I broke his nose with one punch. Before he could bleed, I nailed Gemini in the chest with a river rock. Aric snapped out of his shock and attempted to restrain me. "Celia, what the hell are you doing?"

I struggled against his hold. "They were going to kill you—right in front of me. I was going to watch you die!"

At last his Warriors understood the cause of my outburst. Guilt and shame spread along the planes of their faces. One by one, they slowly bowed their heads. Aric watched them with sympathy instead of anger. "They were following orders, love," he said. "I was dangerous. They had no choice but to obey."

"There's always a choice, Aric. Just like I chose to save you!"

He shook his head. "Celia, this is the way of our Pack."

Aric's statement infuriated me. I broke from his grasp. "Well, the Pack *sucks*. If you think we're raising our baby according to Pack laws, you and your buddies are out of your damn minds!"

Dropping a pregnancy bombshell had a funny way of silencing even the yappiest of werebeasts. No one said anything for a looong time, their blank expressions convincing me that perhaps a singing telegram might have been a more subtle way to go.

Liam rose from his fetal position on the ground. "Baby? Did you say . . . *baby*?"

Gemini shifted his attention to Aric. "You're going to be a father?"

Koda wiped the dried blood on his face with the back of his hand and laughed. "I can see this isn't the first time you've been alone."

Aric's face split with astonishment, elation, and doubt. He dropped his head and stared hard at his feet. When he returned his gaze to mine, heartbreak shadowed his strong features. "Celia, are you sure the baby is mine?"

I picked up another river rock, this time to throw at Aric.

The other wolves scrambled for cover as he caught me in an embrace. I just missed dropping the stone on my foot. "Of course I'm sure, damnit!"

"You haven't—I mean, after the way I treated you .. ."

I took in the light brown eyes of the man who warmed me with his soul and touched me with his smile. "Since the first time I saw you, you've been my love and only lover. There's no doubt that you're my baby's father."

The heat sizzled between us, stimulating our mate bond and allowing me to sense the surge of happiness that sprang from his chest. His lips swept sweetly over mine. But when he dropped to his knees and kissed my belly, I couldn't stop my tears.

I clutched him against me, smiling. "Sorry. This

isn't the way I'd planned to tell you."

"I don't care how you told me. I'm just glad that I know." He rose and rubbed my belly. "A baby . . . I can't believe it. Celia, you've made me so happy."

The wolves collectively howled and approached us, bowing slightly before offering their congratulations and embracing us.

"The first to continue the Connor lineage," Gemini said, clapping Aric's shoulder. "This is cause for celebration."

I stilled, worried he could be wrong. Aric stilled too, for different reasons. His hands fastened on my hips. "Did I hurt you anytime last night or this morning?"

Koda threw back his head, laughing. "Anytime last night *or* this morning? I'm surprised you weren't expecting sooner, Celia."

My cheeks burned. "I'm fine, Aric." I cleared my throat and addressed the wolves. "How did you find us?"

Liam chuckled. "Let's just say CIA ops are not in your sisters' future."

Koda pulled out his phone and hit the notes icon. "They took off a few days ago. Their excuse? They'd won tickets to *The Price Is Right* and were headed to Burbank."

I pinched the bridge of my nose. Shayna loved that show. Koda smirked and showed me a phone number he'd recorded. "Of course, they never erased their caller ID. This is the phone booth you called from. I traced the number to this area. We've been tracking you for days. It was only around dawn that we finally found traces of your scent."

"They've texted from prepaid phones, just to tell us they were safe and claiming Emme won a toaster. We thought they went to search for you, but we never found them." Gemini took in the shack. "And judging by your situation here, they never found you either. Where are they?"

This time it was my turn to lower my head in

shame. "They're in El Salvador. I sent them after Lucinda to force her to cure Aric."

Koda hit Shayna's number before any of us could blink. She answered with true cheerleader jubilation. "Whaddup, puppy?"

His voice grew tight. "I seriously think you're trying to kill me. We're with Celia and Aric. He's . . . cured—and his scars have vanished. Now: Where. Are. You? And if you tell me you won a year's supply of mac and cheese, I'm not going to be happy."

Joyful squealing bounced through the other line as Shayna shared the news. When she returned, she spoke to the gargantuan pissed-off being she affectionately called puppy. "Now, sweet love, don't be mad. We had to help Aric. Especially since you guys tried to kill him and all."

And just like that, Shayna turned the tables on him. Koda cleared his throat before he spoke, although it did little to fade the flush to his skin. "What happened with Lucinda?"

The playfulness in Shayna's tone disappeared. "We killed her the night your scars healed. She didn't leave us a choice. We panicked, thinking we'd lost our opportunity to save Aric. But from everything you say, it sounds like in killing her, we broke the spell that kept the burned *weres* from mending their scars."

Aric leaned toward the phone. "How is Lucinda's death related to the demon that burned us?"

There was some fumbling and then Danny came on the line. "We discovered that both Lucinda and her daughter had raised the demon. Lucinda escaped before the Alliance realized she'd been involved. In awakening the demon, she formed some kind of bond with him, allowing his power to linger after he returned to his dormant state. When she died, the last of the demon's power died with her, allowing the *weres* to finally heal."

The wolves and I exchanged looks. If it hadn't been

for Danny and my sisters, all who had been burned by Ihuaivulu's fire would have remained scarred and Aric would have met a painful death. His lids closed tight. "You saved my life and spared my kind from suffering." He buried his face in his palm. "Dan, I almost killed you. There are no words to describe the disgrace I feel. I beg you to forgive me—"

Danny interrupted, his voice quiet yet firm. "Your actions were only the result of Anara's treachery. But if my forgiveness will help assuage some of your guilt, then, yes, I accept your apology."

"Thank you," Aric said hoarsely. "Thank you all for helping us."

"No problem, dude!" I smiled. Only Shayna could act like taking out one of the most powerful witches on earth was no big deal.

Emme spoke lightly and with a great deal of heart. "Celia loves you, Aric. That makes you our family, too."

Taran swore from somewhere behind her. "If you want to thank us, why don't you start by making an honest woman out of our sister?"

Aric laughed. "I'm trying. This morning I asked Celia to marry me."

That was all it took for my sisters and the wolves to lose their ever-loving minds. "You're actually getting married! It's about damn time. I, for one, have been dying to get off the Aric and Celia drama train."

My mouth sprang open. "Hey!"

Aric wrapped his arm around me. "I'm still waiting for an answer, Taran, especially now that she's told me she's pregnant."

A deafening silence greeted us before my sisters started screaming and crying all at once.

Aric just stared at me. "They didn't know?"

I shook my head. "Danny was the only one I told." The cheer left my mood and voice, silencing the barrage of questions my sisters slammed me with. "I told him after we realized he could somehow block Anara's power. Danny's kept me safe from him this whole time."

The wolves exchanged glances, realizing everything Danny had risked for me. Aric could barely find his words. "You're a hero, Dan. You protected my mate and my unborn child. I'll never be able to repay what you've done."

"It was my honor," Danny said, his voice splintering with emotion.

Aric swiped at his face. "When we return, expect a formal ceremony reinstating you into the Pack. That is, if you're still willing to be one of us after the way we treated you."

"Aric, in your shoes I probably would have acted the same way."

Aric's voice was barely audible. "Somehow I doubt that," he said. Koda disconnected shortly after that, promising to call as soon as they formed a plan. We walked in silence and sat around the extinguished fire. I knew what was coming next, but it didn't make Gemini's question any easier to take.

"Tell us what happened, Celia."

Aric stroked my back. He sensed my apprehension and spoke for me when I wouldn't answer. "Anara used you as pawns to attack Celia."

The ignominy in Gemini's dark almond eyes almost made me weep. He rose slowly, falling speechless.

"It's okay," I said. "I know you didn't mean to hurt me."

Koda matched Gemini's repulsion with fury. "It's *not* okay, Celia. Shit, that day we thought you hurt Emme—it was us, wasn't it? We assaulted both of you." He swore. "And that day we were driving? *Jesus,* you must have been fighting for your life!"

Aric released me and stood, demanding answers in his glare. Gemini lowered his head. "I don't remember what happened, Aric. But if we turned on her, she didn't stand a chance against us. We forced her to leap out of a moving vehicle." He released a shaky breath. "And we pulled out her hair . . . chunks littered the floor and her scalp was bleeding."

"You tore out her hair?"

Gemini nodded. Liam's eyes darted between me and the wolves, expecting one of us to deny what had happened. Koda kicked a huge rock. It landed with a thud across the other bank. "That day at the hotel, was it Anara who tried to break Shayna's neck?"

My jaw clenched. "Yes. He appeared behind Aric when we were holding each other. He told me he'd kill Aric if I didn't get away from him. When I didn't move, he attacked Shayna." My voice cracked. "I never wanted anyone to get hurt."

The pallor in Gemini's skin receded, forced away by his increasing menace. "We've betrayed you in countless ways, and all this time you were protecting your love and ours. We were fools to think you could ever harm them."

Gemini and Koda, while infuriated, covered their faces in deep remorse. Liam couldn't take the guilt. He stared blankly at the ground. "We bludgeoned you . . . and broke your bones. We could have killed you and the baby."

Aric stormed to the forest's edge and punched a hole into a large dead fir, toppling it over. Dirt and mud rained down as the roots sprang from the ground. "I should have been there for you," he growled. "I could have stopped them!"

I staggered toward him. Aric was strong, but the force he demonstrated then was more than I believed him capable of. The wolves followed, appearing to encourage his actions.

My hatred for Anara spilled over into my voice. "Why are you blaming yourselves? None of you would've hurt me if Anara hadn't forced me to break my bond with Aric."

Koda faced me, snarling. "Celia, you were compelled to destroy something sacred to keep Aric from harm. It shouldn't have come to that—his safety and yours is our job. We failed him and we failed you!"

The Warriors rushed me at once—anxious to keep me safe despite the current lack of threat. Aric's warning growl forced them to freeze. Their pent-up restless energy shimmered beneath their skin—like real wolves right before a hunt. My independent side wanted to tell them to back off, and insist I could take care of myself. The side of me that had been terrified for weeks was just grateful they would no longer attack me. Aric gathered me into his arms, more possessive than loving. He failed to look at me. Instead he fixed on the wolves, daring them to approach.

Gemini stepped back slightly; the others followed suit. He rubbed his goatee, irritably. "The desperate measures you took to distance Aric alerted us that something was wrong, but we never imagined the situation involved one of our own. We thought that the vampires had somehow driven you insane."

"The only solace I've had has been with the vampires. Their combined magic overpowered Anara's." I purposely didn't mention Misha's name, but Aric's pained expression told me he recognized Misha as the driving force. I had to be honest. While Misha and his vampires make me crazy, they don't deserve to be the proverbial scapegoats.

"What else did we do to you?"

Liam's deep voice barely registered, making me hate Anara more. I dug my fingers through my hair. "It was hard enough going through it. Don't make me talk about it anymore."

My torrid emotions fueled Aric's rage, his growls grew increasingly menacing. I seized his hands. The way he focused on his Warriors frightened me. His human half could reason that they weren't responsible for their actions, but the infuriated beast within wasn't as forgiving.

Holding Aric soothed him only minimally. His emotions teetered toward out of control, and, short of moving him away, I didn't know how else to calm him. "Aric, please look at me." Fury blazed in his eyes. "I need you to calm down. You're scaring me." He didn't want me to be afraid and tried to tame his beast. But then Liam opened his big yap.

"Celia, the day I found you bloodied and choked . . . Did I do that?"

I *shifted* Aric into the ground as he lunged for Liam. If I hadn't anticipated the attack, I wouldn't have caught him.

"Liam had nothing to do with it!" Aric's head snapped up, expecting me to tell him exactly who'd hurt me. I swore a few times. Revealing the truth had done more harm than good. "It was Anara. That was the day he first came to see me."

Aric broke through the packed ground, enraged. I hugged his waist, ignoring the dirt caking his borrowed clothes. His heart pounded against his rib cage. I didn't know how much more he could take before his wolf would demand his mate be avenged.

He pulled me tight. "You were already carrying our child, weren't you?" I didn't want to say anything, but answered with a nod. He shook against me. "You've been through hell, Celia. And I've done nothing but fail you as a mate."

"Don't say that," I said quietly.

Aric's face darkened to a deep red. And although he remained furious, I sensed the blame he carried. "I should have recognized you were in danger. Instead all I did was add to your suffering."

Tears streamed down my dirty face. "You didn't

know, love. Please calm down."

Liam hurried forward. "He beat her up bad, Aric. Her nose was crushed and forced to the side. And her face was so swollen, I only recognized her by scent."

"Liam—"

"Her back was sliced and her throat was bruised from being strangled—" "Liam, *shut up!*"

Aric broke away from me to crush rocks with his bare hands. They exploded into the air like bits of sand. His strength scared me senseless yet the wolves continued to nod in approval. I rushed to him, but Gemini blocked my way, careful not to touch me directly.

"Leave him, Celia. He needs to embrace his anger. It will help him when the time comes."

My stomach churned with a horrible sense of dread. "Help him do what?"

Koda stared at me with dark, implacable eyes. "Help him and us kill Anara."

Chapter Twenty-nine

My anxiety prompted a sudden attack of morning sickness. Aric halted midstride, worry replacing his need to crush stone. Nothing like projectile vomiting to stop a raving werewolf in his tracks.

In seconds I had more help than I knew what to do with. *Weres* by definition ruled as calculating and vicious predators capable of emerging victorious even when outnumbered. Mine completely panicked. Liam swept me up and flung me over his shoulder, racing me toward the river and holding me over the raging water by the waist. "Shit! She's not stopping!"

Koda, who'd chased us, called over his shoulder. "Damnit, Gem. Boil some water!" Gemini yelled from the safety of the shore.

"What for?"

"How the hell am I supposed to know? It's just what you do when someone's knocked up!" I gripped my knees, trying to catch my breath. Liam "helped" by splashing me in the face with the icy water. I fell back into Aric's arms from the force.

"Liam, stop! You'll give her hypothermia."

"She needs water!" Liam insisted.

I glared at him. "In a glass, Liam. Not up my nose."

Aric led me back to the bank, trying to warm my shaking body with his and barking out commands. "Gem, start a fire and grab a pot from the cabin to boil water."

Gemini blinked back at him. "Okay, but what do I do with the water once it's boiled?"

Koda growled. "I told you, it's the type of shit you do when someone's knocked up!"

These are the future uncles to my child.

Aric clenched his jaw. "It's for Celia. Start searching for some coyote mint to add to the water. It will help settle her stomach."

"Oh. Well that makes more sense." Gemini bolted into the woods with Koda following.

Liam watched me closely. "Damn, Celia. You look like hell. Aren't you supposed to be glowing or something?"

Aric's scowl completely shut him up. *"Just get her some dry clothes."*

The tea the wolves threw together helped reduce the acid that continued to gnaw at my stomach. I returned to the cabin and took time to freshen up so I didn't appear so haggard. Or so I thought.

"She looks pasty," Koda murmured to Gemini when I joined them outside. "Is she supposed to be that fucking white?"

"*She* can hear you." I narrowed my eyes. "I'm pregnant, not deaf."

Liam nudged him. "It must be the hormones. Try not to upset her, she might kill us all."

Gemini cleared his throat upon taking in Aric's death glare. "You look beautiful, Celia."

Liam flashed two very enthusiastic and blatantly dishonest thumbs up. Koda didn't bother to agree. He thought it best to stare awkwardly at his feet. Smart wolf.

Liam's sweats swallowed my legs. I had to roll

them six times to keep them on my hips. Aric chuckled before pulling me to him. "I'm taking you back to my original Den in Colorado. Right now, we're in Oregon's Blue Mountains. We need to hurry. It's a long trek back to Koda's SUV and an even longer drive to Boise, where we're meeting your family."

"You don't trust Martin and Makawee enough to return to California, do you?"

Aric stroked my cheek. "I've known Martin all my life. He and Makawee are honorable, but too much has happened without their knowledge. Something has blinded them to Anara's actions."

Gemini stepped forward. "The Elders of each Pack have a special blood bond. When one uses Pack magic, they all sense it. Given that they failed to notice means Anara must have invoked something darker."

My jaw tightened. After they had ordered Aric's death, I'd lost all trust in the Elders. "How are you so sure they didn't know?"

Gemini softened his gaze. "Celia, you didn't see their reaction when Danny announced that Anara was responsible for your attacks. Their surprise and anguish was genuine, which is why they immediately broke their united bond and removed his power."

Koda stared out into the river. "The power that has been given to us was never meant to hurt an innocent. It was only meant to vanquish evil. That alone sealed Anara's death warrant."

I angled my head toward Aric. "You're taking me to your original Den." He nodded. "What's going to happen when everyone knows we're together?"

Aric's warm eyes could melt chocolate. "Based on everything that's happened, I'm going to appeal to the North American Were Council to allow us to be together. If they refuse, I'm relinquishing my title as a Leader and all the privileges that go along with being a pureblood." He grinned at the wolves. "I tried to release these knuckleheads from their duty to me, but they refused."

Liam tossed a rock at the river, making it skip across to the opposite bank. "We decided to form our own Pack. Hell, we may even start our own Den."

I glanced at them, expecting to see at least some apprehension, doubt—*something*— regarding this life-altering decision, but no. They all seemed determined to follow Aric down this unknown and potentially dangerous path. "Have you all lost your minds? You can't go *lone* wolves."

Koda shrugged. "Technically we're not *lones* if we all do it."

I didn't know what to say. While they weren't purebloods, as *weres* they were obligated to honor their Pack. I didn't know what ramifications their actions would bring nor did I want to find out. I tried to reason with Aric. If I could change his mind, the others would follow. "Aric, you can't do this. Your family name will be tainted and your reputation will be destroyed—and what about your mother? She'll lose everything. I can't be responsible for that."

Aric continued to smile. "My mother recognizes you as my mate. She'll support whatever decision I make. And if she needs to, she can come live with us."

I opened my mouth to argue but he swept me into his arms and silenced me with a kiss. "Come on, sweetness. It's time to leave."

Koda tossed Gemini his pack and finished shutting the cabin door. I squeaked when Aric lifted me in his arms and followed Liam into the forest. "I can walk, Aric."

"No."

"*No?* I've been walking this whole time."

"You've also fallen and cut the shit out of your feet." He smirked. "So long as you're barefoot, pregnant, and mine, you're just going to have to just deal with me fussing over you."

I scowled. "You're going to be in trouble when I get my hands on some shoes."

His smile widened before kissing my lips. "Then I'd better make sure that doesn't happen."

The wolves took off in a dead run, racing through the thick forest in a blur. We reached Koda's Yukon almost two hours later. He started the ignition and phoned Shayna, just to be sure she and my sisters were safe. While the wolves didn't openly admit it, I knew they continued to perceive Anara as a threat.

Aric tucked me into the third row and threw a warm blanket around my legs before reaching for his seat belt. Liam and Gemini shoved the packs in the rear. The moment we were settled, Koda stomped on the accelerator and roared onto the highway. "We'll drive straight through. Shayna thinks we'll get to Boise around the same time. She's bringing Tye as backup just in case."

I leaned forward. "What about Bren and Danny?"

"They're coming, too. Bren's weak but beginning to thrive. Everyone will be safer in the Colorado Den."

Gemini sensed my growing nervousness and tried to distract me. "How many weeks are you, Celia? You're not even showing."

"Almost fifteen." His distraction worked. I smiled at Aric. "I saw the heartbeat on the ultrasound."

Aric's face lit up. He lifted his hand from my knee and he slipped it around my shoulders. "What was it like?"

"Fast, *really* fast. He's a strong little guy." His lips parted. "We're having a son?"

I shrugged. "It's too early to tell, but that's what my instincts tell me."

Koda's eyes crinkled back at me through the rearview mirror. "Do your instincts tell you *were*?"

Aric held me closer. "It doesn't matter . . . I'm going to be a father."

"Fifteen weeks," Liam repeated. I could almost see him doing the math in his head.

"Hey! That means you guys did it the night of the gala." Aric chuckled when I buried my face in my hands.

Gemini shifted in his seat. "That can't be right. You two had a bad argument that night."

Koda threw back his head, laughing. "I told you guys that was all foreplay."

Liam jumped in his seat. "Wait! After the gala you left with the vamp and Aric met with the Elders. That means you got it on *at* the gala. Whoa. Were you like outside or something?"

By that point, I had stuck my entire head inside Aric's sweatshirt. "Can we talk about something else?"

Aric pulled me from beneath his shirt and nuzzled my ear. He wasn't embarrassed, but he knew I was. He tried to spare my humiliation and switched topics, only the subject he picked wasn't much better. "Guess what? Celia brought back four bucks in the time we were in the mountains."

Liam knew I didn't hunt. The news both surprised and impressed him. "No way!"

Aric rubbed my shoulder. "It's true. I wouldn't have made it without her hunting prowess."

Oh, God.

Gemini turned around to smile at me. "Celia, I'm very proud of you."

"No shit," Koda said from the front. "I knew you had it in you, girl. You gotta tell us what happened."

They all perked up, thrilled in anticipation of my riveting hunting tale. I didn't say anything at first and secretly prayed we'd get a flat.

Aric stroked my cheek. "It's okay, sweetness. Don't be shy, tell us all about it."

I swallowed hard and told them exactly how I killed those deer. No one said anything at first, then all at once they burst out laughing. Koda laughed so hard he couldn't drive and pulled the massive SUV haphazardly to the side of the road. Tears streamed down Gemini's face and Liam actually cackled—*cackled* like Dorothy's damn Wicked Witch. Aric released me and faced the opposite window, his back shaking as he pathetically tried to hold in his amusement.

Koda held out a hand. "Let me get this straight. Your strategy was basically to scare them shitless in hopes they'd give up and die."

I scowled at him. "That wasn't my original plan. It's just how things worked out."

"I thought the meat was a little tough." Aric tried to calm down, but his comment only caused an uproarious outburst.

Liam snorted. "That's because she was feeding you the elderly."

I gasped. "It's not funny, I felt really bad about the whole thing!"

Gemini wiped his eyes. "How bad? Did you try to resuscitate? Do any mouth-to-snout?"

The laughter and the comments seemed to last forever. It wasn't *that* funny and damnit all, Bambi's granddaddy or not, Aric ate every last bite.

Koda calmed enough to drive, though they all continued to snicker. I brushed Aric off when he tried to snuggle. "Come on, sweetness. I'm sorry I laughed."

I crossed my arms. "No. You're not."

When he nibbled on my ear, I turned to glare at him. "I hope you enjoyed last night and this morning, because you won't be getting a repeat performance anytime soon." I smiled at his devastated expression. He was probably less bummed when he realized there was no Santa Claus.

Yup, not so funny anymore, is it?

It didn't take long for Aric to win me over. I rested

my head against his shoulder while his arm curled around me. He slid his opposite hand into my super-loose sweatpants and caressed my belly. "Your body is changing," he whispered. "I can feel where our son is growing."

I slipped my hand under his and smoothed my palm over a hard, round bulge. He was right. "Will you be disappointed if we have a girl?"

He grinned back at me. "Are you kidding? Having a little you running around would be precious. I just think you're right—this one's a boy."

I puckered a brow. "This one?"

Aric snuggled closer to me, tickling my neck with his soft lips. "We're going to have a whole brood, lady."

Although the idea of having a gang of children intimidated me, Aric's excitement over our baby showered me with love and hope for our future.

We were two hours into our drive when Koda pulled into a small diner next to a gas station. He tossed his credit card to Liam and shoved his wallet back into the pocket of his jeans. "Fill up, Liam. We'll grab enough food to last us the rest of the trip. I don't want to stop again."

I walked into the diner to use the bathroom and immediately walked back out, unable to stomach the thick aroma of frying food. Liam finished filling the tank and joined me back in the Yukon. I leaned against the leather seat and snuggled against the blanket Aric had given me. Good Lord, I felt tired. Making a person sure took its toll.

Liam played with his phone, sending a text. The gentle tones from his tapping further coaxed me to sleep. "Hey, Celia," he said before I drifted off. "I want to show you something." He handed me his phone to show me a picture of a girl with auburn hair and stunning green eyes. I wasn't sure who she was until I recognized her smile. Liam grinned, brightening his boyish features. "Allie couldn't wait to show me what she looked like without her scars."

It was sweet to see him so happy. He was a good guy and deserved to find his mate even if she wasn't Emme. "She's beautiful, Liam."

"I know." His finger swept over the screen. "I've always known."

The wolves hopped back into the car a few minutes later and we peeled out of the lot. I could take only a few bites of bread from the turkey sandwich Aric had ordered but managed to eat most of the beef barley soup.

Liam unlocked his phone when he finished eating, to show the others Allie's picture.

Gemini straightened as soon as he passed it to him. "Liam. Did you tell Allie where we were?"

"Well, yeah, I—"

He exchanged glances with the other wolves. Their faces hardened and their muscles tensed.

"What is it?" I asked.

Aric pulled me against him. "Nothing. It's just better if no one knows where we are or where we're headed." He tried to sound casual, but I didn't believe him. "You should rest, sweetness."

I didn't rest, especially with the tension swirling around us like a dangerous storm cloud. Koda shoved the rest of his sandwich into a paper bag and tossed it onto the passenger- side floor, gripping the steering wheel tight with both hands. The others, although silent, stiffened their spines, vigilantly taking point in all directions.

And still it wasn't enough to save us.

Less than an hour later, the wolves erupted with sadistic growls. Between their angst and my tigress leaping to the ready, I knew we were in trouble.

A hard force collided against the passenger side of Koda's Yukon. Aric yanked me into a fierce embrace, preventing my head from slamming against the window. I bounced against him as a more vicious blow struck from behind, followed by a hit that caved in the hood.

Koda broke through the front windshield and leapt out. Another strike spun us backward, then another. I caught a glimpse of a large red wolf mauling one of the giant werearms circling us as we careened into the guardrail. Glass shattered from every direction, twisting metal shrilled and squeaked. Aric's arms tightened around me. I held my breath, waiting to die. Through the violent jolts and shudders, Gemini charged out of the demolished vehicle in the form of two wolves, followed by Liam. Aric released my seat belt and hauled me toward the front. The wolves ripped into the opposing threat. But they were outnumbered. I squeezed my eyes shut as the colossal vehicle swayed and tipped over what remained of the railing.

"Stay alive for our child," Aric whispered just before the world spun and crashed around us.

Chapter Thirty

We rolled at an astronomical rate, colliding against the hard and jagged terrain. Yet I failed to feel the force of the blows or any pain. Warm, cushioned softness slinked around me, enshrouding my form. It didn't make sense. I'd seen enough of the pass to know death awaited us several hundred meters down. My skull should have been crushed against the bent frame. My bones should have shattered from the impact. They didn't. Aric's power cloaked me. His strength, love, security—*all* his emotions wrapped around me. The tension dissipated, transforming me into a rag doll, encompassed in the protective bubble his body had become.

I heard his grunts, the thunderous crashing, and the relentless smash of everything we struck. The sounds were muffled, occurring high above me while I remained safely ensconced in a tranquil wave of tepid water. All the while, soothing images of my intimate moments with Aric filled my mind. From our first kiss, to his kiss of my belly when he learned I carried his baby. Bliss was all I knew until one final blow brought everything to an abrupt halt. I screamed when my right ankle snapped.

My head continued to spin although we'd finally

stopped spiraling. I forced open my eyes. Bad idea. My vision whirled in a dizzying blizzard of color. I tried to clear it. I had to. Sprawled beneath me was Aric . . . and he wasn't moving.

His right arm lay at an odd angle and his forearm had separated at the joint. Pieces of his elbow punctured his skin. "Baby, can you hear me?" He didn't answer. I rubbed my eyes hard, it took a few moments, but I was finally able to see him clearly. I bit back a sob. Blood trickled from his mouth, eyes, ears, and nose. Both legs twisted away from his knees. His ribs pierced through his chest like daggers. Somehow he was still breathing—and groaning with each anguished breath.

My human side responded with my nursing training. I straightened his limbs, yet that's all my tigress would allow. I ripped off his T-shirt, removed mine, and instinctively crawled on top of him. He jerked and roared from my sudden weight. It was an asinine thing to do given the extent of his injuries, but my tigress insisted I follow her lead. I concentrated on surrounding him with my love, just as he'd done for me. At first, I couldn't, so panicked I shook. But through my trembles I spoke.

"I hope our son looks like you. I love your eyes...Have I ever told you how striking they are?" Tears formed at the thought. "They would look adorable on our little one." I could picture them vividly in my head—both of us with our arms wrapped around each other, staring at an infant with those same brown eyes I cherished. "Can't you see it, wolf?"

Aric didn't answer. I kept talking. "I was wondering about the baby's room . . . about what colors to use. I thought maybe pale yellow and light green—just in case she's a girl. I don't want to know what we're having ahead of time, do you?" His skin shivered beneath me, I thought he was cold and readjusted my position on top of him. Warm blood streaked across my cheek when I rubbed his jaw. "I want him to have your grin, too. How cute would that look on a little person with no teeth?" He rumbled beneath me. Fear befell me until I realized he'd chuckled. I lifted myself slightly and gasped at what I saw. His bones were mending. They slid below his skin like pieces of a puzzle trying to meet. He must have been in agony, the healing occurring too fast even for a *were*.

Aric's jaw clenched from the pain. He groaned and arched his back. Every muscle around him rippled so tight I feared they'd snap from his bones. "Come back to me," he grunted.

I practically threw myself on him. "Keep . . . talking," he stammered.

My words and emotions had helped, though I wasn't quite sure how nor did I care. I spoke in a rush, telling him what a great father he'd be and how I couldn't wait to hold our baby against my skin. I admitted that I'd dreamed of having a family with him and that I knew our child would love him.

Aric's pain subsided, his breathing relaxed, and he continued to mend at an accelerated rate. When his body finally stilled, I wiped his face and body with my sweatshirt. I met his eyes when they opened. "We have to get out of here, wolf."

I helped him prop himself on his elbows when he nodded. Good God, there wasn't much room. Only warped and twisted metal remained of the SUV. Light poked through the shattered windows, and strips of fabric dangled above us like icicles.

"Can you *shift* us out?"

I shook my head. "Not through the metal and fiberglass. We'll have to climb." I winced from the shooting pain in my leg when I tried to move.

Aric scrambled to examine my ankle. "Shit. How bad is it?"

"I think it's broken." I wasn't *were*. No way could

he heal me.

He swore again. "You wouldn't have been hurt if I'd kept my protection around you."

I stroked his face. "You saved me from death." I motioned to my foot. "*This* is nothing."

Aric pressed me to him, growling when a barrage of angry fists pounded above our heads. What remained of the door was wrenched off. Liam stared back at us, bruised and bleeding. "Anara aligned with the Tribe!"

Aric snarled. *"What?"*

Liam wiped the blood dripping into his eyes. "Koda and Gem were captured." His head jerked behind him. "They're coming for us—they're coming for us now!"

Aric shoved the sweatshirt over my head and lifted me toward Liam. "Take Celia, she's hurt."

They carried me away, stumbling through the chunks of twisted metal and burning wreckage. Barreling down the ravine raced about twenty *weres,* in the form of rams and cougars. A witch holding a staff at her side rode the largest cougar like a stallion. That's when I heard it— the echo of howling wolves.

Aric's and Liam's eyes fired to gold. I would have fallen from the shock if Aric hadn't kept his hold. He yanked me to him, kissing me hard before shoving me into Liam's arms. They locked eyes. "Protect her," he said with quiet rage.

Liam nodded and lifted me into his arms.

"No, Aric!"

He cracked his neck from side to side and *changed,* tearing across the ground toward the oncoming army. The ferocious sounds of beasts colliding shook the earth as Liam darted into the woods.

Liam raced us through the thick pines, faster than I could have imagined. I wanted to beg him to let me go, to let me die with Aric. But I couldn't. Aric had asked me to stay alive for our baby. He suffered to keep me safe. I couldn't surrender to my emotions now.

My head pounded, knowing Aric would be torn to shreds. I wanted to make our enemy bleed, and when I heard the clamoring of hooves and sharp intakes of breath closing in, I knew I'd have my chance. The Tribe *weres* had maintained their beast forms to track and kill us more efficiently. Liam realized and *changed,* flipping me onto his back midstride.

I clung to the loose skin on his neck. As a wolf, he was in his element. His spirit soared and his animal side took over. The wind slapped me hard in the face as he sprinted deeper into the forest. Birds scattered and squawked above us, sensing the impending danger, and leaves rustled beneath his determined strides.

We quickly left the sound of hooves digging into the forest floor, but not the almost silent paws of the cougars. They were faster—and the witch made them more deadly. They closed in, working like a pack to take us down. Liam dodged the snap of fangs and the rake of multiple claws. I *shifted* us away each time they tried a collective tackle, but I was running out of breath and they'd proved impossible to evade.

I was surprised how calm my voice was when I spoke. "We can't keep running, Liam. It's time to fight."

He whined in acknowledgment. I *shifted* us one last time, managing to surface behind them. I emerged as a tigress. The cougar closest to me became my prey. I snapped her neck before she sensed my presence. Liam dug his fangs into the *were* before him. No human would've believed a wolf could defeat a mountain lion so easily. Then again, no human knew Liam. He fought like a true Warrior, taking on the three that ganged up on him.

I couldn't leap with my injured foot. That didn't stop me from cleaving into the flesh of those who neared with all my fury and terror. I used my *shifting* ability to bury another cougar and sever his head, but when I tried to grab another, two tackled me to the ground.

The witch spat chants of venom, forcing me to *change* back. I wouldn't have believed it possible if I hadn't heard the call of wolves grow stronger. A cougar in human form caught me favoring my right leg and kicked me hard in the ankle. I roared and head-butted him in the face.

The witch lifted her staff. "*Enough.* Hold the tigress, she needs to die."

Two cougars fastened their arms around my legs while two more secured my arms. She pointed her staff toward my heart. An antique bottle filled with thick crimson fluid was fixed against the tip with wire. Her eyes dimmed to black as she began her sinister chant. I didn't want those evil eyes to be the last thing I saw so I looked to where Liam continued to fight. Chunks of ripped fur hung from his back and blood gushed from the deep wound in his throat. It pained me to see him hurt and not be able to help. But I'd rather retain the image of his courage than my impending death.

I pushed back the ache in my throat. *I'll be with you soon, Aric.*

It was my last thought before the witch screamed the final curse. Thunder erupted. Lightning flashed. And yet I felt no pain. There was none to be felt. The curse never hit me.

It struck Liam, who lay dead at my feet.

Chapter Thirty-one

The howling of wolves ended. I stumbled forward, angling my head to take in the naked and still form at my feet. I never realized how pretty Liam's amber eyes were, probably because I'd always been distracted by his boyish charm and his noble heart. But there they were, staring up at me, devoid of any sparkle. Strangely enough, he seemed to be smiling. Maybe he was happy his pain had finally ended. And hadn't he suffered in the last few moments of his life?

A flap of skin hung from his throat, spilling the remains of his lifeline. Deep gashes painted his thighs red. Chunks of muscle lay dangling from his arms and he'd lost two fingers.

I let out a laugh—then another, followed by another. The *weres* had released me before the witch cast the magical blow that stopped my friend's heart forever. They stared back at me. Some scowled; others stepped away, unnerved and disgusted by my behavior. I laughed again. Oh yes, Liam's pain was now over, but theirs, theirs was about to begin.

The witch pointed her staff at me. Most of the rich red fluid from the bottle tied to her staff had evaporated.

What little remained reeked of blood and dark magic. She might as well have pointed a damn blade of grass. I exploded into a tigress and tore out her throat in one vicious snap.

My inner beast took over. I relaxed, falling deep within my mind, and watched her unleash our wrath. The pain in my ankle throbbed mercilessly yet my anger surpassed the trifling annoyance in my foot.

I tasted the blood of my enemies for Liam . . . and for his mate.

He wasn't supposed to die. He'd found Allie. He was supposed to get married and make babies and be happy. Because that's what someone like Liam deserved. He didn't deserve to be shredded like meat and struck down like he was nothing. He was someone special. A true friend, a brother, and an honorable Warrior, a *were* with more courage than any of these goddamn Tribesmen could ever possess.

I'm not sure how long I fought. It didn't matter. I never planned to win against an army of opponents. My intention was to fight until my last breath, just as I promised myself I would. I remember something hard beating relentlessly against my skull until the last blow claimed my vision.

It took a long while for me to gather my senses. My lids drooped like weighted steel. Unearthly growls rumbled around me, stirring me from a sleep I couldn't seem to fully shake. I shivered, but not from fright. I'd prepared myself to die. After embracing something so final, what was there to fear?

I trembled against the creeping chill working its way across my bare arms while I lay curled in a ball. The heaviness lifted from my eyes yet I kept them shut, allowing my senses to soar into overdrive. The stench of blood and dark magic crawled against the floor like mist, seeking out its prey while misery and pain sang a mournful tune through bays and growls. Something bad was happening. I needed to assess my surroundings before whoever held me realized I was awake.

Fluid trickled from my ears and the dull ache in my head beat in time with my heart. My bones stiffened. I ached everywhere except in my injured ankle. I must have severed the nerves to lose so much sensation. The thought disturbed me, yet I pushed it aside and listened hard.

Something drizzled like water from an outside drain—*drip, glop, drip*—cutting through the threatening growls. I took a deep breath, scenting the air, and almost choked from a collection of *weres* surrounding me. Only the pure scent of water crashing over stones gave me hope.

Aric.

He was alive. The increasing growls belonged to him, Koda, and the two Geminis.

They'd survived and judging by the intensity behind their snarls, they were furious—and *hurt*.

My lids fluttered slowly, betraying me and alerting my captor. Icy water splashed across my face. I leapt into a crouch, ready to fight, hindered slightly by the long brown slip dress covering my body. It smelled of Makawee. I didn't understand until my glare met Anara's.

We faced each other in the Den's large empty ballroom, which had hosted the gala months before. Anara tossed a pitcher carelessly aside. It rolled along the dark wood floor, colliding against one of the floor-to-ceiling windows that made up one wall. Moonlight beamed brightly against the glass. I'd lain unconscious for a long time.

My eyes swept along the vast openness, taking everything in. What the elegant room lacked in furniture, it made up tenfold in horror.

Martin and Makawee hung bound by their feet from

two crystal chandeliers, gagged and naked. Makawee's long white hair swung as she took sharp intakes of breath. She didn't struggle to free herself and neither did Martin. They stared ahead in a trancelike state as blood dripped from their slashed throats and into the two pitchers beneath them. *Drip, glop, drip.*

Anara kept them still and prevented them from healing, just like he had Bren. With no more effort than it took to glare, he held Aric and his Warriors against a wall with no windows, forcing them to maintain their beast forms. I leaned into my crouch and tried to *shift* my fingers. It didn't work. The bastard constrained us all. He chuckled and gave me his back; it wasn't like he had anything to fear. The wolves in human form surrounding us assured he'd stay safe.

Anara bent to lift the pitcher beneath Martin. Martin shuddered slightly. He remained in a trance, but the rage behind his blank stare was irrefutable. The Elders emitted power so fiercely, anyone could sense it—a command those without magic would misinterpret as confidence and superiority. Those who belonged to the world my sisters and I had stumbled into would recognize it for what it was: an atom bomb disguised as a lily, carefully contained and ready to erupt at will. I'd never cared for such power, but as I extended my senses toward the bound Elders, I really wished they had it back. They seemed weaker, vulnerable, *human.*

"You've made things so difficult for me, Celia." Anara's voice carried no trace of emotion. He poured Martin's blood into a small glass bottle around his neck, similar to the one the witch had fixed to her staff. He then bent before Makawee and took her share.

He corked the bottle tightly and covered it between his palms, lowering his lids with ecstasy. The bottle glowed gold and, although sealed, stunk of the same dark magic the witch had cast. I cringed from the sickening stench of its poison. Anara in contrast moaned with perverse pleasure, high on the magnitude of his prize.

He'd used his packmates' essence against them. That's why they'd failed to suspect his actions and remained defenseless to stop him.

The Pack whined. I wasn't *were,* but I understood the sacrilege behind his actions. My wolves, whose growls hadn't stopped, were incensed. My eyes cut to Aric. Desperation to break free fired the fury in his light brown irises. He refused to bow down to this monster. And hell, so did I.

I straightened. "How long have you been controlling them?"

Anara finished his indulgence before answering. He quivered slightly, relishing the last of the blood's effects. "Since the start of the war. For *weres* to be attacked so easily told me we'd grown too weak as a species." He scoffed. "All our so-called Alphas failed to see the threat to our beloved purebloods. *They* were responsible for their slaughter as much as the Tribe."

Sure they were. "How did you do it?"

He walked over to Makawee and bent to stroke her hair. Her mouth grimaced with distaste from his touch. "She's always possessed too kind a soul, even for an Omega." His voice remained gentle when he spoke of her. "Did you know she took in injured animals she found in the forest?"

I stared back at him. It's not like he truly wanted me to answer. The wolves quieted, remaining furious but needing to understand how a valued Elder had turned against their kind.

Makawee's hair slipped through Anara's fingers as he continued. "Rather than letting the worthless creatures perish as our laws of nature allow, she brought them back to her chambers. Many died, but some—even those too feeble to live—returned to their fullest health. No one understood why nor would she speak of it. One day curiosity got the best of me and I invaded her chambers in her absence. I found a vial with her blood." He shook his head. "Poor Makawee used her spirit to mend another's broken one. I didn't take it with me that day, of course. I chose to wait until the time was right." He smiled almost fondly. "She had no reason to question my scent in her quarters. After all, we met for tea there most nights. Isn't that right, Makawee?"

Aric released a warning growl as Anara abandoned her to stalk to my side. Anara ignored him. "I solicited the assistance of a witch—" He swung his fist, missing my nose when I ducked. The wolves behind me lurched forward and wrenched my arms behind my back, facilitating Anara's next strike. His backhand to my face snapped my head back and instantly swelled my cheek. I spat blood. My wolves went ballistic, thrashing and shaking. But like flies caught in a web there was nothing they could do.

Anara persisted as if uninterrupted. "You might remember the witch. I had Virginia hire her to poison you and set the fire. Excellent wielder of magic she was." He paused to narrow his stare. "Until you tore out her throat." That earned me another shot to the face. My wolves howled with rage and my tigress clawed at my rib cage, fighting to emerge. My breath shuddered in deep gasps as I glared at him. If I could have broken free, I would have sliced through his jugular.

"Once I had Makawee under control, I used our united power to seize Martin. It was almost too easy." He waved his hand casually in Martin's direction. "But that's what happens when you put a non-pure in charge of a Pack where the Omega and the Beta are of untainted blood." Anara peered out the window thoughtfully. "Did you know before coming here, we were all Alphas of our own smaller Packs?" He glanced over his shoulder and smiled at my disbelief. "Then I supposed you don't know once you're an Alpha, your control over your Pack follows you forever."

The color drained from my face. Anara not only manipulated the power of the Squaw Valley Pack but of those other Packs he and the Elders had led. No wonder he was so freakishly strong, he could probably take down a shape-shifter alone.

"That's why the others didn't know who attacked me. They didn't recognize the scents from the other Packs."

Anara clapped in mock appreciation. "Very good, Celia. Perhaps you're not as stupid as I thought." He scowled. "I was going to use my power and elevated position to lead our kind to a new future. But then *you* gave me no choice but to turn sides to survive!" He shoved his face into mine. "Why couldn't you just die! Why must I continue to see your wretched face?"

"I'll fucking kill you! You're dead, Anara—you're fucking dead!"

Aric had *changed* to human, shocking the hell out of both me and Anara. He remained suspended yet his frantic thrashing had cracked the wall behind him. Anara's bemusement told me it should have been impossible for Aric to use his power at all. He meandered to Aric, who continued to bash and flay hard enough to strain the cords of his neck and turn his breaths ragged. Anara touched his shoulder, awe glazing his eyes. Aric wrenched his body away, chipping the plaster behind him and deepening the dent. Anara smiled, admiring Aric like a rare masterpiece. "Such power," he whispered. His face changed without warning, veering toward me with hatred so raw I could taste it. "Wasted on this goddamn abomination!"

Anara rushed me, punching me so hard I flew from the arms holding me and skidded across the floor. "Kill her," he spat.

Aric beat against the wall, his growls loud enough to shatter glass. I whirled to face the advancing Pack led by

Allie. But it wasn't those wolves he'd ordered to kill.

Koda and the Geminis fell from their positions, prowling toward me with their fangs bared and their eyes glowing in that ferocious gold. I stumbled back on unsteady feet, knowing I couldn't win against them.

But when they reached me, they gave me their backs and assumed protective stances. They growled at the human Pack and forced them back. I almost collapsed with relief. In restoring my mate bond to Aric, I'd restored his Warriors' duty to protect me. Anara couldn't make them hurt me now.

An invisible hand grabbed me by the throat and threw me into the corner. "You *whore*. You wasted no time bedding him, did you!" Anara held me and charged my protectors. The Pack of humans howled that miserable song and their stares brightened, fueling Anara's onslaught. His fists flamed gold as he pummeled the wolves, inflicting all the strength of his rage. I shut my eyes tight, unable to stomach the fury aimed at my friends. Their snarls and yelps filled my ears with their anguish until Anara finally beat them into silence.

I slowly opened my eyes, terrified at what I'd find.

Anara stood, gaping at his hands in wonder of his prowess. "Get up." The wolves didn't move. "Get up!"

They rose as much as their injuries allowed. Koda's spine split at the center. He dragged his body along by his front paws. One of the Geminis swayed with his head twisted backward; the other pushed across the floor with one back leg. Slowly and painfully they returned to the far wall. Tears streamed down my face. Aric's movements stalled to a deadly quiet. We locked eyes—a moment to bond, to give each other strength. Of course, Anara took it away.

"Did Aric tell you how many females he's taken in your absence?"

I knew what he was doing and let my glare answer

for me. His head angled toward Aric. "Should I show her?"

"I swear you'll suffer before you die," Aric promised through clenched teeth.

My vision swirled. I blinked to clear it and found myself in a dark bedroom where the aroma of sex condensed in sweltering tides. Sprawled on the bed on all fours was Diane, whimpering with pleasure and saturated with sweat. Behind her was Aric, thrusting himself deeper into her. He moaned her name, making her scream for more.

He obliged her.

Anara's strikes had weakened me. But this image brought me to my knees. I collapsed, sobbing. *"No."*

Thick angry fingers dug into my hair, forcing my attention to the bed. This time Barbara, Aric's former fiancée, lay on her back with her legs draped over Aric's shoulders, eagerly receiving his pleasure. I couldn't contain my distress and cried into my hands, weeping so hysterically I feared I'd pass out.

A gentle voice filled my head. "It's not true, sweetness," Aric whispered. I lifted my head. His transparent image stared at me with tender eyes. A ghostly hand stroked my cheek. "It's not true," he said again. "I love only you. I want only you, forever."

"Forever," I repeated. Aric's soft lips brushed against mine . . . then he was gone.

My gaze returned to the bed. This time it was Anara with Barbara and Diane, his face devoid of pleasure. Only rage loomed. Something exploded in my brain. I screamed as more fluid leaked from my ears. I hadn't quite recovered from the stabbing pain when Anara seized me by the throat with his bare hands. He slammed my head repeatedly into the wall, yelling obscenities and insults.

Aric went mad. Glass screeched and a solid mass collided against the building. Anara dropped me, veering away as I slumped onto my side, coughing blood and struggling to breathe. I didn't know what had happened until I forced my head up and saw angels standing before me.

"Get away from our sister, you son of a bitch!"

Chapter Thirty-two

My family charged in, dirty and covered with blood, with Tye and Bren in beast form leading the way. Danny stumbled in through a broken window behind them, determined yet shaking with fear.

Taran blasted Anara with a barrage of lightning as Shayna launched a dagger into his throat and out through his neck. Emme bolted to me, her blond hair swirling behind her. Anara's wolves *changed* and attacked. She threw out her thin bare arms, sending six flying through the wall of windows with her *force*. Tye and Bren lunged at the others, ruthlessly forcing them back.

I slapped my hands against the floor and pushed up, trying to stand. My head spun. I only made it to my knees before I collapsed. My body had given up, but my mind stubbornly refused to surrender. I rose, careening toward Aric. A large brown wolf tackled me after only a few steps. His front claws dug into my shoulders down to the bone, making me scream.

Bren snapped the wolf's neck before he could kill me. He *changed* and lifted me in his arms, carrying me to where Danny tried ineffectively to pry Aric from the wall. Aric shrugged him off. "Leave me. Get Celia out of here!"

The entire room caved in around us. Glass rained from the speed with which Emme tossed Anara's brethren through the demolished wall of windows. They leapt back in, snarling, hungry, and feverishly seeking blood.

Chunks of ceiling fell like boulders from the strength behind Taran's lightning bolts. She, along with Tye and Shayna, fought their way through Anara's guards. Shayna spiraled in, a windstorm of moving swords, slicing her way through the thickening army of raging *weres*. Taran closed in, compelling the giant beasts back with her fire. She'd almost reached Anara, but she couldn't stop him alone.

"We can't leave them," I told Danny feebly when he pulled me into his arms.

"I have to keep you safe!" he yelled.

As I looked toward the pack of snarling wolves bounding to us, I thought he was attempting the impossible. Emme didn't. She cut through the mob, parting them like waves along the Red Sea. "Run, Danny. You have to save Celia!" She cleared a path across the vast ballroom to a section of windows leading out to the garden.

Danny jetted forward, vaulting us into the cold night. He landed on his knees just as Taran screamed and the sound of flesh tearing from bone rippled behind us. Danny shielded me as the remaining windows shattered in a wash of blue and white flame. My heart sunk into the pit of my stomach. *"Taran!"*

Danny raced across the sprawling lawn, cutting between buildings until he reached our Tribeca. Deep claw marks were cleaved into the side of the SUV and blood was streaked over the hood and splintered windows. He reached for the handle only to jerk back to avoid the snapping jaws of a huge red wolf.

The wolf shoved his way in front of us. My hammer fist met his snout. I brought him to the ground. He shook off the pain and stalked forward followed by three more wolves. A fourth in human form jerked me from Danny's arms and punched me hard in the skull.

Spots fluttered in my vision. I forced myself up on my hands. More wolves arrived, these in human form. I recognized them as the morons who'd mocked and picked on Danny. They encircled him, shoving him between them and taunting him like bullies on a playground. He tried to break through the ring, reaching for me.

The red wolf I'd hit dug his fangs into my scalp and snatched me back. I could barely see straight. My head throbbed from the multiple blows. My limbs flopped against the ground, leaving a trail in the wet grass while he hauled me away by my tresses. He dragged me along, stopping suddenly near a row of firs. I angled my chin enough to see why. A beautiful snow- white wolf bared her teeth with unforgiving ire. Heidi, the last of Aric's Warriors, had come to my rescue.

"No," I told her. "Help Danny."

Danny didn't have the skill or cunning typical of all Warriors. He'd never become the type of *were* to make others tremble with fear. But he'd been my most loyal friend, coming both to my aid and Aric's. I couldn't allow his death. I had the power to stop it. So I gave him the only thing I had left—a chance at life.

Heidi's ears perked up and her head shot toward where he remained at the mercy of the other wolves. There was no hesitation. She charged, ramming them at full speed.

Drool dripped from the wolf's jowls and onto my hair as he raked me over the gravel, the stone steps, and through the debris and destruction littering the main building. Each movement struck me like ruthless kicks. My inner tigress made me tough, but we'd reached our limits and I doubted we could take much more.

Something punctured my wrist, forcing blood to seep and leaving a trail behind me. The *were* following us bent to get a taste. He licked his chops, eager for more. My eyes burned, knowing Anara would willingly oblige him.

Shayna's nightmarish shrieks resonated through the massively thick oak doors and started my tears. She hurt. They all did. Because of him.

The doors were thrown open, an invitation to return to hell. Slivers of wood and glass cut into my skin as the wolf dragged me over the remains of the once grand ballroom.

I passed Bren and Emme first. They were draped over the battered floor where they'd collapsed, from death or bludgeoning—I couldn't tell which. But Emme wasn't healing, and that in itself was a very bad sign. Bren's brown paw was slung over her back. His muscles were flaccid and shriveled from weeks of lying unconscious, and still he'd fought to protect us. Even near to death, he shielded Emme.

Taran and Tye were next. Tye lay as a tremendous lion, his bowels strewn across the space between them. Blood tinged his white fur crimson and his neck twisted away from his body. Nothing in him demonstrated signs of life.

Taran met my gaze, her stark pale face expressionless as white and blue sparks sizzled erratically around her. She'd lost control of her power. She'd also lost an arm. Blood squirted from the bloody stump despite her attempt to tie off the artery with her scarf. She was powerless, weaponless, and terrified. And still not as vulnerable as Shayna.

Shayna stopped screeching and flailing her legs when she saw me, but when I saw what Anara had done to her I thought she had every damn right to continue. Blood drenched her light blue shirt, plastering it to her thin frame. Shards of broken bones jutted from her elbows. Anara had feasted on her limbs, devouring her hands, muscles, and bones while she watched. She choked on her sobs as the wolf lugged me past her. *"Celia."*

Anara kept his back to me as he loomed over Aric. Aric had wrenched himself from the wall and now lay writhing against the floor, his eyes more animal than human. Anara . . . he was mostly animal. He'd doubled in size. His clothes lay in shreds across the floor. Silver fur spilled over his humanoid body and sharp black claws protruded from the soles of his hands and feet. He turned, unmasking his grotesque wolf head. The flask of blood hung against his furry chest. He stroked it lovingly while picking chunks of flesh from his razor-sharp fangs. "I can understand why Shayna was fed to the demons. She's absolutely delicious."

My heart pounded slowly, but with purpose. There was so much strength one could gather from anger. "You *fucking* coward."

His head snapped toward me. "What did you—?"

I drove my fist into my captor's jaw, breaking his hold and hopping to a stand. My injured foot hung loosely, the nerves so damaged I felt no pain when I drove it into the red wolf's side and sent him soaring into Anara. "I said you're a *fucking* coward!" Anara shoved the wolf off him. I limped forward. "Fight me—not with your magic—but like the *were* you pretend to be."

"Celia, no!" Aric's voice was that of a beast.

I kept my focus on Anara. If I looked at Aric, it would've been to say goodbye—to admit defeat—and I refused to deny our baby one last chance to survive. No. I was going to give Anara everything he deserved. "He wants me dead, Aric. If there's any truth to his preeminence bullshit, then he shouldn't have any problem killing me—*without* his stolen power."

Anara ransacked me, but I was ready. I flipped him over, driving my knee deep into his groin. He snapped at me with his jowls, but I was too fast. I knife-handed him right in the eye and yanked it from the socket. He roared in pain. I silenced him with an elbow to the jaw, forcing him to sever his tongue.

The wolves howled, egging on their Leader. Taran, Shayna, and Aric yelled, begging me to run. They didn't understand. A pack of wolves waited outside, ready to maul me if I tried to flee. There was no escaping Anara. Evil like him needed to die. I ignored them and ripped off his ears. He lashed out at me half-blind, scratching me across the chest. After being beaten so many times, tears to my skin seemed like more of a nuisance. I fought. My God, how I *fought*. He kept me from *changing* or *shifting,* but he couldn't stop my punches, kicks, and strikes.

I battled to reach his chest. But Anara whirled and veered, protecting his heart and forcing my blows elsewhere. He bled in rivers and hollered with agony. I was beating him. He knew it. Just like he knew he couldn't allow me to win.

The howling of wolves erupted full blast and launched me across the room. This time, I wasn't getting up. My left leg snapped when I landed. I coiled around it, screaming.

I looked at Aric then, but it was hard. I couldn't stop my tears. I didn't want to die. I wanted to marry him and raise our family. As Anara's paws scraped against the floor toward me, I knew it was no longer possible.

"Don't you touch her!" Aric growled.

Anara moved slowly, healing with every step until his freakish form was whole once more. He hovered over me, smiling with his bloody fangs. He threw back his leg and aimed for my stomach. I rolled to my opposite side, shielding my belly. His foot cracked against my back, making me roar with agony. He paused before leaping over me. Again, he tried to kick my stomach and again I spun and protected my belly despite the horrid pain of my broken body.

He walked around me to meet my face. "Why did

they tell you to run?" I barely heard him over Aric's snarls and my sisters' screams. "Why did they fight so fiercely to save you?" His breath released in frighteningly rapid bursts. "And why do you cover yourself there?" He pointed accusingly at my belly. Everything in his face told me he finally knew my secret. "No," he gasped. *"No!"*

Anara clutched my throat and yanked me up, shoving his distorted wolf face against mine. He shook with all the rage from hell while my arms fell limp at my sides. "Blasphemous whore! I shall make you suffer for your sin."

He drove his claws into my pelvis. And I felt my baby die.

Pain—sharp, burning, and crushing—ravaged my body at once. Warm fluid leaked between my legs, sliding down to my feet and dripping on the floor. Aric howled in anguish. He felt our baby leave me, too. That's when I knew my time on earth was over. I needed to be with our son. But before my eyes could close forever, I thrust my hand at Anara's chest. No, not into his heart—that was never the goal—but at the large vial full of blood he kept so close. I snatched it from the chain around his neck and smashed it against the floor, releasing the essence of the Elders.

And his hold on Aric.

Chapter Thirty-three

The sun shone brightly, warming me and relieving the chill burrowing deep into my bones. I'd returned to the same field from my visions. My fingers slid over the soft brown blanket where I sat beneath a brilliant blue sky. I tucked the skirt of my long white dress to cover my feet, fearful that terrible cold would return to claim me once more.

It was then I noticed the gentle yellow glow of my skin. *My aura,* I thought. The realization made me smile and so did its growing intensity. It called to mind sunny days from my childhood. I relished how happy it made me feel, until the wicked sounds behind me made me veer in alarm.

Dark clouds covered the distant horizon. I remained within the safety of the sun, but I sensed the fury, hate, and violence they carried. I could hear what lurked within them—primal roars, the crushing of bones by powerful jaws, the tearing of fleshy tissue, the ripping of ligaments, and the cries of pain that accompanied such afflictions. Screaming—so much screaming—the wretched squeals from an enormous beast being slaughtered without pity or remorse. I lurched away to stare where the sun made it safe and granted me peace from it all. But then I heard the voices of my loved ones, forcing me to turn back toward the madness.

"Damnit, Celia—don't you leave us!" Bren's voice boomed, commanding me though his sorrow etched into every word. My fingers swept over my chest, expecting hands to be rhythmically pushing down. But there were none and my pain was slowly dissolving.

Emme's voice sounded desperate. "It's not working. I'm losing her!"

The yellow light around me surged. Another joined it, this one white. Makawee's frail and heartbroken voice chanted in that beautiful language she'd shared with me once before.

Taran's hysteria wouldn't allow her to speak. Was she in pain? I couldn't understand why she cried so hard. She was so beautiful and spirited. Didn't she know she'd be all right without me? They all would.

Shayna sobbed. "*Aric*. Celia's dying!"

A long, tortured screech spilled through the black clouds. Thunder and lightning blasted, spreading the ominous darkness like sand. Then silence. The clouds diffused, revealing the same hallowed light protecting me.

The voices should've stopped yet they didn't. More mantras joined the others, this time in Japanese and Korean. I recognized the languages through Gemini's and Chang's voices. Ying-Ying was there, too, singing in that delicately sweet soprano.

Something warm and delicious slid into my mouth. I knew what it was and spat it back out. My shoulders were shaken forcefully, although my body failed to move. "You do not have my consent to pass on. Now take my blood!" Misha ordered. More fluid was forced in. Again, I refused it. On the ground where I'd spat lay diamond hearts and tiny tears.

"Please, baby, please," Aric's voice begged. "Just take the blood."

I could hear how badly he wanted me to drink, but my pain was finally tolerable. I didn't want it back. My body refused to return where it wasn't safe—where it hurt. No. This was better.

Danny yelled. "Aric!"

"Damnit, man—*no!*" Koda growled. "Come back to us!"

Martin's weary voice was barely audible. "There's nothing you can do. He's gone to join his mate."

Aric took form across from me, smiling. "There you are." A thick white sweater draped over his broad chest and tightened around the muscles of his arms. Dark jeans covered his long legs—the same clothes Misha had worn in my vision.

My breath caught. I wanted to smooth my hand over his perfect dark Irish complexion and graze the five o'clock shadow curving along his jaw. The intensity of his eyes brightened when he took me in. I followed his gaze as it traveled down my body, expecting to find our baby nursing from my breast. But my arms were empty.

I rose, searching frantically for our son. Aric stood with me, his voice breaking. "He's gone, sweetness."

A brilliant white light formed in the distance. A baby cooed from within. I moved toward the light. "He's over there, Aric." Every step I took to where my baby waited erased more of my pain.

Before I completely healed, Aric took my hand. "We can't, Celia. There's still much to do."

I tried to pull him forward. "Aric, our baby needs us."

Tears streamed down his face and fell against his sweater in thick drops. With his other and he passed me a goblet filled with Misha's diamond hearts and tears. "Take it."

I lifted it from his grasp, unsure as to why I should do what he asked. "This is his. I only want you."

Aric smiled though his eyes carried so much misery. "It's not our time, my love."

My gaze wandered to where the endearing sounds of our baby beckoned me. When I took a small step toward Aric, a horrible ache stabbed my belly. He released my hand and tucked me against him, except he couldn't alleviate my pain; only our child could.

I stared at the goblet. It promised life just like it promised suffering. I didn't want to hurt anymore and wrestled with my decision. Aric waited, saying nothing.

Finally, I raised the chalice to my lips. The diamond hearts and tears melted into a delicious liquid. I drank for Aric. Not because he asked. But because he'd allowed me to choose.

He held out his hand when I finished. "Are you ready?"

I nodded. My hand met his and we turned one last time to where our baby continued to coo. The lump in my throat tightened. "Will I ever get to hold him?"

Aric squeezed my hand. "Someday, we both will. I swear it."

I believed him, which was why I ran with him, back to the place where our loved ones chanted and wept. I sank deeper into a quicksand of agonizing pain with every push of my legs. Tears leaked from the torture. Yet I didn't slow; I raced faster, leaving the field and all its glory behind.

My body jolted from the feel of razors slicing their way across my body. I jerked up, choking in the middle of the demolished ballroom. The sobs from my sisters and wails of the Catholic schoolgirls drowned my cries of pain. Holding me were the strong arms of my mate, who even in death refused to let me go.

There was strength one could gather from anger. But so much more could be achieved through love.

My memory of what happened upon my return from the field melded into a confusing blur. I remember being bathed and placed in a comfortable bed. IVs were started in both my arms. They bothered me so I yanked them out. Food was offered. I refused to eat. Nothing could fill the vast hollowness within me, so I didn't bother. Voices cut through my fog. Most things I ignored. Some I remembered quite vividly.

Aric growled. "Why is she in so much pain?"

Martin answered him. "The evil one struck her with the sacred power from multiple Packs. Despite our combined efforts there's nothing more we can do. It will take time for her to mend."

"But she'll heal, won't she?" There was a pause before Aric asked more forcefully. "I want to know if she'll heal!"

Makawee's sadness continued to haunt her voice. "Aric, what the evil one did to Celia would have killed most. While I believe she will eventually stop hurting, children . . . are no longer possible."

Shayna must have caught the cool tears sliding down my face. "She can hear you," she whispered.

Aric went ballistic and yelled at everyone to get out. His strong arms pulled me into a tight embrace. My body curled against him, allowing him to release his grief while mine spilled across his chest. This wasn't happening. This wasn't real. Life couldn't be so cruel.

I don't remember sleeping. I only remember waking. Someone opened the door to the room, only to be greeted by a snarling gray wolf.

Emme put her hands out. "Aric, please. We're not going to hurt her. We just want to make sure Celia's okay." Her soft requests were met with more threatening growls. I sat up from the bed and wrapped my arms around his neck. His presence was unbelievably comforting, yet it failed to give me strength to emerge from my depression and relieve my physical agony. I stared blankly ahead, unable to form a single word.

Taran stomped forward. "Damnit, Aric. We love her, too!"

Shayna yanked her back. "Don't, Taran, they need time alone. Emme, leave the food, we'll come back when she's ready for us."

Aric returned to his human form when they left and retrieved the tray of food. I rolled away from it when he placed it on the nightstand. "Please, sweetness. You have to eat, love."

Eventually I let him feed me, recognizing his overwhelming urgency to care for me and keep me safe.

Days passed like hours.

I allowed Aric to continue to dote on me. Every time my needs were met, he would *change* back into a wolf and resume his protective watch over me. He forbade anyone to enter our room. I was too weak to argue and in no mood to entertain, so admittedly, I didn't put up much of a fuss. What concerned me was his need to remain as a beast.

I wasn't sure what day it was, but I needed to leave the bed and tried to rise from my fetal position. It hurt. I didn't want Aric to see how much. I scooted to the edge of the mattress and tried not to flinch. Aric's wolf form was tremendous, but on the large, elevated mattress, he seemed mammoth. I stood and wrapped my arms around my belly, trying not to think about my empty womb. It was hard; my soreness centered around where my baby had thrived.

I swore in my head. Anara had struck me with the ultimate magic of the Packs to ensure Aric's bloodline would remain untainted. I swallowed back my bitterness, not wanting to waste my thoughts on someone so heinous the *weres* would no longer refer to him by name.

I studied the colossal suite while I worked to settle my breathing. A long white couch and two plush chairs made up the sitting room beside a grand picture window. The shades were drawn, but I had no desire to open them, despite the bright sun peering through the cracks. The slate blue walls remained bare, along with the dark wood furniture. Aric hadn't hung a picture, a painting, or anything to make it more his home. To him, it had only been a place to sleep.

A small hallway led to his bathroom. Aric leapt off the bed and followed me when I walked toward it. On either side of the hallway were massive walk-in closets, one was half-full the other empty, save a few hangers. The empty one was large enough to be a bedroom . . . or perhaps a nursery. I shuddered, trying to shake the thought.

I quickened my pace to the toilet and shut the door for privacy, grateful Aric couldn't see me. I wouldn't have been able to hide my grimace or prevent myself from doubling over in anguish. As it was, Aric growled at my sharp intake of breath. He hated that I continued to suffer. But my pain would someday end. My scars? That was a different story.

A spiderweb of hideous red lines marked my lower abdomen where Anara's claws had punctured my skin—a permanent reminder of how he'd robbed us of our child. My pants hid the worst of the damaged tissue, but the embodiment of his torture would haunt me the rest of my days.

Aric followed me to the sink when I stepped out. I looked in the mirror and tried not to cringe at my reflection. Pale skin, swollen from crying, stretched over my thin face. God, I needed more calories. The little food I'd managed to consume wasn't enough for my inner beast. We needed more. I brushed my teeth and washed my face, promising Aric I'd make more of an effort to eat.

Something in the half-filled closet caught my attention on my return to bed. There, on top of a small bureau, lay two beautiful and familiar wooden frames—

gifts once given to me by Aric. When he'd left me, they'd disappeared from the room we'd shared. I'd thought my sisters had taken them to spare me from the memories, but here they were in his possession.

I lifted them and examined the black-and-white photos. The one in my left hand was taken when we first fell in love. We were staring at each other with such intensity, Shayna had captured the loving moment with her camera. In the other, Aric held me while I laughed and he nuzzled my neck. They were both from the beginning of our relationship. A happier time. Never could I have imagined then how much darkness would surround our lives.

A single tear escaped my right eye. "You kept these. After how much I made you hate me, I can't believe you didn't destroy them."

Aric's muscular human arms wrapped around my waist, and he kissed my head. "I felt a lot of anger, sadness, and hurt. But hate? No. You are my love. I could never hate you."

I smiled weakly and returned the pictures to their spots. Aric held my face in his hands when I turned to him, soothing my body with his touch. Deep circles shadowed his sad and tired eyes. He hadn't shaved and his thick dark hair was mussed. Still, he was the most beautiful being on earth to me. I stood on my toes and swept my lips over his. The taste was so sweet, I wanted more. I kissed him softly until our tongues met, igniting our passion in one mighty burst.

Aric's hands traveled the length of my back to cup my backside. Mine were more daring. He stood naked, giving me full access. I took advantage, making him grunt and moan until he tore himself away from me.

I stumbled back from the force he used to separate us. His hands gripped either side of the door frame. The muscles on his back, arms, and legs bulged with growing strain. He lowered his head, panting heavily. "No," he groaned.

I slid numbly to the thick carpeted floor. Of . . . of course he didn't want to make love to me. What would be the point? I couldn't continue his bloodline.

"You don't want me anymore," I acknowledged aloud.

Aric glanced over his shoulder, his eyes widening. He rushed to my side and gathered me in his arms. I wept as my head fell against him. "I'll always want you, sweetness. But you're in pain. You need time to heal." He swallowed hard. "I don't ever want to hurt you again."

I wiped my eyes. "Are you sure? I heard what the Elders said. I can never give you a child."

Aric regarded me with enough force to melt my soul. "I don't need my heart to beat. I don't need to take a breath. As long as I have you, there is nothing else I need."

He meant what he said, for now. But I remembered the joy on his face when I told him I was having our baby. In time, I alone wouldn't be enough.

He carried me back to bed and resumed his wolf form. A soft knocking stirred me from sleep sometime later. I glanced at Aric, surprised when he whined instead of growled. The door opened and in stepped a beautiful woman with white hair cut stylishly to her shoulders. She wore a pale green sundress and a poignant expression. "Hello, son," she told Aric.

Eliza Connor walked around the bed and sat at the edge. I pushed up on my elbows, embarrassed by my disheveled state. She stroked my hair away from my face, reminding me of my own mother's touch. Maybe it was the memory of my mother that started my tears, and perhaps her own maternal intuition drove her to embrace me. "I'm so sorry, dear." She held me for a long while and played with the ends of my long waves.

The position eventually became too painful. She

released me, likely sensing my discomfort, and wiped her tears and mine with some tissues from the nightstand. "I would have come sooner, but I wasn't well." Eliza caressed Aric's fur. "When Martin phoned to tell me about the moon sickness, I fell ill and believed it was time for me to be with your father." She glanced at me and smiled. "But you didn't let something like an irreversible curse stand in the way of helping your mate, did you?"

I smiled weakly when she covered my palm with her hand. "Oh, Celia. What a wondrous gift you've been to my son." Eliza stopped smiling. "Just when I started to recover, I felt Aric leave this earth." She wouldn't look at Aric then, I guess it was too hard. "My poor health returned, so I must ask your forgiveness for the time it took me to arrive."

Aric placed his large head on her lap. I simply nodded. She had nothing to apologize for as far as I was concerned, so instead I asked her about Aric. "Why does he continue to maintain his wolf form?"

"He, like the others, is in wolf mourning." She stroked my hair again. "Soon I shall join them. Our inner beasts are capable of dealing with more physical and emotional suffering than our human sides." She sighed and wept softly. "The treachery and pain you endured, Liam's death, and the death of my grandbaby have been too much for us. We need to rely on our inner animals to help us survive this time. When our mourning as beasts concludes, we will mourn as humans and say goodbye to our beloved Liam. Then we will go on as life intends."

Eliza left our room a while later, taking Aric with her so my sisters could spend some time alone with me. My eyes bugged out when I caught a gander at Shayna's new limbs. Small, delicate arms grew from her elbows, resembling an infant's with hands to match. She waved them at me. "Hey,

Ceel. Don't worry," she added quickly when she noticed my alarm. "They're just growing back."

Taran rolled her eyes and adjusted the long silk gloves she wore. "For shit's sake. Can't you keep those things covered? You're going to freak her out!"

Emme ignored them and rushed to embrace me with her arms and her healing light. She studied me expectantly when finished, until disappointment creased across her delicate features. "I didn't help at all, did I?"

"You kept me from dying. I wouldn't be here if it wasn't for your light."

Emme's gentle green eyes welled with tears. I gathered my arms around her petite frame. It felt good to be strong for someone else. I hadn't liked falling to pieces and Lord knew I'd done it enough over the past few months.

Shayna climbed in bed next to us. "It was a combined effort, Ceel. Everyone needed you to make it." She gulped back some tears and stared at the wall. "Bren performed chest compressions when Aric ordered him to leave the fight. Taran and I couldn't help you." She flexed her still-growing hands to prove her point.

I wasn't sure if they were ready to discuss what had happened, but I thought I should at least ask. "How did Anara die?"

They gawked at me, likely surprised I'd thrown out the bastard's name so casually.

Taran sat beside me. She glanced at my belly, but caught herself and returned her gaze to my face. "In smashing the blood vial, you broke Anara's hold over Aric. Anara used the strength from the other Packs, but it wasn't enough. Aric was too vicious. So that son of a bitch drained every wolf under his control in order to fight Aric. He fried their brains, Ceel. Some are just starting to wake from their comas."

"Then how did Aric do it?" I asked. "He's strong, but he's only one wolf." Emme smiled. "He wasn't then,

Celia."

Shayna bounced on the bed. "Danny came in while they were fighting. He ran to each of our wolves and to Tye, freeing them from Anara's hold just by touching them." She took a breath, trying to contain her enthusiasm. "They healed, and—and *merged* with Aric. It was the coolest thing I ever saw."

Emme nodded. "Danny served like their glue, keeping them together within Aric."

Taran tugged on her glove again, pulling it further up her arm. "Makawee wasn't able to fight. She was too weak since that asshole had been draining her power for so long. She crawled across the floor just to help you. Misha and his family arrived soon after Bren began CPR." A smirk played across her face. "He rushed to your side and ordered the vamps to shield us from the fight. I hate to admit it, but I finally get why you're so close to him."

I couldn't discuss Misha then and focused on Danny's gift. "Danny can manipulate and block *were* magic That's his ability as a blue merle werewolf."

Shayna wrinkled her brow, suddenly sad. "What sucks is he didn't realize how to use it in time to save Heidi."

I jerked up suddenly. My body didn't like me moving so fast and punished me severely. I hunched over and grunted. My sisters gathered around. "I'm okay, I'm okay," I insisted.

The ache gradually receded but their eyes reddened and teared. Their sadness broke my heart. I'd sent Heidi to rescue Danny, not to end her life. It wasn't until Taran explained that I realized their sadness had been over my pain.

"It's all right, Ceel. Heidi's alive." She pursed her lips and glanced away. Aric wasn't the only one who couldn't stand to see me suffer. "She took on the group that attacked Danny. He'd been terrified they were going to kill him, but then his fear turned to anger when they turned on Heidi. That's when he realized how to control his gift."

"I don't understand," I said.

Taran leaned back on the bed. "Danny's ability is more pronounced when he's angry. When he's scared, he can't manipulate another *were's* magic—he can only sense it. That's why he couldn't free Aric when we arrived. He was scared shitless."

"When he grabbed the wolves attacking Heidi, he was able to freeze them," Shayna added.

Everything made sense. When the Warriors had assaulted me, Danny was able to use his power since he was angry that they'd hurt me. That's why he couldn't lift Bren out of his coma: he'd been sad at the time over Heidi's infidelity.

I smiled. "Danny saved us all."

Shayna grinned. "And got himself a mate."

I angled my chin in her direction. "*Heidi* is Danny's mate?"

Shayna laughed. "Yup. Poor dude. His ability to block magic prevented their wolves from recognizing their connection. It had to take her almost dying for them to realize it."

Taran laughed, too. "Yeah, I don't think she'll have a problem staying faithful now." She brushed my hair away from my shoulders with her gloved hands. My eyes trailed up her arms. Sadness claimed her beautiful face when she noticed how they fixed on her gloves. "I guess I should tell you about these, huh?"

I didn't respond. Throughout our conversation, I couldn't help but sense a difference in Taran. She was all attitude, all the time. She didn't do "insecure" and kicked self-doubt repeatedly in the ass. This wasn't the same Taran before me. Something had drastically changed.

She peeled off the glove on her left hand first. It looked normal, healthy. But when she exposed her right, I had to work hard to control my reaction.

From her elbow down, her arm glowed as white as bleached wood, clashing severely against her deep olive skin. Sickly blue veins branched across the length, giving the limb an eerie lifeless appearance. Taran wasn't perfect anymore. And Taran knew it. Her voice trembled.

"Makawee used her Omega mojo and my connection with Gemini to grow it back. It's not something that's normally allowed, but she felt obliged to help." She flexed her fingers. "I'm having trouble working my power. I'm . . . not the same anymore."

"I'm sorry, Taran." I tried not to, but I cried for her anyway. She didn't like it one bit.

Angry tears streaked down her face. "That bastard mutilated your body and killed your baby. Don't you dare feel sorry for me!"

I covered my face and let loose. My sisters wrapped their arms around me. Shayna stroked my hair with her tiny fingers. "Damnit, Shayna," Taran snapped. "Don't touch me with those freak hands of yours, you're creeping me out."

"They're not freaky, they're just little!"

That's the thing about having sisters—you're never allowed to cry or laugh alone.

Chapter Thirty-four

"Hello, Misha."

My senses caught a trickle of him outside Aric's third-story window before the *tap-tap- tap* against the glass signaled his arrival. The time spent with my sisters had left me drained. I carefully crossed the suite and pushed the shades aside.

Misha lounged casually on the sill in dark slacks and a tight black cashmere sweater. One long leg extended across the length of the ledge, the other bent where he rested an elbow. I pushed open the window and screen, grateful it didn't require much strength. Worry darkened his gray eyes and his wicked grin was noticeably absent. I'd lost a lot of weight and blood and had spent most of my time awake crying. I knew what I looked like.

"Why didn't you tell me about Anara?"

A soft warm breeze full of the fragrance of tulips swept against him, pushing a strand of his long blond hair that had escaped the clip holding the rest of his mane. I pushed it back behind his ear. "I didn't want to risk your safety or anyone else's."

Misha laughed, the sound filled with bitterness and lacking any amusement. He turned his head toward the view of the sweeping mountains without really seeing them. "Why do you do that?"

I leaned against the sill. "Do what?"

He glared like I'd missed the obvious. "Trouble yourself with those around you." His eyes traveled from my face to fix on my belly. "Since first making your acquaintance, all I've seen it bring you is despair."

I adjusted my position to rest my chin against my palm. "It's who I am, Misha. I can't help it."

"Well, perhaps you should," he snapped.

It was going to be a long talk. I thought about moving one of the soft, cushy chairs closer so I could sit. It seemed like a laborious task so instead I pondered the many questions swimming through my brain. One slipped from my lips faster than the others. "Why did you come back for me?"

"You should have *called* me when you first fell into danger. I could have prevented all this." He jerked his hand in an irritated wave.

"Weren't you the same vamp who told me to never dare speak your name?"

His scowl deepened. "I was angry. It's possible I might have overstated my meaning."

I shook my head. "No. You meant what you said, Misha." To be honest, I hadn't even thought about reaching out to Misha. Stress and terror had left me somewhat distracted.

I rubbed my tired eyes. There was something I needed to tell him. "When I was dying, I returned to that field in the vision we shared." The muscles of his shoulders tightened slightly, as did his jaw. "This time, Aric was there instead of you. My guess is that it's a place in my mind where I envisioned my greatest dreams . . . with him. I think you joined me there only because you'd just tasted my blood and were using our connection to ease my pain."

Misha didn't say anything. I kept quiet and let him

think about what I'd said. The breeze bustled and the same lock of hair left his ear to curve against his jaw. This time I didn't touch it. He watched me carefully. "Were you already aware you were with child?"

I stared down at my folded arms, remembering the tiny heartbeat on the ultrasound. "I'd found out that same morning." My voice shook, although I worked to steady it.

Misha tapped his fingers against his bent knee, keeping his focus in the distance and taking his time to answer. "I presume there may be something to your reasoning," he finally said.

I'd expected him to argue with me, especially since it was just a theory. But if my belief was misconstrued, he would have told me so. I moved closer to him. He couldn't enter the room without permission, and while Aric had been extremely patient, I think inviting a master vampire into his suite might push him and his beast to their breaking point. I waited for Misha to say more. Instead he returned his attention to where the distant mountain peaks remained covered in snow. I took it upon myself to continue our conversation, knowing much needed to be said. "You didn't answer my question. Why did you come for me?"

Misha's head whipped around and he snarled viciously. It didn't faze me in the least. I knew traces of his anger remained. He took in my lack of fear and huffed. "My family explained how you cared for them in my absence."

I shrugged. "I tried."

"They said you managed the empire as if you were a part of it all along."

"Well, I don't know about that. I—"

"You increased my profits in my absence."

My chin jerked up. "I did?"

He glanced at me sideways. "By sending my strongest to ensure the loyalties of my executive committee members, they discovered those corrupting my empire and disposed of them."

My raspy voice sounded shrilled. "They *ate* your board members?"

Misha scoffed. "Of course. Have you forgotten they are vampires? Subsequently they were also dismissed."

"Did they get severance pay?"

Misha didn't appreciate my humor. *"No."*

"Are they eligible for unemployment?"

Misha tensed again, this time because he fought a smile. I was getting to him, and he didn't like it one bit. I leaned through the window and tugged on his shirt. "Do you love your new bedroom?"

This earned me the glare of death. I glanced around, feigning confusion, and offered the most angelic Emme grin I could muster. "I thought pink was your favorite color?"

"Celia."

"But I never did get your fascination with unicorns. Is that a creature of the night thing?"

My arms extended far enough onto the ledge for him to grab them—fiercely. *"You* protected my family from acquisition from another master, you maintained my realm, you searched for me, and you freed me. You—"

Misha shut his magnificent eyes tight and turned away, but not before I caught the tears that escaped. Master vampires weren't known for their compassion or for their grief; many of their kind believed they were incapable of such pointless behaviors. But Misha wasn't just any run-of-the-mill omnipotent being. He was a friend—*my friend*—who hurt because I did. "You are never to leave this world without my consent. Do I make myself clear?" By this point, his arms had encircled me and I was crying, too.

My world was no longer safe. I risked my life on a regular basis. How could I promise not to die? The shape-shifters were still out there, so were the remains of the Tribe and whatever other scary I'd managed to piss off.

Still, I told him what he wanted to hear although it was a blatant lie. "Okay, Misha."

The door swung open. Aric stood at the entrance to the room holding a tray of cheeseburgers. His eyes narrowed as he watched Misha hold me and stroke my hair while my arms remained securely fastened around his waist. He didn't lash out. He didn't growl. Instead he turned and left, closing the door softly behind him.

Wolf mourning ended after Aric and his Warriors retrieved Liam's body. The time had come to mourn as humans and honor a fallen hero. Aric told me it was a day to celebrate Liam's life, except the tears, the flowers, and the heartache expressed the grief akin to all funerals.

Liam's parents, his mate, and his sister and brother-in-law sat in front of us at the Den's chapel. Liam's sister held her infant son on her lap. They'd passed us on the way in, but I couldn't meet their gazes. The guilt for his sacrifice hacked at my soul like a medieval axe. He'd died for me. No words could explain why I was more deserving of life, because I wasn't.

A large portrait of Liam hung near the altar. His ashes would be taken by his family to Colorado, where they would be spread in a sacred ceremony. Bren held Emme next to me. Aric sat to my right and his mother watched beside him. Gemini and Taran sat on the end of the long pew, close to each other yet strangely apart.

As Liam's best friend, Koda sat in the front with Liam's family. He held Shayna's hand, but kept his arm around Allie. Liam's parents and sister wept openly. Allie remained quiet and unbelievably still. Even though her back was to me, I could tell she was emaciated. The navy dress she wore slipped from her shoulders, exposing the bony prominences of her shoulders. I waited for her to veer around and scream at me, to blame me. I wanted her to strike me, so I could take some of her pain. Her mate was dead and it was my fault. But as much as I expected her to lash out, she didn't so much as glance in my direction.

Koda rose and marched quietly to the pedestal, bowing before the picture of Liam's cheery face. Shayna shimmied across the dark wooden pew and took his place comforting Allie.

Koda gripped the sides of the pedestal while heartfelt tears dripped down his strong face. He took a moment to gather himself then expelled a deep breath. He surprised me by smiling. "Liam never could keep his trap shut," he said. He waited for our laughter to subside before continuing. "Unbeknownst to our Chancellor of Students when I was fourteen, I took his new Mercedes for a spin. Liam and a few of my cohorts came along for the ride." He glanced at Aric and Gemini, who lowered their heads and chuckled. "At fourteen, I wasn't the best driver. Let's just say we ended up in the Poudre River."

"How the hell did they manage that?" someone mumbled behind us.

"Don't swear in church, dear," his partner reprimanded.

Koda rubbed his hands. "It took us about half an hour to drag the car out of the river and another hour to run to Aric's grandfather's house for help. The old wolf got a huge kick out of our dilemma. He called a witch he knew and convinced her to cast a spell to repair the damage to the Mercedes. The witch didn't come cheap, and Aric's grandpa didn't find our situation funny enough to pay the bill without getting something in return. We spent that summer building an extension on his house and then painting the whole damn thing." He shrugged. "It wouldn't have been so bad if Liam hadn't run up to the Chancellor the next day and told him he was glad we didn't get caught stealing his car. Turns out the Chancellor needed his house painted, too."

We laughed again, only to quiet at the river of tears Koda's face had become. He raised his head toward the ceiling and sighed. "My brother, I will miss you. From now, until the great spirits unite us once more." He forced a smile for the congregation. "Yes," he said. "Liam never could keep his trap shut. It was always wide open. Just like his heart."

Aric, Gemini, and Koda joined Liam's family in greeting the attendants at the Den repast. Shayna remained loyally at Koda's side. Aric had asked me to join him, but although I technically was his fiancée, I didn't think it appropriate. Taran didn't join her mate either, claiming she didn't want to leave Emme and me alone. I couldn't help noticing the tension between her and Gemini. They barely spoke and, more disconcerting, they barely touched.

We sat on chairs draped with white linen in the early June sun. Aric kept glancing my way, except he wasn't the only one. Many of the *weres* present, including some of their human family members, watched me carefully. Some stared with curiosity, others with scrutiny.

Taran crossed her legs and draped her gloved hands over the pale blue dress she wore. "If that bitch looks over here one more time, I'm going to char her insides."

Emme had been quiet. As Liam's former lover, she didn't feel she could express her sorrow like she wanted to with Allie so close by. Taran's threat over how Diane glared at me forced her to speak up. "Taran, don't start a fight at Liam's funeral."

Taran's dark waves flipped behind her when her head jerked in Emme's direction. "She's the one starting it. Do you think she's upset about Liam? No, she's mad that Aric dumped her ass."

Diane narrowed her eyes further. I supposed Taran had a point. She stormed to where Aric spoke to his mother and another elderly *were*—and smacked him hard across the face. The brutal strike echoed, causing a stunned silence among the crowd. He shook his head to clear it. I rose, slowly, shocked at her outburst.

She rushed toward me. Aric intercepted her, looming over her. "You can say and do whatever you want to me—I deserve it—but my Celia is off limits."

Eliza took her place next to her son. Her back was to me. I couldn't see her expression, but I saw Diane's. She took a couple of frightened steps back and left. The reception resumed as if undisturbed. It seems some level of violence was expected at a *were* funeral.

Danny left his conversation with Makawee and walked toward our table. Heidi surged out of nowhere, her outrageously large breasts pressed tight against the fabric of her hot pink dress. He lifted her hand and kissed it. His eyes never left hers until they joined us at our table.

I smiled at her. Aric had told me she was the one who'd placed me in Makawee's dress the night we were captured. She didn't remember doing it, as she remained under Anara's control, but I couldn't help but think she'd done so against his will.

Bren swaggered over with his arm around some werecheetah and a bottle of witch's brew at his side. The cheetah snuggled contently against him. I'd wondered where he'd disappeared to. Taran gawked back and forth between them. "Son of a bitch. I can't believe you hooked up at a funeral."

Bren gave her a hard stare. "It's what Liam would have wanted." I pinched the bridge of my nose, knowing he had a point.

The sun had begun to skim across the orange and red sky when Aric knelt before me and took my hands in his. "Liam's family would like a word with you before they leave, sweetness," he said quietly.

I stood with him, knowing I had to face them and

yet wishing I didn't have to. Gemini joined Aric's side, his dark almond eyes locking on Taran. There was something different in the way he regarded her, but I couldn't determine what it was. She pretended not to notice and reflexively tugged the sleeves of her silk gloves. He lowered his head and reached his hand out to Emme. "They wish to see you as well," he said.

Emme shot me a panicked glance as Gemini led her ahead of us.

Aric tucked me against him and escorted me to where Liam's family and his mate waited beside the simple urn holding his ashes. My eyes burned as we closed the distance and I struggled not to fall apart. But my grief and guilt over Liam's death made it impossible to stay strong. By the time we reached them, I was wailing miserably and so were they.

Liam's human mother towered over me and yet she met me with kindness. "Don't weep for my son," she told me as her own tears continued to run. "He died honorably." She kissed my forehead and gazed out into the setting sun. The ache in my chest tightened when I caught her eyes lower to fix on the large portrait of Liam. "He was a good boy, always was," she said remembering. "He'd pick dandelions and leave them around the house for me. 'I know you like flowers, Mommy,' he'd say. Even once he found out they were weeds, he'd continue to bring them to me, knowing they made me smile." Her lips quivered a few times and her voice cracked. "I'd give anything for him to bring me one now."

I gathered her in my arms, my voice shaking. "I would, too. God, I'm so sorry."

I released her into the arms of her husband. Except for his advanced age and a few extra pounds, Liam's werewolf father resembled him perfectly. He smiled while he continued to cry. "Thank you for tearing out the witch's throat for us," he said politely. "I hope you got to eat it before you were captured."

"Um" was the only answer I managed.

Liam's sister, Maeve, passed her child to her husband and threw her arms around me. A tear trickled down her face when she released me. Like her mother, she was also human. "Liam really liked you, Celia," she told me. "He said you were kind and smart and funny." I smiled. "He was also impressed by your sexual prowess. He used to tell us how you and Aric would go at it for hours." My smile faded. His sister didn't look anything like him, but I could tell they were related.

Allie gave me an excuse to turn my crimson face away. She clasped Emme's hands and smiled gently. "The full moon is in two days. I'll be with Liam soon."

Allie was nothing more than a walking skeleton. Her pale skin clung to her sunken face and what remained of her muscles dangled from her bones. When *weres* die, their mates usually join them by the next full moon. Judging by Allie's fragile condition, she would join Liam before then.

Emme squeezed her hands. "Of course you'll be with him. You're his mate for eternity." She reached out as Allie lost her composure and gathered her tight.

It was the moment that Emme needed to release her despair and say goodbye to her beloved Liam.

Chapter Thirty-five

"Will they try to kill us?"

Aric's grip around me tightened. "I don't want you to worry about anything, love."

Okay, not the answer I want to hear.

Koda drove our SUV along the grassy path leading to Mount Elbert, the command center of the North American Were Council. Shayna rode in front with him, gripping his hand tight. She was quiet . . . and scared.

Aric's protective hold on me increased the closer we drew to the base of the mountain. My eyes darted toward Eliza on my other side. She tried to smile when she caught my glance, but failed to conceal the bitter scent of her nervousness.

"Um. This is the part where someone says, 'Don't be ridiculous, Celia. We're not walking into imminent doom.'"

No one laughed at my comment.

"Sweetness, I don't want you to worry," Aric repeated once more.

I angled my chin to face him. "Just tell me what's going to happen."

"I'm going to plead my case before the president

and his advisors. If they deny our union, I'm renouncing my pureblood status."

It sounded simple enough, except the tension thickening in the SUV's cabin convinced me that the ramifications of Aric's actions could be severe.

Koda veered left through a break in the trees. We'd arrived. Just like that. Too late to turn back. *Shit.*

Aric kissed my cheek before helping me out.

"Son of bitch." Taran emerged from the SUV behind us with Emme, Bren, Gemini, and the Elders.

Emme hurried immediately to my side and squeezed my hand. "Do you know something I don't?" I asked her.

She nodded and glanced at Aric. "I'll take care of everything," he assured me before I could ask. "I promise, I will."

Koda approached a giant slab of stone the size of my house. He muttered some words in ancient Ute and then stepped away. The giant slab vibrated, thinning to a clear shield before disappearing completely and revealing a modern fortress. Sixteen *weres* dressed in black capes and dark military fatigues marched toward us in synchronized rhythm. Most were Native Americans and wore holsters on their sides and machine guns draped across their chests. I could smell the gold from the bullets in the weapon chambers, and in the extra clips secured to their belts. It was the first time I'd ever seen *weres* packing heat. But I supposed if their job was to keep other *weres* in line, it was easier to fire off shots than to fight with claws and fangs.

My sisters and I stiffened when they encircled us. None of our *weres* responded aggressively or prepared to fight, except for Bren. He cracked his knuckles as he often did in anticipation of a brawl. In perfect unison, the soldier *weres* turned and led us into the mountain. The backs of their capes depicted the silhouette images of their beast forms in silver embroidery. The group was composed mainly of bears and wolves—except the one on my right. He was a wolverine . . . and somehow appeared the most threatening.

The best way to describe the inside of this Den was a colossal cave crossed with modern comforts and technology. Large brass sconces that flickered like torches lit the open expanse and the multiple levels spiraling high above us. Administrative staff shuffled around the floor or typed feverishly on their flat-screen computers situated atop shiny oak desks.

Everyone dressed in long capes, similar to the guards except in varying shades of earth tones. Those who passed us bowed regally at Aric and Eliza. They nodded back in acknowledgment, stopping only when a cluster of young *weres* knelt before them and the Elders. Each of the young carried a large red velvet box.

Aric and Eliza removed beautiful red capes from the first set of boxes. The capes—satin- lined velvet with flowing trains and trimmed with white fur and jewels—resembled something a king might wear on his coronation. The backs bore silhouettes of wolves howling at a moon fashioned from small black diamonds. If that wasn't bad enough, they pulled crowns, honest to Betsy *crowns*—from the next set of boxes.

Eliza adjusted her dazzling tiara. "Don't worry, dear. It's just a formality."

"Damn," Taran muttered.

Aric had dressed in a black suit and tie and black silk shirt. I'd slipped into a sleeveless maroon dress and silver sandals, elegant enough for a formal wedding, but certainly not enough for a coronation! I couldn't believe he hadn't warned me. As I took him in, I understood why. Aric tugged on the cape the exact same way he pulled on one of his tight-fitting T-shirts. And his command remained no bolder than usual—even with the damn crown. He was troubled by what we might potentially face, but these adornments, all the pomp and ceremony, didn't affect him in the least.

I reached up and kissed his lips. I wasn't sure if it was allowed, but I didn't care. His humility made me proud.

He smiled and cupped my faced. "I love you," he said.

"I know," I whispered.

Aric gripped my hand as the guards escorted us away from the open area and down a long hallway. We entered a large auditorium where rows of seats carved into the reddish-brown stone ascended upward. The twenty *weres* present wore elaborate capes and crowns in different variations and colors. Spongy soft chairs shaped like boulders replaced more traditional seats, strange yet befitting a cave full of supernatural beasts.

The president waited before us on a more traditional-looking throne, its dark wooden back extending several feet past his head. Something about him seemed familiar, but I couldn't quite place it.

We bowed our heads respectfully. He inclined his chin, saying nothing. I watched him closely, careful to keep my eyes averted from his. Four *weres* sat on either side of him, though at least twelve could sit comfortably behind the long stretch of carved marble podium they ruled behind.

The president reigned as a sole lion among the pack of wolves making up his advisors. His crown—surprise, surprise—was the biggest of all and perched on his head like the Pope's miter. Etched in gems into the stone plate before him was his name, President Omar Gris de Leone. My lower lip dropped to my chest. I scanned the room until I spotted Tye. Sure enough, he lounged lazily in the second row of seats nearest to me. He danced his eyebrows and flashed me his dimple. I could have killed him. How could he have never mentioned that the president of the North American Were Council just happened to be his father?

Tye donned a dark blue cape, just like good ol' Dad. I'd never had the chance to thank him for his help. He'd left during the first few days of my recovery, without much said to anyone. And yet as shocked as I was to see him, I hadn't expected to find none other than Destiny cuddled against him. His arm slung around her like the old pals he professed them to be. I feared her ability to predict the future had brought her to help determine Aric's fate. Her presence wasn't a welcoming comfort. And neither was her attire.

Destiny had really outdone herself. She wore neon-pink zebra-printed boots and white and black polka-dot tights. A sparkly silver cardigan partially covered a hot pink minidress that in no way matched her shoes, or the flamingo feathers sticking out of her tight bun. She was, hands down, a walking hodgepodge fashion disaster. And, truth be told, she scared me senseless.

She waved at me excitedly, sending some of her flamingo plumage into the air. I gave her a half-assed smile and turned to the President of the North American Were Council, believing him to be less frightening.

Omar's blond hair draped to his shoulders, just like Tye's. Yet Tye's electric blue eyes appeared to be a unique family trait. His father's were the more typical amber common among *weres*. Father and son carried a resemblance, except Omar's face was fuller and Tye's features sharper. "Shall we commence?" Omar asked.

Aric stepped forward, leading me with him with our fingers linked. "Thank you, Sir President, for agreeing to an audience. I, Aric Connor, Leader to the last remaining purebloods, wish to request an exemption from our laws requiring me to seek another pureblood for a life companion. I have taken Celia Wird as my mate and thereby refuse all others."

Omar responded stiffly. "Anything else?"

Aric didn't appear surprised by Omar's curt

demeanor. "No."

Omar turned the discussion over to his advisor, a tall and striking African American dressed in a cape of deep purple. "And what is the opinion of your Pack Elders?"

Martin walked toward the podium first. His long golden cape flowed behind him. As a non-pureblood, he didn't possess a crown. But his cape was just as regal and decorated with a mixture of black onyxes and clear diamonds. Martin stopped and waited for Makawee to join him. Preserved eagle feathers made the trim on her elegant brown cape, and silver beading mixed with turquoise and red stones created the image of her wolf on the back. Her crown was a Native American headdress, bejeweled with more silver and turquoise, the most splendid of all in my opinion.

Martin lowered his head. "As Alpha of the Squaw Valley Den Pack, I give my consent to their union."

Makawee's chin touched her chest. "As Omega to the Squaw Valley Den Pack, I also give my blessing."

Martin and Makawee waited, their demeanor more serious than I'd ever seen.

When the council remained silent, Martin took a breath and spoke, his deep baritone echoing over the expanse of the auditorium. "Aric Connor and Celia Wird's love for each other has overcome tragedies that would have ended the lives of most. While the current laws in place are for the benefit of our kind, it would be erroneous of me to necessitate them of Aric Connor."

"Do you expect our *were* race to die out, then?" Omar asked Martin.

"I cannot speak for your decision on all purebloods. I can only speak for Aric. Had it not been for Celia's determination and Aric's strength we would have lost the son of Aidan Connor to moon sickness. It's only because his mate fought to save him that he stands before us now."

Gasps and urgent whispers swept around the room. Evidently not everyone had heard of Aric's miraculous recovery. Destiny actually "ooh-ed" with delight.

Despite his intentions, Martin's argument worked against us. Omar smiled smugly. "To have a *were* possess the virility to recover from a bloodlust curse *and* mutilate an Elder leeching the magic from four Packs is a gift, Martin. And such a gift should be passed on to his children— with another pureblood."

Another of Omar's advisors leaned toward him. "Think of how formidable we can become. The world will only benefit through Aric's continued lineage. Mark my words, a new breed of more powerful *weres* will emerge." They were ignoring us at this point, talking mostly among themselves. I felt like I was in vampire court all over again.

Aric gritted his teeth. "Those who have found their mates know what they ask of me is impossible. I will have no other but Celia."

Omar growled. "To deny your obligations as one of the highest-ranking purebloods is disgraceful. You shame your father and his name."

I clutched Aric's hand tighter as he fumed, but it was Eliza who responded to the insult. "How dare you pretend to know my Aidan? Aric has never brought anything but pride to his family."

Omar leaned forward against the podium. "You forget yourself, Eliza Connor."

"And you forget that if my Aidan was here you wouldn't be the one on that throne."

A wave of turmoil erupted around the room. Eliza had just majorly pimp-slapped the President of the North American Were Council. Gemini and Makawee took a firm hold on Eliza's arms. Aric whipped around and whispered tightly in her ear. "Mom, please, calm down. You gave me your word you'd let me deal with this."

My hearing took in the most subtle noises around

me while my tigress paced anxiously inside me, waiting for the next slur, the next threat. Taran flexed her fingers, Shayna reached in her pocket for her toothpicks. Emme delicately placed her back against mine. In their actions, they promised to protect me and strike against those who endangered my safety. I sensed it, and so did the guards as they tightened their circle around us. The wolverine locked eyes with Bren. Bren smiled and blew him a kiss, daring him to make a move.

Martin raised his voice. "Celia herself possesses a formidable and fierce beast. Any child conceived through their union might very well surpass their combined powers."

Aric and I tensed. Martin had phrased his words carefully so the *weres* couldn't sense a lie. The President and his council hadn't been made aware of my pregnancy loss or the irreparable damage to my womb. I stole a glance at Tye. If he knew, he hadn't told them, and I sure as hell wasn't going to volunteer any information.

The wolf to Omar's left nodded. "It's possible they may bear powerful offspring. But it's also possible they'll have only humans." He looked at me. "As potent as she may be, Celia Wird is not one of us. I oppose Aric Connor's request for the good of the world's future."

Another female wolf spoke to Aric. Out of all the *weres* in the council, she was the only one to demonstrate a spark of compassion. "Would you consider making her one of us? It will make the likelihood of producing *weres* greater."

Aric worked to beat back his fury. "No. I will not risk Celia's life."

Another *were* waved away his remark. "If she's as strong as you all claim, then she should survive the *turning* and withstand the pain that accompanies the metamorphosis."

Aric's growls rumbled in his chest. "I will not harm

my mate just because you expect me to breed!"

Omar righted himself. "Then what should we expect of you?"

"The same loyalty and commitment to keep our world safe from evil—just as my family has done since the dawn of time."

Omar angled his heavy brows. "That is not good enough. You cheat your race by not continuing it."

Aric met his eyes. "Then I forsake my pureblood status and all the privileges that entails."

When I was in high school, glares and taunts greeted me every time I stepped into that damned building. The kids hated me because they knew I was different. Some poured paint into my locker, others wrote disgusting things about me in the bathroom, a couple of girls even managed to toss gum into the back of my hair. At that moment, I really missed high school. In high school, I could beat the snot out of anyone who messed with me. I was stronger, faster, tougher. Here, I was a preternatural creature among many, and the many packed ammo.

The entire audience lost their shit, taking Aric's decision as a personal insult and attack. Disgusted growls erupted at an alarming rate. A female *were* rushed from her seat with her nose in the air and her bejeweled crown placed perfectly on her head to spit at Eliza's feet. If it hadn't been for Eliza's grip on our arms, both Aric and I would have jumped her. Our loved ones encircled us to face the guards, although their backs were to us as they attempted to hold back the angry mob.

Omar flashed Tye a knowing smile. He didn't see me notice him over the rising chaos. But I did. I also noticed Tye's lack of enthusiasm at his father's behavior.

Omar roared over the crowd and stared down at Aric with so much superiority, it sickened me. "You're aware of the new laws that have recently come to pass."

Our *weres* exchanged seething glances, but it was

Martin who responded in a low, furious voice. "Do not tell me you still honor the laws suggested by a madman."

Omar crossed his arms over his ridiculously bejeweled chest. "He might have been a madman, but his reasons for the laws passed were just ones. Furthermore, he didn't act alone. Members of *my* council also provided their input and amended the laws to be fair."

Martin's remaining patience melted away, his rage forcing my claws to protrude. He pointed his finger at me. "The evil one tortured this innocent woman for weeks using *our* magic!" His entire body shook with his need to fight. "He took the most sacred of our powers to do his bidding. His goal was to rule the entire *were* nation by commandeering your position. And yet you uphold the laws conjured to help him achieve his aspirations? That's idiocy!"

Omar narrowed his eyes. "I'm neither weak nor a fool. Had the evil one attempted to release his malevolence in my presence he'd have felt my jaws crush his heart." It took all the *weres* on our side to hold Martin back. Omar ignored them to address Aric. "Do you still wish to deny your birthright?"

I clutched Aric's arm to try to stop him, recognizing the malice sizzling in Omar's irises. Something dreadful was about to happen. If I hadn't been so weak and fragile, he wouldn't have kept me blind to the potential danger. But I was too late. He answered Omar without hesitation.

"Yes. I relinquish my title as a Leader and a pureblood."

Omar's stare set like stone. "So be it. Aric Aidan Connor, you are hereby stripped of your supreme status of Leader." Aric kept his eyes trained on the podium. "You will no longer enjoy the comforts of pureblood status and will relinquish your funds, property, possessions, and those of your mother to the North American Were Council." Silently Aric and Eliza removed their capes and crowns and turned them over to an intern who'd remained quietly in a corner. It was so hard not to cry; they didn't deserve this disgrace.

Omar continued, enjoying himself. "And in accordance with our new laws you and your mate are sentenced to a year of hard labor in our maximum-security *were* prison."

Taran couldn't take it, she started screaming and cursing. Violent blue and white flames blazed and crackled around her. Instead of trying to soothe her, primal growls erupted from Gemini. I froze, too astonished to move. Emme cried, large angry tears, ready to launch her *force* at anyone who approached me.

"You call this a just rule!" Koda growled.

"I call it our law," Omar growled back. "Watch yourself."

Shayna stepped in front of me, converting the seven toothpicks in her hands into long gold needles. "No way, dude. No freaking way are you sending my sister to prison!"

Aric placed his hand on her shoulder. "I'm the only one going." He faced Omar again. "The new law also states that as the offending pureblood I can carry out any sentence for both myself and my mate."

I lurched forward. "No! This is how you planned to take care of things?"

Aric gripped my waist, his eyes taming when they met mine. "I hadn't expected the judgment to be so severe. But if two years away from you will guarantee us a lifetime together, I'll do it."

I sobbed into my hands. "No, Aric. You can't do this. It isn't right."

Eliza wept in Makawee's arms while our remaining group exploded in audible protests. "Aric, your chivalrous offer is duly noticed and accepted." Omar's response was simply stated. He was ready to move on.

The wolf who'd regarded us with sympathy cleared her throat. "Sir President, in order for the offending *were* to take on the punishment of his mate, the mate must be deemed worthy of a pardon from a member of the North American Were Council."

Omar's upper lip curled. He obviously hadn't expected anyone to bring this to our attention. He should have, though, if he really wanted me punished.

The wolf surprised me by not cowering at his feet. "Is there a member present who can speak on Celia's Wird's behalf?" she asked the audience.

"I'll speak for Celia." Tye glanced at his father, not bothering to hide his fury while he prowled to my side. The guards parted and allowed him to stand beside me. "Celia is honorable. She doesn't deserve to be sentenced to prison and neither does Aric."

A loud murmur spread throughout the crowd. A plume of pink feathers popped up as Destiny jumped out of her seat and onto the auditorium floor. The guards stepped away from her, too, more out of fear than respect for her position, I imagined. She pointed her finger in my direction. "Sir President, the lion is supposed to mate with the tigress. I have seen it." She thought about her choice of words and let out a giggle. Her face flushed pink, clashing hideously with her hot pink glitter eye shadow and fuchsia lipstick.

"I am well aware of your prediction, Destiny." The edges of Omar's mouth curved into a pleased smile. That's when I realized his intentions. He was sending Aric away so his son could fulfill Destiny's prophecy.

I hissed with all the force of my anger. "You can't lock Aric away just because you expect me to breed with your son!"

The crowd whispered feverishly. Omar glared, resenting me for calling him out. "Aric has broken the law, he will be punished. And there is nothing you can do about it."

"Yes, there is." I *shifted* Aric out of the room. The whole damn place was a giant rock.

No way could they stop me.

I surfaced near the entrance as the entire hall erupted in turmoil. My loved ones clashed against the guards, urging us to escape. Aric broke from my grasp. I leapt to grab him but he pulled away. Each time I tried, he dodged my hands, averting his pained expression from mine.

"Aric."

He bowed his head. "No, love. This will only make matters worse."

Aric allowed himself to be taken by the guards who rushed us. I watched, unmoving as they hauled him before Omar. Another *were* appeared behind me. I felt his presence, but didn't fight him. He didn't grant me the same courtesy and threw me against the stone wall. I cried out in agony from my still-healing body.

The guard abruptly released his hold. I stumbled away from the wall, hunched over in pain. Aric had him on the ground by his throat. *"You may take me, but you will not harm my mate!"*

Aric rose slowly and placed his hands out in surrender. Two more guards arrived as the one on the ground slowly staggered to his feet. Another marched up to me and motioned me forward with his assault rifle, careful to keep his distance when Aric glanced back. "This way."

Almost all of our party had been restrained, including Tye. They stopped struggling, when Aric stood by Omar and heard his words. "I accept my punishment willingly. My only request is a moment to say goodbye to my mate."

Destiny jumped in the air, shaking her arms and feathers. "The lion will mate with the tigress!"

Omar ignored her. "You may bid her farewell, but

make it quick. You've already wasted enough of our time."

The guards stepped away from us. Aric gathered me in his arms. "I'm sorry, but this is the only way."

"But the lion is to mate with the tigress." Destiny's voice held a strong note of confusion, as if no one could understand her.

My tears ran so fast I could barely see him. "Please don't do this. You haven't done anything wrong."

"Forgive me, my love, for failing you once more." Aric kissed me until he was wrenched away at Omar's request. His sad and beautiful brown eyes stayed on me as the guards escorted him toward a small door in the corner of the room. I fell into Shayna's and Emme's arms. After all we'd endured, why was this happening to us?

Destiny stomped her neon-pink boots against the floor as she bolted after Aric and the guards holding him. "You can't do this. The lion is *supposed* to mate with the tigress!" She blocked the door with her body, her gaze whipping between me and Aric. "A new evil is coming. And only their children will be strong enough to stop it."

The room stilled as Destiny's latest prediction struck us like a slap. The problem was, she didn't completely make sense.

Aric's brows furrowed deeply as he struggled to understand. "I'm a wolf," he told her slowly.

Destiny threw her hands in the air, regarding Aric like he was the crazy one. "Don't you know 'Aric' means 'Lion of God'?"

Chapter Thirty-six

It turned out even the President of the North American Were Council was afraid to mess with Destiny. After a lame apology for the "unfortunate misunderstanding," he ordered his guards to release Aric.

Destiny had predicted that "the tigress and the lion will mate" a couple of months ago at the gala. The second part of the prophecy had been "their children will be the ones to keep the world safe from evil." That's not what she said this time. She made it clear the world needed our children—mine and Aric's—against a new evil that would soon rise. I couldn't be sure if she'd done it to help us. But she'd made it a point to look at me when she dropped her latest prophecy bombshell.

Aric and Eliza retained their pureblood status, but after the deplorable way they were treated by the *were* elite present, it failed to hold the same prestige it once had. Omar gave Aric and me his damn blessing to be together—and holy hotness, we couldn't bolt from *were* central fast enough.

My head nuzzled against Aric on our drive to the airport. "It was wrong of you to keep me in the dark."

He gathered me closer. "I wanted to spare you. I

never imagined Omar would be so dishonorable."

Eliza stroked my hair. "But Celia's right. You should have been honest with her, son."

"Mom, look at her. She still hurts. She's not like us."

At first, I scowled at him for singling me out, but then I chuckled when I realized what he meant. "You think I'm a wimp."

Aric blinked back at me. I laughed again, knowing I was right. He couldn't grasp that I'd always been a fighter—even before I'd gained my strength and my ability to control it. One of my earliest memories was when I was three. A big kid shoved me on the playground. My ingrained response was to shove back. And damn, hadn't I spent my entire life doing as much?

The drive to push back harder and not take any shit earned me both respect and fear. Apparently, though, it wasn't enough to impress my werewolf mate or my guardian angel master vampire.

Aric rubbed my arm. "It's not that I think you're a wimp. You're just . . ." I batted my thick lashes at him.

"Yes?"

"Delicate," he finished.

Koda and Shayna cracked up in the front. "Shit, Aric. If you don't want to end up on the couch tonight, you'd better watch what you call her."

"Yeah, dude." Shayna turned around just to wink. "Be nice and count your lucky stars. Some werewalrus could have made you his bitch tonight."

Eliza cleared her throat to cover her laughter. "Watch your language, kids."

"Sorry, Miss Eliza," they told her through their giggles.

Aric escorted me to Misha's house to pick up my

belongings. I tried calling Misha to tell him I was moving out. He wouldn't take my calls or respond to my texts.

It didn't take me long to gather my things. Like Aric's quarters at the Den, Misha's residence had never been my home. Aside from some clothes and a few belongings, there was nothing else to pack . . . except for the box on the bed.

I knew what was inside before I untied the thick satin ribbon and removed the lid. The white dress from my vision rested perfectly against the pink tissue paper. I lifted it and caught Misha's scent.

"The master wanted you to have it." Liz strolled into the bedroom, filing her nails.

Aric glanced up from packing my toiletries in the bathroom. I angled my chin in Liz's direction. "Where is he?"

Liz brushed her nails against her tiny plaid skirt. "He's in Romania." I folded the dress back into the box.

"Romania? What's there?"

"Transylvania. He's gone to find a bride."

I burst out laughing. I'd never realized Liz had a sense of humor. She stopped filing her nails and glared. Apparently, she wasn't trying to be funny. "Oh, sorry." I clasped her wrist when she tried to leave. "Hey, Liz? Where did Misha get this dress?"

She threw back her ice blond hair. "From that boutique in Incline Village."

"What?"

She rolled her eyes. I guess I was interrupting her very important nail filing time. "You were out shopping there sometime before Christmas. Maria noticed you admiring it in the window and told the master. He had her buy it for you as a gift and then forgot about it until that day you got your ass kicked."

"I've never been shopping with Maria."

Liz shoved her file in her pocket. "She wasn't

shopping with you, she was following you.

The master usually has us guard you." She'd had her fill of humoring me and left without saying goodbye.

Aric lifted the suitcases we'd packed and kissed the top of my head. "Are you ready, sweetness?"

I drew the box against me and held it close. "Yes. I'm ready."

I didn't say much on our ride to Dollar Point and followed Aric quietly into the house. My sisters and their wolves were noticeably absent. They likely realized Aric and I needed time alone. My eyes skimmed around the large open family room that led into the kitchen. Shayna's black-and-white nature prints hung beside the stairs in new frames, and the wall had a fresh coat of sage paint. It was as if my back had never been hurled against it and the evil known as Anara had never existed.

But I knew better.

Aric paused on the first step. His grip on the suitcases tightened as he focused on my hands. "If I could kill him again, I would."

I hadn't realized I was stroking my belly. I paused with my hand over the thin fabric of my sundress and made a decision. My breath released in a small sigh. I kicked off my sandals and walked to meet my mate. "Let's go upstairs."

Two dozen fire and ice purple roses sprayed from a crystal vase on my nightstand. I smiled and crossed the suite to take in their inviting aroma. Aric dropped the suitcases behind me and soon I felt his strong arms encircling my waist. "Do you like them? I wanted to give you something to mark our new beginning."

His body so close to mine strengthened my resolve. I turned and ran my fingers across his chest, letting them slide over the dense muscles straining against his tight gray T-shirt. "I love them, but I want something more."

Aric shuddered and clasped my hips. "You should

rest."

"I will. After . . ." I stood on my toes and kissed him. I'd like to say it was a gentle kiss that lasted all day, one that preteens would swoon over. But I wasn't a preteen and I didn't like to lie. Aric clenched me tighter when my hot mouth left his and my teeth found his neck. He reached for the long silver stick holding up my hair and released my long waves to fall against my back. His hand cupped my neck and his lips smashed against mine.

I fumbled to tug off his jeans then dropped to my knees. Aric fell against the wall from the force of my appetite, grunting my name and digging his fingers into my tresses. He ripped my dress off—literally grasped the edge and tore through the soft cotton in one hard wrench. My bra and panties followed, dropping in shreds around me while I devoured my mate. I wanted more of him but he wouldn't let me take. He wanted to *give*.

Aric lifted me, spreading me across the bed before his head dipped between my thighs. My fingers ran through his thick hair as lust burrowed through where his tongue flicked and his lips suckled. My fervor surged, firing upward and releasing my screams.

He entered me before I'd finished, thrusting his hips hard against me and making me cry out once more. "I want you," he rasped. "I want you so much." Our bodies became a tangle of flailing limbs as we rolled, changing positions in a sultry dance until we caved in bliss and exhaustion.

Aric covered us with a soft blanket and drew me against him, sweeping his lips over mine. His fingertips stroked my face as he regarded me with an intensity that made my heart pound. "I'm going to make you happy, I swear it."

His eyes tamed at the sight of my smile and at the sound of my voice. "By being my mate, you already have."

Epilogue

Aric's hand skimmed over the small of my back as we strolled along the shore of Lake Tahoe. "We missed Thanksgiving together last year. We never celebrated your birthday, and Christmas downright sucked without you."

The September sun warmed my face as I leaned closer against him. "We'll make up for it this year, wolf," I promised.

Aric bent to meet my lips with a smoldering kiss. I moaned softly as I curled my free arm around his neck. We'd spent so much time in bed since moving back in together. This kiss reminded me why.

He pulled back, his light brown eyes smoky as he spoke. "Celia, I think it's time we start."

I thought my werewolf lover would guide us back in the direction of the house. Instead he led me around the bend and removed a folded quilt tucked between two boulders. "What's this?" I asked when he spread it along the sand.

Instead of answering, Aric pulled out a picnic basket from behind another large rock and placed it on the edge of the quilt. His dark Irish skin brightened to red and perspiration built along his crown. He hauled me to the quilt, causing me to trip over my feet. He barely caught me before I fell, and lowered me to the center. "Sorry—sorry," he said, stumbling over his words. "There's some . . . stuff in there." He pointed to the basket. "Help yourself—I'll be right back."

I didn't understand what was happening and blinked back at him as he darted away. I tucked my knees against myself and waited, then waited and waited some more. The breeze from the lake pushed back my hair and stirred Tahoe's magic around me, enlivening my inner tigress and inviting her to frolic.

I paused from trying to lull her back to sleep and collect my long curls when I realized where Aric had brought me. This was the section of beach where I first saw him . . . and where his wolf side had recognized me as his mate. I let my hair slip through my fingers.

Oh my God.

I rose slowly, realizing what might be happening and wondering where Aric could be, when the sound of clanging metal had me whirling in the direction he'd disappeared.

Shrill screams followed swearing. Lots and lots of swearing. My claws shot out when I recognized my sisters' distressed voices . . . only to withdraw when a snow-white wolf bolted past me wearing a dress.

That's right, a wolf in a dress. Welcome to my eff'd-up reality. Have a seat, I'll pour you a cup of crazy.

The wolf tore down the beach, kicking back sand with her large paws in her haste to escape . . . my sisters? I watched Taran, Shayna, and Emme race after her, the skirts of their medieval dresses hiked up to their waists and the rose petals from their baskets fluttering in the wind.

"Son of a *bitch*!" Taran ditched the floral wreath on her head and her basket of petals. "Run, Celia, goddamnit, run!" she screamed.

She jetted past me in full foul-mouthed glory with

Shayna and Emme at her heels. The banging sound grew louder. Danny stumbled after them, the knight's armor he wore making it hard for him to maneuver his limbs. "Get back to the road!" he urged.

Four more knights charged behind him on horses . . . wild, bucking horses. I only recognized Koda because his midnight hair hung from his helmet.

Horses clearly weren't taken by werewolf charm. And it seemed my wolves would never become accomplished equestrians. One by one, the horses flung them from their backs like sock monkeys. They landed against the sand in a loud clash of noise, half groaning, half laughing . . . and failing to see the horse thundering toward Emme. I dashed toward her as the large animal continued to kick.

The speed and agility that made me so formidable was hindered by the spasms of pain that continued to claim me. While I ducked away from the horse's legs, and managed to yank Emme from its reach, I couldn't avoid the smack of its tail.

The horse's essence hit me like a thunderbolt and I fell into a violent seizure. The world spiraled around me and what felt like slivers of glass raked against my skin. I clenched my jaw, trying to hold back my cries and work through the misery of my unplanned *change*.

The banging of tin signaled my knight's approach. "Celia, it's okay," Aric said. "I'm here. Just breathe, sweetness. Breathe."

It took several long minutes for the convulsions to recede and my torment to end. I rose on four very long and wobbly legs to stare down at my mate. Aric tugged off his helmet and threw it aside, reaching to stroke my face. Fear darkened his features. "Are you all right?" he asked.

I whinnied to assure him I was fine and nudged him with my nose. He swiped at his face. "This is a disaster."

Gemini took a step forward. "Aric, just ask her," he

said quietly.

My sisters and friends gathered around us as Aric slowly fell to one knee. For a moment, he simply stared. But when he spoke, I could sense his devotion in every word. "Celia, you have been my princess since the first time I saw you. Now, I'd like you to be my queen for the rest of our lives. Will you marry me?"

Big giant tears rolled down my long, fuzzy face. "Scratch once for yes, twice for no!" Bren yelled.

I thought I'd always be ready to hear those words. And there I was, a damn horse. So instead of allowing this moment to be robbed from me, I closed my eyes and took in everything that was Aric—his scent, warmth, love, and all that had brought us together. Someone threw the quilt around me as I felt my body shrink and my bare feet slide along the sandy beach.

For the first time, I'd managed to reclaim my human form following an accidental *change,* and I welcomed it for everything it allowed. Aric tucked the quilt around my naked skin and drew me to him, waiting patiently for me to answer. The lump in my throat tightened. After all the times I thought I'd lost him, was this really happening?

It took the soft graze of his knuckles against my cheek to assure me this was more than a dream. My body trembled and so did my voice. *"Yes,"* I managed.

Everyone assembled cheered when Aric kissed me, including Heidi, who *changed* from her white wolf form to stand beside her mate, Danny. Unlike me and being *were,* Heidi didn't mind being unclothed. In fact, she preferred it.

Three white doves landed a few feet to our left, their loud fluttering wings demanding attention and stirring my inner beast. I broke our kiss, smiling as the little birds closed in. Aric had gone all out!

The one in the center scurried forward, leaving a small trail behind him in the sand.

"Celia Wird," it screeched.

Reader's Guide to the Magical World of the
Weird Girls Series

acute bloodlust A condition that occurs when a vampire goes too long without consuming blood. Increases the vampire's thirst to lethal levels. It is remedied by feeding the vampire.

Call The ability of one supernatural creature to reach out to another, through either thoughts or sounds. A vampire can pass his or her *call* by transferring a bit of magic into the receiving being's skin.

Change To transform from one being to another, typically from human to beast, and back again.

chronic bloodlust A condition caused by a curse placed on a vampire. It makes the vampire's thirst for blood insatiable and drives the vampire to insanity. The vampire grows in size from gluttony and assumes deformed features. There is no cure.

claim The method by which a werebeast consummates the union with his or her mate.

clan A group of werebeasts led by an Alpha. The types of clans differ depending on species. Werewolf clans are called "packs." Werelions belong to "prides."

Creatura The offspring of a demon lord and a werebeast.

dantem animam A soul giver. A rare being capable of returning a master vampire's soul. A master with a soul is more powerful than any other vampire in existence, as he or she is balancing life and death at once.

dark ones Creatures considered to be pure evil, such as shape-shifters or demons.

demon A creature residing in hell. Only the strongest demons may leave to stalk on earth, but their time is limited; the power of good compels them to return.

demon child The spawn of a demon lord and a mortal female. Demon children are of limited intelligence and rely predominantly on their predatory instincts.

demon lords (*demonkin*) The offspring of a witch mother and a demon. Powerful, cunning, and deadly. Unlike demons, whose time on earth is limited, demon lords may remain on earth indefinitely.

den A school where young werebeasts train and learn to fight in order to help protect the earth from mystical evil.

Elder One of the governors of a werebeast clan. Each clan is led by three Elders: an Alpha, a Beta, and an Omega. The Alpha is the supreme leader. The Beta is the second in command. The Omega settles disputes between them and has the ability to calm by releasing bits of his or her harmonized soul, or through a sense of humor muddled with magic. He possesses rare gifts and is often volatile, selfish, and of questionable loyalty.

force Emme Wird's ability to move objects with her mind.

gold The metallic element; it was cursed long ago and has damaging effects on werebeasts, vampires, and the dark ones. Supernatural creatures cannot hold gold without feeling the poisonous effects of the curse. A bullet dipped in gold will explode a supernatural creature's heart like a bomb. Gold against open skin has a searing effect.

grandmaster The master of a master vampire. Grandmasters are among the earth's most powerful creatures. Grandmasters can recognize whether the human he or she *turned* is a master upon creation. Grandmasters usually kill any master vampires they create to consume their power. Some choose to let the masters live until they become a threat, or until they've gained greater strength and therefore more consumable power.

Hag Hags, like witches, are born with their magic. They have a tendency for mischief and are as infamous for their instability as they are their power.

keep Beings a master vampire controls and is responsible for, such as those he or she has *turned* vampire, or a human he or she regularly feeds from. One master can acquire another's keep by destroying the master the keep belongs to.

Leader A pureblood werebeast in charge of delegating and planning attacks against the evils that threaten the earth.

Lesser witch Title given to a witch of weak power and who has not yet mastered control of her magic. Unlike their Superior counterparts, they aren't given talismans or staffs to amplify their magic because their control over their power is limited.

Lone A werebeast who doesn't belong to a clan, and therefore is not obligated to protect the earth from supernatural evil. Considered of lower class by those with clans.

master vampire A vampire with the ability to *turn* a human vampire. Upon their creation, masters are usually killed by their grandmaster for power. Masters are immune to fire and to sunlight born of magic, and typically carry tremendous power. Only a master or another lethal preternatural can kill a master vampire. If one master kills another, the surviving vampire acquires his or her power, wealth, and keep.

mate The being a werebeast will love and share a soul with for eternity.

Misericordia A plea for mercy in a duel.

moon sickness The werebeast equivalent of bloodlust. Brought on by a curse from a powerful enchantress. Causes excruciating pain. Attacks a werebeast's central nervous system, making the werebeast stronger and violent, and driving the werebeast to kill. No known cure exists.

mortem provocatio A fight to the death.

North American *Were* Council The governing body of *weres* in North America, led by a president and several council members.

potestatem bonum "The power of good." That which encloses the earth and keeps demons from remaining among the living.

Purebloods (aka *pures*) Werebeasts from generations of *were*-only family members. Considered royalty among werebeasts, they carry the responsibilities of their species. The mating between two purebloods is the only way to guarantee the conception of a *were* child.

rogue witch a witch without a coven. Must be accounted for as rogue witches tend to go one of two ways without a coven: dark or insane.

shape-shifter Evil, immortal creatures who can take any form. They are born witches, then spend years seeking innocents to sacrifice to a dark deity. When the deity deems the offerings sufficient, the witch casts a baneful spell to surrender his or her magic and humanity in exchange for immortality and the power of hell at their fingertips. Shape-shifters can command any form and are the deadliest and strongest of all mystical creatures.

Shift Celia's ability to break down her body into minute particles. Her gift allows her to travel beneath and across soil, concrete, and rock. Celia can also *shift* a limited number of beings. Disadvantages include not being able to breathe or see until she surfaces.

Skinwalkers Creatures spoken of in whispers and believed to be *weres* damned to hell for turning on their kind. A humanoid combination of animal and man that reeks of death, a *skinwalker* can manipulate the elements and subterranean arachnids. Considered impossible to kill.

solis natus magicae The proper term for sunlight born of magic, created by a wielder of spells. Considered "pure" light. Capable of destroying non-master vampires and demons. In large quantities may also kill shape-shifters. Renders the wielder helpless once fired.

Superior Witch A witch of tremendous power and magic who assumes a leadership role among the coven. Wears a talisman around her neck or carries staff with a precious stone at its center to help amplify her magic.

Surface Celia's ability to reemerge from a shift.

susceptor animae A being capable of taking one's soul, such as a vampire.

Trudhilde Radinka (aka *Destiny*) A female born once every century from the union of two witches who possesses rare talents and the aptitude to predict the future. Considered among the elite of the mystical world.

turn To transform a human into a werebeast or vampire. Werebeasts *turn* by piercing the heart of a human with their fangs and transferring a part of their essence. Vampires pierce through the skull and into the brain to transfer a taste of their magic. Werebeasts risk their lives during the *turning* process, as they are gifting a part of their souls. Should the transfer fail, both the werebeast and human die. Vampires risk nothing since they're not losing their souls, but rather taking another's and releasing it from the human's body.

vampire A being who consumes the blood of mortals to survive. Beautiful and alluring, vampires will never appear to age past thirty years. Vampires are immune to sunlight unless it is created by magic. They are also immune to objects of faith such as crucifixes. Vampires may be killed by the destruction of their hearts, decapitation, or fire. Master vampires or vampires several centuries old must have both their hearts and heads removed or their bodies completely destroyed.

vampire clans Families of vampires led by master vampires. Masters can control, communicate, and punish their keep through mental telepathy.

velum A veil conjured by magic.

virtutem lucis "The power of light." The goodness found within each mortal. That which combats the darkness.

Warrior A werebeast possessing profound skill or fighting ability. Only the elite among *weres* are granted the title of Warrior. Warriors are duty-bound to protect their Leaders and their Leaders' mates at all costs.

werebeast A supernatural predator with the ability to *change* from human to beast. Werebeasts are considered the Guardians of the Earth against mystical evil. Werebeasts will achieve their first *change* within six months to a year following birth. The younger they are when they first *change,* the more powerful they will be. Werebeasts also possess the ability to heal their wounds. They can live until the first full moon following their one hundredth birthday. Werebeasts may be killed by destruction of their hearts, decapitation, or if their bodies are completely destroyed. The only time a *were* can partially *change* is when he or she attempts to *turn* a human. A *turned* human will achieve his or her first *change* by the next full moon.

witch A being born with the power to wield magic. They worship the earth and nature. Pure witches will not take part in blood sacrifices. They cultivate the land to grow plants for their potions and use staffs and talismans to amplify their magic. To cross a witch is to feel the collective wrath of her coven.

witch fire Orange flames encased by magic, used to assassinate an enemy. Witch fire explodes like multiple grenades when the intended victim nears the spell. Flames will continue to burn until the target has been eliminated.

zombie Typically human bodies raised from the dead by a necromancer witch. It's illegal to raise or keep a zombie and is among the deadliest sins in the supernatural world. Their diet consists of other dead things such as roadkill and decaying animals

Read on as the Weird Girls saga continues with **Sealed with a Curse,** the first full length novel in The Weird Girls Urban Fantasy Romance series by Cecy Robson. The excerpt has been set for this edition only and may not reflect the final content of the final novel.

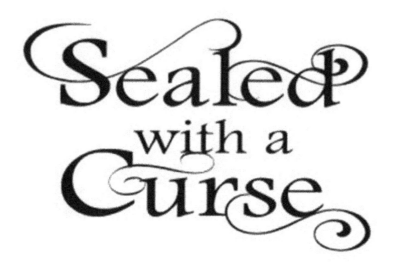

Sealed with a Curse

A Weird Girls Novel
By
CECY ROBSON

Chapter One

Sacramento, California

The courthouse doors crashed open as I led my three sisters into the large foyer. I didn't mean to push so hard, but hell, I was mad and worried about being eaten. The cool spring breeze slapped at my back as I stepped inside, yet it did little to cool my temper or my nerves.

My nose scented the vampires before my eyes caught them emerging from the shadows. There were six of them, wearing dark suits, Ray-Bans, and obnoxious little grins. Two bolted the doors tight behind us, while the others frisked us for weapons.

I can't believe we we're in vampire court. So much for avoiding the perilous world of the supernatural.

Emme trembled beside me. She had every right to be scared. We were strong, but our combined abilities couldn't trump a roomful of bloodsucking beasts. "Celia," she whispered, her voice shaking. "Maybe we shouldn't have come."

Like we had a choice. "Just stay close to me, Emme." My muscles tensed as the vampire's hands swept the length of my body and through my long curls. I didn't like him touching me, and neither did my inner tigress. My fingers itched with the need to protrude my claws.

When he finally released me, I stepped closer to Emme while I scanned the foyer for a possible escape route. Next to me, the vampire searching Taran got a little daring with his pat-down. But he was messing with the wrong sister.

"If you touch my ass one more time, fang boy, I swear to God I'll light you on fire." The vampire quickly removed his hands when a spark of blue flame ignited from Taran's fingertips.

Shayna, conversely, flashed a lively smile when the vampire searching her found her toothpicks. Her grin widened when he returned her seemingly harmless little sticks, unaware of how deadly they were in her hands. "Thanks, dude." She shoved the box back into the pocket of her slacks.

"They're clear." The guard grinned at Emme and licked his lips. "This way." He motioned her to follow. Emme cowered. Taran showed no fear and plowed ahead. She tossed her dark, wavy hair and strutted into the courtroom like the diva she was, wearing a tiny white mini dress that contrasted with her deep olive skin. I didn't fail to notice the guards' gazes glued to Taran's shapely figure. Nor did I miss when their incisors lengthened, ready to bite.

I urged Emme and Shayna forward. "Go. I'll watch your backs." I whipped around to snarl at the guards. The vampires' smiles faltered when they saw *my* fangs protrude. Like most beings, they probably didn't know what I was, but they seemed to recognize that I was potentially lethal, despite my petite frame.

I followed my sisters into the large courtroom. The place reminded me of a picture I'd seen of the Salem witch trials. Rows of dark wood pews lined the center aisle, and wide rustic planks comprised the floor. Unlike the photo I recalled, every window was boarded shut, and paintings of vampires hung on every inch of available wall space. One particular image epitomized the vampire stereotype perfectly. It showed a male vampire entwined with two naked women on a bed of roses and jewels. The women appeared completely enamored of the vampire, even while blood dripped from their necks.

The vampire spectators scrutinized us as we approached along the center aisle. Many had accessorized their expensive attire with diamond jewelry and watches that probably cost more than my car. Their glares told me they didn't appreciate my cotton T-shirt, peasant skirt, and flip-flops. I was twenty-five years old; it's not like I didn't know how to dress. But, hell, other fabrics and shoes were way more expensive to replace when I *changed* into my other form.

I spotted our accuser as we stalked our way to the front of the assembly. Even in a courtroom crammed with young and sexy vampires, Misha Aleksandr stood out. His tall, muscular frame filled his fitted suit, and his long blond hair brushed against his shoulders. Death, it seemed, looked damn good. Yet it wasn't his height or his wealth or even his striking features that captivated me. He possessed a fierce presence that commanded the room. Misha Aleksandr was a force to be reckoned with, but, strangely enough, so was I.

Misha had "requested" our presence in Sacramento after charging us with the murder of one of his family members. We had two choices: appear in court or be hunted for the rest of our lives. The whole situation sucked. We'd stayed hidden from the supernatural world for so long. Now not only had we been forced into the limelight, but we also faced the possibility of dying some twisted, Rob Zombie–inspired death.

Of course, God forbid that would make Taran shut her trap. She leaned in close to me. "Celia, how about I gather some magic-borne sunlight and fry these assholes?" she whispered in Spanish.

A few of the vampires behind us muttered and hissed, causing uproar among the rest. If they didn't like us before, they sure as hell hated us then.

Shayna laughed nervously, but maintained her perky demeanor. "I think some of them understand the lingo, dude."

I recognized Taran's desire to burn the vamps to blood and ash, but I didn't agree with it. Conjuring such power would leave her drained and vulnerable, easy prey for the master vampires, who would be immune to her sunlight. Besides, we were already in trouble with one master for killing his keep. We didn't need to be hunted by the entire leeching species.

The procession halted in a strangely wide-open area before a raised dais. There were no chairs or tables, nothing we could use as weapons against the judges or the angry mob amassed behind us.

My eyes focused on one of the boarded windows. The light

honey-colored wood frame didn't match the darker boards. I guessed the last defendant had tried to escape. Judging from the claw marks running from beneath the frame to where I stood, he, she, or *it* hadn't made it.

I looked up from the deeply scratched floor to find Misha's intense gaze on me. We locked eyes, predator to predator, neither of us the type to back down. *You're trying to intimidate the wrong gal, pretty boy. I don't scare easily.*

Shayna slapped her hand over her face and shook her head, her long black ponytail waving behind her. "For Pete's sake, Celia, can't you be a little friendlier?" She flashed Misha a grin that made her blue eyes sparkle. "How's it going, dude?"

Shayna said "dude" a lot, ever since dating some idiot claiming to be a professional surfer. The term fit her sunny personality and eventually grew on us.

Misha didn't appear taken by her charm. He eyed her as if she'd asked him to make her a garlic pizza in the shape of a cross. I laughed; I couldn't help it. *Leave it to Shayna to try to befriend the guy who'll probably suck us dry by sundown.*

At the sound of my chuckle, Misha regarded me slowly. His head tilted slightly as his full lips curved into a sensual smile. I would have preferred a vicious stare—I knew how to deal with those. For a moment, I thought he'd somehow made my clothes disappear and I was standing there like the bleeding hoochies in that awful painting.

The judges' sudden arrival gave me an excuse to glance away. There were four, each wearing a formal robe of red velvet with an elaborate powdered wig. They were probably several centuries old, but like all vampires, they didn't appear a day over thirty. Their splendor easily surpassed the beauty of any mere mortal. I guessed the whole "sucky, sucky, me love you all night" lifestyle paid off for them.

The judges regally assumed their places on the raised dais. Behind them hung a giant plasma screen, which appeared out of place in this century-old building. Did they plan to watch a movie while they decided how best to disembowel us?

A female judge motioned Misha forward with a Queen Elizabeth hand wave. A long, thick scar angled from the corner of her left jaw across her throat. Someone had tried to behead her. To scar a vampire like that, the culprit had likely used a gold blade reinforced with lethal magic. Apparently, even that blade hadn't been enough. I gathered she commanded the fang-fest Parliament, since her marble nameplate read, CHIEF JUSTICE ANTOINETTE MALIKA. Judge Malika didn't strike me as the warm and cuddly sort. Her lips were pursed into a tight line and her elongating fangs locked over her lower lip. I only hoped she'd snacked before her arrival.

At a nod from Judge Malika, Misha began. "Members of the High Court, I thank you for your audience." A Russian accent underscored his deep voice. "I hereby charge Celia, Taran, Shayna, and Emme Wird with the murder of my family member, David Geller."

"Wird? More like *Weird*," a vamp in the audience mumbled. The smaller vamp next to him adjusted his bow tie nervously when I snarled.

Oh, yeah, like we've never heard that before, jerk.

The sole male judge slapped a heavy leather-bound book on the long table and whipped out a feather quill. "Celia Wird. State your position."

Position?

I exchanged glances with my sisters; they didn't seem to know what Captain Pointy Teeth meant either. Taran shrugged. "Who gives a shit? Just say something."

I waved a hand. "Um. Registered nurse?"

Judging by his "please don't make me eat you before the proceedings" scowl, and the snickering behind us, I hadn't provided him with the appropriate response.

He enunciated every word carefully and slowly so as to not further confuse my obviously feeble and inferior mind. "Position in the supernatural world."

"We've tried to avoid your world." I gave Taran the evil eye. "For the most part. But if you must know, I'm a tigress."

"Weretigress," he said as he wrote.

"I'm not a *were*," I interjected defensively.

He huffed. "Can you *change* into a tigress or not?"

"Well, yes. But that doesn't make me a *were*."

The vamps behind us buzzed with feverish whispers while the judges' eyes narrowed suspiciously. Not knowing what we were made them nervous. A nervous vamp was a dangerous vamp. And the room was bursting with them.

"What I mean is, unlike a *were*, I can *change* parts of my body without turning into my beast completely." And unlike anything else on earth, I could also *shift*—disappear under and across solid ground and resurface unscathed. But they didn't need to know that little tidbit. Nor did they need to know I couldn't heal my injuries. If it weren't for Emme's unique ability to heal herself and others, my sisters and I would have died long ago.

"Fascinating," he said in a way that clearly meant I wasn't. The feather quill didn't come with an eraser. And the judge obviously didn't appreciate my making him mess up his book. He dipped his pen into his little inkwell and scribbled out what he'd just written before addressing Taran. "Taran Wird, position?"

"I can release magic into the forms of fire and lightning—"

"Very well, witch." The vamp scrawled.

"I'm not a witch, asshole."

The judge threw his plume on the table, agitated. Judge Malika fixed her frown on Taran. "What did you say?"

Nobody flashed a vixen grin better than Taran. "I said, 'I'm not a witch. Ass. Hole.'"

Emme whimpered, ready to hurl from the stress. Shayna giggled and threw an arm around Taran. "She's just kidding, dude!"

No. Taran didn't kid. Hell, she didn't even know any knock-knock jokes. She shrugged off Shayna, unwilling to back down. She wouldn't listen to Shayna. But she would listen to me.

"Just answer the question, Taran."

The muscles on Taran's jaw tightened, but she did as I asked. "I make fire, light—"

"Fire-breather." Captain Personality wrote quickly.

"I'm not a—"

He cut her off. "Shayna Wird?"

"Well, dude, I throw knives—"

"Knife thrower," he said, ready to get this little meet-and-greet over and done with.

Shayna did throw knives. That was true. She could also

transform pieces of wood into razor-sharp weapons and manipulate alloys. All she needed was metal somewhere on her body and a little focus. For her safety, though, "knife thrower" seemed less threatening.

"And you, Emme Wird?"

"Um. Ah. I can move things with my mind—"

"Gypsy," the half-wit interpreted.

I supposed "telekinetic" was too big a word for this idiot. Then again, unlike typical telekinetics, Emme could do more than bend a few forks. I sighed. *Tigress, fire-breather, knife thrower, and Gypsy*. We sounded like the headliners for a freak show. All we needed was a bearded lady. I sighed. *That's what happens when you're the bizarre products of a back-fired curse.*

Misha glanced at us quickly before stepping forward once more. "I will present Mr. Hank Miller and Mr. Timothy Brown as witnesses—" Taran exhaled dramatically and twirled her hair like she was bored. Misha glared at her before finishing. "I do not doubt justice will be served."

Judge Zhahara Nadim, who resembled more of an Egyptian queen than someone who should be stuffed into a powdered wig, surprised me by leering at Misha like she wanted his head for a lawn ornament. I didn't know what he'd done to piss her off; yet knowing we weren't the only ones hated brought me a strange sense of comfort. She narrowed her eyes at Misha, like all predators do before they strike, and called forward someone named "Destiny." I didn't know Destiny, but I knew she was no vampire the moment she strutted onto the dais.

I tried to remain impassive. However, I really wanted to run away screaming. Short of sporting a few tails and some extra digits, Destiny was the freakiest thing I'd ever seen. Not only did she lack the allure all vampires possessed, but her fashion sense bordered on disastrous. She wore black patterned tights, white strappy sandals, and a hideous black-and-white polka-dot turtleneck. I guessed she sought to draw attention from her lime green zebra-print miniskirt. And, my God, her makeup was abominable. Black kohl outlined her bright fuchsia lips, and mint green shadow ringed her eyes.

"This is a perfect example of why I don't wear makeup," I told Taran.

Taran stepped forward with her hands on her hips. "How the hell is *she* a witness? I didn't see her at the club that night! And Lord knows she would've stuck out."

Emme trembled beside me. "Taran, please don't get us killed!"

I gave my youngest sister's hand a squeeze. "Steady, Emme."

Judge Malika called Misha's two witnesses forward. "Mr. Miller and Mr. Brown, which of you gentlemen would like to go first?"

Both "gentlemen" took one gander at Destiny and scrambled away from her. It was never a good sign when something scared a vampire. Hank, the bigger of the two vamps, shoved Tim forward.

"You may begin," Judge Malika commanded. "Just concentrate on what you saw that night. Destiny?"

The four judges swiftly donned protective ear wear, like construction workers used, just as a guard flipped a switch next to the flat-screen. At first I thought the judges toyed with us. Even with heightened senses, how could they hear the testimony through those ridiculous ear guards? Before I could protest, Destiny enthusiastically approached Tim and grabbed his head. Tim's immediate bloodcurdling screams caused the rest of us to cover our ears. Every hair on my body stood at attention. What freaked me out was that he wasn't the one on trial.

Emme's fair freckled skin blanched so severely, I feared she'd pass out. Shayna stood frozen with her jaw open while Taran and I exchanged "oh, shit" glances. I was about to start the "let's get the hell out of here" ball rolling when images from Tim's mind appeared on the screen. I couldn't believe my eyes. Complete with sound effects, we relived the night of David's murder. Misha straightened when he saw David soar out of Taran's window in flames, but otherwise he did not react. Nor did Misha blink when what remained of David burst into ashes on our lawn. Still, I sensed his fury. The image moved to a close-up of Hank's shocked face and finished with the four of us scowling down at the blood and ash.

Destiny abruptly released the sobbing Tim, who collapsed on the floor. Mucus oozed from his nose and mouth. I didn't even know vamps were capable of such body fluids.

At last, Taran finally seemed to understand the deep shittiness of our situation. "Son of a bitch," she whispered.

Hank gawked at Tim before addressing the judges. "If it pleases the court, I swear on my honor I witnessed exactly what Tim Brown did about David Geller's murder. My version would be of no further benefit."

Malika shrugged indifferently. "Very well, you're excused." She turned toward us while Hank hurried back to his seat. "As you just saw, we have ways to expose the truth. Destiny is able to extract memories, but she cannot alter them. Likewise, during Destiny's time with you, you will be unable to change what you saw. You'll only review what has already come to pass."

I frowned. "How do we know you're telling us the truth?"

Malika peered down her nose at me. "What choice do you have? Now, which of you is first?"

Photo by Kate Gledhill of Kate Gledhill Photography

Cecy Robson (also writing as Rosalina San Tiago for the app Hooked) is an author of contemporary romance, young adult adventure, and award-winning urban fantasy. A double RITA® 2016 finalist for Once Pure and Once Kissed, and a published author of more than twenty novels, you can typically find Cecy on her laptop writing her stories or stumbling blindly in search of caffeine.

www.cecyrobson.com
Facebook.com/Cecy.Robson.Author
instagram.com/cecyrobsonauthor
twitter.com/cecyrobson
www.goodreads.com/goodreadscomCecyRobsonAuthor
For exclusive information and more, join my Newsletter!
http://eepurl.com/4ASmj

CPSIA information can be obtained
at www.ICGtesting.com
Printed in the USA
LVHW030534260821
696089LV00005B/202